Something in the Past

Something in the Past

TYESHIA CLINTON

iUniverse, Inc.
Bloomington

Something in the Past

iUniverse books may be ordered through booksellers or by contacting:

iUniverse
1663 Liberty Drive
Bloomington, IN 47403
www.iuniverse.com
1-800-Authors (1-800-288-4677)

ISBN: 978-1-4620-3594-6 (sc)
ISBN: 978-1-4620-3595-3 (hc)
ISBN: 978-1-4620-3596-0 (ebk)

Printed in the United States of America

iUniverse rev. date: 08/17/2011

ACKNOWLEDGMENTS

I'd like to dedicate this book to my father June. R.I.P daddy, I know you smiling down at me. I'm going to try my best to keep your memory alive. I'll love you until the day we're reunited!

I'd also like to thank my mother and the father who raised me for everything. I wouldn't be the woman I am today if it wasn't for you guys and I love y'all for that!

To my daughters, Amber and Paris, I love y'all with all my heart. Looking at y'all daily helped motivate me to write this book so that I can provide a better life for you guys. GOD IS GOOD and it's my job to prove that to y'all!

Thank you Jesus for giving me the strength, the motivation and the inspiration to write this book.

(1)

3/16/1994 A New Beginning

When the Dwight Correctional Facility released Jackie they gave her fifty dollars and a greyhound bus ticket to Dayton, Ohio. That was all she had to her name. She had nothing to look forward to outside of the prison walls, and she was so scared to leave that she begged the warden to let her stay. She only got paid thirteen dollars a month for doing the job she was assigned to do while she was in Dwight, but she had a roof over her head, three guaranteed meals a day, and no access to crack or heroin. No one sent her any money during her twenty-one month incarceration, but Jackie had game so she knew how to talk the guards and the other inmates out of anything she felt she needed or wanted. Her room was so full of commissary that she was able to leave her cellmate with lots of it when it was time for her to leave the comfort of their cell. Life in jail was a lot easier for Jackie than her life out in the real world was going to be, but she had no choice but to leave. Her sentence was up and the penitentiary barely had enough room to house the inmates who had to be there, so the warden told her she had to go.

When Jackie got arrested she was a crack smoking, heroin snorting, clothes stealing, drug dealing, prostitute; but she had a roof over her head and a car. Her car got repossessed a week after she got arrested, and the house she shared with her mother and her five sisters got foreclosed seven months later. By the time Jackie got out the only people in Illinois who would help her were all on drugs, living in shelters, so they couldn't be any help to her. She would have to go to the halfway house on the Westside of Chicago if she got paroled there, and there was no way she would be able to stay clean on that side of town. If she started back getting high she

1

knew she would be headed back to jail and she was tired of living like that. So she asked her maternal grandmother, Pam, if she could get paroled to her house in Miamisburg, Ohio.

Pam agreed to let Jackie move into her finished basement, but she told her that she wouldn't be allowed upstairs, she had to get into a Narcotics Anonymous program, she had to get a job, and she had to be out of her home in seven months. Pam was so serious about her conditions that she made Jackie sign a contract stating that she would move out before the seven months if she broke any of the rules. Pam wasn't trying to be cruel, but she moved from Chicago to Miamisburg to get away from her only child, Janice, and her lying, thieving, drug abusing children. She stopped them from visiting her when they first started stealing from her. They started breaking into her house and her car after her husband died, so she moved as far away from them as she could. She didn't know anyone in Ohio and that suited her just fine. She didn't want Jackie coming there, but she knew she wouldn't be able to live with herself if something drastic happened to her because she didn't give her a chance.

Jackie was terrified of all of Pam's conditions. She knew that it was going to be hard to get a job because she was a thirty-four year old, ex-felon, who'd never had a legitimate job in her life. She was ready to stop doing hard drugs, but she didn't think that she needed to join any NA program to stop. She had been to a lot of NA meetings and she felt like they were a waste of time. She'd never had her own apartment and she thought it was going to take much longer than seven months to save up for one, but she signed the contract in spite of her fears.

Jackie had an hour long wait for the Greyhound bus so she decided to buy herself a half pint of gin from the liquor store they passed on the way to the station. She knew that she needed to be frugal with her money, but her nerves were shot and she thought the alcohol would calm her down. She gave the two officers who dropped her off five minutes to get out of sight, then left out the station headed in the direction she saw the liquor store in. She was kind of paranoid so it only took her fifteen minutes to walk the two blocks, buy the gin, and walk back to the station. There was a small restaurant inside of the Greyhound Station and she got a big Styrofoam cup, and a lid and a straw for it from out of there. Then she went to the bathroom and poured all of the gin into the cup. The bus heading to Dayton was there by the time Jackie came out of the bathroom and she wanted to kick herself for not buying something to eat. She hadn't eaten anything since the night before and she knew that drinking on an empty stomach was going to have her super drunk; but that didn't stop her from drinking every last drop of the gin during her eight hour trip.

Pam was waiting for Jackie to arrive and she knew she was intoxicated as soon as Jackie stumbled off of the bus. "Jackie, you smell like a bar! Why would you get drunk as soon as you got released? This ain't gon work unless you're serious about changing your life," she said as she hugged Jackie with a look of disgust on her face.

"Granny, I'm just trying to celebrate my freedom. You said I couldn't do no drugs, you ain't say nothing about me having a little drink," Jackie slurred as Pam released her.

"Well you add no drinking to the list of rules I gave you. Is that brown bag all of the luggage you have? What are you wearing, and where is your coat? It's freezing out here!"

"It wasn't that cold earlier. Mama and nem ain't send me no clothes while I was in the joint, and the County sent the clothes I got locked up in to the house when I got shipped out to the penitentiary. My roommate tried to give me some of her clothes, but they were out of style and its bad luck to take anything from somebody with life out of the pen. The guards tried to give me one of them ugly state issued coats, but I told them I was cool. If you think these blue polyester pants, and this white buttoned down shirt look bad you should have seen how I looked with the coat on. This bag got my toiletries, panties, bras, and socks in it. I'll buy me some more clothes when I get a job," said Jackie as they walked to Pam's car.

"Well, at least you bought your own toiletries because I don't like sharing those kinds of items. But you can't go job hunting in that crap. I guess we can go to the flee market and pick you up a few items in the morning. You look real good with that weight on you and yo skin glowing like it is Jackie. Yo hair grew good too. I hope and pray that you truly are ready to change your life, because the path you were heading down before you went to jail only leads to hell," said Pam as they got into her car.

"I know Granny. Thanks for giving me a chance, I'm gon make you proud of me watch," Jackie replied with a huge lopsided smile on her face. Pam's compliments boosted her self esteem. She was 5'7" and barely weighed one hundred pounds before she went to jail, now she weighed a healthy one hundred and fifty and she thought she was thick. She never had bad skin, but it darkened while she was getting high. It went back to the color of butter while she was in jail. The dimples in her cheeks had sunk in when she lost weight, but they looked perfect in her full cheeks. Her teeth weren't perfect, but they were all hers and she had a real pretty smile. She hated the dirty red color of her long, curly hair but she was happy that her ponytail now reached the middle of her back. She didn't arch her eyebrows while she was in jail, but they had a natural arch to them that complimented her Chinese shaped gray eyes. A lot of the women and guards tried to come on to her while she was in jail so she knew she looked good, but she had bigger things on her mind besides her looks at the time.

"I eat dinner everyday at five so I already ate. I put you a plate in the microwave, you can eat after you clean yo self up," said Pam as she pulled into her driveway and they got out of the car.

"Good cause I'm starving! I ain't ate all day."

"You should have bought you something to eat instead of wasting yo money on them spirits! Take yo shoes off when we get in here. This will be the first and last time you'll be entering this house through this door. There's a door that leads to the basement that you can use. I'm not about to be feeding you for long either. I don't like the way you starting out and you ain't gon be here long if you don't do much better than this," said Pam as she let them in, cut on the light, sat down on her couch, and took off her shoes.

"Ok Granny, I understand. Do you have anything for a headache? My head is pounding," said Jackie with a look of defeat on her face. She could see how things were going to be living with her grandmother already. She wished she hadn't drunk that gin as soon as she got off the bus and saw her grandmother's face, and the way she felt confirmed that feeling.

"Now yo head hurt. Jackie you gon have to make some changes quick, fast, and in a hurry or you gon find yo self in the halfway house they got right here in Ohio! I know they got one because they got criminals everywhere! Tomorrow is Thursday so there's all kinds of business you can handle! I want you up by eight," said Pam as she slipped on her slippers, stood up, and walked to her bedroom.

"Ok, Granny," Jackie yelled as she sat on the couch, put her bag on it, and took off her shoes. "Yo house is real nice; you always did keep a pretty house. My feet sinking in this carpet," she said when Pam walked back into the living room. Pam loved decorating and her house was beautiful and immaculate.

"Thanks. I want it to stay nice, that's why I asked your parole officer to drug test you weekly instead of monthly and he agreed. You going to jail if you fail one, cause I told him that you ain't allowed back in my house with drugs in yo system. I felt bad about doing that at first, but I'm glad I let the Lord order my steps on that move now," Pam said as she looked Jackie in her eyes and handed her a gown, housecoat, washcloth, and a dry towel. "There's a new toothbrush and a bottle of aspirins in one of them pockets on that house coat. Gon head and take you a couple after you clean yo self up. You look like you need them. Come on so I can show where the bathroom is."

Jackie didn't know how to respond to that, so she didn't. She knew that Pam didn't want her there, but she didn't think she would be as hard on her as she was being. She started to feel sorry for herself until she remembered what they said in the self sufficiency class she had to take prior to her release. The class was designed to get inmates ready to live back into society, and one of the things the teacher stressed was that they had to take responsibility for their past, present, and future actions. Jackie knew how her grandmother felt about her living with her before she got there, so she should have been prepared for the treatment she was receiving. She decided to follow her rules, avoid her as much as she could, and to try to get up out of there as soon as possible. She started to feel real lonely and sad until her alter-ego Toni showed up to take over. *"Don't worry Jackie, I got her old ass. You gon head and chill,"* she said to Jackie in Jackie's mind as her eyes changed from gray to green and she followed Pam with the brown bag in her hand. People always thought Jackie she was quiet because she held most of the conversations she had with herself in her own mind.

"Toni, don't get us kicked out. You know she all we got," Jackie silently said to Toni. She had to warn her because Pam was her last resort and Toni was very aggressive.

"I'm not; I know how to handle people like her. I just peeped how tired you is. If you don't want my help I'll bounce like I did while you was in Dwight," Toni confidently replied. She knew that Jackie was going to let her take over the situation because Jackie thought that she was smarter and stronger than her.

"It's cool. I'm glad you came back because I'm real tired and I don't feel like being bothered with Pam. She being real mean," Jackie replied before she went as deep into herself as she could and let Toni take completely over.

Pam went into her room after showing Toni where the bathroom was. The first thing Toni did after she closed the door was fill the cup that was on the sink up with water and took four aspirins. Then she took her bar of soap, deodorant, lotion, toothpaste, hair grease, and her comb and brush out of her bag. Jackie felt petty for taking all of her new personals with her when she got released, but Toni was glad that she did after seeing how petty Pam was being. She brushed her teeth, took a shower, washed her hair while she was in the shower, dried off, and lotioned up when she got out. She dried her hair, parted it down the middle, greased the part and edges and put it in two French braids. Then she put on the gown and housecoat, sat her personal items neatly around the sink, put her dirty clothes in the hamper, and left out the bathroom.

Pam came out of her room as soon as she heard Toni come out of the bathroom. "Come on I'll show you to the kitchen. I already warmed yo food up. Its way past my bedtime so you need to hurry up so I can lock the door that leads to the basement. I put an alarm clock down there and set it for nine, I expect you to get up as soon as it goes off. I want you to get up at eight after tomorrow. The only reason I ain't getting you up at eight tomorrow morning is because the stores ain't gon be open that early; and I ain't bout to be walking around with you looking like that. Yo sister, Angel, sent you a package last week; I put it on the let out bed down there. I was kind enough to pull it out and put some clean linen on it for you. I want it and the linen I put on it folded up every morning after you get up. You can sit the linen on the couch after you fold the bed back up in it. I want you up and out of my house by nine every weekday morning and I don't want to hear you coming back in here until after five in the evening. The latest you can re-enter my home is seven because that's my bedtime and I like my whole house to be locked up when I go to sleep," she said as she led Toni into the kitchen and got her plate of fried chicken, sweet potatoes, greens, and macaroni out of the microwave.

"I got you Granny. That food looks and smells delicious. I ain't had none of yo cooking in years," said Toni as she sat down at the table and started eating the food Pam placed in front of her.

"It has been years since I cooked for any of my grandkids. You look just like you used to look when you was little with your hair like that. That's the Jackie I miss and love, I wish she would come back. You was such a beautiful and sweet child with the most mysterious, enchanting eyes. It was always puzzling to me the way they changed colors so fast. They were that beautiful transparent gray color before you took your shower, now they're green with that mischievous twinkle in them. The only thing you can thank me for is that hourglass figure you got from yo mama. The rest of your looks came from yo daddy. But enough traveling down memory lane, we got to deal with the here and now. I love you, but I will put you out if you don't abide by my rules," said Pam as she sat across the table from Toni and watched her eat. Pam was a petite seventy-seven year old, dark skinned woman who looked like Cicely Tyson.

I can't stand this old ass bitch, thought Toni but she held her tongue and ignored the insults. "I'm gon follow yo rules. You said be up by nine, right?" she asked as she took one of the burgundy cloth napkins out of the napkin holder, wiped her mouth with it, and stood up.

"Yeah you need to be up by nine, and don't ever use any of my decorations to wipe your mouth again. That's why I gave you a paper towel with your meal. I know you ain't bout to leave that plate on the table. Clean up after yo self, you ain't got no maid," said Pam stopping Toni in her tracks. "The sponge I use to wash the dishes is by the dishwashing liquid over there by the sink. Every time I use a dish I wash it out. Every time I take a bath I wash out the tub. If I drop a crumb I pick it up, and I would appreciate it if you did the same. Dang Jackie, you act like you two years old. Do I have to post a set of cleaning rules on the refrigerator? Then act like I don't," she said as Toni shook her head no, emptied her plate, washed it and her fork, and put them in the dish rack.

"The door that leads to the basement is right there by the stove. There's a light switch that controls the lights to the stairs over there too. You might want to cut them on. That door you gon see as soon as you open the door leads to the outside, I'll give you a key to it tomorrow. Now, I'm ready to go to sleep if you don't mind."

"Ok Granny," Toni replied as she walked to the door, cut on the lights, opened the door, and walked down the stairs. *Damn that bitch evil,* she thought as she heard Pam lock the door with a padlock. Toni was mentally and physically exhausted by the time she made it to the bed; so she decided against opening the package that Jackie's sister, Angel, sent her and went to sleep.

Jackie was the one who heard the alarm go off. Toni woke up when Jackie cut on the lamp that sat on the table by the couch. *"Angel sent you that package that's by the lamp Jackie. What is it?"* asked Toni when she felt Jackie picking it up and opening it.

"*It's a picture of my daddy, his diary, and the last letter Timothy wrote me. Seeing my daddy's face is giving me strength. She sent me my birth certificate and my social security card too. I got a lot to do today, but I'm gon get it all done, even with this hangover. I'm glad I didn't get a bigger bottle of that bullshit. You can chill today Toni, I'll put up with Pam.*"

"*Ok Jackie, call me if you need me.*"

"*I will,*" Jackie replied as she kissed the picture of her father, put it back in the diary, put both of them back in the box they arrived in, and sat the box back on the table. Then she took the blanket off the let out bed, folded it up, sat it on the floor, and folded the bed into the couch. After putting the pillows to the couch where they belonged on it, she looked in her bag and got a clean pair of panties, socks, and a bra out of it. Then she sat it and the blanket on the couch and went upstairs.

The door at the top of the stairs swung open when Jackie knocked on it. Pam was sitting at the kitchen table, fully dressed, sipping on a mug of coffee when she walked through the door. "Good morning Jackie. I put a jogging suit in the bathroom for you. It's purple like your shoes. The only sporty shoes I own are orthopedic shoes so I tried to match the jogging suit with the ones you got."

"Thanks Granny. Yo orthopedic shoes probably look better than my worn out Gotta Have It Reeboks," said Jackie as she giggled. She had been worried about her father's picture and diary all while she was in jail; and possessing them gave her a sense of relief and security. Nothing could mess up her good mood, and she felt even better because Pam was being civil towards her. She went to the bathroom, took three aspirins, took off her gown and hung it up on the back of the bathroom door. Then she brushed her teeth, freshened up, took down her hair, put some grease around the edges, brushed it into a ponytail, and put on her underwear, socks, and jogging suit.

When she walked into the kitchen she was happy to see that Pam had sat a hot cup of black coffee in front of her plate of ham, cheese grits, biscuits, and cheese eggs. The coffee helped her battle her hangover and the food gave her the energy she needed to face the day.

Pam ended up taking Jackie to the Sears in the Dayton Mall because it was closer than the flea market. She was a wealthy woman so money wasn't the reason she considered taking her to the flea market to get the clothes she needed. She just wanted to spend as less of it as possible on Jackie. All of the things she bought her were out of season, so she got a deal on them. She bought her a pea coat, a tweed business suit, a big, black, cheap leather purse, a cheap watch, five pairs of Lee jeans, five long sleeved shirts, a pack of white v necked t shirts, a pair of flats, and a pair of Avis gym shoes. She also bought her some new panties, bras, and socks. She made her try on everything before she bought anything and made her keep on the business suit after cutting the price tags off, so she could pay for it. She also made her keep on the flats.

It was almost noon by the time they finished so they went to the food court and ate some Chinese food. "Thanks Granny, I'll pay you back as soon as I get me a job. I knew today was gon be a good day."

"You welcomed Jackie. I don't mind doing things for you if it's productive and you're appreciative. All I want you to do is to try to succeed in life. I know you had a rough start, but it's never too late to better yourself. I was an eleven year old illiterate little girl when I started my career of scrubbing floors, and look at me now. The good Lord will bless you if you work hard to make an honest living. That fast money disappears just as quick as you can make it. You respect the money that you have to work hard for, so you won't be too quick to part with it."

"You right about that. If I had half the money I made in my pockets I could live good for at least three years."

"Ain't no sense in crying over spilled milk, cause it ain't gon change nothing. There's a couple of factories in back of my house you can put applications in. I don't know if they'll hire you, but it's worth a try," said Pam as she stood up with her tray and emptied it in one of the garbage bins that was by their table. "You might as well start job searching this week since you don't have to start reporting to your parole officer or attending your NA meetings until next week. You ain't got a minute to lose! The only way you gon get up out of my house is if you put forth a lot of effort."

"That sounds like a good idea, but in my self sufficiency classes they said that I needed a current state ID or a driver's license before going job hunting. My parole officer told me how to get one here. He said that all I needed was my birth certificate, my social security card, proof of residency, and eight dollars. I'll use the box Angel mailed me for my proof of residence, I just got to go back to the house to get it," Jackie said with more confidence than she felt as she followed Pam out the mall and to her car.

9

"You should have bought that stuff out of the house with you if you knew you needed them. Now I got to take you back home and bring you back to the mall so you can take the bus to the license bureau in Dayton. I bought you a thirty day bus pass before I picked you up yesterday. You might as well learn how to take the bus now, cause I ain't bout to be chauffeuring you around. That's why I bought the thing to save me time and gas. Put them bags in the car and run over there to that bus terminal to get you some bus schedules," said Pam as she opened the trunk, put the bags she had in it, got in the car, and started it up.

Jackie asked one of the bus drivers who was at the bus terminal which bus she needed to take to get to the license bureau, got the schedules she needed, and rushed back to Pam's car. They drove the five minutes it took to get to her house in silence. When they got there Pam took the side door key that led to the basement off her key ring, gave it to Jackie, and waited in the car while Jackie went in and got the documents she needed.

"Get that handbag out that shopping bag and put yo stuff in it. You might want to get your coat out of that bag too. I'm bout to show you where them factories is so you can go bright and early in the morning. They're in back of my house but I think you got to walk down this block to get to them," said Pam when Jackie got back in the car and she pulled off. "Yeah, see there go one of them. The name of it is CTJ. You gon have to walk about a block and a half to get to it, but that shouldn't be a problem for a young gal like you. I guess that's the only factory in this area. I wonder why I thought it was two over this way. Oh, that's probably why, because there are two gas stations over here. You can walk down here when you get done at CTJ and put applications in at both of them gas stations and every other little business in this area. You gon have plenty to do tomorrow. Somebody will hire you if you apply to enough places," she said as she pointed out the different businesses she wanted Jackie to put applications in at.

"I hear ya granny. I'm gon do exactly what you saying. I'm glad it's nice out today; it's at least seventy-five degrees out here. I don't think I'll need that coat," Jackie replied as she took the paper that was stuffed in the purse out, put it in the shopping bag the purse was in, and put the stuff she bought out of the house into the purse.

"This ain't nothing but pneumonia weather; you see I got on a jogging suit and my winter coat."

"Well granny I got on a long sleeved button down shirt and a tweed suit jacket. See, I'm sweating and I ain't even doing nothing. I'll pass on the wool pea coat on top of this ensemble. I might put in some of those applications today if I make it back in time. I got my resume with me, so that should help," said Jackie as Pam pulled up to the bus stop at the mall, and gave her the bus card. Jackie had never worked in her life, so while the other inmates were making resumes out of their work history she invented her one. She got the idea to do it when one of the other inmates asked to use the phone book to find the address and phone number of one of her old jobs. Jackie used the phone book as soon as the other inmate was through with it and made herself a good solid resume. She didn't try to say she was a professional who had a degree or anything; she just said that she worked at a couple of fast food restaurants through out her life. One of the guards typed it up for her before she left, and she planned on using it and the false information on it during her job search.

"Ok, good luck. The number eighteen is the bus that goes by my house, remember to be in by seven. That door in the kitchen will be double locked by 7:01," said Pam as Jackie got out of the car.

"Alright Granny I will," Jackie replied. Then she got on the express bus going to Dayton and it got her downtown in twenty minutes. Downtown Dayton looked very different from downtown Chicago. It was much smaller and it looked like a hangout spot. Jackie smelled weed as soon as she stepped off the bus and she walked past a man drinking a beer out of a tall can of that he tried to disguise with a brown paper bag. She knew that it was beer because of the smell. She only counted two small stores as she walked from the bus to the other bus stop. Downtown Chicago was huge and lined with stores and businesses. The people who weren't down there taking care of business knew not to be down there hanging out. Even the boosters who went downtown to steal out of stores and the people who went down there to pick pockets tried to blend in with the business people in Chicago. They knew that the police would arrest them if they didn't. The people in Dayton were openly disrespectful to its downtown.

Jackie got on the bus that she was told to get on in the opposite direction to get to the license bureau. Her driver's license was valid before she got arrested but she was surprised and happy when they asked her if she wanted to get it transferred over to Dayton. There was a community college right across the street from the license bureau and Jackie went over there to make copies of her resume. She ended up enrolling for the semester that started in September. She was very proud of herself because she passed the entrance exams. She got her GED while she was in jail and she told them that she would bring the certificate back before she started.

It took Jackie a couple of hours to enroll in school, and over an hour to get home. She saw the number eighteen when she got off the bus that bought her from the community college and thought that she would get home faster if she took it to Miamisburg instead of taking the express bus. The express bus took the expressway to get there; the number eighteen took the streets. It was almost five by the time Jackie got back to the house, so she decided to wait until the morning to put in any applications.

She went through the side door and let herself in. She was surprised to see all of the shopping bags in the basement. There was a laundry area down there with a washer, dryer, table, and a shelf above the table. She folded up her clothes, put them on the shelf that was above the table, grabbed her housecoat, and went upstairs.

Pam was eating dinner when Jackie came up. "I've eaten and slept at the same times since I retired seventeen years ago. I have breakfast every morning at seven, lunch at twelve, and supper at five, I think that's how I manage my weight. I try to take good care of this vessel that the good Lord blessed me with," said Pam when Jackie came in. "You're welcomed to join me in the future if you're here around the times I eat. Go ahead and take your bath. I put you a bowl of chicken noodle soup in the microwave. You can warm it up after you come out."

Jackie cleaned up the bathroom after she finished using it. Pam was in her room laying down when Jackie came out, so she ate her dinner alone. She didn't mind because she used the time to tell Toni how her day went. They both went to sleep happy with a positive attitude that night because Jackie had accomplished a lot that morning.

Jackie woke up as soon as she heard the alarm go off at eight. She was feeling so good about the progress that she made the day before that Toni didn't even try to appear. She only popped up when Jackie was feeling lonely and scared and Jackie woke up feeling like she could conquer the world. She put on the same tweed suit she had on the day before after drinking a cup of black coffee and cleaning herself up. She made sure that she had her resumes and ID in her purse before saying bye to Pam and leaving out.

CTJ was the first place she filled an application out at, and that only took thirty minutes. She knew that Pam didn't want her back in the house until after five so she put in applications at every restaurant, hotel, gas station, and factory that she saw. She lied about her work history and her criminal history on half of the applications she filled out, and told the truth on the other half. The woman who taught the self sufficiency class told the inmates to be completely honest on every application they filled out, even if it asked if they'd ever been convicted of a felony. She also said to use the work they did in prison as work experience if that was the only experience they had and to get the contact name and telephone numbers to all of the prospective employers. Jackie wanted to see which way worked better since this was her first time ever going job hunting. She didn't know which way would be more productive but she went home feeling very proud of herself.

The next day was Saturday, and Jackie was pleasantly surprised when she woke up on her own without the screeching sound of the alarm clock. Pam let her lounge around the house all weekend and it felt good not being on the strict schedule she had set for her. Jackie ate when Pam ate, but that was the only contact they had with each other. Pam had a huge collection of books and Jackie enjoyed reading them in the basement by herself. She developed her love of reading while she was in jail. She hated watching television in the recreational area with the other inmates while she was in prison, so she stayed in her room and read during her free time. Seeing all of Pam's books was like seeing an old friend and Pam was more than happy to let her stay in the basement reading most of the weekend.

(2)

Getting Adjusted

Jackie let Toni go to see her parole officer Monday morning because she didn't feel like getting drug tested. She knew that her system was clean so she wasn't worried about dropping dirty, she just felt like the whole process was degrading. Toni didn't mind doing anything Jackie had a problem with doing, so she answered every intrusive question Jackie's parole officer asked her and peed in the cup for him without thinking twice about it. He suggested that she fill out applications for food stamps and public housing and told her the buses she had to take to get to both places. He also gave her a list with every NA meeting in Dayton's information on it and told her how to get to the one that was going to be held at three.

Toni was done filling out the housing and food stamp applications by noon and made it to the bus stop that was across the street from the place that the NA meeting was supposed to be held by two. There was a McDonald's right behind the bus stop, so she went in there to eat and kill some time. She ate her meal at a table that gave her a view of the NA building and filled out a job application. She was there for fifteen minutes before people started going in. She started to go in early too so she could get a seat in the back of the room, but she decided against that idea. She knew if she went in people would try to fellowship with her and she wasn't trying to make any friends who used to do drugs.

Toni walked in the meeting at three on the dot and got irritated instantly. The stench of body odor was strong and she didn't feel like being there. The meeting opened up with the serenity prayer, followed by the twelve steps to the program just like every other NA meeting she had been to. She got disgusted when the other former addicts started telling their horror stories, and mad when they insisted on her introducing herself. She always did hate how you had to introduce yourself as an addict before speaking so she started to leave. She went to get the paper her parole officer told her to get signed from the man she gave it to, and he gave it back to her unsigned. He said that the drug counselor who ran that particular meeting wasn't going to sign any papers until the meeting was adjourned. Toni cussed him out so bad that every person in the room stopped what they were doing to look at them and Jackie had to take over.

"I apologize, I'm not from here and I've never been to a meeting where they made you wait until the meeting is over. Can you put my paper back in the pile with the other ones that have to be signed?" she asked as her eyes changed from green to gray along with her voice, attitude, and facial expression.

"I have never been disrespected that bad in my entire life. If you were a man I would have punched you in your mouth. The only reason I accept yo apology is because I'm trying to work on myself. I don't know how you turn that shit on and off as quick as you did, but it'll be in yo best interest to keep it on off while you here in Dayton. You probably in this meeting because it's court mandated, but a lot of us are here because its life mandated. I don't have a problem with you staying if they don't, but you owe them an apology and the introduction they asked you for," the man angrily responded as he took Jackie's paper from her and put it back in the pile.

Jackie turned around and said, "Hi, my name is Jackie and I'm an addict." She decided to ignore the threats and the suggestion to apologize to the crowd, and was relieved when they all let it drop and replied "Hi Jackie," in unison as she walked back to her seat and sat down.

Jackie didn't say anything else during the meeting and no one said anything else to her. They stood up, held hands, and closed the meeting in prayer. When they were done praying they started giving out hugs. The person who was supposed to hug Jackie stopped in his tracks when he saw her facial expression and she was glad that he got the message. She rushed over to the table to get her paper while the other addicts fellowshipped and got up out of there as fast as she could.

Toni appeared as soon as they got out of the door. *"Man Jackie that was some bullshit. Now I want a drink, or a rock, or something. You seen how them motherfuckers was getting excited when they talked about getting high.*

15

That's why I be hating them meetings. Let's get a beer before we go in, we can drink it downtown like everybody else do."

"Toni you know how Pam is! She gon put us out if she smell anything on us. We gon have to be in her face if we go up to eat," Jackie replied as she walked to the bus stop that was across the street.

"We can grab a couple of ninety-nine cent double cheeseburgers for dinner. We got to go downtown to catch the bus home anyway. We can get a beer from that little store down there. Please Jackie I need a beer. I started to slap the shit out of dude when he was talking that shit to you, but I composed myself. What if we go in and Pam pisses me off? I had a long ass day! I went to Dayton Metropolitan Housing Authority and to the Job Center to put in applications for food stamps and housing after going to see yo P.O. I deserve a beer," Toni pleaded.

Jackie wanted a beer too so Toni's plan started sounding good. She loved Pam's cooking, but it felt good eating restaurant food for the first time in over a year. She decided she was going to have that beer and that burger and went into McDonalds. It was a little after five by the time her bus made it downtown so she took her time walking the half a block to the store. She bought a twenty-four ounce can of Budweiser, kept it in the little brown bag the clerk put it in, and walked to the most secluded bus stop going in the direction she was going in. She sat at the bus stop and drank her beer before her bus came. They ran every hour so she didn't look strange sitting there for so long.

"I feel better now don't you?" Toni asked.

"Yeah, I'm good."

Jackie got in at 6:50 and she could tell that Pam was in a bad mood because she heard her slam the kitchen door and put the padlock on it as soon as Jackie made it down the stairs. Pam's foul mood made Jackie happy that she went against her rules and drank a beer. It satisfied her to think that Pam thought she was going to bed without eating supper and her belly was full from McDonalds. She had thirty-seven dollars left and decided right then and there that she was going to have a drink whenever she felt like it. She thought that Pam didn't appreciate it when she tried to follow all of her rules anyway, so she might as well break the one that she felt wouldn't hurt anyone. She had to go to three NA meetings a week and she knew that she was going to drink after every one of them if they went anything like the one she went to earlier.

Jackie walked to the mall and did her job hunting in there the next day. It was a long walk from Pam's house to there, but it seemed like it took more time and effort to take the bus. She started to get a beer to drink on the way home, but decided against it because she didn't see anyone walking around drinking beer in Miamisburg. She enjoyed the beer the night before so much because Pam didn't know about it. The thrill would evaporate if she got caught because Pam would love it if she got arrested for doing something as dumb as public intoxication.

When Jackie made it in Pam told her that CTJ called and she told them that Jackie could make it to the group interview at nine in the morning. Pam was so happy for Jackie that she went out and bought her a nice black spring business suit for the occasion and made her a cake. Jackie felt kind of bad when Pam presented her with the cake and started singing *For She's a Jolly Good Fellow* to her, but that didn't stop her from craving a beer. She lied on her application to CTJ and she was worried about them finding out the truth.

Toni ended up going to the interview for Jackie and got them the job. It was a group interview and the person conducting it didn't ask any of the applicants any personal questions. They had to take a math test, a personality test, and a safety test after watching a film on safety in the work place. Toni passed them with flying colors so they sent her to Kettering to take a drug test that she passed. After passing the drug test she was given a choice between attending the orientation at nine the next morning or nine Monday morning. She chose to go to the one being held the next morning because her money was down to twenty-seven dollars, and they said that she would get paid for going. There were only two days left in the work week, but Toni was ready to start making some money. They started her out at eight dollars an hour, so if she went to the five hour orientation and worked a full twelve hour day Friday she knew that she would make more than she had when she got out.

Toni was feeling real good about getting the job, but she still had to go to Dayton to go to a two o'clock NA meeting. She made it through that meeting without any altercations, but she still wanted a drink to celebrate. The NA meeting she went to was on a completely different side of town from the last one, but every bus in Dayton connected downtown. She went to the same little store she went to at first and tried to buy some liquor, but she had to settle for beer because regular stores didn't sell liquor in them in Dayton like they did in Chicago. She wasn't finished with the beer when her bus pulled up so she stayed until she did finish it. She knew that she had an hour long wait until the next bus was supposed to come so she bought another beer and drank it before it came.

It was only six when the bus made it to the mall so Toni decided to get off and walk home. She was very tipsy and wanted to walk the beer off before facing Pam. She went straight to the bathroom that was in the basement and brushed her teeth so Pam wouldn't smell it on her breath if she called her up. But she was paranoid for nothing; Pam left her alone for the night and locked the door right before seven.

Toni got up when the alarm went off and went to the orientation because Jackie was too nervous to go. She reported to the office and waited on the supervisor to come and get her. The last time she went to CTJ she found out that it was an automobile factory, so it wasn't necessary to dress in business attire. She wore the Avis sneakers and one of the casual outfits Pam bought her. She knew that the outfit was old fashioned and that no one wore Avis shoes, but she didn't get embarrassed about her gear until the orientation group took a tour of the building. She thought the employees would be wearing uniforms, but they were dressed like people dressed in the streets and she could tell that most of them were younger than her. She wished she would have said something when Pam started picking out the ugly clothes instead of letting Jackie handle the situation completely by herself.

The next day Toni wore one of her v necked t shirts, a pair of the Lee jeans, and her Reeboks. The v neck looked a lot better with the Lee jeans than the flower print shirts Pam picked out. She knew that the Reeboks were out of style and beat up looking, but they were a lot less noticeable in the dimly lit factory than the biscuit toed, bright, white Avis gym shoes. She didn't mind wearing the Avis shoes every where else she went, because she didn't care about the opinions of the people she encountered in those places. This was her first real job and she would have to see the people who worked there every scheduled work day, and she didn't want them talking about her. She normally didn't care what people said about her, but she felt like a self conscious fish out of water in the automobile factory.

She worked in an area with three other people, Marcus, Terry, and Paul. Marcus went to get the parts that the piece of paper that came out of the printer said to get, and sat them on the table. Paul scanned the parts after Marcus sat them on the table with a scanner. Terry put the parts in the rack after they were scanned and trained Toni. The job was real easy and the people who worked in the area seemed real nice. Toni usually stayed to herself and tried not to communicate with anyone besides Jackie, but the people she worked with made that impossible. She had to talk to Terry to let her know that she understood the things she was teaching her, and the rest of them kept cracking jokes and asking her questions.

Toni liked all of the people in her work area but the person she got the closest to was Terry. They were inseparable throughout the entire work day. They took all of their authorized and unauthorized breaks together and Toni felt like she knew Terry's entire life story by the end of the day. Toni was fine with Terry monopolizing the conversation because she didn't like talking a lot, and Terry's story was interesting and she told it in chronological order. She was raised in a predominately white suburb in Ohio called Huber Heights. Her siblings and she had such a hard time trying to fit in that Terry started sleeping with the little white boys she went to middle school with. They would have sex with her, but they didn't want anyone to know. She said that she had very low self esteem until she moved to Dayton around black men who appreciated her features.

Toni couldn't understand how Terry could have ever had low self esteem because she was beautiful to her. Her peanut butter colored face didn't have any scars or acne on it. She had big lips with red lipstick on that looked real pretty to Toni, and she normally hated how red lipstick looked on women with big lips. Her teeth were the whitest and straightest teeth she had ever seen, and her cute little round nose looked like it was made specifically for her face. Her brown eyes were big and slanted, and Toni could tell she had her eyebrows arched because they looked perfect. She had some micro braids in her hair that reached her butt. She told Toni that she had 4 kids, but her shape was so fierce that you couldn't tell that she had any. She had on a black Donna Karen t shirt, some Donna Karen jeans, some Air Force One gym shoes, and her nails were done. Toni thought she was over dressed to be working in the dirty factory, but she did make her want to look a little nicer than she looked.

Terry was part of a large group of CTJ workers who went to a bar located a couple of blocks away from the work site every Friday, and she took Toni with her. She treated her to an order of hot wings, a double shot of Remy, and a Budweiser. Toni had a ball with her, but she peeped how she started trying to get information out of her after she started drinking. Toni didn't care because all she told her were lies. She decided not to tell her any of their business as soon as Terry started telling her own. Toni even lied about things she didn't have to lie about and she was enjoying herself. She invented her entire life story as Terry hung on to every word she said.

Toni was drunk, but she still stayed on her square. She kept a close eye on her watch so she wouldn't break Pam's curfew rule. They got off of work at five, made it to the bar by 5:07, and Toni asked her to take her home at 6:30. She told Terry that she came to Dayton to help take care of her sick grandmother and was getting worried about her. Terry stopped at a gas station before she dropped Toni off, and Toni went in and bought a bottle of mouthwash out of there. She rinsed her mouth out with it before letting herself in the house. She tried to avoid Pam by rushing downstairs, but she called her name as soon as she heard her come in the house. Pam was so happy that she got a job that she didn't ask her where she went after work and Toni was relieved. She told her all about her first day at work, took a bath, and went to sleep.

Terry called Toni the next day to invite her to a barbeque she was throwing, but Toni declined. She told her that she had to stay in with her grandmother because the nurse didn't come on Saturdays, but she really had to go to a NA meeting. The other reasons she didn't go was because she didn't have anything to wear and she didn't completely trust Terry. She didn't mind going to the bar with her after work because everyone who went wore what they wore to work, but she knew they would be dressed nice at the barbeque. She didn't know if she wanted to develop a friendship outside of work with Terry because she had never hung out with someone like her. She talked too much, and she was too loud and too flirtatious for Toni's taste, but she was always nice to her. She introduced her to everyone she knew and included her in their group, but Toni was a loner who didn't know if she wanted to socialize with so many people. Terry told her about each and every last one of them after they walked away from their table, which was another reason she didn't really trust the woman. If she would tell her the people she had known for year's business, what would stop her from telling others hers? They could never be real friends because Toni could never tell her the truth about anything that happened in her life.

Toni handled the next two weeks by herself. She went to work, and to their NA meetings without even thinking about consulting Jackie. She was really enjoying herself. She found out that the crew of people she worked with put on for a fifth of Remy Martin every day and started chipping in after her first payday. They didn't do it the first day they met her because they didn't know if they could trust her. Terry told her about it when she came to pick her up the first Monday after her first day of work. Terry was the person who always went to buy the liquor so she had to tell Toni because she was always with her. They kept the Remy and lots of empty McDonald cups with the lids to them in a cabinet that was in the area they worked in. Toni didn't like the fact that people who didn't put any money on the liquor were welcomed to it, and the group had no problem with stopping them when she spoke on it. It stretched their liquor out and they didn't have to take any unnecessary chances on trying to sneak it in as much. Toni was a fast learner, with a good sense of humor and the group was happy she was put over there with them.

Toni didn't have much contact with Pam. She left out at 4:30 every weekday morning and didn't come back in until her curfew. Pam extended it to 9:30 when she started working because Terry told Toni that there was a lot of overtime available if she wanted some. She explained that they got paid time and a half for every hour over forty that they worked. The calculator started going off in Toni's mind immediately and she wanted some of that extra money. She was already working sixty hour weeks and if she stayed until nine Monday through Thursday with Terry that would be seventy-six hours a week. She didn't know about taxes and was highly disappointed when she saw her check. She was about to go in the office and go off on management, until Terry asked her why she didn't add any dependents to her W4 form. Toni looked confused when she asked her so Terry explained that she used all four of her kids throughout the year so the government wouldn't take so many taxes out. She told her that she should at least use her grandmother as one since she took care of her. Then she led her to the office and showed her how to fill out the form she needed to fill out to make the change. Toni wanted to mention Jackie's two daughters, but she had already told Terry that they didn't have any kids when Terry asked her.

Toni was angry when her paycheck wasn't the $752 she had calculated it out to be, but she got over it when Terry told her that they were going to get it back at the end of the year. She got paid weekly and grossed $497 that first week she stayed over and worked overtime with Terry. She gave Pam $100, bought herself a spring jacket, a couple of decent outfits, and some all white Nike Air Max gym shoes to wear outside of work. She bought herself some cheap steel-toe boots, a couple of packs of Hanes white short sleeved t-shirts, three pairs of blue khaki pants, and three pairs of blue khaki shorts to wear to work. She didn't judge anyone who wore their fly clothes to work; she just wasn't going to be one of them. The uniform she bought for herself was cheaper and less noticeable.

Toni loved working and her new life so much, that she decided to continue taking control of Jackie's life. She kept her past and her private life to herself and got through her workdays letting others amuse her with their life stories. She went in the house whenever she felt like it and got drunk whenever she wanted to. Pam still went to sleep at seven and when Toni found out how hard of a sleeper she was, she cancelled the 9:30 curfew Pam put on her. She never spent the night out or bought any alcohol in the house because she was still afraid of getting caught, but she broke every one of Pam's rules that she could get away with breaking.

(3)

Wow!

Seven months had passed and Jackie was rudely jolted out of the place of peace she had disappeared to deep within herself. She thought she was being violated so she started screaming and clawing at the strange man she felt trying to enter her. He jumped up confused when she started attacking him and she jumped up off the bed and made a dash for the door when he did.

"Jackie what the fuck is you doing?" Toni asked as she led Jackie to the bathroom.

"What am I doing? Shouldn't I be asking you that question? Where the fuck are we and who the fuck was you about to give my pussy to?"

"That's Marcus the dude we work with. Please let me do this Jackie, I'll explain everything later."

"Where is Pam Toni? I knew you was gon get us put out."

"Jackie this is our apartment, we just moved in last week. Chill let me handle this."

"Toni, dude ain't getting no ass tonight."

"Jackie are you ok?" yelled Marcus as he knocked on the bathroom door.

"Yeah, just give me a minute and I'll be out," Toni answered. *"Jackie please just peep how cool he is. We ain't got to do nothing with him tonight; he'll be ok with that. Just let me do all the talking."*

"Ok, Toni but you got a lot of explaining to do," said Jackie as she grabbed a pink silk robe off of the back of the bathroom door, put it on, and let Toni take over as she watched.

23

When they came out of the bathroom Marcus held his hands up in a defensive manner. "Are you ok? I should have kissed you down there first so it would have been a little easier to get it in. You the only woman besides my baby mother I ever even thought about tasting. But you worth it because you choosing to give yourself to me out of every man you've seen these past seven years you chose to be celibate," he said as he gently took them in his arms.

Toni tried to pull away from Marcus until she felt Jackie move forward and soften in his strong arms. *"I feel safe with him, like I know him already Toni. I still don't want to have sex with him, but this just might work. He's the first man I've wanted to have sex with since Juan,"* Jackie silently said to Toni as she inhaled Marcus's wonderful smelling cologne. She didn't know how she felt so connected to the handsome stranger, but she did. He aroused the majority of her senses, and no man had ever been able to do that. He stood about 6'5", was the color of dark chocolate, and had big, pretty, dark brown, almond shaped eyes that made Jackie melt with the long eyelashes that were attached to them. He had deep dimples in his cheeks and when he smiled his beautiful smile, it made her smile. He had sexy LL Cool J looking lips with a goatee shaped up like Morris Chestnut that she instantly fell in love with. She also liked the way his head full of jet black waves were shaped up. He impressed her by having his jeans and socks on when they came out the bathroom. When he picked them up and carried them downstairs to the couch instead of taking them back to the bedroom, he earned her respect.

"I didn't know your eyes changed colors. That shit is so sexy, I don't know which color I like the most. They pretty when they green, but they got that lil devious twinkle in them. When they this beautiful transparent gray color, they look innocent and vulnerable. Like you need me to take care of you. You know I'll take care of you, don't you Jackie?" asked Marcus as he looked Jackie into her eyes and she nodded. He pulled her into his arms, kissed her, stood up, picked her up, and carried her upstairs. She let him spend the night in her bed but they didn't have sex, he just held her all night. She enjoyed herself because she had never been held like that before, but she was ready for him to go so Toni could explain herself.

"Jackie I'm sorry, but I felt like it was my turn to shine. I ain't never did this to you before, but you've done this to me several times and I never complained! There were times I woke up years later and you didn't even try to explain what happened. You asked me to get us the job and I did. I've been

working long hard hours at it, going to our NA meetings, and complying with our parole. I didn't get us put out of Pam's house, we moved out! I accomplished everything you thought we couldn't in half the time," said Toni right after Marcus kissed them and walked out the door the next day.

"But, Toni you're a guest here! I'm not saying that I'm not proud of you, all I'm saying is I deserve to know what's going on with me at all times! These people call us Jackie! Everything you do has to be done in my name so I think the courteous thing to do is to let me know what's going on in my life, especially with my body!"

"You right Jackie, I'm sorry bout that. It won't happen again."

"It's cool Toni; now tell me everything beginning with Marcus's sexy ass."

"Well he's twenty-four, I know that's young but he's real mature. I met him at CTJ, and got to know him because he works in the area I work in. I didn't pay him any attention at first, because you know how we are about men, but he got a real good sense of humor and he kept making me laugh. He has one child. A seven year old little girl name Ashley, and he always comes to work complaining about her mother. You know we know all about custody so I be giving him advice on how to handle his situation. He always flirted with me but our relationship remained innocent, until this broad we work with name Terry started playing cupid. I like him, he seems cool. He pays his child support and still helps me out."

"Everybody we work with seem cool, but them motherfuckers talk too damn much. Everything I told them was a lie. They all sit around talking about sex, so I told them that I've been celibate for seven years. I thought that would keep the men away from us, but that got most of them trying their best to get some. It's like a game to them. They always on the new girl and whoever hits her first is the man. But Marcus seems different; he gives me all of his undivided attention. The rest of them see that I'm interested in him and they still buy my snacks, lunches, and liquor, I mean I don't pay for shit at work Jackie. One of them wants it so bad that he does my job while I be kicking it with Marcus."

"Liquor? Y'all be drinking at work?"

"Yeah, Jackie we be getting wasted at work. They was doing that shit before I got there. Some of them get high in there cars too. Marcus be trying to get me to smoke weed with him, but you know we can't cause we be getting drug tested for parole. You know we'll get locked up if we drop dirty and that would be too embarrassing. I told all of them that we ain't never did drugs or been to jail before. They asked me if I had any kids and I told them no.

Everything them people know about you is a figment of my imagination. I even lied about Pam; I told them we were down here to help our sick grandmother. We just moved out of her house and none of them met her and Terry was taking me back and forth to work. Oh, that's another thing. Pam bought us a 1991 Pontiac Bonneville. It ain't all that but it runs good. I was real surprised when she gave it to me saying how proud of me she was. We only live a half an hour away from her, but she prefers the secluded life she was living before we came. I took her shopping and out to eat for her birthday, and we do talk on the phone every now and then, but I don't see her that much."

"That's cool with me, I felt like I couldn't really be myself around her anyway. Please tell me you got my daddy's diary from her house?"

"Yeah, that box Angel sent you was the first thing I packed up. I put it in one of the drawers on the nightstand by our bed. I didn't feel comfortable around Pam either. She ain't gon never forgive us for what we did to her, so it's best to move on. She be trying, but I can still see the pain and the fear in her eyes when I'm around her. But on a lighter note, we got everything we need so life has been good."

"That's cool Toni but I want to take control for a minute. I ain't trying to get rid of you, but both of us like Marcus so I really need to get to know him."

"That's fair Jackie. I'll go to work with you Monday to teach you how to do the job and to point everybody out. You can enjoy the rest of the weekend by yourself if you want to," said Toni as she showed Jackie their apartment. She was very proud of herself because their apartment looked very nice. Every room was furnished and decorated with expensive furniture and décor and it was all paid for. She put everything from her furniture down to her soap in layaways at the different stores they were sold in when she first started getting letters from Dayton Metropolitan Housing Authority. She paid everything down to zero and had her living room furniture, dining room furniture, bedroom furniture, 64-inch big screen television, black portable bar, and washer and dryer set delivered with in the week that she moved in. She got the idea to do layaways from watching Terry put her kid's Christmas presents in one in July. *"I know these the projects, but it looks nice in here don't it?"*

"It looks real nice in here; I didn't even know these were the projects. How long have I been out of commission and when were you going to wake me up? I know this apartment took at least a year to get," said Jackie as she felt herself getting angry. The apartment was built like a townhouse, with an

upstairs and downstairs. The walls were made out of plaster and the floors were made out of wood. Jackie was used to the projects in Chicago and most of them looked like the ones off the television show *Good Times*. Those walls were made out of bricks and the floors were made out of concrete. The different housing sites she'd been to in Chicago had ten to fifteen, tall, brown, brick buildings in them. The buildings could be seven to twenty-five stories high and could have up to fifteen apartments on each floor. When Marcus left Jackie got a glimpse of the apartment that was across from her and it looked a lot different than what she thought a project would look like. They were brick, but they were attractive looking townhomes connected to each other.

"Jackie it's only been seven months. Today is Saturday November sixteenth; I was gon wake you up before the holidays got here. I forgot all about this apartment until they started sending me letters and making me go to appointments for it. I started going apartment hunting about a week before the letters about this one started coming to Pam's house. You know she gave us a time limit. I been handling everything you know you wouldn't have been able to handle and you still attacking me. Ok, I'm sorry for finally enjoying myself! I told you I'm bout to step back so you can do you," said Toni as she looked Jackie in their eyes in the oval shaped mirror that was attached to the cherry wood dresser in their bedroom, and started crying.

"You did good Toni, don't cry. I'll try to be a little more considerate now that I see how it feels to come back and not know what's going on. But you can never do that again. You need permission to give away my body, especially my heart. I need get to know Marcus so I can make sure he's the right person for me. I can feel the physical connection, which says a lot. I just want to make sure we connect mentally too," said Jackie as she walked to the bathroom and washed their face.

"Thanks Jackie, I tried. The name of these projects is Dunbar Manor. I picked these because they only twenty minutes away from the job. Marcus can't come back over today or tomorrow because this is his weekend to get Ashley. I use these weekends to knock out our NA meetings. Our parole officer don't care when we go to the meetings, as long as we go to them. I like to go on Saturdays because I have to work during the week and the ones that be in session on Saturdays are right in this neighborhood. I'll take you to them today. We don't have anything to do tomorrow so you chill by yourself. Your sisters' call you every Sunday so they can keep you company then. All of them got apartments in the Harold Ickes on the Southside of Chicago. All they really talk about

is the past so it'll be easy for you to keep up with the conversations. You'll see Marcus all day Monday," Toni happily replied as she took the silk hair scarf off their head and un-wrapped their long black hair. She got it dyed black, blow dried, flat-ironed, and clipped into a long full pretty wrap when she got her second paycheck. She liked the way the hairstyle looked so much that she started going to the beautician who did it every Thursday after her first appointment.

Toni got them ready to go to their NA meeting and Jackie was very happy with the way they looked after getting dressed. Their long black wrap touched their elbows, their eyebrows had a fierce arch, and the scarlet red colored lipstick made their lips look extra pouty. Toni put them on a white long sleeved Donna Karen button down shirt, some dark blue Donna Karen jeans, and a pair of black low heeled Coach Shoe boots. It was real cold out so they wore the black pea coat Pam bought them. Jackie hadn't looked cute to herself in a long time so she almost cried when she saw how pretty they looked when Toni was finished getting them ready. She even put them on some jewelry and a big, black, leather Coach purse. Jackie sold her last set of jewelry for crack five years ago and it felt good having a nicer set than the one she had at first.

The NA meetings went a lot smoother than Jackie thought they would go because the same group of people went to both of them and Toni knew everyone. She made up a fictional life story for that group of people like she did for the CTJ employees. Jackie was quiet during the meetings preferring to observe the people in attendance instead of having them observe her. Toni acted completely different from Jackie because she was a much louder and aggressive person. When Jackie was in attendance Toni had to act like she wanted her to act, and that caught a couple of people off guard. They thought she was sick or something. Toni had been in their circle for eight months and they had started looking forward to going to the NA meetings so they could hear the exciting war stories she told in them. They had crime in Dayton, but the crime in Chicago was organized and Toni had those people thinking she used to be some type of queen bee, gang starting, diva in her prime. She did her thing, but not the way she told them she did and not on that level.

When they made it in from the NA meetings Toni took off their coat, hung it up, took of their shoe boots, and put them on a pair of house shoes. Then she grabbed their Remy Martin from behind the portable bar, poured Jackie a triple shot, and left. She didn't mind Jackie enjoying the fruits from her labor because she knew that she wouldn't be there if it wasn't for her. Jackie was grateful for the alone time and decided to take a candle lit bubble bath while sipping on her favorite liquor. This was her first apartment and she wanted to do something she had never done anywhere else, so she stayed naked after she got out the tub, and put on her lotion and deodorant. She hadn't watched television in years and was very happy that Toni had cable installed in all of their rooms. Toni's friend Terry called to ask her if she wanted to go to a club with her, but Jackie declined. She was happier than she had been in years chilling at home by herself.

Jackie got up the next morning and cooked herself some breakfast. Toni had their kitchen stocked with every food that they liked. She even had some insulin in the refrigerator so Jackie knew that she was taking care of their health on top of every other need they had. She started feeling bad for getting mad at her because she did a great job while she was gone, but she stopped herself from letting the guilt seep in. She couldn't let Toni just take over her life without permission. If she would have let her gotten away with doing it this time she would have tried to do it again; and Jackie couldn't afford to wake up like Rip Van Winkle. She pushed the thoughts of forgiveness out of her mind and decided that the reprimand she gave Toni was necessary.

She was very happy with the way Toni had their whole life flowing, and those good feelings soared when her youngest sister, Angel called. It had been years since she heard any of her siblings voices so her body filled with emotions that she managed to control. Jackie knew that Toni didn't cry when she talked to Angel so she didn't want to either. She could tell that Angel was high off of something, but she didn't say anything about it. She felt like she didn't have the right to because she would have been just as high if not higher than Angel if she was in Chicago with them. Her two older twin sisters, Tamika and Jamika, didn't call which didn't surprise Jackie because they had never been close. Her three baby sisters Angel, Jennifer, and Sharon were crazy about her and she talked to them for over seven hours. She tried to discuss the future with each of them during their phone conversations, but they preferred talking about the good old days. She found herself taking the trip down memory lane that Toni told her she was going to be taking and it felt good. It kept her mind off the anxiety she was feeling about going to work for the first time in the morning.

(4)

This Is My Life

After eating breakfast, Toni got them dressed in a pair of long underwear, a plain blue cotton Hanes sweatshirt, and a pair of the Lee jeans Pam bought them. Then she surprised Jackie by slipping on a black Carhartt snowsuit for men, some black ear muffs, and some black steel-toe boots. *"Toni I'm sweating bullets, why we got all this stuff on if we work on the inside?"*

"Jackie you gon be thanking me when you see how cold it gets in that factory. I think it's colder in there than it is outside."

The factory was as cold as Toni said it would be, but they were well equipped. Toni waved to a lot of people as they walked to their work area. *"The black woman with the micros is Terry, she the only woman I kick it with outside of work. The white man with the blonde hair is Paul, he kind of corny but he cool. You already know Marcus. He brings me a cup of coffee every morning, that's why he's approaching us,"* said Toni as they walked into their work area.

The work was very easy so Jackie was able to catch on pretty quick. She was just getting real good when the plant stopped working. CTJ worked for Premium Motors and whenever they had a maintenance problem, CTJ couldn't work until they resolved the issue at PM. Sometimes the problems took minutes to solve and sometimes they took hours. It really didn't matter because the CTJ employees couldn't leave until the end of their shift regardless. They had to be there ready to work whenever the problem got solved. Most of the CTJ workers used shutdown time to kick it and Jackie joined in with them. She started not to drink any of the Remy they had, but the rest of the crew looked like they were having too much fun getting drunk. She sent Toni away, poured her a cup, and tried to loosen up.

If Only For One Night by Luther Vandross came on the radio they had in their area and she surprised herself by dancing with Marcus when he grabbed her. His body felt so good against hers that she didn't want him to let her go when the song ended. "Can I spend the night with you tonight?" he whispered in her ear.

"Damn Marcus you ain't hit that shit yet?" Terry loudly asked before Jackie could answer his question.

"Rather or not he hit this yet is none of your business," Jackie said angrily.

"Well Jackie you have kept my man waiting for a long ass time. We just trying to see who won the bet," said Paul.

"What?" yelled Jackie. *"Jackie chill out they only playing with you. Terry and Paul both know that Marcus has been trying to hit me for months, so they got this fake ass bet going on. It's only a joke,"* Toni said calming Jackie down before she said something they would regret out loud.

"Y'all leave my baby alone, we gon do the grown folks dance when we feel it's time to. Here's a dollar for both of y'all so we can stop going through this every Monday," Marcus said with a laugh as he tried to hand Terry and Paul a dollar a piece.

"Naw, I want to earn my money. Paul gon pay me my dollar when Jackie walks her dick needing ass in here satisfied. I keep telling y'all I'm a sexologist! I'll be able to tell when they do it without them saying shit. Her eyes changed colors this weekend, but she still got that look like she need to be fucked in them," said Terry with and exaggerated laugh.

"You got that I'm tired of just getting fucked look in yours," Jackie replied with a more exaggerated laugh than Terry's. She didn't know how Toni played with them and she didn't care. Her sex life wasn't some workplace joke and she didn't like or trust Terry at all.

"Why would you say that to her Jackie? She real sensitive about the men she's slept with. You need to calm down for real and do like I do. I use their picking as a way to flirt with Marcus. Quit acting like you embarrassed because you ain't gave up the pussy and be proud of it."

"I'll try Toni. This shit is new to me," Jackie replied as Terry's response pulled her out of the conversation she was having with Toni in her mind.

"Damn, you got a nasty ass attitude today! I was just fucking with yo ass like I do every other day. You should have been told me you didn't get down like that instead of trying to hit below the belt and shit," Terry replied with a look of hurt and embarrassment in her eyes.

"I'm sorry, I'm just not in the mood today," said Jackie feeling kind of bad for the woman. She wasn't trying to hurt her feelings but she was getting embarrassed by the childish teasing. The more she got to know Marcus, the more she liked him so she wasn't going to let the woman front her off in front of him. She started enjoying herself once she let her guard down and started reveling in the spotlight being on her. PM shut down at eight and didn't start back up for the rest of the day. She couldn't believe she was getting paid while having so much fun, they even went outside and had a snowball fight.

Terry wanted Jackie to stay and work some overtime with her, but Jackie told her that she was through working all of those extra hours in the freezing factory. Toni had bought everything they needed and she didn't like Terry; so she decided that the extra money was no longer worth what it took to get it. Marcus walked her to her car and asked if he could come over after changing his clothes, and Jackie said yes. She couldn't think of a better way to spend the time Toni used to spend working overtime to get to know Marcus.

"Toni, I'm bout to kick it with Marcus and I don't want you popping in. I appreciate you stepping in when I needed you at work, but I got this," Jackie said as soon as they got in the car and started it up.

Toni got mad and jealous instantly. *"Jackie you full of shit! You just coming back like fuck everything I had going on! I was able to buy all of the shit we needed from working all of that overtime, now you trying to act like you too good to work it! Terry might not be your cup of tea, but that bitch taught me all kinds of shit! I can tell you think that Paul is a lame, but there were times that I got to sit on this ass sipping on Remy because he did my work all day! And now you talking bout don't pop up while you kick it with Marcus! You wouldn't even know him if it wasn't for me,"* she replied as tears started to form in their eyes.

"So that's what this is about. Toni this is your first time getting mad over any decision I ever made and I've made some fucked up ones in the past. I know how much you like Marcus; I can feel it in our heart. But you had your time with him, now it's my turn. You didn't share him so I don't think it's fair of you to ask me to. Damn wipe your eyes, here comes this bitch," said Jackie as Terry walked towards their car. She wiped their eyes and let down the window.

"Girl I feel you on that overtime. I started to stay but PM still ain't up and I was freezing. I don't need the money no way. You know I got the kids Christmas stuff out of layaway two weeks ago. Damn, one of yo eyes gray and the other one is green. You told me yo eyes be changing but I ain't never seen them do it until today," said Terry after she made it to the car.

"I told you, I got these freaky eyes from my daddy. Yeah I thought about that shit though. The money was good, but I got everything I need. Today is one of the coldest days of the year, so we shouldn't have been in there no way. But guess who bout to meet me at the crib?" Toni asked. She liked Terry so she hurried up and engaged in the conversation with her before Jackie got the chance to offend her again.

"Hell naw, Marcus's fine ass! I told you y'all make a cute couple. I would have jumped on that if I didn't have my baby Jerome. Have fun girl, I'm bout to get my ass to the house with my man," Terry said as she gave Toni a high five. Then she got in the blue 1996 Ford Expedition truck that was parked next to them.

"Toni don't tell that bitch none of my business no more. No wonder the bitch feels she can look in our eyes and tell if we had some dick, you telling her every move we make with Marcus. Yeah I'm gon ride this one out by myself. I'll holler at you if I need you."

"That's cool Jackie you wanted to ride it out by yourself anyway. The girl was cool to me and I needed somebody to discuss these feelings I have for him with. She hooked me up with him, so why not her? Well, you do you Jackie. I do think it's time for me to rotate," said Toni before going as deep inside of Jackie as she could.

Jackie drove home with no regrets. Her mind was clear and erotic emotions flooded her body as she took a bath and put her Pear Glace Victoria's Secret lotion on. She started to put on some lingerie, but decided to go with some cute cotton pajamas from Victoria's Secret. She was in the kitchen cooking dinner when Marcus knocked on the door.

A pile of snow blew in when she let him in. "It's getting real bad out there. It took me a hour to get here and you know I only live fifteen minutes away from you. I bought me some personals, clean drawers, liquor and beer in case we get snowed in. I hope you got plenty of food," he said as he sat his bag on the floor, took off his coat, hung it up, and took off his boots. He bear hugged Jackie, and put his cold hands underneath her shirt on her back. She squealed and tried to squirm away but he was strong so she couldn't get away. Then he picked her up, she wrapped her legs around him, and they kissed. He was built like a muscular basketball player so lifting her didn't take any effort and Jackie liked that.

She felt him getting aroused so she jumped down. "I got to check on our steaks, unless you like yours burnt," she said pulling away from him as he tried to grab her. He followed her to the kitchen and put his beer in the refrigerator while she finished cooking. He mopped up the melted snow by the front door while she put their steaks, dinner rolls, asparagus, and baked potatoes on their plates.

Marcus went upstairs to wash up for dinner and Jackie had the table set with candles and wine to go along with their dinner by the time he made it back down. "I hope that food tastes as good as it looks and you as perfect as you seem to be," he said as bent down to kiss Jackie before sitting down to eat. Jackie assumed that the food was good because Marcus ate two plates of it.

They stayed up playing cards and watching movies all night. Work was cancelled the next morning because the snowstorm had reached a level one status. Ohio had accumulated eight feet of snow throughout the night, so Marcus couldn't leave even if he wanted to. The whole town was shut down for three days and Jackie got to know Marcus very well during those three days. She thought she was going to make him wait longer than the five months Toni held out, but she gave in that first morning they didn't have to go to work. Marcus knew how to turn her on better than any man she'd ever been with so she couldn't fight it. He gave her the most sensual massage she had ever felt which had her hotter than she had ever been. He flipped her over and tasted her after massaging her whole body before entering her. No one had ever made love to Jackie before, and he made her feel so special that she cried. He made her feel even more special when he kissed her tears away.

Jackie couldn't imagine sharing Marcus with any other woman including Toni, so she didn't let her come back. Every time she tried to pop in Jackie would say "you are not real" over and over in her mind. She had to do that for about four months, until Toni stopped trying. She hated to do her like that but she just couldn't imagine Marcus with anyone besides her. She made him her everything. She only kicked it with Terry every other weekend when Marcus had his daughter; every other moment was spent with him. Toni used to be with Terry during every break, Jackie spent hers with Marcus. They got so close that everyone who saw them together knew they were a couple, which attracted the other women in the plant to Marcus for some strange reason. Jackie saw them trying to flirt with her man, but she thought that he only had eyes for her. He constantly told her that she satisfied him in every way because she was the perfect combination of a housewife, a hustler, and a freak. She was down to make love to him anytime and anywhere which he enjoyed very much. She wasn't worried about her competition because she thought she had Marcus sprung.

Jackie got off of parole a month after they started dating exclusively, so she didn't have to go to anymore NA meetings. The group that she met in the meetings tried to encourage her to continue attending them, but Jackie refused. They always spoke against drinking alcohol in NA and she liked getting drunk with Marcus. She even started smoking weed with him when she got off of parole. She was happy that she wasn't smoking crack or tooting heroin anymore, but she didn't want to spend the rest of her life completely sober. Most of the friends she met in the meetings were serious about their sobriety, and she wasn't so she stopped dealing with them entirely when she stopped going to the NA meetings.

(5)

Rhonda

Jackie was enjoying her life. She loved her job and the people she worked with. When she got her first income tax check, she got her car painted, put music in it, and rims on it, so she loved it now. She had a man who satisfied her in every way and a nice apartment that she only had to pay $150 a month to live in. She wanted Marcus to move in with her, but he couldn't. His daughter Ashley's mother, Evelyn, had a clause put in their custody papers that said he could only visit with her at his apartment. Jackie was angry about the clause in the beginning, but she got over it because Marcus spent every night he didn't have Ashley with her. A year and a half had passed and the arrangement ended up working out well, because she started going out with Terry whenever Marcus couldn't come over. She hadn't been out in years and it felt good to get sexy and dance. She didn't cheat on Marcus but she liked the attention she received from the men in the clubs. She was a thirty-six year old ex crack head getting hit on by men the young girls wanted, and it felt good.

Her life changed instantly with one phone call from her oldest daughter Rhonda. Jackie had two daughters she hadn't seen in thirteen years, twenty year old Rhonda, and eighteen year old Melissa. The last time she saw them she was giving them to their paternal grandmother, Bertha, after their father, Leon's funeral. She would have let thirteen more years pass if her sister Angel hadn't given Rhonda her telephone number. Rhonda told her that Bertha put her out two years prior to their conversation because she had a baby girl who came out looking just like Jackie. Bertha was so evil that she left the hospital right after she cut the baby's umbilical cord and bought everything Rhonda and her daughter owned up there. She told Rhonda that she saw her baby's eyes change colors three times in the short amount of time she held her so she couldn't bring her in her house. Rhonda went from the hospital to the shelter and she still didn't have an apartment. She asked Jackie if she would help her if she came there and Jackie said yes. The only reasons she agreed to help Rhonda were to see her baby and to spite Bertha, her most hated enemy. Both of her girls came out looking like their father, so Jackie couldn't wait to meet the tiny replica of herself.

Rhonda didn't want to move in with Jackie, she wanted to go to a shelter so she could get her own place. Jackie got the telephone book and gave Rhonda the phone numbers to all of the homeless shelters in Dayton so she could call them in the morning. Then she wired her $300 so she could buy herself a greyhound bus ticket, mail her clothes to Jackie's house, and buy her and her daughter's birth certificates. She told her to make sure she brought their social security cards and her baby's shot record because she was going to need them. When Jackie got off of work the next day she was surprised when she heard Rhonda's voice on her voicemail telling her she was on the bus and would be there by nine. She knew she was trying to come there but she wasn't prepared for her to come that soon.

She told Marcus and everyone else in her work area that her little cousin was trying to relocate to Dayton and she was glad she did because Marcus followed her home. After hearing the message, she let him listen to it and told him she had to pick them up from the bus station. She also let him know that they would be spending the night, so he couldn't. They watched television until it was time for her to pick them up and he offered to ride with her, but she declined. She was going to try her best to keep them from meeting each other. Toni told everyone they knew in Dayton that she didn't have any kids and she wanted to keep that lie going.

Jackie was kind of mad that Rhonda jumped on the greyhound bus without telling her exactly what her plans were, but she calmed herself down on the ride to pick her up. She sat in her car until the bus came fifteen minutes later. She knew which passenger was Rhonda as soon as she lumbered off the bus in her blue stretch pants and her blue and black cornrows braided to the back. She stood 5'2" and looked like she weighed four hundred pounds, just like her father and her grandmother. She was still tar colored and her face still looked the way it looked when she was seven years old. She had a wild bushy uni-brow that looked like it had never been arched. Her eyes were gray and Chinese shaped liked Jackie's, but they were crossed. She had Jackie's cute little round nose, but it looked weird sitting above her big, pink, crusty lips with the white ring around them. Her teeth were small and white with about twelve gaps in them. Jackie hated Rhonda's father and his family so it took everything in her to get out of the car and hug her. She lit up when she saw her grandbaby though. She looked just like her and Jackie hurried up and grabbed her out of Rhonda's arms. She hugged her tight and smothered her with kisses while Rhonda got their bags from up under the bus.

"Her name is Leona and she's two. She'll be three next month on the sixth," Rhonda said as they climbed in the car.

"So she's an Aries if it's April sixth. We gon have to throw you a big party. She is so adorable; I can't wait to spoil her. I might take off work tomorrow," said Jackie as she drove them to her apartment. Her spirits had lifted and she was happy they came.

"I tried to call to tell you that I talked to one of them shelters you told me to call and they want me to be there tomorrow at ten o'clock in the morning. That's why I just came. It sounds like it's a good one because they said they'll give me and Leona our own furnished apartment until I find us one. It's somewhere called Parkside. The lady said it's a bad project, but it can't be as bad as Rockwell and I lived there most of my life. She said they'll help me apply for apartments, jobs, and welfare. I still got some of that money you sent me so I can take the bus to my appointment if you want me to."

"Naw, it's cool I'll take you. I don't mind helping you, but I do have a couple of rules you have to follow if you plan on being in my life. First of all, I don't want anyone to know that you're my daughter. I'm not ashamed of you or anything; I just feel my business ain't everybody's business. I don't want to discuss the past, because I don't regret any decisions I had to make in my life. I don't do hard drugs and I don't want them around me. If you want to smoke some weed or drink some liquor, I'm cool with that. I might even join you. But it took me a long time to get off that other shit and I ain't trying to walk backwards in life."

"I ain't never done no damn crack or heroin in my motherfucking life, and I don't plan on starting. Look Jackie, all I'm trying to do is create a better life for me and my daughter. I'm not trying to ruin your life or make you feel bad about the past. If you don't want people to know who I am I'm fine with that, but don't disrespect me in front of my daughter again," Rhonda angrily replied as they got out of the car.

"I'm not trying to start off on a bad foot with you Rhonda. I just want to start over as friends, because it's too late for me to raise you," said Jackie as she led them to her apartment.

"That's cool," said Rhonda.

Rhonda fed Leona while they were on the bus so they weren't hungry. Jackie tried to talk to her but the conversation felt forced and unnatural. She regretted telling Rhonda her rules because it ruined the mood, but she felt like she didn't have a choice. She didn't want Marcus knowing she had a child who looked like Rhonda. She told Rhonda she wasn't ashamed of her, but she really was. Marcus saw her stretch marks so he knew she'd been pregnant before, but Toni told him that her child was born dead. The lie was easy to go along with because Jackie's kids were dead to her since the day she left them.

Rhonda faked a yawn to get out of the awkward situation and Jackie let her. She gave her towels to bathe them with and got the spare room ready for them. She was in her room faking like she was sleep when they came out. The more she thought about it the more she started to feel like letting Rhonda come to Dayton wasn't such a good idea. She never really liked her and she didn't trust her because she didn't know how much she knew about her past. Seeing her face reminded her of her father and she had always despised him. It was hard to do, but Jackie fought off the demons that tried to creep up from her past and got some sleep. She got rid of the memories by saying "that did not happen" over and over again in her mind until she fell asleep.

Jackie took off of work and took Rhonda everywhere she needed to go. She missed not seeing Marcus for the day, but she wanted to hurry up and help Rhonda get in the shelter. She did not feel comfortable with her sleeping in her house. She dropped her off at the American Red Cross downtown so she could fill out the application she needed to fill out to get into the shelter. She told her to walk down to the blue building three blocks down to put in an application for Section 8 and DMHA. Then she told her to walk two blocks down from there to Main Street when she was finished and catch the number nine bus to the welfare office. She told her that she would take Leona with her and they would meet her there. Rhonda seemed as happy to get away from Jackie as she was to get away from her, so they went their separate ways.

Jackie took Leona to the Dayton Mall and bought her everything she thought she wanted to have. She even bought her a power wheels and a car seat. They went to see the movie *Lion King* and then to McDonalds to eat. Leona was saying Jackie by the time they went to pick her mother up. Rhonda had been waiting for them for over an hour and Jackie could tell that she had an attitude until she saw all of the things Jackie bought Leona. She even bought Rhonda some silverware, dishes, and pots and pans.

It was Jackie's turn to be mad when Rhonda told her that the shelter said she couldn't move in that day. She said that she had to call them everyday to see if they had a unit available. Jackie wanted to punch Rhonda in her mouth because she was smiling when she told her the bad news. "What the fuck is you so happy for? If they don't hurry up and get you a unit you gon find yo ass in one of them shelters that got the row of beds."

Rhonda didn't reply and it's a good thing that she didn't because Jackie was considering putting her out of her car. It took four days for her shelter apartment to come through and Jackie was happy when it did. She spent the time over Marcus's house and realized just how happy she was that they didn't live together. He was kind of messy, and she was a neat freak. She went to bed early, he went late. He liked to sleep with the television cut on; she liked the house to be totally quiet when she went to sleep. She even hated the way he squeezed the toothpaste out of the tube from the middle instead of the bottom. They spent most of the time at her house and she didn't see all of his little flaws until being at his house for so long. She was in such a hurry to go back home that she almost forgot her father's diary and Timothy's letter at Marcus's house. They were the first items she packed when she let Rhonda use her house because she didn't trust leaving them in the house with her. She decided to leave them in the trunk of her car so no one could get a hold of them, after imagining Marcus reading them.

Marcus wanted to meet Rhonda, but Jackie wouldn't let him. She came up with every excuse in the book why they shouldn't meet and she was able to hold the meeting off for four months. The meeting she tried to prevent from happening occurred on a Friday Marcus was supposed to get Ashley, so Jackie wasn't expecting him. She took Leona to Chucky Cheeses to get away from Rhonda because it was July 24, 1996, her father Leon's birthday, and she was taking it very hard. Jackie forgot the significance of the day until she pulled up to her apartment after work and saw Rhonda sitting on her porch crying hysterically. She was mad and embarrassed by Rhonda's behavior, so she rushed her in the house and away from her nosey neighbor. Jackie was very disgusted when she found out the reason for Rhonda's tears so she decided that she needed to get out of there. She hurried up, showered, and left with Leona.

When she pulled back up to her apartment her heart dropped to her feet, because Marcus's car was in her driveway. She hurried up, grabbed Leona, and rushed in the house. She knew something was wrong instantly, but she didn't speak on it. "Hey baby, I see you met my cousin Rhonda. This is her beautiful daughter Leona," she said as she walked over to Marcus and gave him a kiss while searching his eyes to see what he knew.

"Yeah, baby I met yo cousin, she cool people too. Hi Leona, you're a very pretty little girl. Damn she looks exactly like you Jackie, that's crazy how genes skip around family members. But baby I came over to tell you that I got that forklift position you told me to go for. I wanted to kick it with you for a minute, but Evelyn been blowing me up to come get Ashley so I got to bounce," Marcus replied as he kissed Jackie again.

"Alright bay, I'll talk to you later. I feel lucky that I got to see you at all this weekend. Call me in the morning," Jackie replied as she walked him to the door and he left. "I hope you ain't told my man none of the things I asked you not to tell him or anyone else. I see you nice and drunk. Remember loose lips sink ships," she said as soon as she closed the door and looked at Rhonda suspiciously. She couldn't tell what they had been talking about, but she could tell that Rhonda had still been crying and she was very intoxicated.

"Jackie I ain't told that nigga shit. Now can you take me home before my ten o'clock curfew? I don't want to get put out."

"Yeah I'll take you home, but you remember what I said."

"And you remember what I said about disrespecting me in front of my baby. Unlike you, I care about my child."

"I don't give a fuck how you think I feel about yo fat ass. You better hope and pray you ain't made me loose my man."

"Look Jackie, I'm tired, I'm drunk, and I'm depressed. Can you please take me home? I'll give you some air if you feel you need some, but I'm not in the mood for this right now."

"Come on I'll take y'all home, but you remember what the fuck I said," she repeated before driving them home in silence. The thought of Rhonda telling Marcus anything about Leon made her want to punch her in the mouth. She didn't say anything to her when she got out of her car, but she kissed Leona and gave her a big hug.

Jackie was very suspicious of the conversation Marcus had with Rhonda when he didn't come to work that Monday. It wasn't like him to take off, and he usually called her whenever he did. He wouldn't even answer the phone calls she placed to him and she called him at least twenty times. She was relieved when she pulled up to her apartment and saw him sitting on her porch with Ashley. He looked sad and angry and Jackie was beyond relief when she saw that it wasn't directed towards her.

"Evelyn's silly ass sat in front of my house blowing her horn until I came out three o'clock this morning. When I opened the door she sped off and left Ashley on the porch crying in her fucking underwear," he said angrily as Jackie let them in the house. "I was so mad that I didn't feel like talking to nobody. She had some clothes over my house but I took her to the mall and got her some more. I went downtown to talk to the mediator who's been handling our case and told her what happened. Jackie I'm about try to get custody of my baby so I ain't gon be able to see you that much," He said as he held her face in his hands and looked her in her eyes.

"Dang Bay, I am so sorry. First she didn't want you to see her, now she leaving her on your porch in her damn panties! Now what the fuck we gon do? You know that she convinced the judge not to let Ashley spend any nights at my house," she said as he released her and the weight of his words started to sink in. She wanted to be understanding towards Marcus's situation, but she didn't want their relationship to hurt because of it.

"She was acting cool when I first won my visitation rights, but you know she been on some bullshit every since she found out it was your idea for me to take her to court," Marcus said looking defeated.

"Fuck her we gon win in the end. We should try to move in together, if we get my name on the lease she can't say shit. Damn, I thought I was tired of my man not being able to hold me every other weekend. Ain't no telling how long this shit gon last," Jackie said with an attitude.

"Bay I just need you to be there for me and understand the position I'm in. I've kept it real with you from day one. You been knew that my daughter's mother was crazy and silly. You gave me advice on how to handle my situation before we even got together; that's how we got so cool. Please don't flip the script on me, the last thing I need is for you to start trippin' too. You know I can't spend the night over here until I get this shit straightened out. I don't want to risk my chances of getting custody of her by going against any of the court's orders. I'm not going to be able to keep helping you financially either. I'm going to have to buy my daughter everything she needs to live with me. Why you lookin' at me like that? Look Jackie, you either with me or against me, it's up to you! But I got to do what's best for Ashley," Marcus said angrily.

"I'm sorry bay I'm just tired of Evelyn's ignorant ass. I'm definitely on yo team," Jackie said with tears in her eyes.

"Are you sure you down with me because I saw how you was lookin' when I said I can't help you out with your bills no more. Jackie you're a grown woman with a job! Ashley is my child! She didn't choose her mother I did, and she shouldn't have to suffer because I chose to lay down with that trifling bitch. I got to do everything in my power to make her stop hurting my baby, with or without you," Marcus said as he looked Jackie in her eyes.

"Marcus you know I'm here for you and Ashley. I didn't mean to look like that it's just that I was depending on the money you said you was gon give me for my light bill. I'll just work some overtime hours this week and pay it next week," Jackie said as she hugged Marcus with tears streaming down her face. She hated that she wasn't going to be able to see him, but she was happy that it wasn't because of the conversation he had with Rhonda. Jackie really loved Leona and she didn't want to have to cut her out of her life, but she would at the drop of a dime if Rhonda ever betrayed her.

(6)

I Thought he Loved Me

Two weeks passed and Jackie had gotten used to not seeing Marcus as much as she used to. She wasn't even able to see him that much at work because he had to work on the other side of the factory for the forklift position he got. They even went on their breaks at different times. She kicked it with Terry at work and outside of work when Marcus's schedule changed, and started to see why Toni liked her. Jackie didn't agree with the way she cheated on her boyfriend with the different men in the factory, or how loud she was, but she was a fun person to be around. She stopped judging her when she needed her to fill the void Marcus left and started enjoying herself. Terry knew everyone in Dayton, and Jackie had a ball whenever she went out with her.

Terry started going over Jackie's house everyday after going home to change when they got off of work. Rhonda didn't have a television or a radio in her shelter apartment so she came over everyday too. Jackie didn't mind because Marcus had to get Ashley as soon as they got off, so he couldn't come over and Rhonda went along with the lies she told Terry. All they did was sit around talking, drinking, playing cards, and watching TV, but it was better than sitting around missing Marcus. She was also happy that Terry started coming over because she started taking Rhonda and Leona home. She had to ride pass their apartment to get to her house in Trotwood, so she didn't mind.

Jackie missed seeing Marcus like she used to see him, but he made sure he called her everyday to let her know that he wasn't gone anywhere. Her bed was a little lonely at night, but she was alright with that because he hadn't left her. She got a couple of quickies from him the first day he came back to work, so she was cool as far as sex went for the time being. She was secure in her relationship and considered everything that was going on a test of how strong it was.

Jackie knew that Marcus was in love with her, what she didn't know was that she was in love with him. She didn't that find out until it was too late. She was sitting on the picnic table in back of CTJ when Terry walked up smiling. She looked so happy that Jackie thought she was coming to deliver good news, but nothing was further from the truth. "What's up Jackie? I've been looking all over for you. I asked Marcus where you were and he snapped on me. He was in that new girl, London's area. Is he training her or something, because he's always over there? It seems like he been over there everyday for the last two weeks, they been going to lunch together and everything."

Jackie felt like someone had knocked the wind out of her, as her heart started to beat fast, her hands started to sweat, and fear started to creep in. She tried to tell herself that Marcus would not do that to her. He couldn't be that cold hearted to try to get with someone they both worked with. She gave him his freedom; so he could have chosen any other woman in the world. Why would he choose one that she had to look at everyday? The Marcus she knew wasn't that cruel, he was the gentlest man she had ever known.

She didn't realize that she started crying until Terry pulled her out of her feelings by saying; "Girl I know you ain't sittin' up here crying over that nothing ass nigga! What you need to do is check him and that bitch! Shiiit she knew y'all was together! The whole damn factory know that y'all a couple. You need to go in the bathroom, and wash yo face so we can go confront that nigga and that uppity ass bitch! I don't like her no way! The nerve of her to be walkin' around here like she the shit just because she in school! Shit, if the bitch that smart what the fuck is she doing working here with us? I know you don't be on company gossip, but a couple of people asked me if they was fuckin'. The only reason I'm even telling you this is because you my girl, and I would hope that you would do the same for me. Well, what you gon do stand here lookin' stupid or handle your business?" Terry asked before she led Jackie into the plant.

Jackie was discombobulated so she did what Terry told her to do. She was instantly jealous when she saw who Terry was talking about. Jackie didn't partake in the factory gossip, but she couldn't help but notice how all of the men wanted the new young girl. Terry had to train the twenty—four year old law student and she told Jackie about her when she first started working there; but Jackie didn't think anything of it. She felt like Terry was just hating on the girl so she let the words she said about her come in one ear and go immediately out the other. Now she felt threatened by them. London was in her last year of law school. All Jackie had was a GED that she obtained in prison, and she was twelve years older than the other woman. She was also jealous that London didn't have any kids and her figure was flawless. She was a short, petite, intelligent woman with a short hair do that she kept styled. She looked like a dark skinned Halle Berry with dimples which made Jackie think she looked better than her. Jackie was raised to think that light skinned black people looked better than dark skinned black people, so she thought she had London beat which gave her a little confidence. If Marcus hadn't been sitting on his forklift talking to the woman, Jackie would have thought she wasn't his type.

"What's up Marcus? Is there a reason you've been spending so much time over here? Have you been going to lunch with her, because she and I go to lunch at the same time? If you can go with her, you can definitely go with me," said Jackie as she stood on the side of the forklift London wasn't on.

"Jackie don't ride down on me like that, I'm a grown ass man. You letting Terry's phony, nasty, dick sucking ass send you off. Go back to yo area before you cause a scene."

"Fuck you Marcus, it ain't my fault you can't keep yo nasty ass dick in yo pants! You just mad because you got caught up! Jackie is a grown ass woman with her own mind! We was on our way to the break room we wasn't thinking about you. If you wouldn't have been all in London's face everyday you wouldn't have gotten busted," Terry said as loud as she could.

"See how phony the bitch is?" Marcus asked London. "She's the one who hooked us up, now she trying to play like she don't know what the fuck is going on. I'm about to put all the cards on the table because I don't give a fuck no more. I'm sick of this tired ass bitch. Terry introduced me to both of y'all and a couple of other females in here. She sucked my dick when I first started working here, but that's all we did. She's been trying to get me in bed every since then but her house was too nasty for me. Jackie, me and London have been fucking for the past week, and I want to continue fucking her if she'll let me. There, is everybody happy?" he asked before pulling off on his forklift and leaving the three stunned women to sort the mess out on their own.

"Damn Terry, you ain't tell me you and Marcus had a past!" yelled Toni as she took over without Jackie having to ask her to. She saw the fear in Terry's eyes as she squinted hers and they changed from gray to green. She was like a dog when she sensed fear, she pounced on it. "You a stupid ass bitch for getting a nigga you used to fuck with pussy," she said as she poked Terry in the head. Theirs eyes changed back gray as Jackie took their finger from out of Terry's face and took a step back. She was so mad that she didn't realize that she was talking to Toni out loud. "Stop, you know we need this job!"

Terry must have thought Jackie was talking to her, because she got real courageous when she heard her say they needed their job. She got even louder than she was at first drawing an even bigger crowd. "Jackie you can miss me with that bullshit! That was his job to tell you hoes about us! And for the record, I didn't just suck his dick we fucked! You just mad because he played yo ass like a yo-yo! That's what you get because you always bragging on his trifling ass! You thought you had gold but found out it was shit! Then you be the first bitch to talk about the next bitch's man! Remember all that shit you said about Jerome, bitch eat them words cause my baby treats me much better than Marcus treats yo ass! Jerome would have never fucked a bitch that we both work with! You wasn't my friend, not the way you was always trying to put me and my man down! I don't got you looking stupid, yo man got you looking stupid. He's the one who fucked you, not me," she said as she took several steps away from Jackie and talked more to the crowd than to her.

Jackie was so busy checking Toni in her mind that it took both of them a couple of minutes to respond out loud to Terry. *"I told you this bitch wasn't shit! We look as bad as I ever thought we could look. I thought you checked the nigga's past. Put your motherfucking hands down, you better not put yo hands on this garbage ass bitch. We just got off of parole!"*

Toni was walking towards Terry with her hands out stretched like she was going to choke her when she reached her, so she put her hands down like Jackie told her to do. She chose to respond verbally out loud to Terry instead of responding in her mind to Jackie. She got nose to nose to her, so that they were the only two who could hear exactly what she was saying. "Bitch you could have been told me how you felt, and I would have saved my breath. I was just trying to tell yo dumb ass in nice way

47

that I think Jerome is fucking yo teenage girls! If I was over steppin' my boundaries you should have been a woman and told me! You was coming to me asking for my advice about your life. Not the other way around. As far as looking stupid goes, don't nobody look dumber than yo slow ass for letting any nigga who want to hit that nasty shit fuck you for free. You tired ass, thirsty bitch," Toni said with a voice laced with hatred. She had to keep moving forward to stay nose to nose with Terry because she kept moving backwards. When Terry backed into a rack filled with car parts, she just stood there until Toni finished saying what she had to say.

All Terry said when Toni was through was, "Damn is she possessed or something? That bitch eyes kept on changing colors and shit." Toni ignored the comment because Terry said it with a nervous giggle and she didn't say it until she thought Toni was out of ear shot. She didn't say anything while she was in her face.

Toni was about to go talk to London after she was through checking Terry, but the bell rung indicating that their break was over. Tears started to form in her eyes, so she rushed to the women's bathroom that only had one toilet in it before they were able to escape. She locked the door behind her and broke all the way down to the floor as her tears soaked her face. Her stomach hurt worse than it hurt when she used to be sick from heroin withdrawals and her heart felt like it was no longer there. She'd never felt that kind of pain before in her life, but she knew that she had to get through her workday. She let herself cry for five minutes then got up, washed her face, and walked out of the bathroom with her head held high and a mean mug on her face. She saw the questions on the people who worked with her faces, but no one asked her anything as they worked until their next break. Terry and Marcus had both been moved out of her work area and Toni and Jackie were both happy about that now. Neither one of them knew if they would have been able to stop themselves from attacking if they would have had to look at their newest enemies for the rest of the day.

Jackie headed for London's work station ten minutes before the lunch bell rang. She wanted to see if Marcus was going to try to go to lunch with her, and to question her while no one else was around if he wasn't. She made Toni go away because she was still mad at her for not knowing how many women Marcus had slept with in the factory. She was scared to see Marcus back with the woman so her heart was beating hard and fast as the palms of her hands started to perspire. She was relieved when she walked up to find London alone. "Hi London, I don't know rather or not you know me, but my name is Jackie. I'm not trying to check you or nothing I just want to know what's going on with you and my man."

"If you talking about Marcus, we've been seeing each other since I started working here two weeks ago. Terry hooked us up and neither one of them mentioned you. I used to see you with Terry all the time, but she never tried to introduce us so I didn't think anything of it."

"Me and Marcus have been dating for over two years, and I know for a fact that this is his first time cheating. I know that he's going through a lot because of this custody battle he just got into two weeks ago. The only reason he ran to you is because I wasn't really understanding when he told me about his problems. I'm here for him now, and I ain't going nowhere. We were friends before becoming lovers, so I'm gon be in his life regardless of what."

"Look Jackie, I don't do drama so I'm gon back away. I'm not in love with Marcus and it's obvious that you are, so I'm gon wash my hands of this sticky situation and go on with my life."

"That would be what's best for all of us," Jackie replied as the bell rung and they walked to the time clock together. She was real happy that London was giving up because she wasn't going to. She didn't want to be bothered with anyone and she wasn't hungry so she drove to a park and smoked her weed for lunch. She felt like getting drunk after getting high, so she went to the liquor store and bought a pint of Remy. She poured herself a drink into one of the McDonalds cups she kept in her car, and drove back to the job. She sat in in the parking lot listening to *If Only For One Night* by Luther Vandross, and devising what she thought would be the perfect plan to get Marcus back. She couldn't wait until he came back from lunch so she could start working on it. She jumped out of her car as soon as he pulled up and walked towards his. The windows were tinted so she didn't see London until she got out, and she saw red when she did.

"So you leaving me for this bitch Marcus? She ain't got shit on me so it must be because she some type of fake ass lawyer! The bitch was just telling me how she don't love you and how she wants out of this sticky situation! Why did you lie if you still wanted to be with the nigga?" she asked, firing one question after the other at the couple.

"If he was your man we wouldn't be having this conversation now would we?" London asked as she stood behind Marcus.

Jackie was tipsy and angry, so she no longer cared about her job. She tried to get to London, but Marcus grabbed her. When he grabbed Jackie, London went in the factory. "Damn Marcus, so that's how it is now?"

"Jackie you full of shit. Don't sit here crying like you so fucking innocent. Not with all that dirt up under yo nails."

"What are you talking about Marcus? Don't you love me as much as you said you did? All I ever did was tried to be good to you," said Jackie as she pulled away from Marcus and huge crocodile tears started flowing down her face. She was hurt, embarrassed, and furious that he tried to protect the other woman from her. In her eyes he was supposed to ride with her rather she was right or wrong because he was her man.

"Enough of the bullshit Jackie, I know who Rhonda really is and I know what happened to her father Leon. Don't waste your lies on me cause I ain't trying to hear them. Leona looks like you spit her out yourself, so guess who I believe. I know everything so you can cut the innocent act. How can you ask me if I love you when I don't even know you? " asked Marcus as the anger in his eyes turned to a mixture of confusion, pain, and defeat.

Jackie was stunned into silence as she felt her world start to crumble. Her tears stopped flowing as an evil glint replaced them. She didn't try to say another word to Marcus because her problems had just gotten a lot bigger than him. She started to follow him into the factory so she could clock out, but she decided against that. She had to get home and kick Rhonda out of her house and her life before she did anything else to destroy her.

Toni started in on her as soon as they got in the car. *"How in the fuck do he know about Rhonda and Leon? I know you ain't let that fat ugly ass bitch back in our lives. I can't believe you had the nerve to snap on me about not knowing who this nigga fucked, when you let a bitch you know gon try to fuck everything up in. I told you to kill both of them bitches when they came out. I know they yo kids but I knew they was gon be trouble from day one,"* she said as Jackie drove them home.

"I'm bout to kill this bitch now."

"No you not Jackie. She's not worth us fucking our new life up over. We don't even know what all she knows or what she told him."

"I know that she told him that she's my daughter and that's enough."

"I ain't going back to jail over that nothing ass bitch making you lose that nothing ass nigga, Jackie. He wasn't shit no way so calm yo ass down before we

go in here and face this bitch. We gon find out what all she thinks she knows and send her on her miserable way."

"All right Toni I'm with you. Lets go handle this bitch," Jackie replied before taking a razor blade out of the glove compartment and putting it underneath their tongue. Then they got out of the car and went into their apartment.

Rhonda had the TV turned up as loud as it could go with Lil Kim's video *No Time* playing. She was whirling and twirling harder than Lil Kim, as she sang along to the lyrics with a glass of Jackie's liquor in her hand. She didn't notice when Jackie and Toni barged through the door until Jackie grabbed the remote off the couch and cut the TV off. "What's up Rhonda? I thought we agreed to tell everybody that we friends! I thought we agreed that it was too late for me to start trying to be yo mama so we was gon start over as friends! If you didn't agree with what I was saying, you could have told me instead of telling my man all of that bullshit," Jackie yelled in a voice laced with hatred.

"You call the things I told Marcus bullshit? Bitch you call killing my daddy and abandoning me and my sister bullshit? You ain't never been my friend and you never will be! You just ashamed that I'm yo daughter that's why you came up with that friend shit," Rhonda yelled. She looked like she was about to rip their head off as she started walking towards them. Leona pulled her out of her anger filled trance by calling her name and blocking her path.

Jackie put her head down, slipped the blade out of her mouth, placed it between her fingers, and controlled herself from looking shocked. "I didn't kill yo daddy, the streets did. I gave you and yo sister to y'all's grandmother. Shit, I had just lost my husband and I still had the heroin habit that yo daddy gave to me, so how in the fuck was I supposed to take care of two little girls? But all of that shit is in the past, and I told yo fat ass before you came down here that I didn't have any regrets! I still don't feel guilty for any of the decisions I made in my motherfucking life! That nigga is a dead issue! He ain't the first nigga who got killed and he ain't gon be the last one! I suggest you quit listening to that evil ass grandmother of yours and move on with yo fucking life," Jackie yelled wishing Rhonda would give her an excuse to use the razor.

"Bitch you the evilest person I ever met in my life! My Granny wasn't perfect but she took on yo fucking responsibilities! I thought my daughter had thawed out your heart a little bit, but it's still frozen when it comes to me, so I'm gon do you a favor and stay the fuck out of yo life! Bitch from this day forward I won't spit on you if you catch on fire in my face! If you see me or my child walking down the street, walk past us. I didn't ask you for life and I won't ask you for anything else in this lifetime! Me and my daughter is dead to you! Bitch her name is Leona Thompson, after her granddaddy Leon Thompson, she a part of my daddy and me! You can forget that you got a grandbaby, I don't give a fuck how much she looks like you, she'll never be like you," Rhonda yelled as she picked up Leona and her purse and stormed out of Jackie's apartment.

"Bitch I wish you was never born while you talking about you dead to me! Shit I look too good to be a grandmother anyway," Jackie yelled at Rhonda while she was leaving. She was happy Rhonda left like that because she was going to make her stick to everything she said! She didn't know Rhonda knew she killed her father because she was only seven and her sister was only five when she gave them to their grandmother. She knew Leon's mother was turning her kids against her as she raised them, but she didn't know his mother knew she was the one who killed her son. She had to consider her dead husband's family including Leona, as enemies now that she knew they knew it was her who was behind the hit. She had gotten tired of seeing Rhonda's face anyway, because she looked just like her father and he put her through hell. She didn't choose to be with him, she was forced to be with him. She hated him and the kids he impregnated her with. She couldn't help how she felt so she gave them to someone who did love them, because she couldn't no matter how hard she tried.

Jackie and Toni wanted a blow. They sat there for hours after Rhonda left drinking Remy, talking to each other, and listening to the song *Silly* by Denise Williams over and over again. They tried to get rid of the pain from their heartache and the strong yearning for heroin they felt; but neither one of the feelings would go away. Jackie tried calling Marcus seventy-three times, and Toni ridiculed her every time she dialed his number because he wouldn't answer his phone. Thoughts of killing Leon and of Marcus making love to London kept running through their mind until they couldn't take it any more. They both agreed that they had to get out of their apartment. Toni wanted to buy some heroin and Jackie wanted to find out what Marcus was up to, so Toni grabbed their purse, stood up, and fell, not realizing how drunk she was. When Toni couldn't get them on their feet, Jackie did. She was drunk too, but that didn't stop her from stumbling out of the door and buying two twenty dollar bags of heroin out of the dope house she usually bought her weed from.

They wanted to get high before going to stalk Marcus so they went back in after buying the heroin. Jackie wanted to shoot the drug up their veins, and Toni wanted to sniff it up their nose. Jackie won in the end because she made Toni disappear. She hadn't shot up since the seventies, but she didn't forget how it was done. She grabbed one of needles that she used to give herself insulin with and went upstairs to get a pair of stockings. When she came back down, she grabbed a tablespoon from out of the kitchen drawer, emptied the contents of one of the blows onto the spoon, lit the bottom of the spoon with a lighter until the heroin transformed into its liquid form, and drew the heroin into the needle. Then she cut off one of the legs on the stockings, tied it tightly around her left arm, tapped the inside of it until she found a big vein, and shot the heroin into the vein that pooped out. She thought the drug would make her forget everything, but it took her mind back to things she forgot had occurred.

(7)

The Worst Summer Ever!

Jackie nodded off thinking back to the past she thought she erased out of her mind. Rhonda's words took her whole mind, body, and soul back to the summer of 1973. Ironically Jackie's mind didn't take her back to the day she killed Leon, it took her back to the events that led up to the day that Leon raped her of her virginity, family, happiness, and everything else that bought joy into her life. She was a happy fourteen year old child before Leon came along. As she sat on her living room floor with her head laid on her couch, and the rest of her body relaxed in a very deep heroin induced nod, she became that happy fourteen year old child again.

She was no longer in Dayton, Ohio she was back in Chicago reliving the summer that changed her life forever. It started off real good because she had finally caught Juan's eye and he was the finest boy in her neighborhood. Jackie loved everything about him, but she loved his afro the most because it looked good on him. She couldn't get one because her hair was too long and fine, so she kept it styled in Indian hair styles or ponytails. Juan had the perfect hair for a fro and he took god care of it with the black pick with a balled up fist on the end of the handle, that he kept on him. He had sleepy looking, slanted, chestnut brown colored eyes, with long pretty eyelashes. His eyebrows had a natural, high arch that looked masculine on his face. He had perfect skin that was the color of butter and his thin lips were a shade darker than his skin. He was proud of his premature mustache and he possessed a very sexy smile that came with dimples. He was bow legged with a well defined, athletic body that he kept in shape by playing basketball. He was only fourteen-years old, but he stayed dressed fly in his gold chains, bell bottoms, silk shirts, and gators. He even owned a black floor length mink coat. His father kept him dressed like a pimp, because he wanted him to follow in his footsteps.

Juan was the most popular boy who attended their elementary school because of the way he carried his self and he was the only one who had a car. Jackie was pretty and smart but she wasn't fast, so she wasn't the type of girl Juan tried to court while they were in school. She was the valedictorian of their class, involved in every club the school had, and on the yearbook committee; but he acted like she didn't exist until they graduated out of the eighth grade. She was getting all of his attention that summer which made her feel special and excited about entering high school as his girl. They were both going to Marshall and Jackie couldn't wait to enroll. She was going there because her brother and twin sisters went there, and her aunt was the cheerleader coach. The twins were on the squad, so Jackie was going to join it too. Juan was the basketball star at their elementary school, Dodge, and he had plans on joining the basketball team at Marshall. They made a cute couple and Jackie wanted to give him her virginity, but she was making him wait until September third, the day before school started.

Jackie was also elated because her father, Jack, had finished his tour in Vietnam. He wasn't the same man he was before he left and he returned with a heroin habit, but Jackie was just happy that he made it back in one piece. Most of the soldiers who fought in the Vietnam War from her neighborhood came home mutilated or in caskets so she considered her family lucky. She hated that he wasn't in his right state of mind when he came home because he barely ate, talked, took care of his hygiene, or anything else that was normal. He didn't even look the same. He used to be a very handsome man before he returned looking like an empty shell of his former self. He was 6'1" and he used to walk and stand up with his head held high with pride, but he developed a habit of stooping while he was in Vietnam. When he left he was a healthy looking man who was nicely built, but when he came home he looked like he barely weighed a hundred pounds. His eyes used to be big, beautiful, sleepy looking, gray, and clear with a sparkle in them, but now they told a very dark story of a man who had seen too much in his lifetime. His skin was clear and the color of peanut butter prior to his tour in Vietnam, when he came home it was dark brown and covered in abscesses from him scratching and picking at it during his heroin induced stupors. His teeth were rotten and they robbed him of his once, beautiful smile. His nose was still long and pointed and his lips were still thin and pale pink, but both of them stayed peeling.

Jack had always taken care of his wife and their ten children and he didn't stop when he got drafted in the army. He sent the majority of his money home to them, but that alone wasn't enough to support them so he sold drugs to his fellow soldiers while he was deployed. Jack and Janice thought that their kids didn't know that he was selling drugs while he was in the army, but nothing was further from the truth. The oldest four made sure they knew everything that went on in their house. Janice tried to talk in code and privacy when she talked to Jack on the phone, but their kids still knew exactly what was going on from her side of the conversation. They also noticed all of the nice things they were able to afford while Jack was gone. He even bought them a house on the Westside of Chicago and a 1972 light blue Chevrolet station wagon. They didn't look down on him for selling drugs; they looked up to him for it. The area they lived in was infested with poverty and they were happy not to be affected by it.

Jackie was happy for the money Jack sent them, but she was constantly worried about him getting court martialed. She was Janice's fourth child, but Jack's first and they had a very special bond. That was the only reason her oldest brother Timothy, and her older twin sisters Jamika and Tamika, let her in on what was going on with Jack. They felt they owed that to him because he had always taken care of them like they were his own and he never treated them wrong. They were grateful for him, but they really didn't care about the sacrifice he was making trying to support them the way that Jackie did. She was beyond relief when his tour was over and her mother made him promise to give up his occupation as a drug dealer. She really thought that her mother had gotten through to him because she was born and raised on the Westside of Chicago and she heard her tell him all the dangers he would face if he tried to hustle when he came home. Jack didn't know anything about the streets because he was born and raised in Dolton, Ill., a predominately white suburb, and he worked a square job before he had to go to Vietnam. A month before he came home Janice went down to the welfare office and told them that he abandoned her, so she was receiving food stamps, cash assistance, and medical coverage for her and the kids by the time he made it home. Their house was totally paid for and their welfare check was more than enough to pay the bills and the taxes on it, so she thought her father would be more than happy to be back. Before he left, he worked in his grandfather's factory which was the same job he had since he was sixteen. Jackie knew that he hated working there because she grew up listening to his complaints about it. She didn't tell anyone, but she had plans on convincing him to go to school with his GI bill so he could get a job he didn't mind working.

When Jack came home it was easy to tell that he bought drugs with him because he didn't go anywhere for three days, but he stayed high. The only person who came to see him was his mother, Trudy, and Jackie knew she wouldn't bring him any. He stayed in his room those first three days, and Jackie tried talking to him but every time she did he just stared at her as he went in and out of dope fiend nods. Before he got drafted Jackie used to read the Bible to him for an hour everyday after work, so that's what she did the second and third day he stayed in. She hoped and prayed that the Lord's words were sinking into the hard exterior shell he had built around his self. She missed her father while he was gone and having him there physically but not mentally, felt almost as bad as not having him there at all.

Jackie went to his room equipped with her Bible on the fourth day he was home only to find him gone. She was angry at her mother for letting him leave the house by his self and told her she should've left with him. Janice had always found it cute the way Jackie always tried to protect her father and this time was no different. She laughed at her and told her that her father was a grown man which made Jackie even madder. She stormed out onto the porch and refused to come back in until he returned three o'clock the next morning. She was out there for over ten hours and wanted to go back in several times, but she kept catching her mother peeking out the window at her so she stood her ground. She was sleep when he finally came back, but she still questioned him thoroughly when he woke her up and told her to go in. He ignored her questions and the questions Janice threw at him as he walked like a zombie in his heroin induced state to their bedroom. Janice followed him into their room and closed the door but Jackie was still able to hear their argument. She tip toed to her room with a heavy heart full of fear when she heard her mother say that she refused to sleep in the same room with her father because he smelled like a dirty whore. She wasn't naïve, but she didn't know what the awful smell that was coming out of her father's pores was until her mother said where it came from.

Jackie tossed and turned until the alarm clock woke her up at seven. She hoped that the things she heard her mother saying were a figment of her imagination, but when she went downstairs the first thing she saw was her sleep on the couch. She raced back up to make sure her father was still in the house; and breathed a sigh of relief when she cracked his bedroom door and saw him sleeping in bed. She wanted the father she had before the war destroyed him back to help her raise her little brothers and sisters. Janice was an alcoholic who loved to party so she was never much help. If Jack got his act together some of the weight would be lifted off of her shoulders.

Her three older siblings all had summer jobs, so it was her job to walk her six younger ones to free breakfast and free lunch that was served in Rockwell Garden Projects. She didn't want to disturb her parents so she quickly got them ready and led them out of the house. Jackie always talked to her two little brothers and her three little sisters whenever she took them anywhere. She promised her father that she would always help take care of them a long time ago. She knew that the only way she could keep her promise was if she knew what they were thinking and feeling and the only way to find those things out was by talking to them. They trusted her more than they trusted their mother and they told her everything. They had a code of silence that Janice hated because the only way she could find out what was going on with them or who did what was through Jackie.

Jackie was exhausted from being up so late, but she knew that she needed to get up to see if her younger siblings had heard their parents arguing the night before. She was relieved when she read their faces and saw that none of them showed any signs of worry. She was positive they didn't hear anything when none of them bought it up. They had lots of secret talks daily where they disclosed everything that made a difference in their lives, and they had one on the way to free breakfast. All they talked about was Jack getting high and Janice getting drunk, which suited Jackie just fine. They told her everything that went on in their lives, but she rarely told them anything that went on in hers. They didn't know anything about Jack selling drugs, and she didn't tell them anything about the way he smelled or the things her mother said. For the first time, she was happy that Janice often fell asleep on the couch in drunken stupors, because her little brothers and sisters thought nothing of it. On the way home, she made them promise to be on their best behavior.

She contemplated rather on not she wanted to tell her older brothers and sisters what was going on all day. She never got the chance to ask them because she heard her father looking for the car keys before any of them made it home. She was in the living room watching *The Mary Tyler Moore Show* with her little brothers and sisters when she made the split second decision to go see what he was up to. She felt like he was too mentally unstable to be roaming around the streets of Chicago by himself. She already fed the kids, did her chores, and spent a couple of hours with Juan, the only person who would be visiting her so it would be easy to sneak out. Her younger siblings wouldn't tell on her, since she made sure all of their needs were taken care of before she left. Janice wouldn't be checking on anyone for hours because she was in the kitchen drinking and playing cards.

When Jack went back upstairs, Jackie grabbed her Bible and ran out to their station wagon. The door that opened in the back stayed unlocked, so she opened it and hid under a blanket that they kept back there. Jack came out five minutes later and pulled off. Jackie knew that she had gotten herself into a sticky situation when she heard her father and the male passenger he picked up discussing some sort of drug deal. When they got out she peeked out from under the blanket and looked out the window at them. She was shocked and angry to see that they were in the Henry Horner Projects and that the passenger was one of her father's friends from the army. Both of them had on their uniforms and she watched them until they disappeared into one of the tall brown buildings. As she waited for them to come back out, fear started to creep into her stomach and she started to think that maybe the Bible wasn't the weapon she would need if something went wrong. Jack was a devout Christian before fighting in the Vietnam War, so Jackie felt that the Bible and the words in it would have been perfect to use if she would have gotten the opportunity to confront him and his mistress with it. If the mistress would have gotten out of hand Jackie had plans on beating her up, but that wasn't the situation she found herself trapped in.

She got suspicious when she saw a man creep from around the corner of the building the men had entered a couple of minutes after them. Her fear and suspicions rose as she saw that same man run out with a gun in one hand and the same bag that was in her father's hand when he got out of the car, in the other one. The soldier who was with her father was right behind him, and Jackie felt like she was having a heart attack when they ran past the car and into another building. She thanked God that they didn't take the only car her family had with her in it. Then she started praying for her father while she got out and went into the building she saw him go in. The first thing she saw when she went in was him lying in a corner in a puddle of urine, bleeding from his head. She thought the men had killed him, but realized that the wound wasn't from a bullet when she screamed and he looked up.

"Jackie help me up baby. Come on now, we ain't got time for you to get scared on me. We got to get out of here before they come back. The only reason they left is because somebody opened their door. That's daddy's strong girl," he said as Jackie helped him up, wrapped one of her arms around him, and helped him out of the building. "I knew that motherfucker was a snake, but I out slicked his ass. He thought I bought all five pounds with me, but yo daddy is smart Jackie. I only bought one, just in case he was on some bullshit. The only reason they didn't kill me is because they wanted the rest of that China White. I know I didn't finish teaching you how to drive, but I ain't gon be able to see until I stop this cut from bleeding. Just go to that gas station around the corner," he said when they reached the car.

Jackie was more scared than she had ever been in her life, but her body went into auto pilot as she did what her father told her to do. When they got to the gas station she went in, got the bathroom key, and helped her father out of the car and into the bathroom. Then she ran back to the car and got their first aid kit and a towel. She felt like she couldn't breath until they cleaned his wound and she was able to see that it wasn't as bad as she thought it was. "Daddy I hope you finished trying to sell drugs! Daddy one of them had a gun! Do they know where we live?" she asked as soon as they were finished putting gauze on the ugly wound.

"I can't stop now Jackie. This big time dealer paid me to bring back five pounds for him. I wanted that to be my last drug deal, but the man who set me up said that he had a Jamaican who was willing to buy the heroin for twice as much as the dealer paid for it. The shit over there is pure so it wasn't hard to believe that a person would pay that amount. I wanted to sell the dope to the Jamaican, give the other guy back his money, and keep the rest for my family. I just wanted to be able to support y'all until I was able to get a job. I don't like being on welfare, it messes with my manhood. I've always been proud of the fact that I was able to support my huge family without the government's assistance."

"Jackie you know that everyone in my family is white and they have money. The family rumor has always been that mama cheated on daddy, but she's always assured me that she didn't. I don't know how I came out looking like I did, but I believe my mama. They've always looked down on me and said that I wouldn't be anything, so I rebelled in my own way. I had to work in the family factory, but I was so good at what I did that my granddaddy gave me several promotions over my uncles. He was a master manipulator who was able to get a lot of good quality work out of his employees by flaunting my accomplishments in their faces. He didn't hire any black people until he had to, and nothing burned the old timers up worse than having me give them orders. The whole family told me to stay away from black women with children because they might be on welfare. So, I married me a beautiful, dark skinned, woman who had three children when I met her, and I had seven more with her after our marriage. But see, Janice didn't receive welfare. She had a job at the Woolworths that was down the street from our house, and she went to college at night. She dropped out and quit when she started having children for me. I adopted her kids and promised her that I would always take care of her and all of our children, and I kept that promise until now. I've been working in my granddaddy's car factory since I was sixteen, and I might have complained about that job but I don't know what to do with myself without it. Granddaddy died two years ago, and he left the factory to my uncle Jimmy. Before I came home, I swallowed my pride and asked him if I could get my job back at the factory and he said no. They're a bunch of evil people and I'm happy we keep y'all away from them; but it's still hard for me to look myself in the mirror knowing I've become the drug abusing, welfare receiving, loser everyone always said I'd grow up to be."

"I can't cry over spilled milk, but I got to try and clean some of it up Jackie. I got to sell that shit rather I want to or not. If I don't give that man his product or his money, I know he'll kill me. No one knows where we live, but when I went outside yesterday I kept on seeing dude and the guys he hangs out with. I told them that I was getting out two weeks after my discharge date so they don't even know that I'm home. But when that date comes, I know they'll be looking for me. That's why I have to sell the rest of those drugs so I can give him his money back," he responded with a look of pain, regret, shame, and fear in his eyes. "I promise I'm gon make this right Jackie. Please promise me that you'll keep this between us, Janice already threatened to leave me and I don't want to make things worse than they are."

"Ok Daddy, but you gon have to fix this," Jackie replied as they left out the bathroom. She was so discombobulated that she didn't say another word as he drove them home. He kept trying to spark up a conversation with her but she didn't know what to say. Normally she didn't mind when her parents put her in their grown up situations, but she just wanted to be a regular kid that night. It bothered her that her father didn't ask her how she got to the Henry Horner Projects or what she was doing there at two o'clock in the morning. She envied her other siblings because they didn't have to help their father carry the burdens from his sins on their shoulders. She not only had to keep his secret, she also had to act normal while keeping it. She loved him but she wished he would start treating her like a child instead of like an adult all the time. Her older brother and sisters didn't have to help out with Jack's kids like Jackie had to do because their father told them they didn't. Janice stayed pregnant throughout Jackie's early years and Jackie became her little helper as soon as she could walk. Diabetes stuck with her during her tenth pregnancy and that was the only reason she stopped having children. When she stopped having kids she started drinking real heavy, so Jackie still couldn't get a break.

There was nothing Jackie could do about the trouble Jack had gotten his self into so she just prayed a lot and tried not to let it stress her out. She was just happy that the drug dealers didn't know where they lived. Jack tried selling the drugs, but he stopped after three days. Jackie was the only person he had to talk to about the situation, and he told her that he couldn't do it because he wasn't plugged with anyone. Jackie just looked at him like he was stupid, because he knew that before he came home. She heard her mother tell him that the crime in Chicago was organized so he would have to be affiliated with a gang or someone with clout to try to sell anything from pussy to drugs there. At first she was scared when he stopped trying altogether, but her feelings changed because no one ever came looking for him and he was too paranoid to leave the house. The day he told the dealer he was coming home came and went without anyone knocking on their door, so Jackie really thought he was doing the right thing by laying low. After a week passed she started feeling safe, and after two she was a happy carefree teenager again. Janice was a drunk and Jack was a junkie, but they weren't arguing anymore since Jack started staying in the house. He had all the food, toiletries, and drugs he needed to survive for a long time in the there, so Jackie was positive he wasn't going to go out and put his family in danger, but she was wrong.

(8)

Home Invasion

It was after one o'clock in the morning and Jackie got up to use the restroom. When she came out, she heard Janice in the kitchen crying so she went down to investigate. Janice told her that Jack was gone and this was the second night in a row he had disappeared in the middle of the night. The fear that crept up inside of Jackie was so intense that she had to sit down. She felt a tremendous amount of guilt for letting her guard down and not watching Jack's every move. When she heard the car doors slamming her fear mounted. Janice paid them no mind, but Jackie ran to the front room and looked out the window. Their porch was filled with men and one of them had Jack slung over his shoulder, while another one was opening the door with his keys. Janice must have thought it was Jack opening the door because she ran to it when she heard the key opening the door. Jackie saw the look of shock and fear when a big, fat, ugly, dark skinned man hit her mother in the face with a gun. Jackie ran towards the stairs to get her siblings as soon as Janice hit the floor. She felt someone chasing her and when she turned around her eyes met the eyes of the pimp she had been trying to avoid for the past three months.

Jackie and her family lived on Warren and California and the store that Jackie's mother frequently sent her to was located on the next block over, on the corner of Madison and California. That corner also served as a bus stop, and one of Leon's hoe strolls. The Madison bus ran from downtown Chicago to the far west side of Chicago and Jackie used to catch that bus, so she was on Madison quite often. She'd seen the cross eyed man several times over the past four years, and every time she saw him he tried to come on to her. He kept his fro shaped up, and he dressed real nice in his expensive suits, jazzy jewelry, and floor length minks, but he was ugly and old in Jackie's eyes. He was 5'4", and grotesquely obese. His small, beady, brown eyes were crossed and they sat underneath a bushy uni-brow. His nose was big and wide and it flared out rather he was smiling or frowning. His lips were big, and they stayed caked up with dead skin. He was the color of tar and every time Jackie saw him his face was shiny with grease but his hands stayed ashy.

Whenever she saw Leon she tried to act like she was brave, but she was really terrified that a pimp who looked like he was older than her parents was trying to seduce her. He constantly professed his love to her and he knew she was a minor. He tried to give her money and gifts, but she didn't accept them because Jack taught her that nothing in life was free. She was young but she wasn't naïve, she knew what Leon and his brothers were and she didn't want any part of it. Her family wasn't struggling because they had a father who loved them. She didn't want to throw her life away on fast money. She wanted to continue exceling in school so she could become something and help get her family out of the ghetto for good. She was a straight A student and she had dreams of becoming a defense lawyer. She didn't care how many diamonds and furs Leon offered her, she wasn't for sell. She was glad that her father taught her how to love herself, and her mother taught her that her body was priceless, because Leon liked young girls and he'd tricked off with a lot of poor, young, black, thirsty ones in their neighborhood.

Jackie had always been able to reject his advances. When she started walking an extra block to catch the bus and go to the store on the corner of Madison and Francisco, she was able to avoid him. He stayed posted on one of the corners between Madison and California and Madison and Washtenaw to watch his whores, so when Jackie changed up her routine she discovered that avoiding him was easier than she thought it would be. They hadn't seen each other in months and seeing him right on her heels almost caught her off guard, but she made it upstairs and into the room she shared with her twin sisters before he made it to the top of the stairs. "Y'all wake up, it's some men down stairs with guns to Mama and Daddy's heads," she yelled as she shook Jamika. She was so scared that she couldn't stop her body from shaking like a leaf.

"OK, I know its ten kids in this motherfucking house! I want every last one of y'all out in this hallway in one minute or I'm gon tell my brothers to start shooting y'all's parents," Leon yelled as he stood in the hallway. His voice was so loud that all of Janice's kids heard him, even the ones who were sleep. They ran out to the hallway and the oldest boy, Timothy, tried to rush Leon. He didn't look like he was scared of the gun that was in Leon's hand until Leon clocked him on the head with it. He went down hard, but his big, bushy afro broke his fall.

Jackie ran to her brother as he fell to the floor and looked Leon in his crossed eyes as she said, "Please don't hurt him, he didn't mean any harm! He's not from the streets, he's a straight A school boy! All of my mother's kids are!" When Leon saw Jackie a look of recognition crossed his face and she could tell that he knew exactly who she was. The look of hatred that was in his eyes before he recognized her softened and Jackie was grateful that it did. She could tell that he was about to continue to beat Timothy until she said something.

"Gone head downstairs," Leon said after counting the ten kids. Then he made them walk down the stairs in a single filed line in front of him.

Jackie was petrified when they made it down because both of her parents were on their knees with their hands tied behind their backs with the telephone cords. Each of them had a man standing over them with guns pointed to their heads. The other five intruders had their guns aimed at Jackie and her siblings. Both of Janice's eyes were black from blow that was delivered to her head, and she looked like she was about to pass out. Jack was so beat up that his face wasn't even recognizable and the only way Jackie knew that the disfigured man was her father, was because he had his army uniform on. She'd never felt as helpless or as frightened as she felt at that moment. She thought that the men were there to kill her whole family but when the man who had his gun to Janice's head started talking, she realized that their plans for them were much worse.

"Bitch I don't know if y'all know what's going on so I'll enlighten y'all. The man of this house owes me a lot of money for the dope he stole from me. I know he ain't got all of it because he tricked some of it off with one of my brother's hoes tonight. After a lot of persuasion, his weak ass told me that he got robbed for a large amount of it. Jack ain't got no way to pay me back and neither do any of y'all so y'all gon have to work it off. I'm gon start off by putting all the bitches to work as hoes, and I know a lot of niggas who like young pussy. There are seven of y'all so it shouldn't take longer than a month to pay off his debt. If it does I'll send these pretty ass boys y'all got up North to work. If y'all can come up with my money tonight I'll leave y'all's lives just as quickly as I entered it. Janice can you think of anyone in your family who cares enough about you and your kids to pay off Jack's tab? Nobody on his side gave a fuck," said Jason, Leon's oldest brother. He was 6'1" and built like an iron ship. His complexion was the color of tar just like his mother, father, and brothers. His face was smooth with no scars or bumps. He had small, beady, chestnut brown colored eyes, and when Jackie looked in them she could tell he was a low down dirty person. He had a big, flat nose and his lips were big and black. His teeth looked weird in his mouth because his lips were so big and black, and his teeth were real white and small. He was a very mean man and Jackie had seen him loose his temper a couple of times. She couldn't believe that Jason was the dealer her father did business with because he hung out around the corner from their house and she heard her mother warn him against the mean drug dealer.

"My family loves us, but they don't have a lot of money so it'll take us a little longer to raise the money. If I throw card games all week and give you my eight hundred and thirty-seven dollar welfare check I got coming next week, we should have it all by the end of next week. All I'm asking for is a week Jason, please give it to us. Me and my kids had nothing to do with that shit Jack pulled. You know I ain't never did no drugs, I was always a drinker."

"Janice, you know I ain't never gave nobody longer than twenty-four hours to pay me and I ain't bout to start now. I caught Jack at 11:17 last night, so y'all got to 11:17 tonight to get me my shit. You from the streets so I'm sure you've heard of somebody else being in the same position you're in now. Me and my crew gon stay right here until y'all time is up. If y'all can't get the money, we all leave," Jason replied with a nonchalant look on his face.

"Ay Jason, if they give me they gray eyed daughter, I'll pay Jack's tab," said Leon.

"Whaaat? You can fuck that bitch for free, you know we got to break her in before we put her on the stroll anyway," said Jason looking at Leon like he was stupid.

"Naw, you don't understand. I think I love her and I don't want to put her on no stroll. I don't want no man to touch her but me. I want to marry her and I wouldn't feel right harming her or anyone in her family," Leon replied with a goofy smile on his face and his gun still aimed at the family.

"Nigga I want the amount I would have made off that pure dope. I was gon turn them five pounds into fifteen pounds. Then I was gon sell weight to some of my niggas and I was gon sell bags on the streets so you add that shit up and you can buy they lives if they willing to sacrifice Gray Eyes. Shit a motherfucker can't beat that cause you was gon fuck her anyway. And it was gon be way mo dicks running up in that pussy than yours," Jason said as he laughed like he'd just told the funniest joke in the world.

"Naw nigga, Jack said he still had two pounds in here, but I'll pay you for nine pounds for the three he fucked up. That's the best that I can do, and that's fair because you getting three times the amount you paid for them," said Leon to Jason but he was looking at Jackie with lust in his eyes.

Damn, these motherfuckers standing in my face discussing my pussy like I ain't even here! I know my mama ain't gon go for that bullshit though. She knows that I'm thinking about giving Juan my virginity; we just talked about it the other day. She wasn't happy with my decision but she was happy that I came to her. Uhh, I wish that cross eyed monster would stop looking at me like that, thought Jackie as she cried hysterically.

"That's more than fair Leon, I'm cool with the deal if they is," said Jason as he started looking back and forth between Jack and Janice. "What's up, my brother is willing to pay Jack's tab for Gray Eyes. Is y'all willing to give him permission to marry her or is all of y'all gon join my stable? Think about y'all's options because those are the only two that y'all got, and ain't no reneging. Y'all bound to the terms of our agreement like a contract was signed. But instead of me taking y'all to court if y'all break it, I'm gon kill the whole family. Janice you know I got hands that can reach y'all from anywhere including my grave."

Janice was still on her knees when she looked seductively at Leon. "Leon, Jacqueline just turned fourteen so she's inexperienced, but you can have me. I'll divo—"

Jason reached back like the pimp he was and back slapped Janice before she could finish her sentence. "Bitch he didn't ask for yo tired ass pussy, or for her age! He know she young that's why y'all got to give him permission to marry her, but I don't need no permission to sell her young ass," he yelled angrily.

"Yeah, I want this pure, beautiful virgin so I can deflower her. You think I'm gon pay Jason all of that money for a bitch who had ten kids?

The only female I'm willing to pay for in this house is Jacqueline and them pretty gray eyes that been haunting me every since I first saw them," Leon said. And that was creepy because he'd known Jackie since she was ten.

When Jackie saw the look in her mother's eyes, she knew she was sold. Janice had big, pretty, dark brown, Chinese shaped eyes that had a way of revealing her feelings. She was so in tuned with Jackie that she was able to beg her to go with Leon with them. She never said the words out loud, but Jackie saw the fear in Janice's eyes mixed with a glimmer of hope and she knew what was expected of her. "Please don't hurt my family no more! Mama I want to go with Leon. He's willing to take care of me and he gon pay off Daddy's debt. We can get married tomorrow, just please don't hit anyone else! And can we please take my father to the hospital because it looks like he's about to die?" she begged Jason.

"Yeah, we'll drop him off at Mount Sinai if they agree. What's up Janice? Don't you want Jack to live? Look at it like this, you can give up one daughter or I'll take all of y'all," Jason said looking like he was getting madder and madder.

"Jackie are you sure you want to do this baby? You know once you give that away you can't get it back," said Janice looking defeated with tears running out her blackened eyes and down her swollen cheeks.

"Come on now Ma, what other choice do we have? I'll be alright, now tell these men that you gon let me marry Leon so we can get Daddy to the hospital," said Jackie as she tried to be brave.

"Alright Jason, my baby is willing to sacrifice herself for the family," Janice reluctantly said.

"Aight Gray Eyes go put on some clothes and pack so you can ride with us to drop your daddy off at the hospital," said Jason looking relieved.

"Dig this here I just want you to put some clothes on, you can leave the rest of them here. I'm gon send you on a shopping spree as soon as the stores open up in the morning," Leon said sounding ecstatic.

Jackie felt like she was in a very bad dream, like nothing that was happening was real. She had a knot the size of a basketball in her stomach as fear gripped her and her tears blurred her vision. When she ran upstairs to change her clothes, she unknowingly invented herself an alter ego that she felt was strong enough to handle the events that were about to transpire. As she looked in her drawer to find something to wear, she named her alter ego Toni. She couldn't handle giving her virginity to Leon's ugly ass but Toni could. *As a matter of fact Toni gon take that ugly ass, gorilla looking, motherfucker for all he got and use his money to support my whole family including my Daddy's heroin habit,* thought Jackie as she slipped on a pair of dark blue jean bell bottoms with a rainbow on one of the pockets and a blue t-shirt with a rainbow on it.

"Jackie you stay here, I got this," Toni said talking to Jackie in Jackie's mind as she put them on Jackie's Steve Prefontaine Nikes, threw some of her clothes, and toothbrush in a gym bag, and ran down the stairs.

"Can I ride to the hospital with y'all so I can make sure Jack makes it?" Janice asked Jason.

"Hell naw, you ain't no motherfucking nurse, so how the fuck you gon make sure he live?" asked their cousin Fred looking very angry.

"Why she can't ride with us?" asked Leon.

"Because the police gon want to know what happened to Jack so they gon grill whoever brings him in, and Janice might tell them. She looks like somebody kicked her ass too so she can't say she don't know what happened," Jason answered with a look of disgust on his face.

"Well how we gon explain what happened to him?" Leon asked ignoring the disgusted looks on the rest of his crew's faces.

"Motherfucker we ain't goin' in with his ass, we gon lay him on the ground at the emergency room entrance. Damn Leon, quit acting like you retarded. You got ready quick Gray Eyes," said Jason to Jackie as she came back down fully dressed.

"I'm just ready to get my daddy some help," Jackie said as she hugged her mother.

"Janice go look in my top drawer under my t-shirts, and get those two pounds of heroin," said Jack as he held his head down and spoke for the first time since he let the Thompson's invade his home and terrorize his family.

"Do you want me to go and get yo stuff?" Janice asked Jason as she avoided looking at Jack. Jason answered Janice's question with a nod and untied her when she stood up. Jackie could tell that her mother was ashamed of her father and that hurt her to her heart because she had always been proud to have him as her husband. For a brief moment, she found herself more worried about her parent's marriage than her own fate.

When Janice came back down she handed Jason a brown shopping bag with handles. "Y'all help Jack to my Cadillac; I'll be out in a minute. Leon and Gray Eyes y'all ride with me. Janice you probably don't feel lucky, but you is because all of y'all could be dead right now. Best believe me when I tell you that I've known Leon all my life and he's a good nigga who gon take good care of yo daughter."

"If any one of y'all try to go to the police every last one of y'all will be dead before the case makes it to court. As a matter of fact, don't tell nobody what happened here tonight because if I hear about it in the streets, I'll kill all of y'all except Gray Eyes. And y'all know I'm gon find out because the streets gon tell me. They talk even when it looks like all of the people on them have there mouths closed. All it takes is one whisper and the secret that you think you got gets spread like a wild fire. Y'all owe Gray Eyes and Leon y'all's lives. Janice we'll be here in the morning to tell you how we gon do this," Jason said as he backed up out of their house with his gun still out.

Leon carried Jack to the car and Jackie climbed in after them. The windows were down so she was able to hear the conversation the other men were having. "Damn nigga, you know I ain't feeling how that shit just went down," she heard Kevin, the youngest Thompson brother say.

"I know that shit was sloppy, but I'm gon pay y'all good for y'all time. We bout to drop this dope fiend off at Mount Sinai; meet us in Rockwell in a half an hour and I'll straighten y'all out," Jason said to his unhappy crew.

"Leon stay in the back with Jack and make sure he ain't got no ID on him, Gray Eyes you sit up here in the front seat," said Jason as he climbed in his cherry red 1973 Cadillac Deville. Then he pulled off headed towards the hospital, popped in an Al Green 8 track, and sang *Let's Stay Together* like he hadn't just done a home invasion.

He cut down the radio as he pulled up to the emergency room entrance at Mount Sinai. "Leon lay his ass on the ground right in front of the emergency room entrance," he said.

"We just gon leave him like that! Y'all ain't gon even go in and get him signed in? He got insurance through the army, let me go in with him," said Jackie through her crocodile tears.

"Shiiit, girl fuck Jack's ass, he the reason your family in the situation y'all in now. If he make it he make it, if he don't he don't. At least you talked these coldhearted motherfuckers into takin' him to the hospital," Toni said to Jackie as Jason was talking to her.

"Look bitch, you can shut the fuck up and thank God that he at the hospital. I don't usually take a motherfucker to the hospital after I kick they ass! And you can cut that cryin' shit out because the only thing it's doing is making me want to shut you the fuck up! I did a lot of shit that's out of my character tonight for my money, and my brother, not for you. He want yo ass, I don't. I personally think you'd be more beneficial on the track, but I'll honor Leon's wishes and keep my hands off you. But know this, I love that stupid ass brother of mine and if you even think about hurting him I'll kill you myself. I know you don't love him but you better act like you do for yo own good," Jason said as he looked Jackie in her blank, expressionless, green eyes to let her know he meant what he was saying. "Hurry up and get in the fucking car before somebody come out! You standing there looking all stupid and shit," He yelled out the window to Leon.

"Damn bro, you ain't got to front me off in front of my soon to be wife," Leon replied as he climbed back in Jason's car. He didn't usually mind when Jason talked down to him, but he didn't want Jackie to think he was a sucker.

"She can't legally become yo wife until she turn's sixteen. So she ain't about to be yo wife that damn soon, ya dig," said Jason disgusted in Leon for trying to impress Jackie.

"If her mama gives us permission to get married she can. And if she can't then what the fuck am I paying you for?" Leon asked Jason.

"We gon make Janice give you temporary custody of her until she turns sixteen, then y'all gon get married on her sixteenth birthday. Don't worry; I got this shit mapped out already. I got a partner who just went through the shit. You don't have to go to court to get temporary custody of a minor, all a mother got to do is write a letter saying that she's giving you temporary custody and get it notarized. You won't need to show nobody the letter unless you have to use it to prove that you actually have custody of her," said Jason as he pulled in the Rockwell Garden Housing Authority.

"If we ain't got to go to court why do we even need a letter? You think that shit gon work for real?" Leon asked looking confused and angry.

"I know the shit gon work. You gon need that letter in case motherfuckers get to talkin' bout her living with you. You know how nosey people is in the projects. And what if you have to take her to the doctor? That letter along with her medical card will allow you to take her. If a teacher gets suspicious you can show them the notarized letter, and if that don't shut them up, we can get Janice to tell them that she gave you custody. You know Janice gon do whatever we tell her to do to save the rest of her family. She ain't gon give us no problems, cause she knows we ain't to be fucked with. Now if you finished with the third degree, I would like to go to yo crib first so I can collect my bread," said Jason as the trio got out of his car and walked in one of the big, tall, brown, ugly buildings.

"I'm glad this motherfucker works because I ain't feel like walking up them stairs," said Leon as they got on the elevator after it took a long time to come.

Damn this motherfucker smell like piss. I know this ain't where they live. All that money they got. This about to be worse than living at home, thought Jackie in disbelief.

"Honey, we're home," Leon said to Jackie as he opened up the door to his apartment. "You can put yo shoes behind the door."

Leon lived in the projects, but you wouldn't know it if you never stepped outside of his apartment because it had all of the newest gadgets and décor. It was constructed like all of the other apartments in the high rise building with hard brick concrete walls and cold concrete floors but his paint, rugs, and decorations covered his up. When Jackie stepped inside she was treated to a gush of cold air. She was amazed because she'd never been inside of a building that had air conditioning that wasn't a department store, and she rarely went to those. Her school didn't even have air conditioners. When she took off her shoes her feet sank into the plush blood red carpet. The walls in the hallway leading to the living room were also blood red, and he had a red light bulb in the light fixture in the hallway. The hallway was kind of long and Leon had long plastic red and orange beads hanging between the entrance that led to the living room. The same carpet that was in the hallway was in the living room too, but the walls in the living room were the same color orange as the beads that welcomed people into the room. Beautiful, black, velvet paintings of attractive Negros hung on the orange walls. One of them caught her eye because one of the girls in it looked just like her, gray eyes and all. There was a plush, black, Italian leather pit sofa and a 35' inch wooden floor model TV in the living room. Jackie had never been surrounded by such luxury.

"Let me give you a tour of your new home," Leon proudly said to her. He saw the amazement on her face and it filled him with pride.

"Damn nigga, can you give her a tour when I leave? Pay me so I can pay Fred and nem for they time. Take her to the bedroom so we can conduct our business," Jason said feeling disgusted in Leon for acting like Jackie chose to be there.

"Come on Jackie let me show you our honeymoon suite. I hope you like it, I feel like I've been preparing the whole apartment for you. If you don't like any of the decorations or furniture we can change them with no problem. I just want you to be comfortable," Leon said to her as he led her to the room they were going to be sharing.

"Thank you," Jackie whispered as reality mixed with fear took over. The room that Leon led her to was decorated beautifully. The bedroom furniture was made out of cherry wood and it looked very expensive, especially the sleigh bed with the matching foot stool. The vanity, the wood around the mirror on the vanity, and the chair that went to the vanity were all made out of the same expensive looking cherry wood that the rest of the bedroom furniture was made out of. All of the bedroom furniture looked like beautiful antique pieces with there clawed feet and the black detailed carvings that decorated them. The vanity had a medium sized, oval shaped, double sided mirror and it was stocked with all types of new bottles of perfumes and makeup. The bedroom walls were painted cobalt blue, and the velvet drapes, the velvet bedspread, the satin sheets, and the velvet cushions that were embedded on the vanity chair and the foot stool that sat the end of the king sized bed, were the same exact color as the walls. There was also a deep, snow white Persian rug that complemented the room nicely.

Jackie got the chills as she took it all in because it seemed like Leon really did decorate the room for her because up until that very moment, cobalt blue was her favorite color. She wore that color blue whenever she could, which was often because she had a lot of clothes that color. Her whole family and all of her friends knew how much she loved the color but she didn't know that Leon knew it too, and she felt violated. Leon thought she would love the room because it was decorated in her favorite color, but she hated it and she hated him.

"I want to go over to Fred's apartment with you," Leon said after he left Jackie in the bedroom, walked back into the living room with Jason, and opened up his safe to pay him the money he owed him.

"Naw nigga, you need to gon head and break yo Philly in. You know you gon have to break her in the same way you break hoes in don't you? You gon have to take some of that strength away. Shit, she seemed like the strongest one out the whole family. Leon, she didn't choose to be with you, so you gon have to be able to control her. You don't want her to run away from you," Jason said as he counted the money Leon handed him.

"You right, I do need to stay in here with my wife so we can make love. I know she ain't choose to be here, but I think she gon enjoy it here. She gon be happy to give herself to me because I saved her and her whole family, so I think I'm gon pass on getting her hooked on that shit. I don't want no bitch who strung out on heroin to be my wife. Man you really don't understand the way I feel about her, but it's cool because I paid you what I owe you and whatever happens from here on out is on me."

"Aight nigga don't say I ain't warn you, that bitch ain't used to being controlled and she got too much mouth on her," Jason replied as he headed for the door.

(9)

Home Sweet Home

Leon was happy that Jason left so he could finally be alone with Jackie. He had dreamt of this moment for a long time and he didn't want to delay it for another second. When he walked into the bedroom he was surprised to see Jackie sitting on the bed, hugging her knees to her chest, crying. "I know you had a tough day but I'm gon erase all of those bad thoughts out of yo pretty little head. Jack gon be all right and you ain't gon want for nothing no more. I'm gon buy you whatever you want and all of yo lil friends gon be jealous of you. Shit, yo sisters might even see the green eyed monster when I finish spoiling you," he said as he sat on his bed and tried to rub her back. When he touched her, she pulled away from him like his touch burned her and started shaking and crying uncontrollably. His feelings were hurt which angered him, so he walked out of the room.

An hour passed and Jackie was relieved because she thought Leon was going to let her be for the night. She decided to try and get some sleep, and laid down underneath the blue velvet blanket. She was sleep on her back for about twenty minutes when he reentered the room, snatched the blanket off of her, put his right hand around her neck, and gently squeezed his middle finger and his thumb. He was able to cut off her air circulation using two fingers, so she could imagine what he could do with his whole hand.

"You can't even breathe and I ain't even using all of my strength! I control everything you do from this point on, even how much air you get in them young lungs of yours. See, I den paid for you. That daddy you always bragged about sold you to me! I remember you said yo daddy was a war hero and he would kill me if he knew the things I said to you. You said yo mama taught you how priceless yo pussy was. Jack dope fiend ass ain't shit, Janice drunk, welfare receiving ass ain't shit, and you came from them so you ain't shit either! You's my property and if you ever try to leave me I'll kill every member of your family slowly. Everyday that you gone I want you to think about me killing yo mama or daddy or maybe I'll start with one of yo brothers, or sisters. You can think that fat meat is greasy if you want to, and try me. I want you to because the more I think about the way yo lil punk ass brother kept looking at me; the more I want to kill his ass first. Yeah, he gon be the first one to go, the one who kept lookin' at me funny. If you decide to run, I don't know what all I'm gon do to him; but I can tell you that I'm definitely gon cut his eyes out. You keep that image in yo head because that's the first thing I'm gon do to him. Now I'm bout to give you something that's gon stop them tears from falling down that pretty face of yours! All they doing is making my dick soft, which makes me want to kick yo ass. I know my dick and he gon get hard everyday and I ain't gon have the strength to fuck you, make my money, and kick yo ass everyday," Leon said to Jackie with his fingers still around her throat, which hurt like hell, and made it impossible for her to breathe through her nose. She was hyperventilating as she tried to breath through her mouth, but the snot that oozed out of her nose mixed with the tears that continued to fall made that hard to do. She was too scared of Leon try to wipe any part of her face, so she tried to make herself stop crying.

Jackie thought she was scared when the men came into their home, but that fear was nothing compared to the fear she was feeling as Leon talked. She closed her eyes real tight and subconsciously made her whole body real still and stiff as she tried to get Toni to take over. *"Toni please stop these tears from falling! I'm trying but it ain't working and I don't want him to hit me. He real mean, don't you hear the things he's saying about me and my family."*

"Girl, fuck his fat ass he the one who ain't shit. You know yo daddy wasn't like that before he went to war; he used to take good care of y'all. Just go to sleep and dream about the good times you had with yo family. Naw don't even think about yo family, think about Juan's fine ass," Toni said to Jackie as she opened their eyes after feeling Leon remove his fingers from around their neck. Her eyes filled with anger as they changed from gray to green, but Leon didn't see the fear leave and the anger take over because he was too busy taking off his belt. After taking it off, he wrapped it around her arm, hit the inside of it until a vein popped out, picked the needle that he

bought into the room with him up off of the bed, and injected every drop of the lethal mixture that was in that needle into Jackie's fourteen-year old vein.

It took the cocaine and Spanish fly mixture less than a minute to take effect, and when it did it hit Toni and Jackie like a ton of bricks. *"Damn that feels good, don't it girl you can really relax now,"* Toni said as she rolled their eyes to the back of their head. The Spanish fly had their vagina hot, wet, and throbbing. Toni was controlling their body and she decided to rub their vagina through their jeans to try to put out the fire down there. She felt powerful, like she was in control of the situation. She looked into Leon's ugly crossed eyes and hypnotized him with the lust that the Spanish fly had put into hers. The cocaine had her feeling like she was superwoman and she wasn't afraid of Leon anymore. She knew he was going to rape them in a matter of minutes but she refused to feel like a victim. "Leon go wet us a towel in warm water so I can wash our face," she said not realizing that she had said us and our in her sentence; but Leon didn't notice because he'd been watching her rub her vagina and his penis was doing his thinking for him. "And cut off that light when you come back, don't nobody feel like looking at yo ugly ass."

"Yeah baby, anything you want," he said as he ran out of the room with glee. He didn't need the light anyway because she had lived in his mind for years and he knew that he would never forget her face. He hated that he had to give her any drugs, but he liked the effect that the ones he gave her had on her. The heroin that Jason wanted him to use would have given him complete control over Jackie, but Leon hated the way it had his whores throwing up and having loose bowels and he didn't want that for Jackie. He was so happy that he was whistling when he walked back into the room and handed her the clean, warm, wet towel.

"Toni I'm scared, I don't like how those drugs making me feel. Juan is the only person that ever made my privacy feel special, and he never made it feel like it was on fire. I know that Leon's real ugly ass don't turn me on. I ain't breathing right and his hands ain't even around our neck no mo! I feel like I'm about to black out and my mind ain't working right! Toni he's taking off his clothes!"

"Jackie close your eyes and go with Juan. We didn't ask to take the drugs, he made us take them so try and let them help you relax. I refuse to let him win by feeling guilty on top of everything else I feel. He made us take them so I'm gon enjoy them. Just think about Juan Jackie," said Toni as she felt

Jackie leave and Leon disrobe her. She kept her eyes closed as she felt him open her legs and lick her vagina. She closed them even tighter preventing any tears from falling when she felt him enter her. Two minutes later he grunted, ejaculated on her stomach, rolled over, and fell asleep.

Toni was still wired, high, and horny off of the drugs so she spent the next three hours masturbating. Her hand was wet from the blood and cum but she couldn't help herself. The Spanish fly had her hot down there and she did not want Leon humping on them again.

The next morning, Leon woke Jackie up out of her drug induced sleep by opening her legs and entering her again. When he finished he ejaculated on her stomach again. "Damn that's some good pussy; I ain't never had sex with a fully developed virgin before. It felt so good having some tities lick with that tight twat. I planned on getting me some more before that shit knocked me out like it did. Don't worry daddy gon keep that shit nice and wet," he said after using his penis to spread his semen all over her flat belly. Then he got off of her. "Go look in the hallway closet and get some clean towels. Wash up in the bathroom sink and when you get through; soap up a clean towel so you can wash my dick."

Jackie thought she was at home, sleeping in her bed, dreaming about Juan until Leon pulled her out of la la land and into reality by thrusting himself into her over and over again. When she got out of the bed to wash up like she was told, she touched her stomach, felt Leon's semen on her fingers, and almost threw up. She was afraid to throw up in Leon's room so she held it down until she got to the bathroom and threw up in the toilet. After throwing up, she rinsed out her mouth with some mouthwash and went to get a towel out of the hallway closet. Her vagina felt tender, moist, open, and sticky so she couldn't wait to wash up. She grabbed a white wash cloth, went back into the bathroom, soaped it up, scrubbed her vagina and almost fainted when she saw the blood on the towel. *"Toni we're bleeding. That fat, ugly, motherfucker made us bleed and he wants me to clean our blood off of him when I'm finish getting it off of us."*

"Girl why you ain't wake me up when he first told you to wash his dick? You know damn well you can't handle that! It's cool I'll take care of the gorilla in the next room. Yeah, see I like to hear you laugh. We gon be alright, just trust me," Toni reassured Jackie as she rinsed out the towel and finished washing the soap off of them.

"Leon I need to take me a shower after I finish washing you off," Toni said as she gently washed his small, soft penis. She didn't want to touch it, but she knew that she wasn't going to be able to control him if she continued to be afraid of his penis. She peeped that he would give her the world if she could pretend like she liked him. She knew that she could do it as long as she stayed high; she just had to convince Jackie to see things her way.

"You can take one, but hurry up because Jason is on his way over here so he can take us to handle that business. I'm gon get me some mo of that pussy tonight. I would get me some right now but we got a lot of shit to do today, so don't get lost in there," Leon called after Toni as she grabbed their bag and headed for the bathroom.

When Jackie emerged from the shower both of her personalities were present and were having an argument because Toni wanted to ask Leon for more drugs, and Jackie didn't. As Jackie brushed their teeth, slipped on their clothes, and brushed their hair into a quick ponytail, Toni talked to her, *"Damn Jackie, why you don't want me to get us anymore drugs. You want me to handle all of this shit and I don't mind doing it, but I can't do it sober. We can escape in our minds while we high. We can't kill Leon's fat ass cause he too strong, so we got to deal with his bullshit rather we like it or not and I rather do it high."*

"Man Toni I don't want to get hooked on that shit, you see how my daddy did us over it and I ain't tryin' to be like him. It's one thing for him to force us to take drugs, but it's another for us to ask him for them. I don't want to be no dope fiend and I definitely don't want our pussy to ever be that hot again. That shit wasn't natural! Before he gave us them drugs his touch repulsed us, and after he gave us them drugs you acted like you liked him."

"I did not like him touching us, I just liked being in control of the situation. You heard what he said. If we would have kept on crying he would've kicked our ass! So I acted like I liked the shit, made him nut quick, and got it over with. He would've killed us if I would have let yo weak ass handle the situation, so don't try to play me like I want his cross eyed ass Jackie. And he didn't give us the same drugs that Jack be using. That shit be having Jack off his square and looking sleepy. I was alert and we both felt good," Toni said to Jackie as she looked in the mirror and noticed how green their eyes were when she was in control of their body.

Jackie took control while Toni was still looking at their eyes in the mirror, and Toni noticed how they changed to a beautiful, transparent looking, light shade of gray when Jackie was in control. *"Alright Toni, but I don't want none of that stuff that made us hot down there. I want you to ask him how many drugs he gave us, what kind of drugs he gave us, and what each one did to us. I know we were given at least two drugs because our pussy stayed hot longer than we felt high. I ain't gon lie, I didn't mind being in la la land myself. Toni I'm sorry for being selfish. I'm asking you to take control over the situations that I can't handle, but I don't want you to have the tools that it takes to deal with the shit. If you ask him for the drug that took us to heaven, I'll take it."*

When Toni came out of the bathroom Leon was already dressed, talking to Jason in the living room. *"Damn, what the fuck is he doing here already? I just spent all that time trying to convince you to let me ask Leon's fat ass for some more of that shit only to have this big, black, ugly, motherfucker stand in my way. Leon act like that dude his daddy, but he ain't our daddy and I ain't about to treat him like he is! Fuck that! Leon got plenty of that shit and I want some more,"* she said to Jackie as she stormed into the living room. She had a strong craving for the cocaine that had her feeling so powerful and she wasn't about to let Jason stand in her way. "Leon I need to talk to you in private," she said a little too strong.

"Don't mind me foxy, I know what you need to talk to Leon about. Gon head and hook her up with some more of that girl minus the stuff that had that twat so hot Leon. She hooked already, and I thought she was so strong. I can recognize that look in any set of eyes, even them pretty green ones. Shiiit Leon let me get some of that cocaine too since you like giving it away. You should've gave her what her daddy like, like I told you to do. I would never get a bitch strung out on no expensive ass cocaine, shit that's the pimp's drug," said Jason with a huge smirk on his face. He loved getting women strung out on drugs because he felt that was the only way they could be controlled.

"Money ain't a thang when it comes to satisfying my wife. I'm happy she likes the same drug I like so we can get high together. She my soul mate and I'm gon school her so she can be the coldest bitch out on the streets of Chicago. And I ain't talkin' bout her walkin' the streets like no hoe, I'm talkin' bout her runnin' them alongside her man. You can start callin' us Bonnie and Clyde because that's how it's about to go down. Can you dig it my nigga? She gon earn her keep and a lot mo! She already book smart and if I mix that with some street smarts, we gon be unstoppable," Leon said to Jason as he got up off the couch, and walked around it to enter his small but nice looking kitchen. "Just because I'm willin' to support her habit don't mean I got to support yours too. Don't get me wrong, I don't mind gettin' high with you but I didn't give you yo habit like I gave her hers," he said as he took a plate with a razor blade and a bag of cocaine on it out of a kitchen cabinet, then walked back into the living room.

"Alright Clyde," said Jason with a sarcastic laugh.

"What's that? Leon please don't give me the drugs my daddy be taking. I wasn't trying to be disrespectful, I just didn't know that yo brother knew you gave me some drugs last night," said Jackie as her eyes turned gray and she took control over her body. *"Toni you gon make him take his brother's advice and have us taking that shit that had my daddy fucked up if you don't quit being so damn bossy! We ain't in control, they is!"*

"Baby didn't you hear what I just said. I ain't giving you that shit, this is the same drug that had you feeling good last night; it's just in another form. I gave you two drugs, cocaine and lil bit of Spanish fly to loosen you up. If you perform your wifely duties and satisfy me whenever I get horny, I won't have to give you no mo of that Spanish fly. I didn't like how it had you playing with yo pussy after I pulled my dick out anyway," Leon said as he poured some of the cocaine on the plate, formed three thick lines, took a dollar bill out of his pocket, rolled it up, snorted one of the lines with the bill, and passed the plate to Jason.

After snorting his line, Jason passed the plate to Jackie, and she snorted hers. The cocaine numbed her lips and burned her nostrils, but she felt like she was as powerful as Toni; until she heard Jason tell them to get up so they could get Janice to write that letter. Her head started spinning and her nose started to bleed as she stood up. She didn't feel the blood trickling down her chin and she couldn't seem to form the words that made it possible to communicate out loud. *"Toni we got to go home and face my mama and my daddy if he out of the hospital! Damn, what they gon think of me when they see me high as a kite?"*

"Shiiit Jackie, fuck Janice and Jack they the reason we in this situation! We ain't ask Leon's fat, greasy ass, for nothing last night! I want all them motherfuckers to see the shit we going through for they asses, and I want them to appreciate us for it," Toni responded as Leon laid them on the couch, went and got a cold, wet towel, put it on their nose, and changed their shirt after he stopped the bleeding and cleaned the blood off of them.

"Toni I'll always love and respect my parents and I'll never hurt them intentionally no matter what they've done to me! I understand why you're angry because I'm a little angry myself, but the Bible says to honor thy mother

and thy father and that's what I'm going to do," Jackie told Toni as she floated out of the apartment with Leon and Jason.

"Girl the Bible also says that parents aren't supposed to provoke their kids into disrespecting them; and if you ain't been provoked I don't know who has! If you want to go in there all respectful and shit you handle it, because I could care less what Janice, Jack, or anybody else in that fuckin' house thinks of me! Now I wish you would leave me alone because I don't feel like asking Leon's real ugly ass for shit while his daddy is around and I don't feel like wasting my high on yo weak ass either! Damn that piss is strong," said Toni as they rode down the elevator. Toni didn't like how Jackie wanted to respect her parents, so she went deep inside of her and decided to let her handle the situation by herself.

Jackie couldn't believe her eyes when they pulled up to her parent's house because her seventeen-year old twin sisters, Jamika and Tamika, were on the porch smiling up in the boy of her dreams, Juan's face. Her thirteen and twelve-year old brothers, Dwayne and Jack Jr., were playing their daily game of dice at the bottom of the porch steps, and her eight and nine-year old sisters, Sharon and Jennifer, were bouncing their red ball back and forth between each other right outside their gate on the sidewalk like they did every other day. It seemed like her family was going on with their everyday lives while she had to sacrifice hers for them. They knew what she went through the night before for them but they didn't care.

"Can I stay in the car? I don't think I can face my mother while I'm high like this," Jackie said to Leon. She didn't want her brothers and sisters to see that their normal behavior wounded her heart like an arrow had been shot through it. She thought Leon would agree since Jason drove his own car and they were alone, but her heart sank when she heard his response.

"Naw, I want you by my side. Janice and Jack needs to know that you can do anything I let you do from now on. I'm yo mother, yo father, yo sister, yo brother, yo lover, yo husband, and yo teacher! In other words, I'm yo everything and if anybody got a problem with that they can holla at me," Leon said with authority as he got out of the car and opened up the passenger door for her.

Jackie had never been as embarrassed as she was when she walked passed Juan and saw the questions in his eyes. She felt dirtier than she felt while she was being raped because she could feel that Juan could feel that her innocence was gone and she no longer belonged to him. Juan's father had been grooming him to be a pimp since he was little, and he knew everyone in the pimp game. She wished she hadn't let Toni talk her into asking for any drugs because she felt like Juan and all of her siblings could tell that she was high. Her humiliation rose when she heard the twins giggling as she followed Leon and Jason into her parent's house. They didn't even bother to knock on the screen door; Jason just opened it up like their house belonged to him.

"Janice get some paper and a pen and get yo ass down here so we can handle this business," Jason yelled as he walked through the door. He thought Juan was one of Janice's kids so he didn't try to be discrete .

Jason's voice pulled Janice out of her heroin induced nod. She grabbed a notebook and a pen off of her dresser and ran down the stairs. The right side of her face was swollen, her lip was busted, and both of her eyes were black and swollen; but Jackie could still tell that her mother was high and that bought her some sick sense of satisfaction. She was happy that she wasn't the only member of her family who was suffering and she vowed to take care of her mother as soon as she could.

"Hey baby, are you alright? I called the hospital this morning and they said that Jack was going to make it! I acted like I didn't know what was going on and I was only calling because he didn't come in last night. They said he should be released by tomorrow at the latest," Janice said as she hugged Jackie tightly. She knew Jackie was high, but she was afraid to speak on it because she didn't want to upset Jason or Leon.

"This ain't no damn family reunion and we didn't come over here to hear about Jack's sorry ass. I want you to write a letter saying that you give Leon Thompson temporary custody of Jackie. You need to sign it and date it. You can say that you feel she'll be better off in his care because you and Jack have heroin habits and he's a good member of society. My buddy let me use his notary kit so we don't got to go nowhere, we can take care of everything right here," Jason said as he peeped Janice slurring her words and nodding in the middle of one of her sentences.

(10)

Losing Beauty

After Janice wrote the letter, Leon and Jackie left and to Jackie's relief, Juan was gone. Leon took her to his whorehouse on the North side of Chicago. He made her stay in the car as he went inside to get his bottom bitch, so she could take Jackie shopping for new clothes. Her street name was Beauty and she was the most beautiful, stylish woman Jackie had ever seen in her life. She was a 5'5" black, white, and Filipino woman. Her hair was in a thick, black, long ponytail that touched her butt. Her eyes were slanted and jet black and they sat up under her thin, jet black eyebrows that had a natural arch to them. Her nose was small and pointed, and her lips were full and pouty. Her complexion was smooth and it looked like the color of coffee with lots of cream in it. She wore heavy, black eyeliner and cherry red lipstick. She had on a tailor made fire engine red, light silk, v necked, mini dress that hugged her body and showed off her perfect full breasts, her ample round butt, her flat stomach, and her beautiful, thick, scar free legs. Her over sized, red, Channel purse, and her 6', red, leather, Channel opened toed high heel shoes matched her dress perfectly. She walked and carried herself like she knew she was worth a million dollars.

"Beauty you take good care of my wife and tell that dick sucker that he owes me! I spends good money with him and I sends him good clientele! I'm tired of not getting some type of discount! He act like he Versace or somebody, I discovered his bitch ass," Leon angrily said.

"Look Daddy, the last time I told him that shit he embarrassed me in front of the whole store by saying my man wasn't willing to take care of me properly, and maybe I should get me a pimp who wouldn't have a problem with his prices. So, I would appreciate it if you handled him because I ain't strong enough. If he liked pussy maybe I could get somewhere, but he just like every other jealous bitch I've had to encounter in my life," Beauty said as she got the car keys from Leon and got in on the driver's side.

"Alright I'll handle him myself. But if he don't try to offer you no deal, I'm gon quit doing business with his ass," he said as he reached into his pocket and gave Beauty a large knot of money.

"What's yo name honey and how old are you? Leon aught to be ashamed of his self," Beauty said as she pulled off.

"My name is Jackie but I ain't gon tell you my age because Leon would have told you if he wanted you to know," Jackie said not trusting the woman.

"I ain't mean no harm baby girl, I was just trying to make conversation. You just look and dress like you kind of young. But you gon look totally different when I get done with your makeover," said Beauty trying to cover up being in Leon's business with a subject change and a smile.

Beauty wasn't lying when she said that Jackie was going to look totally different when she was done with her. She took her to a small boutique where a gay seamstress took her measurements so he could make her a whole new wardrobe. "Girl, you ain't working with much in the tits and ass department, but you gon look like a beautiful, petite, brick house when I finish with yo lovely wardrobe. Beauty I want to see you in my office when you finish trying on that dress," said the flamboyant seamstress, Stevie, after he finished taking Jackie's measurements.

"OK, I'll be with you in a minute," said Beauty as she came out of the tiny fitting room. She had on a beautiful hot pink, spaghetti strapped, floor length, silk dress. "I don't really like long dresses but I think I look foxy in this," she said as she grabbed a small mirror off the wall, took a small vial of cocaine out of her purse, shook a pinch of it on to the mirror, took a razor out of her mouth, formed a line and gave it to Jackie. "Leon told me to give this to you. Here's a new straw. I'll be right back because you're shopping spree is far from over," she said as she strutted after Stevie.

Beauty took her to Bloomingdales on Michigan Ave. and bought her all types of designer purses, shoes, boots, jewelry, and clothes. She even bought her a floor length mink coat and it was hot outside. After the shopping spree she paid for Jackie to get her face made up at one of the makeup counters and after that, she took her to her beautician on the Southside of Chicago and had her blow dry and feather Jackie's hair. She also ordered Jackie several wigs from the beautician in the shop who specialized in making customized wigs. Jackie didn't recognize herself when she looked in the mirror and she wasn't sure if she liked what she saw, but she enjoyed the bond that she formed with twenty-one year old Beauty.

Beauty took a chance and taught Jackie a lot of her game that first day. She let her know that she wouldn't have schooled her if it hadn't been for the innocence she saw in her eyes. She knew that the girl would be eaten alive by the streets if she didn't help her, and Leon was a representative of everything that was evil and mean in them. She wasn't in the position to save Jackie, so she tried to help make living with Leon easier on her. He was a sucker for love and Beauty taught Jackie how to stroke his ego and how to pretend like she enjoyed having sex with him. Jackie was amazed when she saw Beauty pull the razor blade out of her mouth to chop up her cocaine, so Beauty taught her how to keep one in her mouth while talking and how to use it if she was forced to. Before she took Jackie home to Leon, Beauty took her to her apartment to teach her how to reinvent herself with different wigs, accents, clothes, body languages, makeup and contacts lens.

Leon taught Jackie everything he knew about the streets and when September rolled around, he decided that it was unnecessary for her to attend high school. The school sent Janice several letters about Jackie's attendance, but she told them that Jackie ran away from home and there was nothing she could do about it. She told them that she was alive, but out of control. The school reported the situation to the police and left it alone. Jackie didn't mind dropping out because she had become everything that she despised, including a drug addict. During school hours, she got high, helped Leon and Beauty bag up dope, and counted money. Beauty's constant presence was the only thing that kept Jackie sane. She rarely went outside and she wasn't allowed to see her family at all, but she had Leon sending them money on the regular.

Beauty was the only person Leon trusted to be around Jackie, and he liked the fact that they were getting along so well. He even angered his family by letting her quit working in his whorehouse up north, and she was one of his best moneymakers. Then he made them even angrier by firing the family members he had making his dope runs, bagging his dope up, and collecting his money. He gave their jobs to Beauty and Jackie and he paid them good; which angered the competing pimps who had been waiting on the opportunity to possess Beauty. Beauty was very street smart and good at her new job, but they felt like she was a whore so she needed to be on her back making money for one of them. But Leon discovered her and made her, so she belonged to him and he wasn't to be fucked with. His brothers would help him before they would help his cousins, and his cousins knew it.

Beauty and Jackie were a lot smoother and smarter than Leon's former employees were, with their smooth talk, their many disguises, and their sex appeal. They were able to negotiate drug deals with the most notorious gangsters in the United States of America without anyone knowing what was going on. Most of these transactions took place at the most popular boxing matches during that time. They were made in front of the cameras right in the front row with all types of federal agents and policemen watching the men they were doing business with. Beauty was an international whore when she was a prostitute and even though prostitution is illegal, the policemen who were observing the gangsters wanted to catch the men buying or selling drugs, not pussy.

Leon and his two women were selling major weight to all types of gang leaders throughout Chicago, drama free, without the police even blinking at them. The streets were very peaceful and prosperous and everyone was happy those first two years, especially Leon. He envisioned his dream and he executed it perfectly without anyone's help. He knew that some of his family members had been using and getting over on him for years, so he couldn't wait to fire them. He wasn't as stupid as everyone thought he was, and he was happy when he was able to prove it to them.

For Jackie's sixteenth birthday, Leon taught her how to drive and got her a driver's license and a phony ID. He also bought her a cute, canary yellow, 1976 Corvette, and threw her a big party at the Cotton Club downtown. She already had all of the diamonds, furs, clothes, and every other materialistic item she could have wanted. Leon gave her something that she hadn't felt in years by giving her the car, the license, and the fake ID and that was freedom. She knew that the threat of him killing her family was still very real, so she couldn't leave him for good but she could get some air.

Everyone was invited to Jackie's sixteenth birthday party, including her whole family. Her brothers and sisters invited Juan and a lot of her old friends. Jackie told Beauty all about Juan on one of their long drives, and when Beauty met him at the party she said that he was as fine as Jackie told her he was. Beauty felt real sorry for Jackie after meeting Juan. She knew that Jackie was young but seeing her family and her first boyfriend showed her the life that Leon snatched her out of. She felt so bad for Jackie that she crossed Leon for her by getting Juan's phone number. When Leon released Beauty from being his whore, he released her completely. She was allowed to talk to any man that she wanted to, be in a relationship with any man that she wanted to, or sell pussy to any man that she wanted to as long as none of them were his enemies. He treated her like he would have treated any of his business partners, male or female. He didn't even sleep with her anymore because he respected the friendship that she had with Jackie too much.

After the birthday party, Leon started letting Jackie and Beauty go out together. He was thirty-five years old and didn't like the club scene anymore, so he didn't go with them. He figured that both of the women knew not to cross him. They thought that he trusted them, but he kept several pairs of eyes on them that they didn't know about. Beauty called herself surprising Jackie a week after her birthday party, by having Juan meet them at the club. She took her to one on the Eastside of Chicago and Juan was the first person that Jackie saw when they pulled up. Her emotions went through a whirlwind when she saw him. She was happy, sad, excited, scared, disappointed and ashamed all at the same time.

Beauty got rid of all her fears by simply saying, "Bitch, I know you ain't scared! You was taught by the best so you are the best. Hold yo head up high and make that motherfucker feel like it's a privilege to be in yo presence, and not the other way around. Handle yo business because this is the only night I can get you out of the house all night long. I told Leon that I was giving you a surprise slumber party at my pad after we leave the club, so he agreed to let you out for the entire night," she said with the biggest and prettiest smile Jackie had ever seen on her face.

As Jackie's mind drifted back to that night her body got real stiff, and she felt the overwhelming fear, guilt, and pain all over again. She started crying uncontrollably as she poured the other blow that she bought from the dope dealer in Dunbar Manor on a spoon. Then she turned it into it's liquid form by lighting a lighter underneath it, took the needle that had been in her arm all that time out, filled it back up with heroin, tied the stocking around her other arm, found a good vein in that arm, and shot that blow into her body. She didn't bother to wipe the blood and puss that was running down her other arm off as her body went through the whirlwind of emotions and her mind flooded with the horrible memories from that night.

◆ ◆ ◆ ◆ ◆ ◆ ◆

Jackie remembered taking Beauty's advice but she was a little more afraid of Leon than Beauty was, so she told her that she couldn't be seen out in public with another man. They decided to skip the club and go directly to her house. Beauty got out and told Juan to follow them to her condo up north and when they pulled off, he pulled off. Beauty made sure that Jackie knew exactly what they were going to tell Leon the next day as they rode to her house. She didn't want to leave out any details because Leon didn't believe in sharing his women, and she did not want to feel his wrath if he found out the true events of the night.

The spy who Leon hired for the night was his youngest brother Kevin. He didn't know what was going on when Beauty got out to talk to the young wanna be pimp, so he decided to follow them anyway. He didn't want Leon mad at him so he was going to make sure his woman was doing exactly what she was supposed to be doing. He got suspicious when they didn't go to the club, but he relaxed when he saw them pull up to Beauty's condo. He figured that Beauty must have told her about the slumber party when they pulled up to the club, and they must have changed their minds about going inside. Beauty was allowed to do whatever she wanted to do, so Kevin didn't care when Juan got out of his car and followed them into Beauty's building. When he didn't see anyone else pull up for the "slumber party" three hours later, he went to a payphone and called Leon who made it there in fifteen minutes.

Leon was embarrassed by the situation so he didn't want anyone to know. He felt he could handle it by his self because he had the element of surprise on his side, and there was only one male in the condo. He had an extra key made for his self the day he paid Beauty's deposit on her condo and he let his self in with it. He wasn't trying to invade her privacy when he got the key made, but they were business partners and he didn't know if he would ever need to get into her condo while she was gone. He didn't care about her privacy or anything else that night, he wanted to know what was going on with his wife.

Beauty was sitting on the couch getting ready to snort another line of cocaine when Leon came through her door with the key. She was about to go off until she saw that it was him, and his appearance shocked her into silence. "Bitch I made that name Beauty and I'm about to take it back," he said as he chopped her throat with a very sharp machete. That one cut went through most of her arteries, bones, and veins in her neck; so when he pulled the machete out, her face looked like it was about to fall all the way off. After killing her, he sliced all the skin off face with a butcher knife he got out of her kitchen.

Juan and Jackie's moans of pleasure led him to Beauty's room. They were so high off of cocaine and so wrapped up into each other that they didn't see, hear, or feel Leon's presence when he entered the room. Juan was caught completely off guard when he grabbed a fistful of his hair and slit his throat while he was still inside and on top of Jackie. Jackie had her eyes closed so she didn't know Juan's throat had been slit until she felt his blood squirting on her face, and thought he was ejaculating on it. When she opened her eyes she felt Leon snatching Juan's limp body from up off of her, and saw his neck wide opened. She fainted instantly but Leon's punch to the face bought her to. He was about to strike her again until his mother, Bertha, told him to stop.

Kevin was the only brother Leon fired when he promoted Beauty and Jackie. Leon didn't know it but he was still angry and humiliated from that, so he was happy that the women were betraying him. He knew Leon was going to do something crazy and he wanted no parts of it. He told him that he had no dog in that fight and let him go in by his self. Their mother was the only person who could talk some sense into Leon so she was the only person Kevin called after Leon went in. She made it there twenty minutes later.

"Get yo hands off of that damn girl and help me clean up this big ass mess you made," Bertha yelled. She was the same complexion as her sons and all of them looked like her in their own way. Her skin was smooth, beautiful, and real dark, but that's where her beauty ended on the inside and out. Her eyes were small, round, chestnut brown, crossed, and beady, and they set below a very, black, bushy uni-brow. Her lips were big and crusty with a white ring around them. She was 5'9, obese, and so lazy that she never put a bra over her big, saggy breasts and rarely picked her big, nappy afro. Her four sons gave her plenty of money but she didn't spend it on nice clothes or on trying to beautify herself.

"Put that boy in the tub and cut his body up and when you finish with him, cut up Beauty. Hurry up cause we only got four hours before the sun comes up! I bought some big black garbage bags with me so we ain't got to worry about that. I already called the clean up man. He'll be her in a hour to help, but we have to have at least one of the bodies ready," Bertha said with authority.

"But Mama, what about this bitch? Her and Beauty played me like everybody said they would and I loved her. She deserves to die too! I don't even want her no mo! She damaged now because she let another man enter her," Leon said as tears flowed down his blood splattered face.

"Boy you killed the people that needed to die! You ain't even got yo money worth out of this ungrateful little bitch! You gon take her out to the house you bought yo grandma and get the bitch pregnant! I want me some pretty grandbabies and she's the perfect bitch for the job with them pretty gray eyes of hers. Get yo trifling ass up, put on some clothes, and help my boy cleanup yo mess you low down dirty tramp," she turned around and said to Jackie as she hugged Leon.

Jackie was sitting on her living room floor in Dayton, Ohio with a small stream of blood mixed with puss rolling down her arm. The heroin along with the images in her head had her feeling like she was in Beauty's bathroom covered in blood, helping Leon cut up her friend's bodies all over again. She even smelled the blood as she sat there with her eyes shut tightly, her hands balled up, and her body as stiff as it could go.

Leon did what his mother told him to do and took Jackie to his grandmother's house in Rantoul, Illinois that night. As soon as they entered the house he led her to a spare bedroom. She was happy when he took a needle full of heroin out of the purple Crown Royal bag he bought with him. She didn't care what kind of drug was in the needle, she happily stuck her bloody arm out so he could tie his belt around it. She willed a big vein to appear as Leon popped the inside of her arm and felt euphoric as she felt the drug for the first time. Toni tried to pop up but Jackie wouldn't let her because she wanted to feel the weight of her guilt on her own.

Leon regretted not taking Jason's advice the first night he got her. He told him the only way to control Jackie was to get her hooked on heroin, but Leon didn't listen and Jackie betrayed him just like Jason said she would. He wanted her dead for the humiliation he felt because of her actions. He didn't let her wash Beauty and Juan's blood off until she came on her period five days later, and he only did it then because she was fertile. She stayed on for three days and he had sex with her everyday that she was on. The day she came off he taught her how to turn heroin into its liquid form and how to shoot up, then he left. He took his grandmother with him because she didn't approve of the treatment Jackie was receiving, but there was nothing she could do about it. When he left; he left her plenty of food, toiletries, alcohol, and heroin. He didn't come back until a month later when she came back on her period.

Jackie was only sixteen but she could have easily passed for a twenty-four year old because of the toll the drugs, guilt, pain, and grief were taking on her. Leon blacked both of her eyes and broke her nose when he hit her in the face the night he caught her in bed with Juan, so she also looked beat up. She didn't take care of herself unless he came and made her eat, wash up, and fix herself up. The only human contact she had was with Leon and she hated to see him coming because she knew he was only there to try to impregnate her. She felt nasty, violated, and sick to her stomach whenever he had sex with her while she was on her period, but there was nothing she could do about it. She hated having sex with him at first; but doing it while she was on her period made her disgusted in herself. Feeling him shoot his sperm inside of her made her feel worse than feeling him ejaculate on her stomach used to feel.

She wanted to commit suicide, but Leon told her he would kill her whole family if she even thought about killing herself. So, she just sat around dazed and high all of the time. She didn't want to think because the only thoughts she could conjure up were very bad ones. She didn't talk to him or herself, she was just there and Leon preferred it that way. He still wanted to kill her, but he also wanted to give his mother the pretty grandbabies she desperately wanted, so he only slept with her during her most fertile moments.

After three months of having sex with Jackie during her periods, Leon finally got her pregnant in the month of November. Bertha came out there to live with Jackie and made her stop taking drugs and drinking alcohol cold turkey. She ignored the agonizing cries that erupted out of Jackie's body whenever the pain from the heroin withdrawal reared its ugly head. The heroin withdrawal had Jackie throwing up lime green poison and shaking like a leaf. It also had her bowels real messed up and loose and if Jackie accidentally shitted on herself or threw up before she made it to the toilet; Bertha would make her sit in it for hours and clean it up herself. Then she would beat her for making the messes.

Bertha made Jackie take a shower every morning and the water that came out of the shower head felt like tiny arrows hitting her sore body. Jackie didn't have an appetite but Bertha made her eat the three meals that she prepared for her daily and after she ate, she made her take a walk with her unless it was raining or snowing. The only prenatal care she received came from Bertha, and she acted like she enjoyed seeing her in pain. She gave her prenatal vitamins that she purchased from a pregnant drug addict daily, but she mentally and sometimes physically abused her daily too. Jackie hated being pregnant. She kept morning sickness, her back constantly hurt, her breasts stayed tender, her feet stayed swollen, she was getting fat, she had stretch marks all over her stomach, and she had a huge monkey on her back that wouldn't go away. She hated the life that was growing inside of her and everything it represented. Whenever she was alone and felt the creature inside of her moving, she would punch her stomach. The only time she talked was when Bertha said something to her that needed a response. She constantly relived Beauty and Juan's murder and she used to wake up screaming until Bertha beat her one night for waking her up.

Jackie delivered Rhonda Thompson at 11:37 AM on August 27, 1976. She had her in Leon's grandmother's house with the help of a midwife and Bertha. After Jackie saw all of Leon's features in her child, she didn't want to touch her baby. Rhonda came out weighing twelve pounds and she tore Jackie's vagina up. The midwife stitched her up with a needle, some thread, some iodine, and some ice. The ice was supposed to numb Jackie's vagina but it didn't work and she felt the needle every time it was stuck in her.

Rhonda was the ugliest baby Jackie had ever seen in her life and she couldn't believe that she came out of her. She actually shed tears when

93

she saw her for the first time and even though she didn't want to hold her, Bertha laid her on her chest anyway. Bertha was a little disappointed that the baby didn't look more like Jackie, but she loved her anyway. She was happy that she inherited Jackie's eyes even if they were crossed. They were still gray and Chinese shaped. She came out kind of light but her ears were very dark so Bertha knew she was going to be dark skinned, and she didn't mind. Rhonda had Jackie's little cute round nose, but it looked funny above her big lips. Bertha knew that Jackie was going to hate the baby and she wasn't going to take care of her properly, so she continued to live with them so she could raise Rhonda. She had other grandchildren but they were all boys so she spoiled Rhonda rotten. She always wanted a little girl but the Lord never blessed her with one and she felt like her prayers were answered when Rhonda was born. She couldn't make Jackie love the baby, but she did try to make her breastfeed her. Jackie tried to, but her body wouldn't produce any milk because she was so stressed out and depressed.

Leon came to see his first child the night she was born, and he was ecstatic. He never had any kids before because of the way he looked. He thought he wouldn't be able to love any child that he produced, but his heart filled with pride, joy, and love when he saw the tiny replica of his self. The baby even made him forgive Jackie and right after he saw his child he filled the room Jackie gave birth in with teddy bears and dozens of red, white and pink roses. The next morning, he bought her a beautiful three carat diamond engagement ring.

Leon decided to move into his grandmother's house with Jackie, his mother, and the baby. The house had four bedrooms so there was plenty of room for them. Bertha turned one of the rooms into a nursery as soon as she moved into the house, and redecorated the master bedroom for herself shortly after. Leon bought his grandmother another house because he knew she wouldn't approve of the way they were living. He loved being home so he stayed in unless he had to go to the city to handle business or to take Rhonda to see all of her relatives.

Jackie hated when Leon was home because he started back having sex with her on the regular, and he acted like they were a happy little family. She liked it better when he hated her, because the feeling was mutual and he didn't touch her as much. He started giving her heroin again and that helped keep the monkey that was on her back at bay, but she was very depressed. She didn't have to worry about taking care of the baby because

Bertha and Leon did it with no problem. They didn't care nor did they find it strange that she didn't have any type of bond with her daughter, and she lived in the same house with her.

Jackie didn't have any contact with the outside world and she thought her family thought she was dead; because that's what Leon and Bertha told her whenever she built up enough courage to ask them about any of them. Jackie's family knew she was still alive there was just nothing they could do to save her. They didn't know where she was located or how to get in contact with her, but they figured that she had to be healthy because they saw her baby girl several times. Leon was still going over their house bringing them money and supplying Janice with heroin.

Janice started getting high the night Leon took Jackie with him. He came back to their house while Jackie was asleep that night, and offered Janice some heroin. She didn't want to snort it, but he told her it would make her feel better and it did. She accepted the drug because she couldn't deal with the tremendous amount of guilt she felt for releasing her daughter to the man she had been protecting her from. Leon gave the heroin to her so he could have complete control over their household.

Jackie's five sisters sympathized with Leon, and they couldn't believe that Jackie betrayed him the way she did. Leon was a pimp and he had been in their naïve little minds every since he infiltrated their family. He paid the mortgage, all of the bills, made sure that they kept food, fed Janice and Jack dope, and showered all of them with expensive gifts, so they felt like they owed him. They loved Jackie, but they thought she was biting the hand that was feeding all of them so she deserved the punishment Leon was imposing on her.

Her four brothers felt like Leon better be happy that Jackie was still breathing because if he would have killed her, they would have killed him. They had the opportunity to get him several times because he came to their house alone all the time. They knew there would have been repercussions if they killed Leon, but they would have taken that chance if he would have killed their sister. Leon was sleep on them, they weren't the same little boys who allowed him to come into their home and take over. He didn't know what was going on with them because they didn't hang out in his hood, they didn't ask him for anything, and they didn't accept anything from him. Leon didn't care because he wasn't trying to control the boys; he wanted to control the girls. He already had control of their parents because they depended on him to support their heroin habits. The boys never disrespected Leon, but they had been longing for some type of revenge on him for years.

Everyone in the streets thought he killed Jackie when he killed Juan and Beauty. Neither one of the victims received a funeral because their bodies were never found, but everyone knew they were dead. Kevin never entered Beauty's condo but he told at least ten different versions of the events that transpired in there. Leon's intermediate family knew that Jackie was still alive but their mother gave them strict orders to keep that piece of information between her kids. She didn't want Leon to appear weak in front of anyone, including his cousins.

A year after having Rhonda, Jackie was pregnant again and that pregnancy was just as hard as the first one. Bertha made her stop getting high again and Jackie hated living with them sober. She thought Leon was going to help her, but he helped Bertha enforce the strict routine. The only thing he helped her do was clean her and her messes up when she went through her heroin withdrawal. Even though he helped keep her clean, his presence made it worse because he acted like he couldn't keep his hands off of her. Jackie thought she was fat and ugly during her pregnancy but Leon thought she was the sexiest woman on earth during that time. She had a beautiful glow, flawless skin, fuller breasts, and her hair grew real long. She wasn't fat like she thought she was because she only gained weight in her breasts, stomach, and butt. Leon and Bertha ignored the empty look and the pain in her eyes. Her happiness and well being didn't matter to them; they felt like her only purpose in life was to make babies for them.

Mellissa Thompson was born September 15, 1978 at 3:53 AM. The same midwife that delivered Rhonda delivered her. Bertha and Leon were present and they helped too. Jackie couldn't bond with Mellissa even though she came out prettier than Rhonda. Her complexion was the same color as Rhonda's was and you could tell that she was going to be dark when she got older; just like you could tell Rhonda was going to be dark when she got older. Her lips were big and her nose was like Jackie's, but Mellissa's eyes didn't come out crossed, they came out the same color brown as Leon's and Chinese shaped like Jackie's. Mellissa's birth weight was the same as Jackie's was as a newborn, which was 5 pounds and 7 ounces. She didn't tear Jackie's vagina so Jackie didn't need any stitches, but that was the only easy part of the delivery.

Jackie hated Leon and she felt like her kids were a product of the hate that she felt towards him. She'd been raped and forced into motherhood.

If she had a choice she would be in college studying to be a lawyer, not a mother of two at the age of eighteen. But she didn't have a choice and Bertha made her help raise her kids. Her body couldn't produce the milk to feed them, but there were lots of other things that Jackie could do to help raise her kids and Bertha made sure she did them. She did everything for Rhonda, but she needed Jackie's help when she had Mellissa and Jackie didn't have any choice but to give it to her.

(11)

The Wedding

Jackie jumped up off of the floor in her Dunbar Manor apartment and stumbled out to get her father's diary from out of her trunk. She wanted to remember how she killed Leon after all of the bad memories that she had tucked away in a dark corner of her mind came flooding out. Thanks to Rhonda, she had unwillingly thought about a lot of people, places, and things she hadn't thought about in years. Now she wanted to think about the revenge she got on the people who made her life a living hell!

♦ ♦ ♦ ♦ ♦ ♦ ♦

October 18, 1982, was Jackie's wedding date, but she wasn't proposed to like a traditional bride. She was threatened into it with the letter her mother had written eight years before the wedding. She dreaded the day she was going to have walk down the aisle with Leon, but she was ecstatic when she saw all of her siblings and her mother in the pews. She felt as good as she looked when she saw her family for the first time in years. She had on a beautiful long, white, satin traditional wedding gown that Stevie designed for her with a veil that went with it, and her hair was styled in a up-do.

Leon had on a white tuxedo and held the wedding ceremony at his childhood church. He only invited his brothers and Jackie's intermediate family to the wedding ceremony because they were the only people that he felt needed to be there. Bertha walked her down the aisle and gave her away, six-year old Rhonda was the ring bearer, and four-year old Mellissa was the flower girl. Jackie didn't know who was going to attend the wedding or what to expect until the day of it because the whole wedding party besides the preacher, lived with her. She didn't even see her wedding dress until Leon bought it to her the morning of the wedding because Stevie came to the house, took her measurements, and left without saying one word to her. Beauty was the only person in Stevie's professional life who knew he did drugs; so she became his supplier and they had been scamming Leon and his associates for years. When he lost Beauty; he lost a friend, a business partner, and his drug connect. He blamed Jackie for her death and he really didn't want to make anything for her, but he was a dope fiend who had a habit to support.

There were more people at the reception than there were at the wedding, and most of them, including Leon and Jackie, were high and drunk. Jackie's brother Timothy stayed sober because he had a mission to accomplish and he intended on accomplishing that mission. Jack and Janice were very good steppers and they taught all of their kids how to step at a young age. Jackie hadn't danced in years and she was more than happy to be her big brother Timothy's stepping partner when her father's favorite song *Mercy Mercy Me,* by Marvin Gaye came on.

"Baby girl I want you to meet me by the punch bowl so I can give you yo daddy's diary and this letter I wrote you. I don't want you to read either one of them in front of anyone including Leon, and I don't want you to read them while you're high. Read both of them all the way through and then decide what you want to do. Start off by reading my letter because it'll clear a lot of things up for you. If I don't hear from you before the deadline, I'll know what you're decision is. Think long and hard about the things that I've put in that letter because they can change your life," Timothy whispered in Jackie's ear before the song went off.

"Where is my daddy?" Jackie asked Timothy as he took the diary out the back of his tuxedo pants and handed it to her. She put it in her purse and looked at Timothy with a confused look on her face.

"Just read that shit Jackie, its gon explain everything," he said as he gave her a hug and walked away.

Jackie and Leon flew to Hawaii after their reception. They'd been there for three days when she finally got the chance to read Timothy's letter. Leon had been trying to get her out of their hotel room since they got there, but she kept telling him that she was sick. He stayed in with her the first two days but she convinced him to go to the luau the hotel was throwing on the third one. He believed her when she said she was sick because she wasn't getting high as much as she normally did. He decided to take her advice and go to the luau, because he didn't come all the way to Hawaii to sit in the hotel room. Jackie opened Jack's diary, pulled out the letter that Timothy wrote to her, and began to read it.

October 15, 1982

Dear Jackie,

Let me start off by telling you how much I love and miss you. I've thought about you and the sacrifices you've made for our family everyday you've been gone and I pray that you're in good health. Leon destroyed your life by taking you out of our home and making you grow up too fast. He destroyed the rest of our lives when he took you, but he walks around like he saved us. He's got our mother and sisters believing that bullshit. He came back to our house the night he took you to "talk" to Mama and when he left, she was high off of heroin and he's been feeding her that shit every since then.

He's been having sex with Jamika and Tamika for the past six years and can't nobody tell them anything about him. They finished high school, but their dreams of going to college flew out the window when he bought them a condo on the Eastside, and introduced them to cocaine and the street life. They've been pregnant several times but they aborted most of their kids and left the ones they didn't kill in the hospital. I know that they're twenty-five years old, but Leon has been working on them since you left by bragging about the way he takes care of you and by giving them expensive gifts.

Angel's seventeen and Jennifer is sixteen and both of them got expelled from school for selling Leon's weed in school a year ago. I wouldn't be surprised if he had sex with them too because they don't listen to anyone but him, and he also showers them with expensive gifts. Sharon is fifteen now and she dropped out when Angel and Jennifer got kicked out. Mama don't even try to raise her kids anymore, it's like she's given up on life. Leon pays the taxes on the house, all of the bills, and supports her heroin habit so she puts on her rose colored glasses and lets him make the household decisions.

All of Mama's boys moved out. When we lived there we watched over our little sisters because we knew Leon was a pedophile. He wanted you when you were only fourteen years old. But, he didn't try anything with anyone until that shit happened with my boy Juan. After that, he went for our older sisters. I tried to talk some sense into the twins but they told me they were grown and I needed to stay out of their business. I bought the problem to Mama, but she cussed me out for stirring up trouble.

I moved out six years ago because I ended up going off on Leon and the twins for flirting with each other in front of me. It was sickening how gullible they were. He told them that having twin girlfriends had always been a fantasy of his, and he wanted to pick them instead of you but he didn't think they would go for it. When I heard him mention your name something inside of me snapped and I hit him in his mouth. He pulled out his pistol, hit me in my mouth with it, made me open my mouth, and put his pistol in it. Mama calmed him down by apologizing for my behavior over and over again. Then she told me that I had to leave her house if Leon decided to let me live. When she said that; he took the pistol out, laughed, told her that she didn't have to put me out, and left.

I was eighteen years old and had been saving all of the money I made working at McDonalds for two years. I also had a steady girlfriend who had been trying to get me to move in with her for over seven months, so I decided to move out. I was attending the University of Chicago at the time, and living at home with Leon around interfered with me getting good grades. I told myself that the rest of them would be fine without me.

When I left Angel was twelve, Jennifer was eleven, and Sharon was ten and I thought that Leon wasn't interested in them. Dwayne was sixteen, Jack Jr. was fifteen, and Phillip was fourteen. I wasn't worried about them because Leon ignored them. I think I was the only one of Mama's sons that he paid any attention to, and that was because he hated me. I told myself that I could help them more if I didn't live there anymore, but I think I was really just trying to save myself.

I know you've noticed that I haven't mentioned Jack. Well sister, that's because he died six years ago. Leon said that he didn't tell you and he didn't want us to tell you. He didn't say why he didn't want you to know, he just forbade us from doing so. I don't know if it's actual factual, but the word in the streets is that he's the one who killed Jack. One of his former prostitutes said that she saw him going under his hood to make a bag of dope out of battery acid. Then she said she saw him give the bag of "dope" to Jack and two hours later, she saw an ambulance speeding around the corner to our house. I believe the prostitute because Leon paid for the funeral and everything, so why wouldn't he want you to know? Why didn't he want you to mourn your father's death properly? That's fucked up ain't it? He requested you to pay off Jack's drug debt, but he turned around and killed him anyway.

Dwayne, Phillip, and Jack Jr., were all attending Westinghouse high school, the same school I graduated from, so I thought they would graduate too. When I left Dwayne was a popular, basket ball playing, junior who earned good grades. He was following in my foot steps and Phillip and Jack Jr., were following in his. My plans were to finish college successfully and make something of myself so I could show them that it could be done. I thought I was leading them on the path to success, but I didn't notice when they stopped following me. I became absorbed in my own life and my own problems. My major was criminal justice and I had been going to school for two years before I found out that I couldn't get into that field because I had a couple of assault and battery charges on my record.

I went to jail for defending myself. Students from Lucy Flowers High School used to come up to Westinghouse damn near every day after to school and pick fights with us. Don't get me wrong motherfuckers from Westinghouse used to go up to Flowers to pick fights too, but I wasn't one of the ones who went up there on that bullshit. But that didn't stop them from hitting me when they came to return the favor. I used to take out all of the frustrations that I had for Leon out on whoever put their hands on me, so you know I was whipping ass. I used to pretend that my opponents were Leon, and I would get so carried away that it would take the police to pull me off of whoever I was fighting. I got caught at least five times, but the two times that stuck occurred when I was seventeen. I thought I was still being charged as a minor for those fights, but in Illinois you get charged as an adult for felonies at the age of seventeen.

I used to visit Mama and the kids all of the time, but I stopped after I found that out. I was depressed because I owed money for that shit and I couldn't even use the shit that I did learn! I felt sorry for myself and I didn't feel like being bothered with anyone else's problems but my own. I hadn't planned on McDonalds being my career choice, but I couldn't quit because we still had bills that had to be paid. I wasn't about to waste anymore of my time or money on college so I dropped out. It wasn't fair Jackie! I had avoided becoming a pimp, a dope dealer, a gang banger, and a lot of other things to better myself, and that was the thanks I got.

I was so busy feeling sorry for myself that three years went by, and I didn't know what had become of my brothers and sisters. I left home in the summer of 76', stopped visiting in 78', and didn't see any of them again until last year on November 16th. Dwayne came into the McDonalds I worked in and said that he needed to talk to me. He came about fifteen minutes before I was supposed to get off so he waited on me. I thought we were about to take the el to my house until he led me to his brand new midnight blue 1981 Mercedes Benz. I tried not to act surprised but he had on all types of jewelry, some fly gear and the keys to the luxury car. I wanted to ask him all types of questions, but he started answering them before I got a chance to ask him anything.

He said him, Jack Jr., and Phillip were Black Gangster Disciples and they had dropped out of school years ago to start hustling. He also said that they got an apartment together. I told him I was sorry for leaving them and it was my fault that they had joined the gang; but he said they were in the gang before I left home. They hid their gang activities from me because they knew I wouldn't have approved. I thought I was keeping an eye on them when I lived at home, but I guess I was always wrapped up in my own little world. They all hung together but I had my own friends and when I think about it, I never paid that much attention to them. Leon ignored them, and I guess I did too. I always kept a girlfriend, a hobby, and tons of homework. I was on the basketball team and Dwayne was too so I thought they wanted to be like me, but nothing was further from the truth. I called myself going to school for a better opportunity in life, they went to get girls, gangbang, and sell drugs. I'm not judging them or their way of life because they're doing better than me from the looks of things.

After telling me about the boys, he started telling me about the girls. He's the one who told me about your upcoming wedding and about the twins living in the apartment Leon got them. I don't know if he was running game on them, but he told them that the only reason he was marrying you was because the police found parts of Juan and Beauty's bodies and he knew you couldn't be forced to testify against him if y'all was married. He also told them that you helped cut up their bodies, so you're an accessory to their murders. (I always felt bad about Juan getting killed because I was the one who invited him to your sweet sixteen party, and I know that's how y'all hooked up).

Dwayne was also the person who told me about our other sisters working for Leon. He said that he just found out that none of them were going to school, and the reason why they weren't in school a week before he came to see me. Mama won't do nothing about it, it's like Leon's been controlling her mind every since he came into our lives. Those are her kids, and she's the only one who can peacefully stop Leon from ruining their lives, but she won't even try to.

Now Jackie, the rest of the stuff I'm about to tell you are their gang's secrets and we can get our brothers killed if they get caught telling anyone. If you don't want to help us and you want to continue to live with the man who stole all of our futures that's fine, but please destroy this letter and be safe and precautious when you're out in public with him.

There's a hit out on Leon and his brothers because they opened up a couple of dope spots on BGD territory when the niggas who ran the spots went to jail. Everything was fine at first because they weren't in any gangs and they were paying the extortionist fee that was demanded. The soldier who collected the weekly fee was King David's (the leader of their gang), youngest son. Leon shot him in the head when he came to collect his father's money a couple of days before Dwayne came to see me. When the job was offered Dwayne, Jack Jr., and Phillip asked for it without anyone in their gang knowing they had personal animosity against the Thompsons. Getting the chance to kill them was a sweet deal, but getting paid to do the job was even sweeter. They also accepted the job because they knew that any other soldier sent to do it would have no choice but to kill you too. It was best that they didn't mention your relationship with Leon because they would have never gotten the job.

King David gets released from prison May 24, 1983 and he doesn't want any of them executed until he gets out. He wants Leon killed last so he can feel the pain of having his family members executed. We've been following Jason, Eddie, and Kevin around for the past couple of weeks and we know their routines so we can get them easily. We've been following Leon too, but getting to him won't be that easy because the only places he goes to alone is Mama's house, the twins apartment, and the house that he shares with you out in Rantoul. We don't want to kill him in Mama's house or the twin's apartment because we would probably have to kill them if we tried to do anything to him in front of them. And we don't want to kill him in front of the kids at y'all's house. We could get all of them out in the open but King David wants their baby fingers, their index fingers, and their middle fingers cut off so it'll look like the Black Souls did it. The BGD's have been in war on and off with the Souls for years and King David wants the heat that the murders are going to generate from the police on them.

We discussed it and we think that you can kill Leon. I know he's either been brainwashing you for years or threatening you for years, because you would have left him as soon as you turned eighteen. I still think you can do it though. I remember how repulsed you used to be when he used to try to get with you. I even remember the first time you came home crying because of the things he said to you. I don't know how you feel about him now, but I remember how much you used to despise him and you have more reasons to hate him now. I want you to summon up that hate you got for him and get that motherfucker! All of his dope spots, whore houses, drugs, and hoe strolls that ain't on BGD territory will be turned over to you. You'll get all of his money and property legally since you'll be his wife when he get's killed. It's good that King David wants him killed last because the police won't suspect you. They'll think it's just another gang hit on his family.

If you decide to do it, you're going to have to start working on him now! Tell him that being in the hotel during the honeymoon made you realize how much you miss being alone with him; and that you enjoyed the break you got being away from the kids and his mother. Insist that he starts taking you to hotels every weekend, and role play during y'all excursions. Use all of those wigs and different disguises you and Beauty used to use so you can't be identified by anyone. Start off by entering the hotels with him and then tell him it'll be more romantic if he allows you to meet him in the room. If you do it like that, you won't have to be in the hotel employee's faces. Get him to take you to different hotels and motels so you can choose the one that you'll be more comfortable killing him in. You can read Jack's diary to decide which method you want to use to kill him because it's full of silent techniques. I taped the knife he used to carry inside the back cover of his diary just in case you want to use it. Try to wear gloves while you're in the hotel and if you can't, wipe down everything you touch with a wet towel before you leave.

Jackie I know tolerating Leon sober is hard, but you're going to have to if you decide to carry out the mission. You don't want your mind cloudy because you might mess up and reveal something to him or his mother. Everything that I told you must remain a secret, even your father's death.

Dwayne was leery about telling you our plans because we don't know how you feel about Leon. But after some convincing from me, we all decided to take a chance on telling you because we love you very much and your safety is at risk. I reminded them of the hatred you used to feel towards Leon; and I told them that you might want to avenge Jack's murder because he was your father too. I hope I wasn't wrong about you and your love for us outweighs the love you might have developed for him over the years. We'll know if you warned him because you're the only female sibling who knows about our plans to get them. The Thompson's are going to get killed rather you warn them or not because King David has a lot of money, power, and soldiers and he wants them bad. The only thing your warning will do is get our brothers killed too. The hit is already in play and it's going to happen with or without your help, so you might as well do it and get your freedom from him, his ugly ass mama, and those kids.

I know you had those kids and they're a part of you, but for some reason I can't imagine you loving them. I apologize if I'm wrong and I'll accept them as my nieces if you choose to raise them, but if you don't want anything to do with them, I'll understand and accept that decision too.

Well sister, I've got to go now but I'll see you at your wedding. I hope and pray that we'll be reunited soon. I don't think you should contact me until King David gets released from prison, but if you need anything before then, feel free to call. My phone number is (312) 555-8807. It's a cell phone so I'll be the only one answering it.

    Love always and forever,

    Timothy

    The things Jackie read in Timothy's letter devastated her. She was hurt, grief stricken, and angry, all at the same time. She felt like a piece of her heart and soul instantly evaporated when she read about her father's death. It was hard for her to breathe and she immediately felt the pain from losing him physically, mentally, and emotionally. What hurt her the most was the fact that she didn't get a chance to say good-bye to him. She didn't even get to go to his funeral and mourn with the rest of her family. The last time she saw him was at her sixteenth birthday party and she didn't pay much attention to him then. She was still hurt and angry at him for letting Leon take her out of their home. Guilt seeped in when she thought about the way she pulled away from her father when he tried to hug her at the party. She never got the chance to tell him that she forgave him and still loved him in person so she told him in her mind and in her heart.

    Jackie read her father's diary from cover to cover before Leon came in from the luau. She finally understood why he started using drugs and was able to let go of the ill feelings she felt towards him after reading his most inner thoughts. The things he saw in Vietnam would make anyone want to get high, hell she couldn't even deal with Leon sober. Timothy wasn't lying when he said that Jack's diary had several ways to silently kill a man in it. Jackie was lying down on the hotel bed trying to figure out which one to use to kill Leon when he came in from the luau around three o'clock in the morning.

    He was drunk and high as ever when he stumbled in, took off his clothes, plopped down on the bed, and fell into a deep sleep. He was so drunk that he didn't notice her crying. She had to stop Toni from killing him as soon as he started to snore; and she didn't even realize she had returned until she heard her talking to her.

    "Quit crying Jackie, we can kill him right now! Let's use Jack's knife and gut his fat ass from his dick to his throat like Jack saw that Vietnamese soldier do to his friend."

    "Naw Toni if you gon help me kill him we have to wait and do it exactly like Timothy told us to do it," Jackie replied as she made herself stop crying and wiped her face and eyes with the sheet she had over them.

"*Girl fuck Timothy! He ain't the one who got to live with this gorilla for the next seven months. I say we do it now while we got the chance to. He drunk and he laying on his back, so he won't know what's going on until it's too late.*"

"*If we do it now, how in the fuck we supposed to get home? He got our passports, our plane tickets and everything else we gon need to get out of Hawaii. And on top of that, we'll get caught and I ain't trying to spend the rest of my life in jail for killing his big, fat, ugly, greasy ass. Besides, I want all of that money Timothy said we can get. I wanna do it smart, Toni. If we ain't gon do it right I don't wanna do it at all.*"

"*Alright Jackie, I'm with you but did you decide how we gon do it?*"

"*Yeah we gon get him like that prostitute got that soldier who was threatening to report my daddy.*"

"*Jackie, I don't wanna put no razor in our pussy! What if we cut ourselves down there? That shit will hurt like hell.*"

"*Toni we ain't gon cut ourselves if we start practicing how to control the razor with our vagina as soon as we get home.*"

"*How the fuck do you practice controlling a razor with your vagina Jackie?*"

"*That midwife taught me how to do kegel exercises to get my vagina muscles back strong after I had my kids.*"

"*What the fuck is a kegel exercise?*"

"*This is a kegel exercise,*" Jackie told Toni as she tightened and relaxed her vaginal muscles.

"*That shit just might work; we just have to be careful when we put it in! Jackie I would love to bounce up and down on Leon's dick with a razor in our pussy slicing it up with every stroke we make. I want to ride him so we can see the expression on his face as his dick is being shredded to pieces. I don't even mind waiting no more because we gon have to practice controlling the razor like you said. I want to use Jack's knife on him too, as a tribute to him.*"

"*Trust me Toni, we gon definitely use my daddy's knife on his fat ass.*"

"*What about the twins Jackie? Ain't you mad at them? I know you don't love Leon, but they still wrong for fucking him.*"

"*We gon get them back by killing him. Who gon pay them bitches rent when he dead? Who gon support their cocaine habits? I'm not! Them hoes been jealous of me since I was little because of my hair and my eyes so I'm not that surprised by their actions. They gon be the only ones in my family who gon suffer when this fat piece of shit is buried six feet deep. I hate Leon, but I still feel hurt and betrayed knowing I've been sharing him with two of my sisters,"* Jackie told Toni as a tear rolled down her cheek.

"Don't cry over his ugly ass Jackie, we gon get him when the time is right."

"I ain't crying over him, I'm crying over the things he did to my family. He killed my daddy and didn't have the decency to tell me he was dead. He turned me, my mama, and my sisters out on drugs, which is something none of us would have ever done if we hadn't met him. He caused division and turmoil within my family as he turned them against each other, and didn't think twice about doing it. How could he profess his love for me and have sex with me, knowing he was having sex with my sisters? How could he be so low down and dirty?"

"Jackie we bout to do the same thing to him that he did to us, but worse; every time our brothers kill one of his brothers, we gon act like we hurt. Like we there for him and shit. We gon act like we love him, our kids, and his mama just like he pretended to love you and yo family. We gon be the perfect wife, mother, and daughter-in-law for the next seven months until we get our revenge. It's gon feel good watching the pain Leon and his mother gon feel when they start losing their loved ones. It's gon feel damn good destroying his family worse than he destroyed ours. We gon get the last laugh, not him."

Jackie started working on Leon the very next day by initiating sex. Leon was pleasantly surprised when she woke him up by pulling his penis out of his boxer shorts, stroking it until it got hard, and climbing on top of him. He didn't know that Jackie knew how to ride a dick, but here she was riding him like there was no tomorrow. She always acted like she hated sex in the past, but he guessed those days were over because she had the biggest smile on her face as she bounced up and down on his dick. "Who taught you how to ride a dick baby girl?" he asked when they were done.

"You did Daddy. You think I don't be seeing how those women be pleasing their men in those porno movies you always watching? I remembered you tried to get me to try to ride you, but I didn't think I could do it. I'm a married woman now and I know I got to satisfy you sexually so you won't stray. Leon, I've loved you since the day you rescued my family from Jason and I love you even more for marrying me. I know that I didn't show it at first but I was young, dumb, and confused. Now I plan on being the best wife and mother a man could ask for. I'm tired of being depressed and I'm tired of getting high all the time. If you don't mind, I'd like for you to help me get off of drugs," she said using all of the acting skills Beauty taught her.

"Jackie I don't mind helping you get off of drugs if that's what you want to do, but we gon have to wean you off slowly because I didn't like how sick you use to get when Mama made you stop cold turkey. Damn, if I would have known marrying you would bring you out of that depression, I would have done it a long time ago. I love you and I'm going to be the best husband in the world. All I ever wanted was for you to love me and our kids as much as we love you," he said with tears in his eyes.

"Well I do, and I'm really enjoying our honeymoon. I didn't realize how much I missed spending time with you alone. I think we should try to get away every weekend. We don't have to leave the country or nothing; we can just go to hotels in the neighborhood. I know your mother won't mind watching the kids if you ask her to," she said as she wrapped her arms around him.

"Them hotels charge too much, but I wouldn't mind taking you to a motel every weekend. It does feel good not hearing the kids crying and Mama nagging. Yeah, we can definitely start getting away. You starting to get sick ain't you?" he asked as he got up to get her some heroin.

"Yeah, but I only need a little bit. I been trying to cut back since our honeymoon started," she said as she started to shake.

"He so cheap, all that money he got and he talking about how expensive hotel rooms are," said Toni as she looked at Leon with disgust.

"Shit Toni that's even better. Motels don't have as many cameras or staff as hotels do. Look how many doormen, maids, and people we had to pass before we made it to our suite. That's one of the reasons I didn't want to kill his fat ass in here. Plus we all on camera, we ain't gon bump into those problems at no cheap ass motel," Jackie replied with a smile on her face as she felt Leon tie something around her arm and inject her with the heroin.

They spent three more days in Hawaii and Jackie almost had her heroin habit kicked. When they got back to Rantoul, Illinois Leon started giving her methadone to help her get off completely. She took the methadone for a week and then she stopped taking it because she didn't want to develop a methadone habit. She also stopped drinking alcohol because she knew that she talked too much when she drank. She tried to be completely sober but she couldn't, so she started smoking weed to help her relax. She felt like the weed would help her accomplish her mission. She had to be high, especially since she had to pretend like she loved Leon knowing he killed her father.

When they returned from Hawaii Jackie was a changed person. She kept a smile on her face and she became the perfect wife, mother, and daughter-in-law she could be. She kept the house spotless, did everyone's laundry, spent quality time with her kids, and she cooked all of the meals. Leon and her daughters were happy that she appeared to be happy, but Bertha didn't trust her sudden attitude change. Before they went to Hawaii she couldn't stand her kids, Leon, or Bertha and now she acted like she was Joan Cleaver or somebody. Bertha used to have to make her comb her kids' hair, dress them, feed them, and bathe them; but now she did those things with no problem. She even started reading to them, playing games with them, and all types of other things mothers do with their kids. Bertha used to see her grimace whenever Leon touched her, but every since they came back from their honeymoon she was the one being affectionate and insisting they get away every weekend.

Three months passed since they returned from Hawaii and they went to the motel every weekend since getting back. Jackie was real happy because she had finally convinced Leon to buy her all types of costumes, lingerie, trench coats, and wigs by saying she wanted to spice up their relationship. He destroyed all of her old disguises when she cheated on him; and when she first asked him to get her some more he didn't want to because they reminded him of Beauty and the things she taught Jackie. But after three months, their little rendezvous started getting boring so he surprised her by taking her on a shopping spree to get all of the things she wanted. He enjoyed watching her try on all of the different costumes and lingerie, and she enjoyed the fact that her plan was going the way she wanted it to go.

After the shopping spree Leon and Jackie came in together, but Jackie stayed in the living room while Leon took her shopping bags to their room. Bertha came in a couple of minutes later and when she did Jackie got up off the couch, kissed her on her right cheek, and said, "Thank you so much for watching the kids Mama, we had a ball."

Bertha tried to keep her feelings to herself but she lost it when Jackie tried to call her mama. "Look bitch, you might got everybody else around here fooled but I can see right through you. You around here smiling all of the time, but you know what? I've noticed that that phony ass smile never reaches them evil ass eyes of yours! I ain't never seen nobody's eyes change colors so fast and I don't trust yo little possessed ass. See, the eyes never lie because they the window to the soul, and yo soul ain't right. I don't know what you got up yo sleeve but I got my eyes on you. All three of them! The good Lord blessed me with a third eye and it's been giving me a strong warning about you every since you came home from y'all's honeymoon. When I used to look into yo eyes I used to see fear, but now I see pure evil! I ain't yo mama so don't you ever fix that pretty little mouth of yours to call me that again or I'll bust it wide open," Bertha yelled as she enjoyed the surprised look that entered Jackie's eyes.

Leon came back in the living room when he heard the commotion. "Damn Mama, Jackie's trying her best to do right and you getting on her for it. She doing everything we want her to do without anyone asking her to, and you still got complaints. I'm the one who told her to start calling you mama and she said you would get mad. So I'm the one you should have cussed out, not her! You got her crying just because she called you mama. You act like she called you a bitch or something," he said angrily.

"I'm just trying to look out for you and yo kids and you got the nerve to cuss me out over this bitch! What about when she fucked that young boy? Who was there for yo dumb ass? I was that's who! Who had to stop you from killing her? Oh, that was me too, wasn't it? Do you really expect me to believe that girl went from hating you to loving you just because you married her and took her to Hawaii? Well I ain't the one! You can believe that bullshit if you want to, but I ain't no fool and her fake ass tears don't faze me one bit! I would leave yo dumb ass here with the bitch, but I love my grandbabies too much to leave them here with y'all. She'll been and killed one of them and yo stupid ass wouldn't even see it coming. You ain't got to worry about me saying shit else to her or about her, but I meant what I said! I ain't her mother and I don't want her calling me mama! You should have listened to her when she said I wouldn't want her calling me that! I guess she knows me better than you do," Bertha said before she stormed out of the room, went into her bedroom, and slammed the door.

"I told you she hated me! I know I messed up that one time, but haven't I been punished enough? I know I haven't been a perfect mother, but she's wrong for saying I would kill my kids. She hates me and I ain't never did nothing to her. I'm trying to stop doing drugs and everything, but she'll never respect me or love me. If you can forgive me Leon, why can't she?" Jackie asked him through her tears.

"It don't matter if she forgives you Jackie because I do. I love you, I trust you, and you're the woman that I'm going to spend the rest of my life with, rather my mother likes it or not," Leon replied as he wiped her tears away with his hand and wrapped her in his arms.

"And the award for best actress goes to Jacqueline Wright. Man Jackie you got his ass wrapped around your finger! When did you learn how to make yourself cry? I can't stand his fat, ugly ass mama, she thinks she's so smart, but like Leon said it don't matter if she don't trust us cause he do. I almost cracked up laughing when he put her in her place. We should kill her fat ass too for talking all that bullshit," Toni said with a huge smile on their face.

"Naw, we gon need her to get them kids after we kill Leon. I decided that I definitely don't want nothing to do with they lil spoiled, ugly asses after he's gone. Them little bitches is bad as hell. I been trying to spend some time with them to see what I want to do with they asses when this shit is over and done, and they helped me make my decision. Shit it be taking everything in me not to knock their fucking heads off when they be demanding shit. Especially the oldest one; she too fat, old, and ugly to be crying all the time. But don't worry, Bertha gon get hers when she got to live with all the pain she gon feel after all her sons get killed," Jackie replied as Leon stopped hugging her.

Jackie decided to avoid Bertha but she kept on acting like the perfect wife and mother. She couldn't wait to get her revenge! She felt like May 24th was never gon get there, but it did and she was more than ready to do her part. She had been putting a razor blade inside her vagina every morning for the past seven months, and she knew she could control it. She walked around, doing her kegel exercises, with the razor blade inside of her all day. She took the razor out every night and during the time they spent at the motels so she wouldn't cut Leon when he wanted to have sex with her. She was so excited that the day had finally come that she got up at four o'clock that morning, snuck the phone into the bathroom, and called Timothy, "Is the job still available," she whispered into the phone.

"Yeah lil sis, it's still going down," Timothy said and Jackie hung up. She didn't know if he was finished talking, but she didn't want to get caught on the phone because she had never used it before. She heard all that she needed to hear and she was relieved that the hit was still in play because she couldn't imagine living the rest of her life pleasing Leon and their kids. May 24th fell on a Saturday and she wasn't looking forward to spending yet another weekend with Leon, but she had to do what she had to do.

(12)

The Murders

When Leon and Jackie came back from the motel Monday morning, Bertha was sitting on the couch rocking back and forth and crying hysterically. "Jason's dead, they found him and his girlfriend at her house yesterday! Whoever did it cut off his fingers and shot him and her in the head! Kevin went to identify his body this morning. Why did they kill my boy Leon, why?" she asked through her tears.

"I don't know Mama, but I'm gon find out who did then I'm gon kill them! Y'all sure it was him? I can't believe my big brother gone! Noooooooooo," Leon wailed as an ear piercing scream escaped his body and he punched the wall.

"Girl look at them. They ain't so strong now is they? This shit is hilarious, I never thought I would live to see them two gorillas cry! Do you think Leon gon find out who did it?" Toni asked Jackie as she got kind of worried.

"Girl naw, by the time he figures out what's going on, he'll be dead too. I'm glad they started with Jason because he was the one who started all of this shit in the first place. I hope that bitch is burning in hell right now," Jackie replied as she hugged Leon from behind.

Jackie thought pretending like she loved Leon was hard, but that was nothing compared to consoling him and his mother and pretending like she was sad over Jason's death. She loved seeing them in pain, but she had to act like she was in pain too. And on top of that, she had to take care of her kids by herself because Bertha had to make the funeral arrangements; and she acted like she was too stricken with grief to be bothered with them. The way they acted really made her hate them, and she couldn't wait to kill Leon so she could finally be free from all of them. Leon and

115

Bertha really disgusted her; they didn't care when they destroyed other people's lives and families but they wanted sympathy when something happened to one of their family members.

Leon tried to call his brother Eddie the next day and got worried when he didn't answer his phone; so he went to the city to check on him. Jackie knew her brothers had succeeded in killing Eddie when she heard Bertha scream after receiving a phone call from Leon three hours after he left. She was alone in her room so she was able to laugh before going into the living room to check on her. "What's wrong Ms. Thompson is everything all right?" she asked as Bertha hugged her.

"Them motherfuckers killed Eddie! We know it's the same people because they cut off the same fingers, and shot him in the head too. Leon found him in his apartment when he went to check on him. He said that it had to be the Black Souls because the fingers they cut off formed their gang sign. Jackie why they trying to take my boys from me? They ain't did nothing to nobody! All they ever did was help the community! Look how many people they employed and this is the thanks they get," Bertha said as tears mixed with snot ran down her face and onto Jackie's back.

Bertha's words had Jackie speechless, all she could do was hug the woman and she didn't want to do that. *"Is this bitch serious? Them no good bastards of hers ain't helped nobody but themselves. She got to be playing; talking about they ain't did nothing to nobody. I bet everybody in the hood glad they dead! At least they think it's the Souls. I can't wait until it's my turn to inflict some pain on this ugly ass bitch,"* she said to Toni as Bertha released them.

"It ain't fair Jackie. I lost two boys in three days. Jason was my oldest boy and he was only forty-eight, Eddie was right up under him and he was forty-seven. I guess I'm gon have to bury them together. All I got left are my babies. Kevin is forty-three and Leon is forty-four. Speaking of Leon, I got to go so I can meet him in the city. Now, you take care good care of my grandbabies, we'll be back in a couple of hours," she said as she grabbed her purse and left out the door.

Bertha had Jason and Eddie's double funeral Friday, May 30, 1983 and Jackie was surprised to see her whole family there. Her mother and sisters looked like they were genuinely sad, but her brothers looked like they were pretending to mourn the Thompson's deaths in Jackie's opinion. She figured they didn't look genuine to her because she knew they were the ones who killed them.

"We gon get Kevin after the funeral, we want you try to get Leon this weekend. If you can't do it we gon have to, because King David wants all of them him dead by next week. The Thompson's didn't start a war with the Souls like he thought they would. Instead, Leon requested a meeting with King Pee Wee, the leader of the Souls. That meeting is supposed to take place Tuesday, and if they put two and two together they'll figure out King David is behind the hits. If that happens the peace treaty that's been in play for years will be over and the BGD's will be in war with the Thompsons and the Black Souls," Timothy whispered in her ear at the burial.

"Damn Jackie how the fuck we supposed to convince Leon to go to the motel this weekend and he just buried not one, but two of his brothers? You know his mama don't trust us! I was thinking we at least had until next week to get him. We can't do it in the house or we going to jail," Toni said to Jackie.

"We ain't gon panic just yet. Let's just stay calm and see how it plays out. At least we know that somebody gon kill his big ass," Jackie replied as she got into the limo with Leon.

She didn't have anything to worry about because after the re-pass Leon pulled her to the side and said the best words she ever heard come out of his mouth. "Jackie I still want to go to the motel tomorrow night, we just gon go to one we ain't never been to. One of the niggas in my crew is related to King Pee Wee, the man who's over all the Black Souls. I had him set up a meeting with him for next week. He assured me that there wasn't an authorized hit out on us and he's in the process of getting to the bottom of this shit. We should be safe, but I still want to switch motels just in case dude is on some bullshit. We only gon spend one night there because I don't want to leave Mama in the house by herself with our kids. I know I'm being selfish but I need at least one night away from her cries. I need you more than ever Jackie; please say you'll go with me?"

"Of course I'll go with you Daddy, but I think we should leave out after we put the kids and your mother to sleep. We can slip some sleeping pills in your mother's beer to help her go to sleep. She hasn't slept a full night since all of this started happening, so I know she needs the rest. We don't even have to tell her that we're leaving because she won't approve, and she'll be worried about us all night. We can sneak out tomorrow night and sneak back in Sunday morning," said Jackie hoping she had convinced

Leon that she was trying to look out for Bertha, and not trying to develop an alibi for herself.

"That's why I need you Jackie because you're smart and considerate. You looking out for my mother even though she's been treating you like shit. When this is over with I'm gon make her start respecting you more. Marrying you was the best decision I ever made. I wasn't completely faithful to you before our wedding, but I promise I've only been with you since I made you my wife. I'm sorry for everything I've done to you in the past and I want to thank you for being here for me and my mother during our time of need," Leon said to Jackie as he hugged her tightly and cried.

Leon's words infuriated Jackie so she couldn't wait to rid the world of him. She couldn't even bring herself to respond to the bullshit he let come out of his mouth. *"He ain't gon be sorry for what he did to me until tomorrow night,"* she said to Toni.

The next night Leon put two sleeping pills in his mother's beer and waited on her to fall asleep. Jackie took a bath and put on her nightgown after she fed her kids, bathed them, and put them to sleep so Bertha wouldn't think she was going anywhere. She dozed off in her bed until Leon woke her up around eleven and told her that Bertha was sleep. She went into the bathroom and put on her nurse's costume, which consisted of a short white button down dress, some white thigh high stockings that connected to her garter belts, some white stilettos, a small white nurse's hat and her long straight-haired red wig. She chose the nurse costume because it also came with a black leather bag. After Jason got killed, she filled the bag with a black plastic garbage bag, a roll of duct tape, some leather gloves, Leon's machete, Jack's knife, a pair of balled up socks, a black wig, and a change of clothes. When she finished putting the costume on she put on some makeup that was a lot lighter than her complexion and dark brown contacts into her eyes. Leon wasn't in his right state of mind, so he didn't pay any attention to the fact that Jackie put on her disguise before they went to the motel. She normally changed into her costumes while they were in the various motels they went to.

Jackie was more than ready to kill Leon, but she was still nervous because she had never killed anyone before. She was second guessing herself on the ride to the motel, but Toni was there to give her the motivation she needed. *"Jackie you can do this, shit you have to do this! Your brothers are depending on you. This fat piece of shit ain't did nothing but hurt you since the day you met him. If you don't kill him somebody else will and when they do, they might kill you too. Look at how they did Jason's girlfriend! I know you ain't willing to die over Leon! And on top of that, you don't want your kids to see him get killed! He took your pussy when you was only fourteen so you have every right to take his dick,"* she said to Jackie as Leon pulled into the Palace motel, a rundown motel located on the far Westside of Chicago.

"I know this one ain't as nice as the ones we usually go to, but I feel more comfortable here. I'll be right back after I pay for the room," Leon said as he got out the car.

Jackie was relieved when he didn't make her go in with him to get the room, but she was also scared because he chose a motel on the Westside. *"What if he knows my brothers killed his brothers? Toni I'm scared! Why did he come here? What if somebody recognizes me? What if he bought me here to kill me?"* she asked Toni as fear ran through her entire body.

Toni slapped Jackie's side of their face as hard as she could. *"Damn Jackie, get a hold of yourself! That motherfucker don't know shit because he would have tried to kill yo brothers if he did! If he wanted to kill you he would have done it somewhere private, not here where the cashier can recognize him! Now you can and you will accomplish this mission. Do it for your family, Beauty, Juan, and yourself! If you can't do it, I will! I ain't been walking around with a razor in my pussy for seven months for nothing,"* she said as Leon walked out of the office and motioned for them to follow him with his hand.

"Naw Toni I got this. He destroyed me and my family not you or yours," said Jackie as she grabbed her bag and got out of the car.

Jackie got into character as soon as Leon locked the door. "I got to use the bathroom Daddy, but I'll be right back. When I come out I want you asshole naked, laying on your back, waiting on me to ride that big dick of yours," she said as she walked into the bathroom with her bag in her hand. She took it with her because she didn't want him looking in it while she wasn't in sight. She closed the door, and took the change of clothes, the leather gloves, and the black wig out the bag and sat them on the toilet. Then she took the brand new razor blade out the breast pocket of her nurse's uniform, and carefully inserted it into her vagina. She put the razor in the pocket when she decided to wear the uniform three weeks ago. She didn't put the blade inside of her when she got ready because she didn't want to cut herself. She nicked her vagina one day while she was practicing sitting down with it inside of her. She eventually learned how to control it sitting and standing; but she didn't trust riding in a car with it inside of her because the bumps in the road could have messed her up.

When Jackie came out the bathroom she sat the black bag on the floor by the bed and did a striptease for Leon. She took off everything except her stockings, her garter belt, and her stilettos. This was her first time ever dancing for him and he was fully erect by the time she finished her routine; like she hoped he would be. She squeezed her vagina real tight so she could keep the blade in place, and slid down his rock hard penis. She felt the blood oozing out when she came back up. For the first couple of minutes she didn't see any reaction in his face as she bounced up and down on his penis cutting him deeper and deeper with every stroke. But when he did feel the pain, she got to see the agonizing facial expression she had been waiting to see.

Leon didn't feel the pain in his penis for several minutes because he took some cocaine when she went in the bathroom and it had his whole body numb. When the pain did hit him he felt it in every part of his body including his nails. He screamed at the top of his lungs and pushed her up off of him. When he pushed her off of him the blade cut her and fell onto the bed. She didn't feel the cut due to the adrenaline rush she was feeling mixed with the fear she felt over the possibility of getting caught. She knew she had to shut him up before anyone heard him screaming as loud as he was. She grabbed the bag and took out the socks preparing to stuff them into his mouth, but he fainted when he touched his penis and felt how bad it was shredded up. She put the socks back and grabbed her father's knife and the roll of duct tape instead. Then she cut his penis all the way off with it. He came to when he felt Jack's knife cutting through his flesh and he managed to mutter the word, "why" before she stuffed his penis into his mouth and taped it shut.

"Why? I know you not wondering why I'm bout to kill you! There's a list of reasons why I'm bout to send yo fat, ugly, low down, dirty, no good ass to meet yo maker! You took me from my family when I was only fourteen, stole my virginity, my dignity, my future, and my entire life! You killed my daddy, and didn't have the decency to tell me he was dead. You killed the only friends I had in this world and made me help you cut up their bodies! You turned me, my mother, and my sisters out on drugs, and had sex with them! And you and yo ugly ass mama made me have your ugly ass kids! But all of that shit is personal; I'm also doing this for business. You fucked up when you shot King David's son in the head when he came to collect his father's extortionist fee. You and yo brothers lived y'all lives taking shit that didn't belong to y'all and now all of y'all dying for it. You live by the sword you die by the sword," she said as she took his machete out the bag, chopped his head off with it, and started giggling hysterically. After decapitating him, she cut off his middle fingers, his index fingers, and his baby fingers with her father's knife. She put all of Leon's body parts into the black plastic bag then put the bag into the leather bag; and went into the bathroom to take a shower. She giggled during the entire process.

The giggle turned into a very loud laugh when she was in the shower and noticed that she had cut her vagina; but she stopped when she realized that the razor blade was missing. She knew she didn't take it out of her vagina so she had to find it. When she finished showering, she put a towel in the pair of panties she bought with her. Then she put on the shorts, the t shirt, and the black wig she left on the toilet. She didn't realize that she forgot to bring a change of shoes with her until it was time to change into them. She was about to wear the stilettos but they were soaked in blood, so she rinsed them off in the tub and remained barefooted. After she was dressed, she washed her father's knife and Leon's machete. She put on the leather gloves before using the towel she washed up with to wipe off everything she touched. After wiping down the room, she put the machete, the stilettos, the nurse's outfit, the red wig, and the bloody stockings into the black bag. She looked for the razor blade for about ten minutes and when she couldn't find it, she had no choice but to leave it. She made herself feel better by assuming that it was lodged into Leon's penis. She took his keys out of his pants pocket, grabbed the bag, and left out the motel two hours after they entered it. She considered taking his wallet, but she didn't because she wanted him to be identified.

She didn't see anyone as she walked to the car so she thought the coast was clear. The first thing she did was find a payphone to call Timothy. "I just did it," she said as soon as he answered the phone.

"Alright baby girl. Where you at?" he asked.

"I'm by that McDonalds on Madison and Karlov. I need you to take me home before his mother wakes up. I convinced him to slip some sleeping pills in her beer, but I don't know how long she gon be sleep. I got his car, but I want everybody to think he snuck out of the house without me so I need to leave it parked somewhere in the city," she said getting nervous because it was after three o'clock in the morning and she knew the sun would be rising in a couple of hours.

"I'll be near there in fifteen minutes," he said.

"Stay on the phone with me Timothy. I'm a fucking wreck," she pleaded. She didn't feel bad for killing Leon, but she was scared of getting caught.

"I can't Jackie; you need to drive away from there because there might be cameras around there. That's why I said I'll meet you near there in fifteen minutes. I want you to drive over to the next block on Monroe and Karlov. There's a vacant lot over there we can leave the car in. Pull yo self together baby girl. The hard part is over, but you gon have to act normal so his mother don't think you had anything to do with his murder," he said before he hung up the phone and raced out of his apartment.

Jackie drove to the vacant lot Timothy told her to go to, cut off the lights, and took the keys out of the ignition. Leon had a big key ring with a lot of keys on it, and Jackie wasn't sure which one went to the house in Rantoul. She took the car keys that went to the Cadillac off and slipped the key ring with the rest of the keys on her wrist. She was relieved when she saw Dwayne and Timothy pull up in Dwayne's car ten minutes later. She grabbed the leather bag and jumped out when they pulled into the lot. They were listening to *The Message* by Grandmaster Flash and it was the first time Jackie heard rap music. Both of them got out and hugged her before they all climbed into the car. Dwayne turned down the radio when they got in. "We gon just leave that nice ass car? What year is that Caddy, an eighty-two? We should take that motherfucker I'll have it pimped out for real," he said in an animated voice.

"That car will get us caught, because it's the car Leon was last seen in. We gon leave that pretty motherfucker right where it's at," replied Timothy. While he was still in school, he had to dissect a case for homework where the police officers caught a suspect in a murder investigation because he went joy riding in the victim's car. He wasn't about to let Dwayne make the same mistake.

"Damn, I hate to leave it but you right. Leon's fat ass used to get a new Cadillac every year. I thought he got rid of his eighty-two when he got that eighty-three! But anyway, we proud of you baby girl. I ain't gon lie, I didn't think you could do it until I talked to Timothy," said Dwayne.

"Killing him was easy after the shit he did to us I just hope his mama or them kids ain't woke. I want that bitch to be my alibi. The fingers King David wanted are in this bag with his head," Jackie replied.

"Damn you a beast! You cut his head off too? You just gave me a new level of respect for women, because I lost it after watching Leon take control of Mama and the twins minds. You lived with him for years and you didn't let him get in yours. I didn't understand how a pimp got his hoes until Leon came into our lives. He was in the process of getting our little sisters too. Jackie, I always regretted not being able to save you, and I wasn't about to let that happen to our little sisters. Our big sisters told us to step off when we tried to save them, so I wasn't about to let them bitches be their role models. On the real Jackie, I knew we was gon bring you home but I ain't know you was gon help us get you back. I can't believe we bout to get paid $10,000 for killing the Thompson's. We killed Kevin's bitch ass as soon as he finished saying bye to Jason and Eddie. Jackie I'm glad I know where yo heart at and who side you on, because we gon have to kill his mama if she ain't sleep when we drop you off," Dwayne said trying to cover their tracks.

"That's all we getting for killing five motherfuckers? How we gon split that shit five ways? I bet I don't ever do another hit for King David's cheap ass," said Timothy. He was mad at his self for not finding out how much the job paid ahead of time. He was so happy to get the opportunity to kill Leon that he didn't think about the money until the job was done.

"Nigga you ain't kill nobody no way! You planned everything but me, Jackie, Jack Jr., and Phillip put in the work, and we still willing to give you an even cut! Motherfuckers kill for King David for free so I doubt if he need yo services in the future. Jackie do you have a problem with the two stacks you getting for killing the man you hated?" asked Dwayne. He was extremely loyal to King David so he didn't appreciate the way Timothy was talking about him.

"I would have killed that motherfucker for free, but I don't want to kill his mother because I need her to raise my kids. I don't want nothing to do with them, but I don't want to send them to no foster home. I know Bertha loves them and she'll take care of them better than I can. I'll think of something to say if she's woke. It'll be my ass on the line if she suspects anything, not yours so let me handle her. Do one of y'all got a joint? I need something to calm my nerves," Jackie said. She thought the job paid more too, but she wasn't mad. She was just ready to get to the house to make sure Bertha was still sleep.

"Yeah, I got one. Jackie we gon let you handle your situation anyway you want to handle it. We can get rid of everything you got in that bag if you want us to," Timothy said. He was mad at the small amount of money they were getting for killing the Thompson's; and he was even madder that Dwayne wanted Jackie to kill Leon's mother. She just killed her husband for them and that was going to haunt her for life rather she knew it or not. He took a psychology class so he knew a person's first murder always haunts them unless they're a psychopath. He knew Jackie wasn't a psychopath, so she couldn't have enjoyed seeing the life leave out of Leon's eyes.

"You can get rid of everything in this bag except for Daddy's knife. Damn, I don't see it," she said as she looked through the bag and realized she left her prized possession. She was so busy looking for the razor blade that she forgot to get her father's knife from out of the bathroom sink.

"Damn was yo fingerprints on it?" asked Dwayne. He was worried about the police linking Jackie to him. He was against using her in the first place and the thought of her making a critical mistake like leaving her fingerprints at the crime scene angered him.

"Naw, I wiped down everything that I touched like Timothy told me to do. Them motherfuckers made me wipe down everything I touched after they made me help them cut up Beauty and Juan's bodies, so I knew how to do it. I'm mad because I left my daddy's knife. I ain't even get a chance to tell him goodbye. I ain't even know that he was dead and I left one of his favorite items in the world. Well at least I still got his diary. Reading that motherfucker was like reading his mind," she said as she took a long pull off the joint Timothy gave her.

"You ain't lying! After I read it, I started missing the father we had before he went to the army," said Dwayne.

"Me too! But what kind of music was y'all listening to when y'all pulled up?" asked Jackie trying to change the subject. She was happy that she killed Leon successfully and didn't want to ruin the moment by thinking of the things her father had to endure while fighting in the Vietnam War.

"That was rap music. Damn, Jackie everybody listen to rap nowadays. Did you like what you was hearing?" Timothy asked.

"Yeah, that's why I asked what it was. Was dude saying don't-push-me-cause-I'm-close-to-the-edge?" she asked as she rocked from side to side. The marijuana had calmed her down and she wanted to hear the song all the way through.

"Yeah, that shit deep too. His name Grandmaster Flash and the name of that song is *The Message*. He talkin' bout living in the ghetto. You want me to put it back on?" asked Dwayne.

"Yeah, would you? I ain't never heard nothing like that. I can't believe they actually letting a nigga express his self like that," she said before the beat came in.

They listened to *The Message* over and over until they made it to Rantoul. When they pulled up to the house, Dwayne took the tape out of the tape deck and handed it to her. "Here you can have this. They got a couple of good songs on there," he said. He felt sorry for his sister because he realized how isolated Leon had her from the rest of the world when he found out that she didn't know what rap music was.

"Thank-you! Man I love and miss y'all so much; but I'll be home within the next month," she said with tears in her eyes.

"We love you to baby girl and remember; the hard part is over," said Timothy before she got out of the car.

Jackie was as quiet as she could be as she tested key after key until the fifth one opened the door. When she entered the house, the first thing she did was tiptoe up the stairs and peek in Bertha's room. She was happy to find her in a deep sleep. Exhaustion, grief, and the sleeping pills did there job. Bertha hadn't slept for more than two hours since she found out Jason had been killed. Jackie was scared that one of her nightmares had woke her up because she had been having them every since her sons started dying. She figured her kids would still be asleep because they rarely got up before nine; but she felt better when she peeked in on them and knew that they were.

After the long ride home and walking up the stairs, the nick that she got in her vagina was throbbing. She went to the bathroom and looked at the towel that was inside her panties to see how bad she was bleeding. There was only a small amount of blood on the towel, but she wanted to make sure the cut healed properly. She took one of her disposable douches, took the top off of it, and rinsed it out. After she was sure the vinegar and water was completely rinsed out of the bottle, she filled it up with warm water, screwed the top back on, sat on the toilet and squirted the warm water inside of her. She did that until the water that streamed back out of her came out clear. Then she took a tampon, soaked it in peroxide, and stuck it inside of her for a few minutes. When it stopped bubbling and burning, she took another tampon and coated it real good with some triple antibiotic ointment and replaced the peroxide soaked tampon with the one that had the ointment on it. She didn't know if the wound would heal properly, but at least it was the only one she sustained during the murder. All she had to do was walk normal and the wound would go unnoticed since Leon was dead. After taking care of her injury, she got a drink of water, and put on the long nightgown that Bertha saw her in before she fell asleep.

It was after five o'clock in the morning and she was exhausted so she went to sleep. She couldn't wait to see Bertha's face when she discovered Leon missing. She was going to act more surprised than Bertha was going to be by his absence, and then she was going to help her look for him. For years both of them acted like her father was living, knowing he was dead so she was more than ready to deceive Bertha.

It was after ten o'clock in the morning when Bertha woke her up. "Jackie wake up baby. Please tell me you know where Leon went! One of his cars is gone and he ain't nowhere in this house," she said as she shook Jackie's shoulders.

"Naw, I ain't even know he left. He didn't tell me he was going anywhere. He knows I've been worried about him every since everything started happening. I don't even remember him coming to bed. I went to sleep right after I drank the tea he gave me and I been sleep every since then. I think he put something in that tea because I went to sleep early but I still feel exhausted and weird," Jackie replied with a long drawn out yawn.

"I think he put something in that beer he gave me because I feel weird too. Damn, I was about to ask him if he talked to Kevin because I ain't been able to get in contact with him. The girls woke me up about twenty minutes ago and something told me to call him. I tried calling his house phone and that big ass cell phone he keeps on him and my baby ain't answering either one of them. Now Leon's ass is gone! I told both of them to tell me their every move and the company they gon be around every since this bullshit started! They ain't gon be happy until I die from being stressed out. Well, they should be ok because Leon told me about a meeting they having Tuesday. But that's if we can trust King Pee Wee. If they took my last two boys away from me fuck a street code, somebody's going down," she said as she walked out of the room.

Jackie got up, put on her robe, and followed Bertha to the living room. She watched television while Bertha tried calling Leon and Kevin several times. Then Bertha called the police and cussed them out when they told her she had to wait forty-eight hours before she could file a missing person's report for them. Jackie was happy that she was so engrossed in her telephone conversation because Leon's death was being reported on the news. She knew his body was going to be discovered at checkout time, but she still wasn't prepared to see it being reported on the news.

She thought Bertha didn't hear the news report, but she heard every word that was said. "I bet that's one of my boys, I can feel it in my gut. They still ain't answering their phones and the police still ain't doing shit to help. I'm bout to go to Kevin's house and make sure he's alright. If he ain't there, I'm going to the morgue to make sure the man they just found ain't him or Leon. This ain't fair, a mother is supposed to die before her children, not the other way around. Ain't I suffered enough Lord? Jackie you stay here with my grandbabies so they don't see anything they shouldn't see. I can't sit around here waiting no forty-eight hours, I'm going to find my sons dead or alive," she said through her tears and snot.

"Bertha you don't need to be alone, I'll go with you. We can drop the kids off with my family so they don't witness anything. Leon is my husband and I want to make sure he's alive, waiting around here is going to drive me crazy too," Jackie said.

"Alright baby. I want to thank you for everything you been doing for us. You been a big help around here," Bertha said as she embraced Jackie. Then she helped get her granddaughters ready.

"Damn Jackie, why you tell her we was gon go with her? That long ass ride gon have our pussy aching and I'm still sleepy," Toni complained.

"We have to keep up with her to see what she tells the police. I told you we gon do this right," Jackie replied as she went into her room and grabbed some panties, a bra, a t shirt, some gym shoes, and some jogging pants. Then she went into the bathroom and took out the tampon. There wasn't any blood on it so she used her finger to put some more triple antibiotic ointment on the cut inside of her vagina. After that she brushed her teeth, washed her face and slipped on her clothes. She also put on a maxi pad just in case the cut started bleeding again.

Bertha had a green 1981 Chevy and she told Jackie to drive them to Chicago in it. Jackie didn't have to worry about trying to hold a conversation with her because the first thing Bertha did when she got in the car was cut on the radio, popped in a Phil Collins tape, and fast forwarded to his song *In the Air Tonight*. They listened to the entire Phil Collins tape three times before they made to Jackie's mother's house. "Jackie I'm gon wait out here for you. I don't have the strength to move right now. Rhonda and Mellissa y'all be good, we gon be back to get y'all as soon as possible. Now give Granny a kiss," said Bertha as she turned around in her seat to kiss her grandkids.

It was a beautiful June day and Angel and Jennifer were sitting on the porch when Jackie pulled up. She was surprised that her kids knew them so well. When she took them out of their seatbelts and opened the car door both of them jumped out the car and ran into her sister's arms. Jackie grabbed the bags that Bertha packed for them and followed her kids to the house that held so many good and bad memories for her. "What's up y'all?" Jackie asked as her sisters put her kids down and hugged her. Jackie didn't say anything but when she hugged her sixteen year old sister, Jennifer, it felt like she was pregnant.

"You know there ain't shit you can do with Jennifer if she already fucking, kicked out of school, and pregnant. She think she grown and if she fuckin' yo other two baby sisters probably fuckin' too. Fuck what Timothy talking about, we bout to move home and get this money, not babysit no wanna be grown ass teenagers! We've sacrificed enough of our lives for these fast ass heffas," Toni said to Jackie and Jackie was listening to her and her sisters at the same time.

"Hey Jackie! What you doing on this side of town? How long y'all staying here? Mama gon be so happy to see you! She miss you too much," said Angel.

"I can't stay for long today. I just came to see if I can pay y'all to watch my kids for me. Leon didn't come in last night and his mother wants me to help her look for him. But I'll stay for a couple of hours when we finish," Jackie replied.

"Yeah we'll watch our nieces, and you ain't got to pay us. I feel so sorry for Ms. Bertha. It looks like she's aged twenty years since the funeral. That's messed up how she lost two sons in the same week. I hope Leon alright cause I can't imagine what she gon do if he ain't," Jennifer said as tears started to form in her eyes.

"Where's Mama? I wanna speak to her before we go," Jackie said trying to change the subject.

"I don't know where Mama went; she was gone when I woke up. You probably see her while y'all looking for Leon. Me and Jennifer the only ones here, but don't worry we got yo kids," said Angel.

When Jackie got back in the car Bertha was crying hysterically. "I know they dead Jackie, I'm just praying that the good Lord proves me wrong. Kevin lives in Rockwell, we can go there first," she said through her tears.

Jackie cut back on the radio and drove to Rockwell Gardens. Kevin lived in an apartment in the same building that Jackie used to live in with Leon. They used to live on the seventh floor and he lived on the first one. Bertha had a key to his apartment and she let them in when their knocks went unanswered.

Jackie knew that Kevin was dead so she thought she was prepared to see his corpse; but nothing could have prepared her for the stench of death that hit her when Bertha opened his apartment door. "Maybe we should call the police Bertha, you don't want to see him like that," she said as she tried to prevent her from entering the apartment by holding her back.

"Let me go Jackie, that's my son in there," Bertha replied as she pushed Jackie away from her and ran into Kevin's apartment.

Jackie couldn't stand the smell that was coming out the apartment so she went outside, drove to the corner store, called the police, and reported the murder. *"Damn Toni, don't nobody deserve that. We should have just stayed home like you said,"* she said as tears started to well up in her eyes.

"Fuck that! You was right! Them niggas got what they had coming to them and she deserves to feel all the pain that she's feeling for raising them the way she did! We here for one reason and one reason only, and that's to see what the police know. You can cry, but don't cry for them. Cry for yourself and all those years they stole from you! This shit is almost over. You can go on with your life as soon as the funeral is over," Toni said as they pulled back up to the projects.

When Jackie went back to Kevin's apartment the hallway was crowded with nosey neighbors. Bertha was inside hugging his decaying corpse as she cried and cussed. A couple of people were in there with her trying to pull her up off of him, but every time they got her loose she ran back to him. Somebody called Bertha's sister, Anita, and she was finally able to coax her out of the apartment. "Come on sister it's gon be alright, he's with God now," she said.

Hearing her sister's voice helped calm her down and drained her at the same time. "Nita, why did they take my boys from me like this? How can I heal when I keep feeling this pain over and over again? I know they with God, but I need them with me! How can I breathe when they ain't? Please tell me you seen Leon? He disappeared sometime last night and I got a bad feeling that the man they was talkin' about on the news is him," Bertha said through her tears, as she let her sister lead her out of the apartment.

"Come on y'all get out of our way, this ain't no damn show. Bertha, I ain't seen Leon since the re-pass but I doubt if that man was him. Come on we can wait over my girlfriend's house until the police get here," Anita said as she led Bertha through the crowd of people to the apartment across the hall from Kevin's. Anita had been living in the apartment building behind Kevin's for over twenty years so she knew almost everyone who lived in Rockwell. She knocked on the door and when the lady opened up it she said, "Reese my nephew across the hall from you got killed. Can we call the police and wait on them in here?"

"Yeah Nita, but you know I don't like no police around me. Y'all can wait for them in here, but I don't want y'all calling them from my house. Then they'll be asking me all kinds of shit and I don't know nothing about nothing," said Reese with a frown on her face.

"I already called the police," said Jackie.

When Anita heard Jackie's voice a look of confusion flashed across her face because she thought Leon killed her years ago. But now wasn't the time to bring that up. "Give me a hug girl, I ain't even know that that was you," she said to her after they entered Reese's apartment. Jackie gave her a phony hug, but she didn't want to touch the woman because she didn't like anyone in Leon's family

Bertha tried calling Leon's cell phone several times while they waited on the police to come. Reese refused to let them call the police back from her house so Anita went home and tried calling them back a couple of times. Every time she called they told her that a unit would be there as soon as possible, so she went back to Reese's house to wait with Bertha.

They were sitting in Reese's living room when the news came on. The story about the man in the motel came back on and Bertha felt helpless so she looked in the phone book that was by the phone, and called the channel seven news station. "I had four sons, two of them were found dead last week and I just found another one in his apartment. All three of them were shot in their heads and all three of them had the same fingers missing from their hands. I have a strong feeling that the man who was found in that motel is my fourth son. Can y'all please try to help me because the police ain't? I found my son over two hours ago and the police still ain't got here. Thank you, he lives in Rockwell Gardens in building 2417 apartment 103, I'll be outside his door waiting on y'all," she said into the phone.

"Yeah you wait on them on the other side my door. I'm not trying to be mean Bertha, but you wrong for using my phone to call the news. I don't want nothing to do with that shit. If motherfuckers see you giving a fucking interview in my house then me and my kids lives could be in danger," Reese said angrily.

"Aw, bitch fuck you! You the nosiest bitch down here and you expect me to believe you didn't hear or see shit! My son lives right across the hall from you and you ain't hear no gunshots, no screaming, no arguing, or nothing? That's what I'm supposed to believe, right? You mean to tell me you didn't smell the scent that's been coming out of his door? What if it was one of yo sons laying in there with they heads blown off? How would you feel? You've known all of them their whole lives and you don't even want their killers caught," Bertha screamed.

"Oh, now that the shoe is on the other foot you want to act all righteous and shit! What about when yo sons was around here fucking up the neighborhood? You damn right I've known them all of their lives, and they terrorized the Westside for over twenty years. Them evil motherfuckers would kill a person for blinking at them, and when they did y'all made sure there wasn't no witnesses! Now you want me to risk my motherfucking life and the lives of my children because somebody got they asses back for doing Lord knows what to them! I said it before and I'm gon say it again, I ain't seen or heard shit! And don't send no motherfucking police or no damn reporters to my fucking door! Now all of y'all get the fuck out of my house," Reese yelled as she held the door open for them, and slammed it shut when they left.

Reese's baby sister used to hoe for Leon and he used to punish her in the cruelest ways. He kept what he called a bitch beater on him which was a device made out of seven wire hangers that he twisted together. He beat Reese's little sister with it whenever he felt like she needed to be disciplined. He also took a twelve gage bullet, emptied out the gun powder, filled it with salt and pepper, and shot her in her chest with it because she tried to run away from him. When she got released from the hospital, their eleven big, black, muscular uncles escorted her out of the hospital doors and took her back to Mississippi with them. Reese couldn't believe it when Bertha and Anita had the audacity to ask if they could wait for the police in her house, but she was cool with Anita so she allowed it. But she didn't feel sorry for Bertha or any of her sons. They had done so much shit to the poor, black people in the ghettoes of Chicago that Reese wasn't surprised when Bertha didn't remember what one of her sons had done to her sister. She couldn't have remembered or she wouldn't be acting like Reese owed her or her sons something. The fact that Bertha didn't remember Reese's baby sister pissed her off even more.

"Yo girl ain't shit Nita and you know it! How she gon put us out and talk about my boys like that? If the police wasn't on their way I would have kicked her ass in her apartment! I'm gon get her though! I might not do it today or tomorrow, but I'm gon get the bitch one of these days," Bertha said through her tears. She was very angry and overwhelmed with grief.

"Man Bertha, she ain't mean no harm. She just don't want the police asking her no questions. You know how it is down here, ain't nobody gon talk to the police and they damn sho ain't gon talk to no reporters. You act like you forgot where you at, ain't nobody trying to have no trouble knocking at their door," Anita replied.

Before Bertha could respond the reporters made it there, "We're looking for the woman who called about her sons being murdered," said the black female reporter, Brenda Walker, who was sent to broadcast the story.

"That would be me, my name is Bertha Thompson," Bertha said as she shook the woman's hand.

"Hi Bertha, I'm Brenda Walker and I'm going to be covering your story," said the reporter.

"Thank you, because I felt like no one cared before you came. I have the keys to his apartment if you want to show the world what they did to my boy."

"That won't be necessary Mrs. Thompson; we don't want to be responsible for contaminating the crime scene. I'll show his apartment door, but I'd like to do the actual interview outside. Teddy get a shot of us in front of the door and then tape us walking outside," Brenda said to her cameraman.

Before the interview could begin the police rode up and all of them except of one, walked past Bertha headed towards Kevin's apartment. "Bertha, I need to talk to you," said Chief Joseph Monroe, a fifty-five year old, red haired, white, heavy set policeman. He used to be on the Thompson's payroll until five years ago, when he was promoted from a narcotics detective to his current position. He worked for Bertha before he worked for her son's and had been a loyal employee of theirs for over twenty years.

"I'm gon give you that interview, but I need to talk to the police first. Finding the people responsible for the deaths of my sons is my first priority," Bertha said to Brenda Walker before she went to see what Chief Monroe wanted. Brenda and her cameraman followed the other police in the building to try to get the inside scoop on the murder before the media got barred from the crime scene or the other television stations made it there.

"What do you want Joe? We been too good to you for my son's deaths not to be investigated right. It took you motherfuckers over two hours to get here," said Bertha as she walked away from the building with the police chief and Jackie.

"You should have called me personally Bertha. I just found out yo boys were being executed. I'm sorry to tell you this, but the man who was found at the Palace motel was identified as Leon. His wallet was on him and the victim's fingerprints matched Leon's fingerprints. There was a witness who says he saw a nurse entering the motel with him, so we're following up on that lead. Now that I'm on the case we're going to do everything we can to find his and his brother's killers," said Joe as he hugged Bertha.

"No, no, no, no, no, not all of my babies! Joe the police know who's doing this, and it ain't no damn nurse! It's them motherfuckin' Black Souls! The fingers they leaving on my boy's hands forms they gang sign. Why y'all not getting them? Why? Noooooooooooooo," screamed Bertha as she pulled away from Joe, fell to the ground, and started banging her head on it.

Jackie and Joe pulled her up. "Bertha we've been putting a lot of heat on the Souls and so far, we haven't found any solid evidence against any of their gang members. You know I know everyone who has juice on the streets of Chicago, and that includes King Pee Wee. He said none of his soldiers are responsible for your son's murders and he doesn't usually deny the hits he puts out on people. Everyone knows their gang sign so anyone could have amputated your son's fingers to frame them. We want to get the right people, and we're going to get the right people," said the police chief.

Bertha punched Joe in the mouth as soon as the words crept out of it. "You working for them motherfuckers ain't you? Is that why you quit working for us, to work for our competition? You greedy, no good, son of a bitch! You probably helped them bitches kill my boys. Me and my boys helped feed yo ass before you called yo self breaking free and going straight. They could've turned yo crooked ass in or killed yo sorry ass, but instead they gave you yo life back by letting you walk away. The police didn't properly protect them, so the least y'all can do is find the monsters who killed them," she said as she continued to throw punches at Joe. He tried to stop her, but she was like a strong, angry, crazy pit bull in attack mode. She looked bad all of the time, but she looked plain old scary that day. She had blood all over her jogging suit from hugging Kevin's dead body, and there was blood trickling down her forehead from banging it on the ground. She was crying uncontrollably and her tears mixed with blood and snot. She was very angry, and when she got angry, her eyes bugged out, her nostrils flared, and her big, crusty, lips poked out.

The police turned Brenda Walker and her cameraman away as soon as they tried to enter Kevin's apartment. They left the building but not the scene. Brenda wanted that interview Bertha promised her and if she didn't give it to her, she knew that there was a possibility she could get one from one of the officers on the scene. Brenda Walker came there for a story and she didn't plan on leaving until she got one. She saw when Bertha started banging her head against the ground, but her cameraman didn't have his camera rolling. She made sure that he had it aimed and ready when she started beating up the chief of police. The camera didn't pick up what was being said, but the fight was interesting enough without words. Bertha got in a lot of good licks, but several police came to their chief's rescue when they heard the commotion. It took every last one of them to get her off of him and into a pair of handcuffs. Joe tried to tell them not to arrest her, but they didn't care what he said. She was a black woman, on television, beating up their white chief in front of several laughing witnesses. She was definitely taking a ride to the police station. The only reason they didn't beat her up was because they knew she had just lost all of her sons and the media was out there taping everything. Brenda Walker was so bold that she made it no secret that she was reporting live. When the police finally got Bertha pinned down and her hands behind her back, Brenda bent down and put one of her business cards in her right hand.

"Jackie pick my purse up off the ground, put this card in it, and follow the police car to the station so you can bail me out. Mrs. Walker I'll be in contact with you," Bertha said while lying on her stomach on the ground. Her head was turned sideways and she saw when the people from the morgue arrived. As one of the policemen put his knee in her back and the handcuffs on her wrists, she saw the wheels to the gurney that was about to take her son's body away roll past her.

"Damn, we should have stayed at home or over my mama's house! I can't believe we out here with this ignorant, ugly ass bitch! She making motherfuckers happy her sons dead! How you gon cuss people out for trying to help you? Ain't no telling how long it's gon take them to let her ugly ass out and I wanted to see my mama before we went back to Rantoul," Jackie said to Toni.

"Girl, it's a good thing we here because it sounds like the chief don't think the Souls killed Leon or his brothers. You heard what he said about the nurse, and I was sure no one was out there. We have to stay close to this bitch so we can know exactly what's going on. Even if they don't think we was involved in their murders, we don't want them to know your brothers were involved in them either. We doing the right thing by keeping our mouths shut and our ears open. When this shit is over with, we gon have plenty of time to see yo mama and whoever else we want to see. For now we need to stick around and see the progress of their cases," Toni replied as they got into the car, and followed the squad car that carried Bertha to the Harrison and Kedzie police station.

"Girl I know, it's just my pussy throbbing, I'm embarrassed to be seen with this bitch, and I just don't feel good. I'll be glad when this shit is over with because I'm kind of scared. I'm just ready to live the rest of my life without them people in it! Did you see Leon in the hallway with the rest of them people when we came back from calling the police? It didn't even look like his neck was cut or his head was cut off! He was staring at us with that same scared look he had in his eyes right before we cut his head off," said Jackie as they parked Bertha's car, got out of it, and walked inside the police station on Harrison and Kedzie.

"Girl do not go crazy on me! That motherfucker is laying up in the morgue headless and dickless," replied Toni as they waited on Bertha to be processed in.

A policewoman was in the middle of fingerprinting Bertha by the time Chief Joseph Monroe made it to the station. The policemen on the scene wouldn't allow him to leave Rockwell Gardens until the medical examiner who was there to check Kevin's time of death, examined him. "I want Bertha Thompson released this second! I'm the victim in the crime she committed, and I'm the chief of this precinct! That black woman just lost four of her sons to gang violence and a bunch of white police officers are going to be seen on the five o'clock news escorting her away in handcuffs! Imagine how we're going to be portrayed next year which also happens to be election year. There's going to be a lot of heat from above, on top of the heat we're already getting from the NAACP for all the black on black crime that's constantly being unsolved in the city of Chicago. It took us over two hours to make it to that crime scene, and we're fifteen minutes away! Now go get Ms. Thompson, drop all of those charges, apologize to her, and bring her to my office. And try not to screw that up," he yelled as he walked to the back of the police station where he knew most of the other police officers would be.

"The chief said to release Ms. Thompson immediately. Ms. Thompson we apologize for the way you've been treated by the officers in the twelfth precinct during this disturbing time in your life. We understand your grief but you can't use violence as a way to deal with it, especially towards an officer of the law. Chief Monroe would like to see you in his office," said the officer who was sent to retrieve Bertha. He handed her a roll of brown paper towels and a liquid that gets the ink used to fingerprint people off of their hands. Then he led her to the chief's office.

"I'm sorry Bertha, blah blah blah," was how Bertha interpreted Joseph Monroe's words. She had never been arrested before and she felt more degraded after being strip searched than she felt the first time she turned a trick. The officer made her take off all of her clothes, raise her breasts, lift up her feet one at time, pull apart her butt cheeks with her hands, and bend over. Then she made her stick her hands straight out, stand up with her legs spread apart, and cough while she squatted and came back up three times. After that; she made her take the shoestrings out of her shoes and the strings out of her jogging suit so she wouldn't kill herself, and allowed her to put her clothes back on. After putting her clothes back on she told her to bend over and run her fingers through her hair. When she finished, she had to go to a desk so the officer sitting there could get all of her personal information. She was supposed to go to a cell after she got fingerprinted. If she would have made it to the cell, she wouldn't have been able to get bonded out until her fingerprints were sent off and returned back with a status saying she didn't have any warrants. It was Saturday so her prints wouldn't have been sent off until that following Monday.

Bertha should have been grateful towards Joe for dropping the charges and stopping the process, but she wasn't. She was pissed off. The only reason she didn't show any anger was because she was afraid of getting rearrested and strip searched again. Joe thought everything was fine, but Bertha had been planning her revenge on him every since they put those handcuffs on her and she saw that gurney roll past. She knew she couldn't do anything while she was in the police station, so she decided to entertain Joe by answering his bullshit questions.

"Now Bertha, Leon lived with you, his wife, and his daughters, right?" was the first question Joe asked.

"Yes," Bertha answered trying to say as little as possible to Joe, her newest enemy.

"That's his wife out there in the lobby isn't it?" he asked. He recognized Jackie as Leon's wife because he was a guest at their wedding reception.

"Yes," she said.

"Leon Thompson, the victim from the motel's wife is out in the lobby waiting on the release of her mother-in-law. I need someone to escort her to my office. And for Christ sake, bring me a first aid kit and a clean, wet towel for poor Ms. Thompson," Joe said speaking into the walkie-talkie he took off his hip. "Does that bruise on your head hurt?" he asked Bertha.

"No," she lied. Her head was hurting just as bad as the rest of her body; but her pride hurt more than the pain she felt everywhere else.

"That's good; I guess it looks worse than it actually is. Here wipe your face off so you can tend to that cut. I sent for your daughter-in-law because this interview will be easier if I do it with both of you guys present since you both lived with the deceased," he said to Bertha as she wiped her face off with the face towel the officer bought her. Then he handed her a mirror that he kept in his desk drawer and the first aid kit so she could clean and dress her wound.

"Hi Mrs. Thompson my name is Chief Joseph Monroe. I'm going to be leading the investigations of the Thompson murders from now on. I have a few questions for you and Bertha concerning Leon's whereabouts on the night of his murder. It's standard procedure to question the victim's intermediate family because sometimes they can shed some light on the reason someone would want to cause harm to the victim. Neither one of you are suspects in his murder so both of you can stop this interview whenever you feel the need to. First of all, did either of you see what time Leon left the house?" he asked.

"No," Bertha replied with a blank look on her face. She stopped crying and the cut on her head stopped bleeding. Looking into Joe's face helped her decide how she was going to get revenge on him, and she felt stronger because of it. She felt like he wasn't trying to catch her son's murderers so she wasn't about to waste her breath with long drawn out answers. She refused to show him anymore weakness. She used every ounce of pain she was feeling from the loss of her sons and turned it into anger and hatred for him

"I didn't see him leave either. I think he waited until we both went to sleep before he left. I'm sorry this is just so overwhelming, I can't believe he's really gone," said Jackie as big crocodile tears fell from her eyes. She wasn't crying because Leon was dead, she was crying because she was scared of getting caught. She knew she had to play the grieving widow's role right, or she could become a suspect. She felt terrified and uncomfortable in the chief of police's office answering questions about Leon's death; but she didn't show it.

The average person wouldn't think Jackie was nervous, they would think she was a very beautiful, distraught woman who had just lost her husband. But Joe had been a cop for a long time and his instincts told him that she could've been involved. "A witness at the scene of the crime told the detectives that there was a light skinned, nurse with long red hair with Leon when he entered the motel. The witness also said she was about your height and build Mrs. Thompson," Joe said as he squinted and looked Jackie from head to toe several times.

"First of all, I know Jackie ain't no damn nurse. Second of all, I saw her in her bed sleep before I went to sleep, and third of all, I woke her up looking for Leon. Unless she can be in two places at one time, she ain't yo nurse," said Bertha using air quotations when she said the word nurse. "And if her body fits the nurse's description, mine definitely don't. We're leaving now! If you got any more questions for either one of us you can contact my lawyer," she said using air quotations around the words questions and lawyer.

(13)

Them Yo Kids!

They went home after picking up the girls and didn't make it in the house until three o'clock the next morning. Bertha was so angry at the police for arresting her and for the way they were handling her son's murder investigations; that she called the number Brenda Walker had listed as her cellphone number as soon as she walked through the door. Brenda Walker woke up out her sleep and got up out her of bed to meet Bertha at her house in Rantoul after their telephone conversation. She lived three hours away from Chicago in the opposite direction of Rantoul so it was going to take her over five hours to get there, but the drive would be worth it if Bertha had the evidence against the Chicago Police Department that she said she had in her house. She got there nine o'clock Sunday morning and got her first career promoting interview.

Bertha started off by telling her about the lives that her son's lived and how she knew they weren't angels, they were survivors. She said a life of crime was the only life they knew growing up black, poor, and in the ghetto. Then she talked about their murders and how she felt they were executed by the Black Souls because the fingers that were missing formed their gang sign, a fact that the police were ignoring. She also told Mrs. Walker about the meeting Leon was supposed to have had with King Pee Wee Tuesday.

After talking about the way her son's were murdered and who she felt murdered them, she asked the community for their help in solving their murders. She told the community that they were the only hope she had left because all of the Chicago Police Departments were corrupt and they didn't care about black on black crime. She said that the hood had to stop honoring its code of silence or the murders that occurred in the hood would continue to go unsolved. She gave the reporter the names of the policemen who used to work for her and her sons, and the things they did for them without incriminating herself. She said Chief Joseph Monroe was handling her sons' murder investigations the way he handled the murders he let her son's get away with, and that she believed he worked for the Black Souls now. She gave her three boxes full of ledgers filed in chronological order with the policemen names, what crimes they were paid for covering up, and how much they were paid. She even had the receipts from the money her son's deposited in their bank accounts. She claimed she found the items after going through Leon's things, but that was a lie. She started making ledgers when the police started working for her. She taught her son's how to keep records and how to deposit money into the policemen's bank accounts, so they could get receipts in case they ever needed them. Whenever they filled a box, she put them up. She had dirt on judges, prosecutors, and a few politicians too but she wasn't in war with them so she didn't mention them to the reporter. Bertha knew what she was doing was dangerous, but she felt like she had nothing to lose because all of her sons were dead. If she had to join them to bring their murderer's to justice, then so be it.

Bertha was so engrossed in giving interviews and the murder investigations that Jackie took over the task of planning the double funeral. The only requests she had for Jackie was to have the media there and to have their caskets opened. She wanted to show the world what was done to her sons the same way Emit Till's mother had done. Jackie happily agreed to honor Bertha's request. Bertha kept accusing the Black Souls of murdering her sons, so Jackie wasn't afraid of getting caught anymore. Planning the funeral became a fun game to her. She loved seeing Bertha feel the pain she was feeling, but she stayed consoling her and acting like she was just as hurt. Every time she hugged her she was smiling and making fun of her with Toni. Bertha thought they were bonding and getting closer during the process of planning the funeral, but Jackie was using the opportunity to plan her escape.

Jackie had to go to Chicago every weekday in the week before the funeral to handle everything. The Tuesday after the murder, she went over Anita's apartment to help her write the obituaries. While she was there, she heard Leon's cousins planning a business meeting. The only solid details she heard were that Bertha didn't know anything about it, and it was supposed to take place nine o'clock on the night of the funeral. She knew that she needed to be there so she told Bertha about it when she got home and Bertha called her nephew Fred. Jackie tricked her into telling her everything about the meeting as soon as she got off the phone with him. Bertha was mad when Jackie told her about the meeting her nephews were planning for the night she was burying her sons. She was pissed when she called them and they told her that the meeting was being held to see who was going to take control over the whorehouses and dope spots her sons left. She felt disrespected and discombobulated and the only person she had to vent to was Jackie. The news knocked her completely off her square so she didn't realize that Jackie was fishing for details about the meeting that should have been irrelevant to her. Bertha told her everything from how weak and vulnerable her sons' crew was without them to the address the meeting was going to take place at. It was going to be held at one of Leon's old whorehouses on the North Side of Chicago. Jackie still had all of the house keys she took on the night she killed Leon so she decided to see if any of them went to the whorehouse the meeting was going to be in. She went at four o'clock the next morning and was pleasantly surprised when the third one she tried opened the door. She told her brothers about the meeting and the key, and they all agreed that the meeting would be the perfect time for her to take everything Leon left.

Jackie enjoyed watching Bertha mess up her son's murder investigations with the interviews she gave to Brenda Walker. She found it funny when they started making everyone angry. They pissed off the people in the streets because she was breaking the code of silence. They angered the people in the community because they reminded them of the havoc the Thompson's wrecked in their neighborhoods. And they angered the police because every officer she named in her interviews was being investigated by Internal Affairs on paid leave. The interviews also scared any potential witnesses from coming forward because the cases were so public that they knew their identities wouldn't stay secret and they didn't want to get killed because of their input. The police stopped following the nurse lead after Bertha told on their fellow officers. After those interviews the police worked on the Thompson's cases, but not properly.

Jackie knew the coast was clear when the police stopped coming to their house asking questions. She was so happy when the day of the funeral came that she stayed up all night. She waited until Bertha fell asleep and took everything out of Leon's two safes and put the contents from out of them into one of his Luis Vuitton suitcases. One of the safes had his money and his current ledger in it, the other one had his jewelry and his drugs in it. She used the rest of his luggage to pack up everything she owned accept of the things she planned on wearing to the funeral. Then she put everything in the 1983 Cadillac he bought right before he got killed. The funeral was going to be at ten in the morning, Jackie was ready by four. When the limousine arrived she insisted on driving the Cadillac saying that she felt closer to Leon in it.

The funeral was packed, but the only person who seemed genuinely sad was Bertha. Jackie sat on the front pew on one side of her and her sister Anita sat on the other. She tried to put her head on Jackie's shoulder so she could console her, but Jackie pushed it off as hard as she could. Bertha gave her a strange look, moved closer to Anita and cried on her sister's shoulder. She tried to ignore the fact that her sons' funeral was like a circus with all the media and street characters in attendance. Everyone appeared to be performing for the cameras trying to get their five minutes of fame. She really regretted having the media there because some of the people who came gave interviews outside of the church before the funeral was over or her sons were buried. They didn't even stop when the pallbearers carried the caskets out and led the congregation out for the burial. Jackie didn't know what she enjoyed more, the media making a mockery of Leon and Kevin's funeral or seeing Bertha' s overwhelming amount of grief flowing out. The whole event was hilarious to her and Bertha heard a giggle escape but said nothing about it. Jackie wouldn't have cared if she did because she was no longer afraid of her.

The re-pass was held at Bertha's mother's house and as soon as it was over, Jackie walked up to Bertha holding her kids' hands. "I'm going to live with my mother and I don't want to raise y'all's kids." One day Jackie was in Chicago making the arrangements for Leon and Kevin's funeral and while she was there, she visited her mother and asked her if she could move back home. Janice was more than happy to say yes.

"What the fuck you mean you don't want to raise our kids? Them yo kids! They came out of you! You the one who had them," Bertha said as looks of confusion and anger crossed her face.

"I'm not about to waste the rest of my life raising these ugly ass kids y'all made me have. Bitch having them was yo idea, so you gon deal with them! You should be happy because they can remind you of yo ugly ass son, lookin' like him and shit! You know what? If you don't want them, you don't have to get them. I'll just take them to the foster home in the morning. That's why I had the funeral on a Tuesday, so if you didn't get these heffas I knew I could get rid of they asses the next day. But I'm not wasting another day being in the presence of any of you motherfucking Thompson's," Jackie replied as her gray eyes filled up with hate and turned green. Toni tried to pop in but Jackie didn't let her. Leon had controlled her life for over ten years and she wanted complete control now that he was buried.

"I bet you was that nurse they saw with Leon the night he got killed. I knew you was acting when you was walking around there pretending like you loved all of us so much! You hated Leon, me, and yo own damn kids! Now that I think about it, I'm sure you had something to do with his murder! I can feel it in my gut," Bertha yelled.

"First you was sure it was the Souls who killed Leon, now you blaming me! At first you said there wasn't a nurse now, you saying she was me! You told the police that I was at home all night with you, now you saying I was with Leon! Which is it Bertha? You can't have it both ways! Like you said, I couldn't be in two places at one time! You don't know what the fuck happened to yo damn sons, but you do know what's gon happen to these ugly ass granddaughters of yours if you don't get them," said Jackie as a giggle escaped. She found the situation very funny all of a sudden so she started laughing hysterically in Bertha's face. She was laughing so hard that she had to let go of her daughter's hands to hold her stomach while she laughed.

"It'll be my pleasure to raise my grandbabies and I'm gon do it better than yo trifling ass ever could. But know this, I know you had something to do with my son's murder and if I ever get any evidence, you going down," Bertha replied as Jackie stopped laughing and stood up. She raised her hand to hit Jackie, but Jackie grabbed her hand before the blow landed with her left hand and slapped her as hard as she could with her right one.

"It ain't what you know, it's what you can prove bitch! If you ever raise your hand to hit me again you'll be joining your sons in hell," she said before she turned around and walked out of the house without saying goodbye to her kids.

Jackie's family came to the double funeral and the re-pass, and her brothers were outside waiting on her while she gave her kids to Bertha. "I want to go to Mama's house to change out of this dress before we go

143

handle that business. Y'all changing or keeping on them suits?" she asked. Leon's grandmother's house was located right down the street from Jackie's mother's house on Jackson and California, and her brothers didn't live that far away either.

"We'll go with you to change, but we gon keep on our suits," said Jack Jr., looking and sounding like Jack Sr. All four of her brothers were dressed in black from head toe in their Armani suits and hats

"Y'all should keep them on because y'all look like some gangsters in that shit. Jack and Phillip ride to the house with me since all of y'all rode with Dwayne," said Jackie with a genuine smile on her face. She was happier than she had been in years. Leon was buried, the investigation was over, and Bertha knew she had something to do with his death. To put the icing on the cake, she was free from Bertha and the kids they made her have.

"Damn it ain't that much room in this motherfucker, I guess I'll sit back here with all of yo fly ass luggage," said Phillip as he climbed in the back seat. Jackie had an enormous wardrobe so she needed every piece of Leon's seven piece luggage to pack it all. She never went anywhere, so she didn't realize how many beautiful clothes Leon had bought her over the years until she packed them up. Some of them were designed for her and the rest of them were made by popular, expensive designers. She had several mink, fur, and leather coats with the hats that matched them, and she had hats that matched several of her outfits. She also owned an astronomical amount of expensive shoes and boots in a variety of fabrics, lengths, styles, and colors. She had lots of designer purses and sunglasses that matched her outfits and shoes as well. All of her wigs were custom made and every piece of jewelry she owned was made with expensive and exquisite diamonds. She was even amazed by all of the expensive makeup and perfume she owned.

"Nigga yo bony ass can fit," said Jackie with a laugh. It was the first real laugh she had enjoyed in years and she felt happiness through her whole body, heart, and soul.

"Where my grandbabies at?" Janice asked Jackie as she walked through the door with her brothers following close behind her with her luggage in their hands.

"Bertha asked me if she could have custody of them, and I told her yes," Jackie lied.

"Jackie that poor woman has been through enough. She ain't gon have the energy to raise yo babies. You shouldn't have agreed to that. And besides, I was looking forward to them living with us. I barely got a chance to see them when Leon was alive," Janice said as she scratched herself and went in and out of heroin induced nods.

"Mama that lady was in tears when I tried to take her grandkids out of that house. She said they was the only piece of her son she had left. Don't worry, you gon get to see them all the time. Angel which room is mine?" Jackie asked after lying to her mother, she had no intentions of ever seeing her kids again.

"We fixed up the room you used to share with the twins for you. Jackie I'm so happy you home! When you first left I used to dream about this day, but after so many years I never thought it would happen," Angel replied with tears in her eyes.

"Well it did and I'm happy too," said Jackie as she walked up the stairs headed for her old room. Their house looked exactly like it did back in 1973 when Jackie first left, and it was ten years later. The living room still had the same brown, orange, and green checkered, worn out, sofa, loveseat, and chair that was there when she left. The dining room was connected to the living room, and it still had the same scuffed up dark brown, oak wood table and chairs set that Janice bought from the thrift store when they first moved in. The walls in both rooms still had the wooden paneling and the wooden floors Jack had professionally installed when he purchased the house. The room Jackie shared with the twins was still painted robin egg blue and all of her Jackson Five posters were still hanging on the walls. The furniture still consisted of a wooden bunk bed, a twin sized bed, and a ratty, old dresser with a big square mirror on it. The floor had the same thread bare throw rug on it that was there when she was an occupant of the room.

Jackie's emotions hit her like a ton of bricks when she walked into her room and for a split second she felt like the last ten years of her life had never happened. "Just sit my bags down anywhere, I'm bout to change. I'll meet y'all downstairs in a minute. Oh, I almost forgot to ask if one of y'all got a throw away gun and a silencer I can use until I buy me one tomorrow," Jackie said to her brothers as they sat her luggage down in her room. She had unknowingly picked up some of Leon's slang along the way.

"Yeah I got a little twenty-two you can get rid of, but I ain't got no silencer," said Jack Jr.

"Are you sure you want to takeover Leon's dope spots Jackie? Ronald Reagan got this fake ass war on drugs going on and the only casualties in it are poor black people. I know you heard Leon complaining during election years because the police get real hot around that time. They have quotas they have to meet so the statistics look like the crime rate is going down to get voters to vote for the most popular candidate. Well, imagine it being election year everyday and the only people being targeted and arrested by the police are poor black people. Some are innocent, but most are guilty because they don't have a choice but to sell drugs. Reagan passed laws that prosecute people harshly if they get caught with the smallest amount of drugs. I know a nigga who just did a year because he got caught with a baggie with drug residue in it. And you know white people do just as many drugs as black people do if not more, but the police only looking in the ghettoes for the drugs. They ain't doing they drug raids and drug sweeps in the suburbs. It makes me wonder if they convicting the people who got the large quantities because the streets of Chicago stay flooded with drugs. I think Reagan be letting motherfuckers bring that shit in America. Niggas ain't got no airplanes to fly that shit in, but we the ones who getting punished the hardest. Every time I see his ugly ass wife on TV saying "just say no" I think of how hypocritical they are," said Timothy. He wanted Jackie to know what was going on before she decided to get in the drug game. He kept his brothers up on the new laws rather they wanted to hear about them or not because he didn't want them out in the streets stupid. If Jackie was going to be out there he was going to school her too.

"That nigga always be talking about conspiracy theories in the government and shit. Look Jackie, them motherfuckers is strokin' niggas with long ass prison sentences, but you'll be alright if you let the workers I'm gon give you work yo corners and bag yo drugs up. I look at the situation like this; they the cops and we the robbers! They got to do they job just like we got to do ours," said Dwayne. He wanted Jackie to takeover because he had been bragging about her and he felt she could do it with his help.

"Yeah, I still want to takeover. I put up with that nigga for ten years and I want everything he left out here because I deserve it. I ain't got no education because of him, so I can't get no decent job. I didn't get to see high school, but I did get schooled on how to sell drugs and pimp so that's what I'm gon do. I ain't go through all of that bullshit to end up broke with a drug habit. I want that nigga's money and his power and I'm willing to take it if I got to. That twenty-two will be perfect. Fuck the silencer if you ain't got one because I can use a potato," said Jackie. Leon used to take her target practicing when he had her and Beauty working for him, and he always made her practice with a twenty-two.

Jackie put on an all black Gucci satin, halter topped, bell bottomed jumpsuit and some low heeled black Gucci sandals. She chose the jumpsuit because it had deep pockets and the twenty-two could fit in them easily. She kept on the long black straight haired wig that she wore to the funeral and retouched her makeup. She grabbed a pair of black leather gloves and her purse, and walked down the stairs. When she made it down she took a potato out of the refrigerator, got a paring knife out the kitchen drawer, and carved some of the inside of it out. Then she rinsed her hands, dried them with a paper towel, slipped on her leather gloves, and walked out the door. "We might as well ride in the same car. We can take Leon's car since we going to talk to his people," said Jackie as she checked to make sure that the twenty-two her brother handed her was loaded. She forced the potato on the tip of it and slipped it into her pants pocket, and got into the car with her brothers behind her.

When Jackie and her brothers made it to the meeting it was after ten o'clock, and they heard people yelling before they made it to the porch. Jackie used the house key to let them in, and everyone was shocked into silence when they saw her and her brothers walk into the room. Her brothers had their guns drawn and aimed at the nine men and one woman who were sitting down at the long table. One of the rules of the meeting was for everyone to leave their guns out in their cars so no one would be tempted to use one if an argument got too heated. Dwayne and Phillip had machine guns and Timothy and Jack Jr. had nine millimeters, so they had a huge advantage over the other people in the room.

"Sorry I'm late. For those of you who don't know me, let me introduce myself. My name is Mrs. Leon Thompson. The men behind me are of no concern to you; they aren't here to hurt you. They're here to protect me and to make sure I receive what's rightfully mine. My husband might have been buried today, but I wasn't. He told me that he wanted me to take his place if anything ever happened to him, and I intend to do just that. I'm not here to decide what happens to what the rest of the Thompson's left out here; I'm only here regarding Leon's shit. I have his ledger so I know those of you who owe him money and how much he had on the streets and I want it all. I don't want any of his dope spots or hoe strolls that are located in K-town and I suggest y'all leave them alone too, because the BGD's ain't playing over their territory. Does anyone have any questions, concerns, complaints, or objections to the things that I've said?" asked Jackie as she took turns looking the people at the table in their eyes.

China looked at the men on both sides of her and was instantly disgusted at the fear she saw when she looked into their eyes. She wasn't scared of Leon's wife and she wasn't about to give up the power Leon gave her six years ago, when his girlfriend and Beauty betrayed him. She refused to go back to whoring and if the woman claiming to be Leon's widow wasn't willing to promote her or let her keep her current position, there was going to be a problem. "Me have lot a questions. Me been loyal employee of Mr. Leon for many years and he give me lot a promotions that me demand to keep," she said proudly with her heavy Chinese accent. She was the only female besides Jackie in the room, and she was the only one who had the balls to stand up to her. She felt like Leon and his word was dead if it didn't benefit her.

"Ain't yo name China? You started out working for Leon in one of his whorehouses didn't you? You were very loyal to him, weren't you? I remember he told me how you saved him a lot of money by telling on this soldier who used to shop with you. Do you remember that?" asked Jackie as she walked towards China, and China nodded yes to the questions.

"Yes, me remember it very well. The guy had been shopping with me for weeks and he tried to get me to sell heroin that he stole from the Thompson's. Your husband and him brothers beat the shit out of him," said China getting animated as she told the story.

"Me never liked that weird—," was all that China could get out before Jackie took the twenty-two out of her pocket and emptied the clip into her head. Leon's cousin, Tommy was sitting next to her and pieces of her brain, scull, and potato pieces, mixed with blood splattered on the right side of his face. Jackie wanted to kill China every since she read about her in Jack's diary. She couldn't believe her eyes when she saw her sitting in the meeting, and she couldn't believe her luck when China said that she was indeed the infamous one who told on her father. Her brothers told her that she needed to kill someone at the meeting to show them she meant business, and China was the perfect target.

"Any motherfucker that moves out of their chair is going to get exactly what that oriental bitch just got! Listen up and listen good cause I'm only gon say this shit one time! From this point on Mrs. Thompson is the new owner of the dope spots and hoe houses Leon left out here! She'll decide who she's going to keep on her payroll, and who's going to be relieved of their duties! She plugged with the Black Gangster Disciples and we nation wide! We on these streets, we in them police stations, we in the D.A.'s office, and the list goes on and on. If any one of y'all think about breaking the code of silence, you'll be dead before that thought makes it to court. We got her covered on that gangster shit too! If anybody goes to war with her, they going to war with us! Am I making myself clear or do we need to make another example out of one of you motherfuckers?" Dwayne asked the group of scared men. He got a huge adrenaline rush as all of the men nodded their heads with no hesitation. They were all in there late thirties to early fifties and had all done a lot of dirt in their day, but the new breed of criminals had them scared. They would kill a person for stepping on their gym shoes.

"Which car was China driving?" asked Jackie after she went through her purse and found a set of car keys.

"She was in that cherry red Mercedes Benz that's parked out front," Leon's cousin, Fred, said in a shaky voice. He hoped and prayed that Jackie and her brothers didn't recognize him because he recognized them. He was with Leon and his brothers the night they invaded their home and he knew it was a mistake to let them live. Now he was scared for his life. He didn't know how they pulled the hits off, but he was positive they were the ones who killed his cousins.

"Y'all get up and move this table up off of this rug. Now two of y'all roll that bitch up in it and follow Mrs. Thompson outside. She gon open up China's trunk so y'all can put her in it. Mrs. Thompson give me your car keys, I'm gon drive your car and I want you to follow us in China's. Roll her body up tighter than that Fred and Tommy! You motherfuckers know how to do this shit, so don't fucking play with me. Every last one of y'all know how this shit is done, so don't play me for no fool or we'll be rolling one of y'all asses up next," Timothy said angrily.

Dwayne paid some young BGD's to get rid of China's car and body around three o'clock the next morning. The rest of the Thompson's crew fell off real bad after the meeting. Jackie's brothers saw how weak they were and decided to take everything they had. Jackie kept her word and only took Leon's things. She let his mother keep the house out in Rantoul, but that was all she gave her.

That meeting was the beginning of Jackie's criminal career and she enjoyed every minute of the good times while they lasted. Leon and Beauty taught her the dope game and the pimp game very good, and she got paid well throughout the eighties. She didn't have to kill anyone else because the streets knew she killed Leon and China, and they invented and speculated her doing other hits including the other Thompsons. She was a smart, pretty, cold blooded, cold hearted hustler who was well respected and highly feared on the streets of Chicago.

Every man wanted her to be the Bonnie to their Clyde, but Jackie didn't have the desire to be in any type of relationship with any man. She went celibate after killing Leon and directed the men who threw themselves on her towards her sisters and the beautiful whores who worked for her. Leon stole the joy of sex from her when he took her virginity, and then he took it again when he killed Juan while his penis was still inside of her. She used her beauty and her brains to turn the most powerful gang leaders, dope dealers, and hustlers on the streets of Chicago into business associates, customers, and connects. She loved the attention and respect she got from the men, but the only men she trusted, befriended, or let get close to her were her brothers and the workers they provided her with. She had all of her sisters working for her and they were the only women besides her mother and her whores that she dealt with.

Jackie was feeling herself for a long time and she thought that nothing or no one could bring her down. It seemed that way until her brother Timothy gave her some crack to try on her cocaine customers in 1985. The new drug felt like a blessing at first because she made a lot of money from selling it. She made so much that it compensated for the lost she took when all of her whores quit working for her and started working for it. Crack changed the entire pimp game, because the urge for it was so strong that the whores no longer wanted to give the money they worked so hard for to their pimps. They wanted to use all of it to buy crack, so crack became their pimps. Crack made the loyalist whores run off with their daily profits, and they were willing to take any ass whipping their former pimps could dish out for it. Their high came quick and left quick, so every penny they made left as soon as it got into their hands. It was harder trying to keep and control her whores, so Jackie did the next best thing and supplied them with the drug that had replaced her. She was still getting their money, and she was getting it without the headache so everyone was happy.

Jackie was the most successful female hustler on the streets of Chicago during her reign. She was respected more than any of the other female hustlers because she wasn't having sex with any men. She wasn't gay, so she wasn't having sex with any women either. She was scared to have sex because HIV and AIDS had hit the scene, and she wasn't trying to catch anything that didn't have a cure. She also quit shooting drugs up her veins and went back to snorting powder versions of her drugs of choice because of the deadly disease.

Being celibate had her very focused on her business, but she had fun too. She missed out on all of her teenage years when Leon took her, so she made up for lost time. She went out partying every night with all of her brothers and any of her sisters who weren't pregnant. They went anywhere that was jumping. They didn't care if the party was thrown in a nice exclusive club, in one of the projects located out south on the low end, or at a picnic that was thrown outside by the BGD's, they were there. When they weren't at somebody else's party, they were throwing one of their own and their parties were legendary. They threw their parties at the house on Warren and they didn't charge their guests to get in like some people did. They had an open bar that stayed stocked with top shelf liquor and the platters of food, weed, heroin, and cocaine stayed in circulation all night long. They kept rap music, house music, pop music and R&B music blaring throughout the house at all times. All of their guests were so happy to be invited that there was never any violence which was very rare for a house party thrown in their neighborhood.

Jackie was having a ball until she started doing crack. When she started doing it, she understood the urge her former prostitutes had for it because it got her too. Timothy told her not to use crack and she didn't until July 21, 1988, the day her brothers killed each other. She started back doing cocaine the night she killed China and since she had a dealer's habit for it; she didn't think it could provide her with the escape from reality she felt she needed on that dreadful night. She didn't want to start back doing heroin so she opted for crack since its main ingredient was cocaine, her drug of choice. The crack was stronger than any other drug she had ever done and its evil claws grasped her as soon as she took that first hit. She spent the next three years of her life and every dime she had trying to feel the feeling that she felt the first time the potent drug entered her system.

She had so much money coming in that she didn't realize how much was going out. She stayed at her mother's house so she didn't pay rent, but she paid the taxes on it. She also had it renovated when she first moved back home and professionally decorated every year that she lived there and was able to. She was a shopaholic with a big heart, and when she went on shopping sprees she treated her mother and her three baby sisters too. She pushed Leon's 1983 Cadillac until December of 83 when she traded it in for a 1984 Lexus. She got a new Lexus every year after that. She went to one of the most exclusive beauty shops in Chicago and she still had Stevie as her stylist until she couldn't afford those luxuries any more.

(14)

It All Falls Down

The BGD's split up into two separate gangs, Black Gangster Disciples and Gangster Disciples and Timothy was responsible for the split. Dwayne was so proud of his family that he bragged to King David about the way they took over the Thompson's empires; and the roles they each played in the hits. King David was always on the lookout for strong soldiers who weren't afraid to kill, so he told him to invite Jackie and Timothy to join the gang. Jackie wasn't into gang banging so she declined King David's offer but Timothy accepted. He told Jackie that the only reason he joined was to take as many of King David's soldiers as he could and start a gang of his own.

He thought he could earn their little brothers respect if he succeeded. He hated that they looked up to another man more than they looked up to him, but the only person he would admit that to was Jackie. They had always been real close and their bond grew stronger during the years they were apart. They both felt like outsiders when they came back into the lives of their younger siblings; so they tried to help each other through the awkward transition. Before Jackie was snatched out of their home, she helped raised her little brothers and sisters. When she left Timothy looked out for them until he was forced out. It was hard for them to come back and see their little brothers and sisters traveling down a path to self destruction; and not be able to do anything about it. Their little brothers were all over eighteen so they were grown. Their little sisters were all sexually active by the time they made it home, so they were grown as far as the streets were concerned. They accepted some of the advice Timothy tried to give them, but they did whatever they wanted to do most of the time. Jackie didn't try to advise them because she had none to give. She hated to see her little sisters having children at such young ages, but she had two before she made eighteen so she felt like she couldn't tell them not to. Seeing the power King David had over her little brothers broke her heart, but there was nothing she could do about it. She was happy for the powerful street connection it provided her with because she felt like she deserved it. She sacrificed her entire life for her family so she was ready to start living for herself. She sympathized with Timothy and listened to his plans, but she didn't let the distance she felt around her siblings affect her happiness.

Jackie watched Timothy's plan from start to finish and she was amazed when he started executing it a month after joining the BGD's. She used to jokingly call him Nostradamus because everything he planned happened exactly like he said it would. He found out his old college buddy, Miguel, was Pablo Escobar's nephew while they attended the University of Chicago together. He didn't turn him in, nor did he tell anyone besides Jackie who he was. He never asked him for any money and he saw him make lots of it selling drugs to all of the white college students. Miguel started to get too much clientele so he propositioned Timothy with a business deal after he joined the street gang. Timothy was the only friend he had in America and he trusted him more than he trusted anyone there. When Timothy told him about his plans to start his own gang, he told him how they did it in Colombia.

Timothy bought two kilos from Miguel and he gave him two. The two he gave him was a great gift, but he also taught him how to make crack which turned out to be an even better one. Miguel never tried to sell crack in America because he was sent there to get a master's degree in criminal justice and selling crack would have interfered with him reaching that goal. He knew how it made the people who got addicted to it behave and no amount of money was worth the heat he would generate if he introduced it to the college kids. Timothy let King David try some out on his customers and he became his supplier when the gang leader saw the effect it had on them. They were the only ones in the city of Chicago who sold crack so they made a ton of money. Crack was a lot cheaper than cocaine but the urge was a lot stronger so the money came quicker and the clientele became larger. King David was so busy enjoying the good life that he didn't realize what Timothy had done until it was too late.

King David tried to make Timothy a governor but Timothy declined and asked if he could start another branch of the gang instead. King David gave him his blessing and Timothy named his gang Gangster Disciples, or GD for short. The majority of the BGD's followed Timothy because he fronted them crack and made them entrepreneurs. When they were BGD's they worked for King David and most of the profits went to him, so Timothy's offer was hard to refuse. He had an endless supply of crack and word spread about the new drug and the new gang quickly. Thousands of people tried to join the GD's and Timothy welcomed them all regardless of age, race, or gender. They set up shop all over Chicago which caused a lot of gang wars. He was stepping on a lot of toes and he didn't care because all he wanted was power. He made killers out of the members of his gang and he was constantly recruiting them. They even forced some people into joining by intimidation. Timothy got his strength in numbers and he was obsessed with keeping it going so he told his female members to raise their kids to be GD's. He had his youngest members selling drugs and killing people because they wouldn't be prosecuted as bad as the adult members would be. There was so much blood shed when Timothy started the GD's and brought crack to the streets of Chicago that the police were afraid of patrolling them. Crack heads were a new breed of drug addicts and GD's were a new breed of criminals and no one knew how to control either one of them. The streets had gotten very dangerous and it was like a war zone with soldiers as young as eight years old protecting, patrolling, and selling drugs on them.

Jackie was scared that someone was going to murder Timothy but she never thought it would be one of her other brothers. Her little brother Jack Jr. was the only one who joined the GD's which frustrated Timothy. He had thousands of members and couldn't get his own brothers to join. Jackie tried to make him look on the bright side of things so she constantly reminded him of his success. He helped make all of them a lot of money and she thought he should be proud of that instead of being worried about the way Dwayne and Phillip felt about him. If they wanted to follow King David for the rest of their lives that was on them as far as Jackie was concerned. She was making major money off the super drug and the only way she was going to continue getting paid was if she kept Timothy on his square. At times he acted like he was superman and could conquer the world, and there were times that he was very unsure about his self. Jackie even tried to get her brothers to join Timothy's gang but they just didn't want to. After she tried to get them to join and they refused, Timothy cut them off and moved on. He refused to give them anymore crack so they had to start back working for King David. They stopped talking to him after that which made Jackie happy because she didn't have to listen to him complain about them anymore.

Three years passed and Jackie got used to her two younger brothers not talking to her two older brothers. She felt uneasy when she called Timothy and he said he was on his way over Dwayne and Phillip's apartment to talk to them. She told him to be careful, but he wasn't worried at all. He was happy because he thought they were finally about to join the GD's. The GD's had more people, more money, and more power on the streets than the BGD's so he thought his little brothers had finally come to their senses. She calmed down when he told her that Jack Jr. was going with him. She forgot all about the meeting until she turned on their street and saw their apartment building surrounded by police. There were four apartments in their building but something told her that the trouble was going on in her brother's apartment. She parked her car, jumped out and ran to the building.

When she made it to the building her brothers neighbor Karen walked up to her and said, "Jackie I heard a lot of gunshots go off in yo brother's apartment, and I don't think nobody was in there but them. The police been trying to talk whoever's in there out for over an hour."

"You sure girl?" Jackie asked with a look of anguish on her face.

"Yeah, I'm sure. Go talk to the police and see if they'll tell you what's going on," Karen replied.

"I'm sorry ma'am but you can't cross this line," said the police officer who was blocking the entrance.

"I have to get in there to check on my brothers, they live in apartment 2a on the second floor," Jackie said hysterically.

"The sister of the suspect has arrived, do you want me to send her through?" the policeman blocking her path asked an unknown voice through his walkie-talkie.

"Yeah, we need her," replied the voice.

The policeman who was at the yellow tape escorted Jackie to the negotiator. "I'm sorry to tell you this, but it looks like one of your brothers has killed your other three brothers and he's threatening to kill himself. We need you to try to convince him to surrender peacefully. If he doesn't give his self up we're going to have to go in eventually. He's been answering the telephone, but we haven't been successful in talking him out of the apartment," said the negotiator as he dialed their home phone number on his cell phone and handed it to Jackie.

That phone call was the beginning to Jackie's road down self destruction. She begged Jack Jr. not to kill his self and talked him into turning his self in. She promised to bond him out of jail and to get him the best lawyer money could buy. She followed the squad car that carried him to the police station on Harrison and Kedzie, but they told her that she wouldn't be able to bond him out that night because he was a violent criminal who was a danger to his self and others. She didn't know how she was going to tell her mother and her sisters that her brothers had killed each other and Jack Jr. was being charged with all of their murders at the present time. She had a large quantity of crack in her trunk and she was tempted to smoke some before going home, but decided against it.

"Mama, Timothy, Dwayne and Phillip are all dead," she said to her mother as soon as she entered their house.

Jackie was crying hysterically and Janice was sitting on the couch in a heroin induced nod, so she thought she hadn't heard Jackie correctly. "What you say about my boys?" she slurred.

"Mama they dead, and they killed each other," Jackie screamed through her tears.

"They can't be dead because I just saw Timothy and Jr.," Janice said as she started to shake and tears started to fall from her eyes.

"Jr. ain't dead but he's in jail for their murders. I had to talk him out of killing his self! When I talked to him he said that Timothy killed Dwayne so Phillip killed Timothy. He said he had to kill Phillip because Phillip was trying to kill him. I'm sorry Mama but it's true, I saw the coroner come and I followed the police to the station when they arrested Jr.," said Jackie through her tears.

"This shit is yo fault Jackie! My boys loved each other before yo evil ass came back! Now I know how Bertha feels! First you got rid of Leon and his brothers, and now you've gotten rid of my boys! Why did you come back here? Everything was fine before you came back into our lives trying to make us feel guilty for your life! I hate you," Janice yelled. She knew that Jackie didn't have anything to do with her sons killing each other, but she didn't have anyone else to blame so she lashed out at Jackie. She already blamed her for the tremendous amount of guilt she felt for releasing her to Leon, but she didn't have the courage to voice it until now.

Seeing Jackie's face everyday for the past five years was a constant reminder of the tragic event that changed all of their lives, and she secretly resented her for it.

Janice's words stung Jackie's mind, body, and soul. She thought that everyone in her family was happy that Leon and his brothers were dead; and she thought they were definitely happy to have her home. She grabbed her mother's crack pipe off of the coffee table and left back out of the house. She got an eight ball of crack out of the trunk, sat in her car, and smoked some for the first time. The crack numbed her whole body and offered her a brief escape from her mother's cruel words and the tremendous amount of pain she felt from the loss of her brothers. She couldn't think about anything but it so she stayed in her car and smoked all night. The next day Janice came out to the car and apologized for saying the things that she said to Jackie. Jackie accepted her apology and got high with her, but her words cut too deep so the apology couldn't repair the damage that they did. Janice tried to take the words back, but she couldn't and they played over and over again in Jackie's mind.

She started to move out of the house, but decided against it. Her father paid for that house and she had the right to be there just like the rest of them. The twins moved back home when their brothers killed each other, because they couldn't afford to pay their rent without them. There was a lot of tension in the house with the seven women living there, but all of them refused to leave. Jackie and Janice were the only ones who didn't get pregnant during the time they all lived together, but somebody stayed pregnant between the other five women. Everybody started getting high off crack, including the three youngest girls. Jackie didn't want them doing drugs, but she felt like she couldn't tell them not to do crack when she was doing it herself. All three of them had kids that they took care of, steady boyfriends, and got welfare. They were grown women who took care of themselves and that suited her just fine. She wasn't going out like Timothy did trying to control grown people who didn't want to be controlled. Jack Jr. told her that King David sent Dwayne and Phillip to talk Timothy into disassembling the GD's and reuniting with the BGD's which started the argument that made them kill each other.

None of her brother's had life insurance so Jackie paid for their triple funeral. Dwayne only had $103 to his name when he died and Phillip only had $52. Timothy's girlfriend stole all of the money and drugs that he left behind as soon as she heard he was dead. They never saw her again;

she didn't even have the decency to attend the funeral. The GD's started out helping with Jack Jr.'s legal matters but at the end of the day, it was Jackie who bonded him out of jail and got him the best defense lawyer in the state of Illinois.

Jack Jr. was just following Timothy when he joined the GD's. He wasn't built for the streets so he didn't have the heart to become the leader of the GD's after Timothy's death. He was facing a lot of years in prison when Timothy first died, so he dropped his flag and squared up. He didn't make it to their funeral because he was transferred to the crazy hospital after spending one night in the Cook County Jail. He was suicidal at the crime scene, so they put him into protective custody and added him on the suicide watch list as soon as he made it to the jail. He ended up being suicidal in there, so they refused to let him out into society immediately because he was still considered a danger to his self and to society. His trial couldn't even start on time because he spent the first eleven months in the crazy hospital. He wasn't released from there until the psychiatrist who examined him daily said he was fit to go to trial, and could be released into the custody of his family while going through trial. Jackie bonded him out as soon as they released him from the mental ward.

He moved out to Dolton, Illinois with his paternal grandmother, Trudy, to get away from all of the riff raff. The BGD's had a hit out on him for killing Phillip, and the GD's didn't respect him anymore because he dropped his flag. His paternal grandfather, Jonathan, died two years before Jack Sr. died. Everyone accept Jackie went to their grandfather's funeral and Trudy had been trying to get Jack Jr. to move with her every since then. Jack Sr. was strung out on drugs and he looked like he was. Jack Jr. looked like her son looked before he went to the army so Trudy wanted him with her bad. She felt a tremendous amount of guilt for letting Jonathan and her whole family mistreat her son throughout his life. They accused her of cheating when her son came out looking mixed and there was no way she could tell them different. She tried to shield her son from their cruelty, but she resented him too in a small way. They were all shocked when they went to Jonathan's funeral and his entire family was black. Trudy was happy that she got the chance to show Jack Sr. that she wasn't the whore everyone made her out to be before he died, but she regretted that she never got the chance to help him. She was more than happy to take Jack Jr. in and she spoiled him rotten during the four years his trial went on. In her mind he was her son Jack and he had just came back from fighting in the Vietnam War.

Jack Jr. was sentenced to five years for the unlawful use of a weapon, but he would have only had to do three at the most. The murder charges they had against him for killing Timothy and Dwayne were dropped. His defense lawyer subpoenaed the morgue's files that had forensic evidence in them that proved there were three different guns used by three different men. Jack Jr. didn't touch any of their guns, so the crime scene investigators knew which gun each brother used. After proving who killed who, the lawyer had the first degree murder charge they had on him for killing Phillip dropped. He was able to prove that Jack Jr. killed Phillip in self defense because Phillip aimed his gun at him right after he killed Timothy.

Jackie was looking forward to getting the money she bonded Jack Jr. out with back because she was broke by the end of his trial. He was supposed to turn his self in on August 2, 1992, but he ran. Jackie was hurt and angry at him for running because he knew she needed her money and she wouldn't get it back if he ran. She was strung out on crack, working on other people's dope spots, renting out her Lexus to dope dealers, whoring on Madison and California, robbing her johns, boosting clothes and anything else she could do to make the money it took to support her habit.

Jackie went from being a millionaire to being broke in four years, and she thought that she could become a millionaire again if she got the $100,000 she paid to bail Jack Jr. out of jail back. When her brothers first killed each other she went into a depression and getting high, planning their funerals, and taking care of Jack Jr.'s legal problems consumed her. Three months later, she tried to reclaim her territory and collect the money from the drugs she had out on the streets prior to their deaths. The BGD's who worked for her robbed her for the twenty-seven dollars she had in her pockets, her 18k, 20 inch, gold dookie rope chain, her18k bamboo earrings, the 18k gold rings she had on all of her fingers, her black lambskin leather jacket, and her black Gucci shoe boots. They were about to take her Lexus but she told them that the repo man was looking for it. After robbing her they told her they were taking over. They also said that their loyalty only extended to her brothers and since they were dead, her muscle was dead. There was nothing Jackie could do about it, so she just thanked God that all she had on her was twenty-seven dollars and they didn't kill her. She started to bring her "workers" some more packs of drugs to sell, but something told her not to and she was glad that she didn't. Her bankroll started to dwindle while she was hustling and she understood why Timothy told her to never smoke crack if she was going to sell it. When she wasn't able to sell drugs anymore and was still smoking them, her bankroll disappeared right before her eyes. She wasn't even able to continue to pay Jack Jr.'s lawyer but Trudy continued to make the payments.

The main reason Jackie went with Leon was to stop Jason from putting her, her mother and her sisters out on the hoe stroll, but all of them ended up out there anyway. This revelation came to her on a cold winter night. She was standing around a steel garbage can with burning wood in it with her mother and all of her sisters trying to catch tricks on Leon's old hoe stroll. It was the first time all of them were out there together, and Jackie hated competing with them for tricks, especially her mother. She also hated their conversation because all they wanted to talk about were the good old days when the men Jackie sent their way used to take them on exotic trips and spoil them rotten. They weren't in gangs, so they were allowed to date any man they wanted to regardless of what gang they belonged to. They dated most of the gang leaders in Chicago. She got tired of hearing how the street famous men had proposed to each of her sisters. If they loved them so much, why were they on the corner with her trying to catch tricks?

Jackie didn't say anything because she knew her sisters would say she was jealous because she didn't get the opportunity to enjoy dating any of the powerful men. She went from being celibate and acting like she was too good to have sex with them, to fucking them and their friends for crack. It took the men years to get Jackie into their beds, but when she started selling her body for crack anyone who was willing to pay got to have sex with her. Her fear of AIDS went out the window and she didn't care who the men slept with first, as long as they were paying her so she could support her crack habit. Her clients didn't know she was doing crack in the beginning. She told them she was selling her body because she got robbed and her dope spots were taken from her. Her little black book had a lot of street famous names in it and she was able to charge them a nice fee, until she got caught smoking crack and let it take complete control of her. When that happened she lost all of her customers and started selling her body on the hoe stroll; and by that time anyone who looked at her could tell she was a crack head.

Jackie caught all types of cases during the four years Jack Jr. was going back and forth to court, so she was on probation when she thought she was going to get her money back. Her problems with the law weren't the only ones she had to worry about. Her 1988 Lexus was in jeopardy of being repossessed, the electricity and heat in their house was cut off, and they were behind on paying the taxes on it so it was in jeopardy of being foreclosed. Jackie used to make sure that the bills got paid, but her mother and sisters were stealing from her every chance they got. She got tired of being the only one who cared about the roof over all of their heads. She had a real bad crack habit that she had to support herself, so she got selfish and only concentrated on her own habits.

Jackie thought that things were looking up for her because she was on the hoe stroll three weeks before Jack Jr.'s sentencing trial and she saw Timothy's connect, Miguel. She got in the car with him and didn't recognize who he was until he told her that he remembered her and she was too good to be out on the stroll. She broke down crying and told him everything that had been going on in the last four years of her life. He told her if she got the $100,000, he would sell her the best cocaine in the city and match whatever quantity she purchased. He said he was still affiliated with the gang Timothy started and he could get her some GD soldiers to sell her drugs and some corners to sell it on. Then he took her home, gave her $3,000, an ounce of pure heroin, and an ounce of pure cocaine.

Jackie was street poisoned so she was addicted to the respect and the power that came with having money just as much as she was addicted to crack. She was tired of being a crack head because it seemed like everybody disrespected them. She was famous on the streets of Chicago at one point in time, and she missed that street fame. Whenever she bought some crack from one of the little disrespectful thugs on one of her old corners, the first thought that ran through her mind was *they just don't know who I am* when they disrespected her. She decided that she was going to stop doing crack as soon as she got her money, and become the bad bitch she was used to being. She used to think that crack was cheap until it made her money; respect, mind, and pride disappear right before her very eyes.

Jackie knew she wasn't going to get her money when she didn't see Jack Jr. or his lawyer in court; but she still waited in courtroom 101 on twenty-sixth and California until she heard Judge Bryant call his name.

She stood up and looked around the courtroom after Jack's name was called and when the judge told the bailiff to issue a warrant for his arrest she spoke up. "So Your Honor, if y'all issuing a warrant does that mean I don't get the money I bonded him out with back?" she asked.

"Miss I'm sure you were told your bond would be forfeited if Mr. Wright missed any of his court dates; and since this is a court date the bond that was posted for the absent Mr. Wright will be confiscated," said Judge Bryant with a scowl on his face. He hated when people made outbursts in his courtroom, but he was happy to tell the woman that her money wouldn't be returned to her. It was obvious that she was on drugs and he felt like the money she used to bond the defendant out with would be put to better use if it was used to help the state find and arrest him.

Trudy came to court and Jackie would always be ashamed of the conversation she had with her. Trudy was a thin, sixty-one year old, 5'5" white lady, with piercing, big, blue eyes, a small, pointed, thin nose, pale, pink, thin lips, pale, wrinkled skin, and silver hair that she kept in a tight bun. She had on a navy blue business suit and old fashioned navy blue pumps. Jackie walked right past her, sat on the bench in front of the one she was sitting on, and she still didn't recognize her until she felt her tap her on her shoulder and call her name. "Jacqueline, I need to talk to you," she whispered in Jackie's ear after the rude outburst Jackie made in court.

"Grandma where is Jack?" Jackie asked as she followed their grandmother out of the courtroom. Jackie had on some white ankle socks, some of her little sister Angel's Guess blue jean shorts, Angel's purple Guess t-shirt that went with the shorts and some purple and white Got To Have It Reeboks. She had her hair pulled back into a ponytail. She thought she was doing good by keeping up with the changing styles and that she looked cute, but nothing could've been be further from the truth. She was only thirty-two years old by the end of Jack Jr.'s trial, but she looked like she was at least forty, with her empty, distant, looking eyes with the huge bags under them. The bags under her eyes looked like they weighed more than she did because she was 5'7" and only weighed one hundred pounds. She used to boost clothes from the big Marshall Fields on State Street but she couldn't fit any of the ones she got before she smoked up all the money and drugs Miguel gave her, so she took one of the size zero outfits that she gave Angel back. She still had a nice amount of tits and ass but the rest of her looked like it had disappeared, her gray eyes looked bugged out, like they were too big for her face and her dimples looked like they had sunk into her cheeks.

Trudy felt like Jackie's clothes, language, and tone of voice was very inappropriate for the courtroom, but she had bigger things on her mind. "He was afraid of reentering any of the jails in Chicago because the police officers who arrested him tortured him severely and made him write a confession saying he killed all of his brothers," Trudy said with great, big, crocodile tears in her clear blue eyes.

"Grandma that nigga running game on you, if he got tortured, why didn't he tell me?" Jackie asked as they stood in the hallway outside of the courtroom.

"He was ashamed to tell anyone what happened until I saw how bad he was shaking this morning and forced the truth out of him. He started off by telling me how they took him down to the basement of the precinct and pistol whipped him real bad. After pistol whipping him, they put a plastic bag over his head until he felt like he was about to suffocate. Then they shocked him with some sort of device that looked like a black box with alligator clips attached to it. They put the alligator clips to his earlobes and cranked up the device; and the electric currents from that machine shocked him so bad that he chipped his teeth as they rattled. When your brother still refused to tell the prosecutor that he killed all of his brothers; those bastards took the clips off of his ears, made him pull down his pants, attached the clips to his testicles, and shocked him down there too. He was in so much pain after being tortured that he wrote down everything the prosecutor wanted him to write down. He told that big shot lawyer you hired what happened to him and he got the confession thrown out, and the murder charges dropped, but he didn't do anything about the abuse Jack endured."

"Jacqueline, he tried to come to court so you could get your money back, but I refused to let him after he told me what those monsters did to him. I went to law school so Jack has agreed to let me represent him. I'm going to file a civil suit against the city of Chicago on his behalf. I got his file from his lawyer this morning and told him that his services are no longer needed. He had the statement that Jack Jr. gave him about the abuse and the pictures that were taken at the jail. He had a black eye, his face was swollen, and the marks from the alligator clips on his earlobes were visible in those pictures. I used my Polaroid camera and took some pictures of his testicles this morning because as hard as it is to believe, the marks are still down there as well. He's also afraid of what those two gangs that are after him will do to him if he enters any prison in Illinois. I know you wanted your money but after hearing everything I've told you, I'm certain you can understand why I didn't allow him to attend his sentencing hearing this morning," said Trudy, with hope, mixed with fear in her big, watery, blue eyes. Jackie's eyes had changed from gray to green three times as she talked to her and the evil that lurked behind them scared Trudy.

"How in the fuck do you know what I understand? You don't know me, you don't know Jack, and you don't know shit about the street life. We didn't even know that yo white ass was still alive up until a few years ago, and now you want to use Jack Jr. to help ease the guilt that's eating away at yo conscience for the way y'all did our daddy. Why did you have to interfere with our plans? Jack Jr. told me about his fear of the gangs and I told him to do his time in protective custody. Grandma, the only thing that I understand is you the reason I don't have my motherfucking money in my motherfucking hands right now. I don't give a fuck about Jack Jr. getting tortured. He ain't the first nigga them motherfuckers tortured and he ain't gon be the last nigga they torture! There ain't shit yo old, wrinkled ass can do about it," Jackie said. The Chicago police had been making murder suspects confess to murder by torturing them for years. Jackie heard Leon and his brothers come in their apartment laughing at the way the policemen on their payrolls tortured their enemies and made them confess to murders they had committed lots of times. They even used the same techniques that Jack Jr. described to their grandmother so she knew he wasn't lying, but she wanted her money. She felt like he was in a street gang, and the dope game, so he threw bricks at the penitentiary everyday for a living. He knew there was a chance he might get caught for some of the dirt that he did. Jackie told her brothers the stories that the Thompson's used to brag about when she was reunited with them; so Jack Jr. knew that if he ever got caught there was a good possibility he would be tortured by some dirty, prejudiced policemen. She didn't feel sorry for him at all, he murdered their brother and he acted like he deserved to be free just because he got roughed up.

"I was only trying to help I—," Trudy tried to say but Jackie cut her off.

"Oh, you trying to help? Can you help me by giving me the $100,000 that it cost to bail Jack's bitch made ass out? Or can you give me back all the money that I paid that big shot lawyer you fired? Or can you stop the police from making me give them some free pussy when I try to sell some tonight? What the fuck you looking so shocked and disgusted for? I'm a crack head and I got to support my habit some type of way! Thanks to you I ain't got shit but two dollars to my name and that's for bus fare," Jackie said as tears started to form in her eyes. Her tears weren't for Jack Jr., they were for her. She was a selfish, heartless crack head, who felt sorry for herself as she felt her last chance at making it big again evaporate. As her dream started to leave, reality started to seep in, and the strong urge for crack crept in. She was going to stop doing crack if she got her money, but since she wasn't going to get it, the monkey on her back started pounding on it, as it demanded to be fed. Jackie loved her brother but somewhere along the way her addiction to crack wouldn't allow her to care about anything but feeding it. She was mad at their grandmother for convincing Jack Jr. not to turn his self in and she was mad at him for listening to her. Jackie would have never felt that way before crack entered her life but it was in her life and it controlled every part of her, including her emotions.

"I don't carry money around with me, but I can write you a check for $2,000. I can also see if they'll let me put my house up for Jack's bond and give you back your money, but you'll have to wait until morning court is adjourned which should be about three o'clock. I have to inform Judge Bryant of Jack's change of counsel and I want to file a motion to have his warrant lifted because the police used excessive force when they apprehended him. They're not going to lift the warrant today but if they do, I'll make sure you get your money," Trudy said. She felt sorry for Jackie, but the anger that she felt towards the policemen who violated Jack Jr. outweighed the pity she felt for her. She knew that she wasn't going to be able to exchange the deed to her house for Jackie's bail money; and she really didn't care because she felt like Jackie was going to use the bond money to buy drugs anyway and saving Jack Jr. was a much better cause. She intended to make everyone who harmed her grandson pay for what they had done and she wasn't going to give up until they were punished for their actions. They thought he was just another poor, uneducated, low life, law breaking nigger when they violated him; but they would have thought twice about doing what they did to him if they knew how hard Trudy was willing to fight for him.

"I don't think they gon let you put yo house up, but if they do I'll give you back yo $2,000. But writing me a check won't help me because drug dealers don't take checks. If you really want to help me out you can get some money out of the ATM machine down the street," Jackie said as she sweetened her voice and softened her eyes. The dope fiend inside of her told her that the $2,000 her grandmother was trying to give her sounded better than nothing. She could use it to buy a nice quantity of cocaine from Miguel and explain what happened in court to him. Maybe he would have some sympathy for her and match what she bought from him and front her at least a kilo.

"I'm afraid I can't do that Jacqueline because that's not the bank I do my business in and I don't have the time to go to the one that my money's in. I've got too much to do in this courthouse to even think about leaving right now. I've got complaints and motions to file and I've scheduled a press conference with a couple of my media friends, so if you'll excuse me I really must get started," Trudy said as she hugged Jackie and hurried up and disappeared into one of the many courtrooms. The only reason she was going to write Jackie a check was to get her out of her face because she wasn't going to waste her money to support anyone's drug habit. If she had to write the check she was going to put a stop payment on it; but things worked out for the best because she was able to get away from Jackie before she realized she didn't get the check or the cash. She felt that she could have done a much better job raising Jack, but the one thing she never did regret was refusing to help him support his drug habit.

Damn I forgot to get the fucking check, Jackie thought devastated by the revelation. She felt stupid because she stayed up smoking crack with the little money she had left the night before with her mother. She was expecting her money the next day so the only thing she saved out was bus fare to get to the courthouse and back home. She didn't drive because she didn't want the repo man to take her Lexus while she was in court. She only had two dollars when she walked out of the courthouse and she was feigning for crack harder than she ever had. She stumbled out and went across the street to catch the California bus to Jackson and California, so she could beg one of the GD's out there to let her sell a couple of packs of dope.

Luck wasn't on her side that day, because she had just convinced the GD to let her get on, and her first customer turned out to be an undercover policeman. As soon as the "hype" walked away with his drugs, police cars pulled up from all four directions in the four way intersection and bombarded her. She didn't even get a chance to smoke a rock before the officer grabbed her and threw her on the gray bubble detective car in front of the small red store on the corner. He asked her if she had anything on her that could harm him but she was in a daze. She couldn't believe she was going to jail on the day that Jack Jr. was supposed to be going and she wanted to kill him as she heard the familiar words to the Miranda rights come out of the officer's mouth. Jackie was on probation so she didn't get a bond and the judge gave her four years that she had to serve in the Dwight Correctional Facility. She only had to do one and a half years; and in that short period of time, the police caught Jack Jr., her car got repossessed, and her mother and sisters got evicted from their house. They were living in shelters trying to get housing in the projects and she didn't want to join them so she went to Miamisburg with her grandmother Pam.

(15)

Mistreated (Dayton, Ohio 8/4/1997)

Jackie would have killed Rhonda if she had been standing in her face for making her heart hurt the way that it did from losing Marcus; and from thinking about all the painful memories she had tucked in the back of her mind. She tried not to think about her brother's murders more than the murders she committed. You reap what you sow and God made Jackie's pain and grief ten times worse than he made Bertha's. Jackie's brother's killed each other. Bertha knew that Jackie killed at least one if not all of her sons so she had someone to blame for their deaths; and the thought of her getting revenge on Jackie is what kept her alive. Jackie didn't have anyone to blame for her brother's deaths but three of her brothers, and they were all dead. She knew Jack Jr. wasn't lying when he said he killed Phillip in self defense because the police said the same thing after the lawyer and the forensic evidence proved it. While she was locked up sometimes she regretted helping Jack Jr., but then she would reprimand herself for having those thoughts. If she wouldn't have bonded him out he would have been killed in jail. If she wouldn't have retained a good lawyer for him a public defender wouldn't have even tried to make the corrupt Chicago Police Department tell the truth and Jack Jr. would have gotten life for the three murders.

Jackie still felt like Jack Jr. was a victim after he played her. She saw how all of that money and power changed Timothy; and she knew the strong influence he had over Jack Jr. She also witnessed the loyalty that Dwayne and Phillip had for King David. Her brothers weren't the only young, black victims that the mean streets of Chicago had devoured. She developed a strong hatred for gangs and crack while she was in prison, because she felt like they were the downfall of her family. She felt that gangs were no better than cults and they recruited people under false pretenses because they took her family and turned them against each other. She wasn't trying to blame any GD's or BGD's for the deaths of her brothers, but she felt like they wouldn't have killed each other if they would have never gotten caught up or affiliated with any gangs. Timothy started the GD's and he was dead and gone but they were bigger and stronger than ever, and they were still keeping the streets of Chicago flooded with crack. King David succeeded in getting rid of the founder of the GD's but he couldn't get rid of the gang itself because the rest of it's members were just as strong as their leader was and it had already taken on a life of it's own. Jackie believed in spirits and she felt that evil spirits kept gangs, violence, and drugs alive in the ghettoes and projects of the inner cities.

Her hatred for Rhonda grew ten times stronger than it was before she left. She hadn't thought about her brothers, crack, gangs, Leon, Bertha or none of the other things that she spent the last twelve hours thinking about in years. She was mentally exhausted so it felt like days had passed since the confrontations she had with Marcus and Rhonda occurred. She had to be at work by six thirty in the morning and it was already five. She decided to go even though she wasn't in her right state of mind. She went back to the dope man and got two more twenty dollar blows before she took a shower and got ready for work. She had plans on doing the dope after work, but Toni convinced her to do one when Marcus didn't answer his cell phone. *"Girl, fuck that nigga! You got a lot more to worry about than him! Did you hear all of that bullshit yo fat, ugly ass daughter was saying? I told you to kill that bitch when you first had her but you got rid of me instead,"* said Toni as she gathered the materials that Jackie used to get high with the night before. *"You might as well gon ahead and get one of them thangs ready because I'm gon have to get high to get us through the bullshit you got on our plate now!"*

"Toni, I don't want to get all the way back on the wagon! I only bought them dopes so I can have something in case I get sick. You trying to come back and run shit! Where the fuck was you at when I needed you the most? I lost three of my brothers and you wasn't nowhere to be found so I think I can handle this shit without you," Jackie said as she took the stocking that Toni tied around her arm off.

"Jackie, every time I wasn't around you replaced me with something else! First it was Beauty, then it was heroin, after that it was the power that

the streets gave you, then it was crack, and Mr. Marcus has been yo latest distraction! I ain't mad about the situation, but don't try to make me feel bad for not being there for you when you felt like you didn't need me! Look, I ain't trying to argue with you because I'm on yo side, but if you expect me to go into that factory and not slap the shit out of Terry, Marcus or his new little girlfriend then I'm gon have to be high," said Toni as she retied the stocking around their arm, turned the heroin into it's liquid form and shot it into the biggest vein that jumped out when she thumped it.

Jackie got on highway seventy-five going north by the BP on Dryden Road and saw Marcus and London in the car on the left hand side of her when she eased her way into traffic. She usually enjoyed riding to work, but when she saw Marcus with the new girl, it felt like someone had snatched her heart out of her chest and threw it out the window. She actually had to pull over to the shoulder of the highway to catch her breath and to eject the Luther Vandross CD out of the CD player. She listened to that CD every morning but the lyrics to *Here and Now* bought on the waterworks. She didn't realize she was crying until she tasted her tears because she thought she was all cried out from the day before. The tears actually stung her eyes and face as they rolled down her swollen face.

Jackie's eyes were swollen, puffy, red, and irritated; but she was still able to see Marcus's car when she pulled back into traffic and there were at least four cars in front of it. She thought they were headed to the job, but Marcus's car was the only thing she saw when she rode past the BP Gas station on the left hand side of Buyer's road. She was beyond angry when she pulled into the same gas station they were in, and ran her car into the front of his. Marcus was in the car when Jackie hit it and he was about to jump out when he realized what happened, but she wasn't finished. She popped her trunk, got out of her car, grabbed the steel baseball bat that she kept inside of it, and started busting out his windows with the bat. She started with the window on the driver's side and pieces of glass flew into his left eye when the window shattered. London was inside the gas station and she didn't come out until the policewoman who was parked across the street at the Shell gas station drove over and apprehended Jackie.

"Damn Jackie, what the fuck is you doing? The dope was supposed to have calmed yo ass down! Bitch, we bout to go to jail," said Toni as she saw the policewoman drive across the street with her lights on.

"Drop the bat and put your hands in the air," said the officer as she drew her gun and aimed it at Jackie. "Do you have any drugs, weapons, or anything that will hurt me on you?" she asked as Jackie dropped the bat, and the policewoman threw her against her police car.

Jackie shook her head no and she knew she was definitely going to jail when the policewoman started telling her, her rights. After she finished telling Jackie her rights, she patted her down, checked her pockets, put her on a pair of handcuffs, and into the backseat of her police car. After closing the door, the policewoman went to talk to Marcus and several of their co-workers.

Jackie didn't notice that almost everyone they worked with was out there and had seen everything that happened; until she saw the policewoman taking statements from them. She was happy that she left her other bag of dope at home because she would have really been embarrassed if her nosy, backstabbing co-workers would have seen her with it. Seeing them sobered her up and made her realize exactly what she had just done and how much trouble she was in.

She felt stupid, scared, embarrassed, angry, and hurt all at the same time. She had just messed up her car and she knew her insurance company wasn't going to pay to get it fixed. The police and a lot of other people who were obviously willing to testify against her, witnessed her using it to maliciously cause damages to someone else's car. She only had two out of her nine attendance points left, so if she spent more than two days in jail she was going to get fired. If she got fired she wasn't going to be able to get her car fixed. Her rent was cheap so she could get her grandmother to pay it for a couple of months, but if stayed in jail for too long, DMHA would find out and she could still get evicted rather the rent was paid or not. And on top of all of that, she knew that she had lost Marcus for good.

"Ma'am can you tell me what's going to happen to my car and if I'll be released today," Jackie asked the white policewoman after she got into the car and drove her to the Miamisburg police station.

"You weren't worried about that car when you rammed it into that guy's car, so don't worry about it now. You're a violent person and a threat to society so you won't be getting released from jail any time soon if I have anything to do with it," the tall, white, lanky policewoman replied as she parked the car in back of the station.

That was Jackie's first time being arrested in Ohio and she immediately noticed how nice and clean the station there was compared to the ones that she had been in, in Chicago. They didn't strip search her, they fingerprinted her. That surprised her because when a person got arrested in Chicago they strip searched them and made them cough and squat three times before they even thought about fingerprinting them. After fingerprinting her, the arresting officer sat her on a bench, and handcuffed her to the steel ring that was attached to the wall in back of the bench. The Miamisburg Police Station didn't have any holding cells which shocked Jackie. Every police station that she went to in Chicago had at least five cells with steel bars, a steel bunk bed, stainless steel toilets, and stainless steel sinks in them. She was the only inmate in the whole Miamisburg police station and that made her happy, because she had to put up with other inmates every time she was arrested in Chicago. She kept a cellmate, and if her cellmate wasn't one of the inmates rattling the bars and yelling for an officer, some other inmate within her earshot would do it. She was a dope fiend and when she couldn't come down off of heroin or crack in peace all hell used to break loose. She had a couple of fights and a lot of arguments with other inmates and correctional officers in the jails in Chicago. It felt good to be able to focus on her problems and her case without developing any new ones.

She was transferred from the Miamisburg Police Station to the Montgomery County Jail in Dayton two hours after she got arrested. She would have to go to court in Miamisburg because that's where she committed her crime, but she had to be held in Dayton where she could be accommodated. She liked that procedure better. Whenever she caught a felony in Chicago, she had to stay in the police stations for three days waiting on her fingerprints to come back before being transferred to the Cook County Jail. She didn't like being locked up in the County, but she hated being locked up in any of the police stations more. First of all, they didn't issue out any soap or toothpaste to the inmates so they could take care of their hygiene. Anyone would stink after three days of not washing up or brushing their teeth, but a dope fiend throwing up lime green poison everywhere would stink even more. They kept it real cold in the police stations in Chicago, and the only way an inmate could get a blanket, a pillow, or a mattress to go over there hard steel beds was in their dreams. So even though Jackie didn't want to be in anyone's jail, she preferred to be in the jails in Ohio over the ones in Illinois any day.

When she made it to the Montgomery County Jail she was more shocked than she had been at the Miamisburg Police Station; because they still didn't strip search her. In the Cook County Jail not only was she strip searched, and made to squat and cough several times, but she also had to lift her naked breasts, and spread her butt cheeks as well. And to top it off, she had to do it with about fifty to seventy other naked female inmates who didn't get the opportunity to wash up either. After the search, the correctional officers would give the inmates blue DOC uniforms, wait until they got dressed, and bring three huge German Shepherd dogs who were trained to sniff out drugs into the bullpens to search the inmates. Jackie felt like the dogs were unnecessary because the inmates had been strip searched thoroughly not once but twice. They would tell the inmates to give up any drugs or contraband that they had on them because if the dogs smelled anything on anyone they would bite whatever part of that person's body the drugs were on. After warning the inmates the correctional officers would give them a half an hour to get rid of whatever they had on them. After the half hour, they would make everyone turn around and put their hands on the walls. Then they walked the huge, scary looking, ferocious dogs around the room and had them sniff all of the inmates. Jackie never got bit and she never saw anyone else getting bitten after the strip searches, but she used to be terrified every time she felt the huge German Shepherd's noses on her.

When she first got to the Montgomery County Jail a female corrections officer patted her down and the only thing she had to take off were her shoes. After the first search, she was led through a door into a room that looked more like a doctor's office than any county jail she had ever been in. The room had three bullpens with glass doors for the male inmates to the right, but most of them were outside of the bullpens, sitting in chairs, watching TV. The left side of the huge room had a huge black, circular desk, with computers and telephones on it and correctional officers behind it. They told her to follow a line that was painted on the floor that led her to a small area on the left hand side of the room, and the other female inmates. Two of them were talking on the two payphones that were provided for the females. The rest of them were sitting in chairs watching cable television like they were waiting to be seen by a doctor, instead of waiting to get their fingerprints taken. They had two small bullpens located by the waiting area, but they were only used during shift changes and when an inmate acted up.

Jackie was surprised that the inmates were outside of their cells, and the female inmates were so close to the male inmates. In the Cook County Jail the inmates were held in filthy, overcrowded, bullpens. They tried to keep them clean, but a lot of the inmates who were arrested in Illinois were dope fiends and that green poison was coming out of their bodies rather they wanted it to or not. So the trustees, inmates who worked for the jail and got extra privileges for doing so, had to clean up lime green throw up along with the garbage from the inmates who refused to use the garbage cans to dispose of the food they didn't want. The bullpens had four wooden benches, two steel sinks, and one or two steel toilets in them. There was a concrete wall and no door on the side of the toilets to protect their privacy. They kept the male and female inmates locked up in bullpens on different sides of the building unless they had to go to court in the same courtroom and if that was the case, they were held in separate bullpens. Most of the bullpens had concrete floors, three concrete walls, and a glass wall in the front that had a large, glass, sliding door attached to it. Whoever constructed the building made a wide hallway that was used to separate the rows of bullpens that faced each other and to transport the inmates to and from the bullpens. The hallways had cameras in them and the correctional officers were able to monitor the inmates through the glass doors so they knew what was going on inside the bullpens at all times. They didn't stay in the bullpens with the inmates, and they definitely didn't have the inmates outside of the bullpens with only a desk separating them from the correctional officers. The Montgomery County Jail treated their inmates like human beings which was more than Jackie could say for the jails in Illinois.

She was mentally and physically drained so she dozed off in one of the chairs until her name was called to get photographed and fingerprinted. After she was finished with that, the officer asked her if she wanted to make a phone call and she shook her head no. She had family in Chicago and in Dayton, but she didn't want to call any of them because all that would do is put them in her business. Her family wouldn't bond her out rather they had the money or not. And she doubted Marcus or Terry would bond her out after the confrontations she had just had with them less than twenty-four hours ago. She knew she wasn't getting out any time soon when she heard all the felonies they charged her with and the $70,000 D bond they gave her. She only needed ten percent of the bond, but she didn't have any way of getting $7,000 so she tried to get herself mentally ready for a long stay in jail.

Jackie had all the money that she owned on her and it wasn't nearly enough to pay her bond, so she had to go upstairs. She was disappointed when she had to go up without being seen by a doctor. In the Cook

County Jail, every inmate was given a thorough physical examination and they were checked for hepatitis, all STD's, and any other communicable diseases before they were processed in. The first time Jackie ever saw a gynecologist was in jail and she was terrified when the he gave her, her first pap smear. She was afraid, but she was also amazed because he knew that she had had a baby and he was able to see the healed up cut that she had in her vagina. She also learned that she had Diabetes the first time she was incarcerated, so she felt like those examinations were important. She wanted to be checked for STD's after seeing Marcus with London and after finding out he slept with Terry. She needed her insulin and she had plans on asking the nurse that she thought she would be seeing for some methadone too. To make matters worse, she was about to be around a bunch of women who hadn't been checked out by any doctors either so they could have anything.

She was so mad at not being seen by a doctor that she didn't realize that she was allowed to change into her green DOC uniform in a bathroom stall with a door on it, until she was escorted to a steel elevator. That blew her away because inmates weren't given any privacy in the Cook County Jail until they were properly searched and dressed in their blue Department of Corrections uniforms. Stepping off that elevator was the moment she forgave her brother, Jack Jr. He didn't deserve the torture he had to endure when he was arrested. None of the inmates deserved to be treated the way they were treated in the prisons and jails in Illinois. She didn't realize how degrading and disrespectful the strip searches were until she was arrested without going through them. All of the blunt brutal force, hatred, humiliation, sexism, and racism, wasn't necessary to apprehend a suspect. A Chicago policeman had actually told a news reporter that some of his fellow officers liked to round up two thousand pounds of nigger and hope that they got the right one. She knew that there were prejudice people everywhere; but to be so blunt about being prejudice when you're supposed to be working to protect the people that you're prejudice against, was just wrong.

Thinking about the police in Chicago made her hate the gangs there even more! Part of the reason they were supposed to have been started was because of the way the police treated poor people. Chicago was segregated, and the police didn't protect or serve the minorities who lived in the ghettoes and projects. They were prejudiced, crooked, mean, and corrupt so no one trusted them. The people who ran Chicago thought that the best way to deal with poor people was to make them live in the city stacked on top of each other, educate them and their kids poorly, and make them think that welfare was more profitable than working by not giving them the opportunity to get a job. Crime ran rapid throughout these areas as the people who lived in them invented every hustle they could think of to try to make ends meet, and to support the drug habits they developed in their quest to escape their reality. Different gangs were formed to protect the people in their neighborhoods from the police, and rival gangs. They provided illicit jobs for the people and gave them a false sense of unity and love. The leaders of the gangs lured young, hungry, vulnerable kids into their organizations by letting them "work" for them; and by providing them with all of the necessities they needed including the love their drug addicted parents didn't give them. But they didn't love them; they turned them into cold blooded, drug dealing, disrespectful killers. Jackie was able to clearly see what was going on for the first time in her life.

(16)

Picking Up The Pieces

When Jackie went into her cell, her roommate was already in there so she introduced herself. "Hey girl, my name is Jackie and I don't like discussing my case with people, but we can discuss anything else if you feel the need to talk. What's yo name?" she asked the short, fat, pretty, young looking, light skinned woman as she held her hand out for her to shake.

"My name is Jane'en and I don't like discussing my case either," she replied as she shook Jackie's hand.

"When do we go to the store? I had my whole paycheck on me so I can go today if they let me," Jackie said as she made up the top bunk with the dull gray wool blanket, and the thin worn out sheet the correctional officer gave to her.

"You just missed it, we went yesterday. You can have this new stick of deodorant, and this bar of soap. You can use my lotion, toothpaste, and powder whenever you need to. You're welcomed to my food too, but I would prefer if you asked me before you went in it," Jane'en said.

"Look honey, I'm strictly dickly. I don't play them dyke games, so if you trying to be all nice and shit because you think you gon get some coochie, you got another thing coming," Jackie snapped.

"I don't play them dyke games either, because I'm a Christian. That's the reason I offered to help you, because Jesus would have and I want to be like him. I ask myself What Would Jesus Do in every situation I'm put in," Jane'en said. "Look, I didn't mean to offend you I just know that going without good toiletries and good food for a whole week is hard and as a Christian it's my duty to share what I have with you. So like I said before, you're more than welcomed to share my commissary with me and I also have a Bible you can read. Have you accepted Christ as your Lord and Savior? If you don't know him, I would love to introduce him to you."

"I wouldn't mind meeting him later. I'm sorry about snapping on you earlier, I just wanted you to know where I was coming from. I'm still fresh from the shower I took this morning, but I do accept your offer. Can I have a couple of pieces of candy, a pencil, two stamped envelopes, and some paper so I can write a couple of letters? I'll get you anything you want when I fill out my commissary slip. Like I told you, I had my whole paycheck on me so it won't be a problem," said Jackie as she waited for Jane'en to gather the things that she asked for.

"You don't have to do that. When I give I give from my heart, and Jesus blesses me. I don't give people loans or lend them anything because that causes confusion if they can't pay back the loan. When I give, I give from the heart, forget about it, and know that I'm stacking up my blessings in heaven. Giving makes me feel good because it warms my heart and swells my body with the presence of my God. Here, you can have all of this candy because I really don't need it," Jane'en replied as she handed Jackie a pad of paper, a pencil, three stamped envelopes, and a bag full of candy. She had the biggest smile on her face and Jackie saw a light in her that she knew had to have come from God.

"Thank you," was all that Jackie could get out because she felt her heart swell as the girl talked. It was like God was talking directly to her through Jane'en, because she said the words that Jackie needed to hear before she wrote her letter to Jack Jr. She'd never met anyone as unselfish as Jane'en was, so Jackie didn't really trust her. As she climbed in the top bunk, she made a mental note to make a list of all the items Jane'en gave her so that she could order them when she filled out her commissary slip. She was going to follow the rules of the jails she was used to being in. She had been locked up with a lot of females who claimed they were "Christians" but they didn't act like they were. Her mother taught her not to accept anything from anyone the first time Leon tried to give her an expensive gift. She told her that nothing in life was free and Jackie believed this to be true since she had to pay for everything she ever received in her life. She took a candy bar out of the paper bag Jane'en gave her, rolled the bag up, sat it on her windowsill, laid on her stomach and started writing her letter to Jack Jr.

August 4, 1997

Dear Jr.,

I'm so sorry for the way I've treated you these past few years, and I forgive you for not going to court. I should have been by your side no matter what. I really didn't understand how bad prisoners are treated in Illinois until I got locked up in a different state. The way those officers did you was really wrong. I am so ashamed of myself for putting money and drugs above the love that I have for you, grandma, and my race as a whole. I hope you can forgive me and realize I'm not that person anymore. I've left crack alone and I've grown a whole lot since the last time you saw me.

What happened to our family Jr.? I know that Leon played his role in destroying us, but the most destruction occurred after his death. We used to be a strong, loving, caring, tight knit, African American family with lots of black pride. We used to look down on drugs and gangs, but we ended up letting them consume our lives. I feel as distant and lonely from y'all as I felt when I was with Leon. When I was with him, I used to dream of coming home but I never imagined that things would turn out the way they did. Well, that was then and this is now.

I guess people change as they get older, but you know what Jr.? Sometimes I miss the little girl that I once was. I sometimes wonder where she went, and wish that I could go back to being her. I wish our father would have never fought in the Vietnam War, or gotten hooked on heroin. I know you have a lot of things you wished had never happened too, but we've got to move forward in life. If only we could turn back the hands of time, but that's just wishful thinking.

I didn't support the fight that you and grandma were fighting against the legal system in Illinois at first, but I do now. I understand why y'all doing what y'all doing and I'm proud of y'all for having the guts to stand up to such a strong enemy. Jennifer, Angel, and Sharon used to write me when I was locked up in Dwight, and they kept me posted on what was going on with you. They told me you only had to do thirty days before grandma got all of your charges dropped. I ain't gon lie, I was mad at first because they still revoked the money that

I put up for your bond, but now I'm proud to be a part of the history y'all creating. I also heard that y'all been all over the news and grandma filed a civil suit against the Chicago Police Department, and the City of Chicago for the pain, suffering, and distress they caused you. I hope you win the suit because you deserve to win. It's going to be a long, tough battle, but don't give up because y'all got a lot of people rooting for y'all. When you get justice it gives other people who were done wrong by the courts, the government, and the system hope that they can get justice too.

Well, I'm going to end this letter with plenty of love, pride, and determination.

Love Always,

Jackie

P.S. I'm not ready to discuss why I've been arrested down here yet.

"Jane'en, what address do we use for our mail?" Jackie asked her roommate after she folded the letter, put it in the envelope and put Jack Jr.'s name and her grandmother's address on it. She knew not to lick the envelope because all mail leaving out or entering any jail had to be examined.

"This address is 330 W. Second Street Dayton, Ohio 45422," Jane'en replied. She was on the bottom bunk reading her Bible and thanking God for a quiet roommate.

After finishing Jack Jr.'s letter, Jackie felt a huge weight lifted up off of her shoulders. She finally understood what her mother was talking about when she used to tell them that forgiveness is for the person doing the forgiving. She used to try to tell them that being angry at others only hurt you because the person you're angry with has went on about their business and left you with the bad feelings. It felt real good to forgive Jack Jr. after so many years and she hoped he could find it in his heart to do the same.

She was afraid to write Marcus but she knew that she had to, so she started on his letter.

August 4, 1997

Dear Marcus,

I want to start this letter off by apologizing for everything! I don't know what came over me this morning when I saw your new girlfriend in the car with you. I was so angry and hurt that I couldn't help it. You're the first man I've ever given my heart to, so the pain and emptiness that's replaced your presence is unbearable. I now know what people mean when they say that there's a thin line between love and hate, because I love you so much that I hate you for taking your love away from me.

I had full coverage insurance, so my insurance company will handle the damages that I caused to you and your car. I just wish I had something to fix the damages that I've caused to my life. I should have told you about my kids, and the circumstances surrounding them and my dead ex-husband a long time ago. Rhonda wasn't lying about me giving them to their grandmother when their father died, but I didn't have a choice. I know this is going to sound horrible, but I hate those kids and I hated their father.

My father owed him a large amount of money for running off with his drugs. He asked for my hand in marriage to pay off my daddy's debt when I was only fourteen years old. I consider those kids a product of rape and hate, and their faces are a constant reminder of their father. I knew their grandmother was poisoning their minds and turning them against me, but I didn't know she would go as far as telling them I killed their daddy.

I didn't kill their father and I don't know who did. Don't get me wrong, I was rejoicing on the inside when he was murdered but I had nothing to do with it. I've never been charged with killing Leon or anyone else! I didn't know that Leon's mother, my kids, or anyone besides them thought I had anything to do with him getting killed.

I hope you can understand why I didn't tell you all of these things after reading this letter. I try not to think about Leon, my kids, or the childhood I had to sacrifice for the rest of my family. Leon and his family were some evil, powerful, well connected people in Chicago and they would have killed my whole family if I wouldn't have gone with Leon. I don't regret anything I've had to do in my life to survive, but I am ashamed of some of the things I was forced to do. I know I was just a child and I didn't have a say in the matter, but the shit is still embarrassing. My father was a good man and he never touched drugs before he was drafted into the army and sent to Vietnam; so I blame the government more than I blame him for the way he turned out.

Before I met you, I'd never been in a real relationship and my heart had never felt true love. Leon spoiled me rotten and he showered me with the finest gifts that money could buy, so I was accustomed to the good life. I didn't date for years after he died but when I did; I only dated men who could take care of me the way I was used to being taken care of. You're the first man that I've dated with a square job, and you're the first one I ever trusted with my heart. I didn't even know that you owned it until you crushed it. If I ever figure out how to repair it, I know I'll never be able to give it to another man.

This shit hurts so bad that it's hard for me to breathe. I'm sitting in jail and I can't think of anything but you and the love we used to share. Marcus, please come back to me! I love you, I need you, and I know that you love me too. You can't fake the kind of love we had, so I know you loved me before Rhonda turned you against me. I understand why you wanted to leave me alone after the cruel lies she told you, but I'm begging you not to throw away our beautiful relationship over them. You've been with that girl less than a month, so I know you can't possibly love her as much as you once loved me. I saw the love and the pain in your eyes when you said that you knew who Rhonda was, so don't fool yourself into thinking you're over me because you're not. She'll never be able to love you the way that I do, no one will! I never thought I would beg a man to be with me, but I can't help it! I'll sacrifice my pride for my heart any day! I love you and I don't think I can live without you!

Can we please get back together and put all of this bullshit behind us? Please take me back and love me the way you used to! I'll do anything you want me to do if you take me back; all you have to do is ask.

Love always and forever,

Jackie

P.S. Please Don't Forget About Us!!!

"*Girl, why are you begging that nigga? Fuck him if he wants that bitch,*" said Toni.

"*It ain't his fault that he found out about my past the way he did. I just want to try to be honest with him, tell my side of the story, and hope he takes me back and forgives me,*" Jackie replied as tears flowed down their cheeks.

"*You call that letter you just wrote being honest with him? You need to stop playing and realize you ain't gon never be able to be totally honest about yo past with anyone! I ain't trying to be hard on you and I know that you love him, but if he loved you he would have asked you what was going on before he took Rhonda's word for it. He didn't know who she was and had never even seen her before that day! Look, you can go ahead and mail the letter, and then you'll know that you tried your best to get him back. I just don't want you to get yo hopes up too high because things can go either way,*" Toni said.

"*Toni I know you feel how much pain has swelled up in our heart!*"

"*I feel it and it's cool to try to get him back because if you succeed you can convince him to drop the charges,*" said Toni as she tried to think of a way to get them out of their legal problems. She could care less about Marcus, or the pain that Jackie felt over losing him. She had to make sure their mind was operating properly.

A whole week had passed since Jackie sent out the letters that she wrote to Jack Jr. and Marcus, and she hadn't heard anything back from either one of them. She had to be in court in three days and she tried not to call anyone during the whole week she was there; but she broke down and called Marcus early that morning. She didn't get a chance to say everything she wanted to say because he had a block on his phone, but she heard him say "Hello" and he heard her say "I love you". All Marcus said on the telephone was hello, but the sound of his voice was enough to flood Jackie's body and mind with all kinds of images of them together. She was happy for the first time during her week long incarceration in the Montgomery County Jail. She was imaging Marcus's face when she heard Toni talking.

"*Have you noticed that our roommate ain't ate nothing since we been here? She goes out on the deck for every meal just so she can give away her breakfast, lunch, and dinner trays. She got a lot of food that she bought from commissary, but she ain't ate none of it either and she ain't no small girl. She gave us all of the candy and gave the rest of her food to them broads out there. I've asked her if she gets hungry a couple of times and she said that Jesus fills her belly up. Her Pastor and part of his congregation is coming to preach today and she wants us to go to with her. I think we should go,"* said Toni. She noticed how Jane'en stayed positive and filled up with the Holy Ghost, so she thought God could heal Jackie's broken heart.

"Now that you said something, I can tell that Jane'en has lost a lot of weight. I peeped that she ain't ate no food too. I sat the commissary that I bought to replace the commissary she gave us on the table that the rest of her stuff is on and she ain't touched none of it! I feel good and I wouldn't mind going to the Chapel with her. She do seem like she at peace with herself and I feel real good since I talked to Marcus," Jackie replied with a big grin on her face. She didn't know how love felt until she lost it. She couldn't eat, sleep, or concentrate on anything. She walked around the jail in a zone while the past and the present continued to cross paths in her mind.

Jackie wasn't in her right state of mind but when Toni was in control, she was on point. *"I ain't never wondered why another inmate was in jail, but I really wonder why Jane'en is locked up. I'm gon ask her tonight, and I'm gon ask her Pastor to pray for us. You ain't been noticing her, but I have. She walks around this jail happy with an inner glow that everyone can see. I don't like how sad you've been over Marcus so I'm gon try to get you some help. She gets more visits than anyone, because her Pastor comes to see her whenever he wants to. She reads all of her mail to us; but you be so busy feeling sad that you don't be paying no attention to the words that are sent to her. Her boss wrote a letter to her judge saying she's a hard working employee who'll have a job waiting on her when she get's out. He said he's a Christian and God told him to save her job for her. She ain't worried about nothing because she said God gave her everything that she has, and all of it's covered with the blood of Jesus Christ. She's been trying to teach us about Him since we got here; but this pain in our heart hurts so much that I can hardly keep up with the things she say, and you can't keep up with them at all,"* Toni said as tears started to well up in their eyes. She wiped them away before they walked out of their cell.

Jackie was surprised when she went to the room that they referred to as the Chapel, because Erica, a girl that worked with her was there. Erica used to try to get Jackie to visit her church all the time, and this was the third time Jackie saw her with her church doing missionary work. She lived in Dunbar Manor and she saw them down there a couple of times barbequing for the residents, giving their kids book bags filled with school supplies, and teaching all the residents the word of God. She didn't have her kids with her, so she didn't attend the events but she had to walk through them to get to the corner store.

Jackie didn't believe in coincidences and she felt like God made Jane'en her roommate and Erica her co-worker because both of them were like rays of lights in dark places. Erica used to come to work everyday with a smile on her face every morning; and she spoke to everyone rather they spoke back or not. She was a married, Christian woman who carried herself like one. She bought her Bible to work with her everyday and read it at every break. She was a good employee who was never involved in the factory gossip. She was very pretty, but the men they worked with were scared to hit on her because they respected her too much. She was thirty-seven, but she didn't look her age and everyone said she looked like she could be Nia Long's twin sister. She had a nice disposition and she didn't cuss so people didn't cuss around her. A lot of people in Dayton knew her because of her family's church, and she invited everyone she encountered the opportunity to visit it.

Jackie felt her body swell up with joy when she saw Erica, and she was surprised and happy that she knew Jane'en. Erica was greeting the inmates as they came in the room and Jackie was ecstatic that she was at the door because it felt good to hug someone she knew; and who knew part of what she was going through. She didn't tell Jane'en or any of the other inmates why she was in jail. Toni was the only person that she discussed anything with; and she knew that wasn't healthy because she knew Toni lived in her mind.

As soon as everyone was seated, Erica put a CD that had the instrumental music to the Clark Sisters song, *You Bought the Sunshine,* in the portable radio that was in the room and started to sing. Jackie was blown away because she didn't know Erica had such a beautiful, powerful voice. She sounded just like the lead vocalist, and Jackie felt like God told Erica to sing that song because it was the only gospel song that Jackie knew all the way through. The first time she heard the gospel song was in a club and she liked it when she thought it was a secular song, but she loved it after she found out it was a song praising Jesus.

Jackie really enjoyed the service and she felt like the Pastor was talking directly to her. His name was Pastor Washington and he preached based on Matthew 6:22, 23 about an inner light that Christians have and she wanted that light. When he finished his sermon, she went up to the alter call and gave her life to Jesus Christ. Jackie heard several alter calls the few times she went to church when she was little and during her previous incarcerations, but none of them tugged at her heart the way Pastor Washington's did. He invited her to visit his church after she got released and to join it if she liked it.

The church service was just what Jackie needed to heal her broken heart and tears of joy flowed down her cheeks as she walked back to her cell with Jane'en. "Jane'en I know we said we wasn't gon talk about each other cases, but I've got to ask what you doing in here? I'm sorry, but you don't seem like the type of person who would commit any crime. You walk around here all day helping people out, holding Bible studies, and every other positive thing a person can do in jail. And girl, why you don't eat?" asked Jackie as they entered their cell.

"You're my roommate and it's like we live together; so I can tell you why I don't eat. It's because I'm fasting, which means I can't eat any solid foods. I can drink a little water, but I try not to. I pray aggressively when I'm fasting and the spirit of God feeds me. When you fast it's a sacrifice and a gift to God, so you can't let other people know that you're fasting. You fast to get blessings in Heaven and to cleanse your soul. If you try to get attention by showing the world you're fasting, God says that you already got your reward while on earth. You're not supposed to act like you're weak from the lack of food, you're supposed to wash your face and act like you normally act. You can tell the person you live with what's going on because they can't help but notice the change in your eating habits. Your roommates are going to ask you what's going on, and you don't have to lie about it."

"Now, about my case. I wasn't always a Christian Jackie, and I did a lot of dirt in my past. I guess you can say that my past caught up with me. I was born in Dayton, but I moved to New York with this guy I was involved with eleven years ago. He had me transporting drugs from New York to Dayton, and we got caught one day. That was my first time being arrested so I was given a bond. I had money on me, but not enough to bond myself out; so I called my family and they paid the rest of it. I left New York and never returned after I got bonded out, so the state of New York issued a warrant for my arrest. I knew they were going to issue a warrant, but I figured I would be all right if I squared up and never went back there. I got me a job, gave my life to Christ, and joined the church that my family has been attending since I was a baby. I guess God was ready for me to clean out my closet because my taillight went out two weeks ago and a police officer pulled me over. When he ran my name the warrant popped up, so he arrested me. I didn't catch another case here so I'm just waiting to see if the state of New York is going to expedite me. I'm not scared, worried, or anything else because I know that I'm going to be all right in Jesus name. Now it's your turn. What are you in here for?" Jane'en asked.

Jackie started to lie but she decided not to since she had just gotten saved. She didn't grow up in church but she did know the Ten Commandments and "thou shall not lie" was definitely one of them. "My ex-boyfriend called his self leaving me for this broad we worked with, so I ran my car into his while he was in it," she said.

"Girl, you're too pretty for that! Do you know how many men would love to have you on their arm? I'm fat and I used to have low self esteem until I let God into my life. I used to let men use me until I learned my worth. But you're beautiful and you got a pretty shape so you ain't got no excuse," Jane'en with a serious look on her face.

Jackie ended up telling her all about her relationship with Marcus, about her brothers killing each other, and how her words had inspired her to forgive Jack Jr. for not going to court. She didn't tell her anything about Leon, her kids, or anything else that could incriminate her; but she felt good talking about the things that she did discuss. The only conversation she had about her brother's killing one another was the one she had with her mother. When Janice accused her of causing their deaths, Jackie never discussed them again. It was easy talking to Jane'en and she felt good discussing her feelings about her brother's deaths, because they had been bottled up inside of her for years.

Marcus and Jack Jr. never wrote Jackie back, and Marcus came to her first court date. He wasn't asked to testify, but his presence spoke volumes. He wouldn't look at Jackie so she felt like he didn't accept her apology. She just knew he was going to testify against her when her trial started. But Jackie wasn't hurt or sad because she had prepared herself for this and her heart was filled with the Holy Ghost. She lost her job, freedom, and dignity because of Marcus and she refused to lose her faith in God because of him too. God healed her broken heart and she wasn't about to allow the same man who broke to break it again.

The day after Jackie went to court Jane'en got expedited to New York City and Erica came to visit her. She was kind of down because Jane'en was leaving, but the visit lifted her spirits. Erica told her that CTJ fired her, but there was another factory called Respect Tool and Die on Heid Avenue that was hiring. She didn't know what happened to Jackie's car but she said that she would call all of the towing companies to see if she could locate it. She put some money on her books, offered to pay her rent for her, and said that she would go to her next court date with her. Jackie was more than happy to accept the offers that Erica made. She still hadn't told anyone in her family besides Jack Jr. that she was in jail because she didn't want to ask them for their support unless she desperately needed it.

She stayed in jail for two more months and Erica continued to visit her every week. She also prayed for her earnestly, paid her rent, came to all of her court dates, and kept money on her books. Marcus didn't attend anymore court dates after the first one so all of the charges against her were dropped, but she had to pay a $2,000 fine. She was thankful that she still had her apartment and for her freedom, but she lost her car and her job. She had a tough road ahead of her; but she knew she would be all right by God's grace. Erica told her whenever a negative thought entered her mind all she had to do was say "no weapon formed against me shall prosper"; and she was saying those words a lot after her release from jail.

She was released on a Friday and Erica took her to Respect Tool and Die Monday. They gave her a drug test and hired her the same day she filled out her application, but she didn't start working until that following Monday. The work she did at Respect was back breaking and a lot harder than the work she did at CTJ, but she was just grateful that she had a job. She didn't mind the dollar cut she had to accept because she was able to have a fresh start without everyone judging her. All she talked about with her new co-workers was God, Jesus, and the Holy Ghost. She acted the way she saw Erica behaving at CTJ, but she was more zealous than her. Jackie was a new Christian and she loved the feeling of Christ being in her life so much that she felt the need to tell everyone she worked with about him, which pushed a lot of them away from her.

Her car was totaled and her insurance company refused to get it fixed due to the circumstances. They didn't even want to pay to get Marcus's car fixed, but they didn't have a choice. She was in jail for over two months and the towing fees were astronomical, so she left her car at the towing company that towed it. She rode the bus to and from work until Martin, a Christian she worked with, offered to take her back and forth for a small fee. The church van picked her up from her apartment in Dunbar Manor and dropped her off to all of the church functions. She missed having a car, but she knew that the Lord was going to bless her with another one when he felt she needed it.

Jackie was truly enjoying life as a Christian, and she only socialized with them. Erica and the Christian group she was in made sure they showed Jackie how much fun Christians could have. Jackie didn't think she would enjoy herself at the events they took her to, but she went with them anyway and had a nice time at them all. They went to plays, carnivals, amusement parks, bowling, skating, the zoo, and lots of other places Jackie had never been in her life. Her mother didn't pay for her kids to go on any field trips when the school sponsored them, and she didn't take them anywhere herself. The only places she went to when she was with Leon were nightclubs, boxing matches, and whore houses. When she got away from him, the only extracurricular activity she had outside of hustling was partying. It took her by surprise by the way she enjoyed living a good, clean, wholesome life and she loved the company she now surrounded herself with. They stayed engaged in intelligent conversations concerning the state of the world. They showed her how the Bible prophesized what was going on and how Jesus was on his way back. They were an intelligent bunch but they also had good senses of humor, and most of them were naturally funny. They knew how to have fun without cussing, going out to nightclubs, drinking, smoking, or doing any type of drugs. She was learning what her purpose in life really was and felt like she inherited a whole new family during her Christian walk. She forgave everyone who did her wrong and let go of every grudge she had. When she got away from Leon, she knew she was still missing something in her life and she finally understood that it was God's presence. He answered all of her prayers and filled her heart, mind, life, and soul with the joy she desperately needed.

She decided that she wasn't going to be the type of Christian who just talked the talk; she wanted to be the kind who walked the walk. She started by throwing away all the liquor she had behind her bar and the bag of heroin she bought before she went to jail. Marcus contacted her three months after she got out and tried to get back with her. He told her that he had to go to the first court date because her insurance company wouldn't have paid to get his car fixed if he wouldn't have gone. He knew the district attorney would drop the charges if he didn't attend any of the other ones, so he didn't. He said that he accepted her apology when he read the letter, but he was too hurt and angry to tell her. He claimed that he loved and missed her and asked if he could come over to make love to her. She was grateful that he accepted her apology and flattered that he wanted be with her again, but she declined his offer. She told him that she was a Christian so she couldn't be with him unless he married her. He let her know that he wasn't ready for marriage, but he could always use a good friend. Jackie spent all of her time with the Christian group she joined, but she called and checked on Marcus at least once a month.

(17)

Scandal!

Jackie rode back and forth to work with Martin for eight months and the arrangement was going fine until he tried to have sex with her on a Friday after work. He didn't come on to her too strong, but his actions confused her and made her feel dirty. They had Bible study that night so she asked her new friends for their advice because she didn't know what to do about the awkward situation. She was in tears because she considered him and his wife good friends and she knew that she wouldn't be able to be around them without telling on Martin. She didn't want to continue to ride with him and she didn't want to start back riding the bus because it got her there an hour early or fifteen minutes late. Respect Tool and Die only gave their employees five attendance points and they deducted a half of one for being tardy. After telling the group about her problem a deacon everyone called Deacon Jenkins offered to give her a 1987 Ford Taurus he said he didn't use. Jackie was uneasy about accepting the car without paying the man for it, so she offered to pay him in installments but he refused her offer. The rest of the group advised her to accept the car and to distance herself from Martin.

Bible study was held that Wednesday and that following Sunday, Jackie stood up and told the church her testimony of God delivering her from jail, prostitution, and drugs. When service was over, one of the sisters who was in the little Christian social group she was in approached her after they got outside. "Jackie, I don't know if you know this, but you don't have to tell the church all of your personal business. People in church gossip just like everybody else. Catholics go to a confessional every week and confess their sins to a Priest who prays to God for them. When Jesus came back he gave Christians the power to pray directly to his father, God. So you see, you can pray to God yourself and He'll listen to you and He'll answer you. I know that you're a true Christian so you'll know his voice when you hear it in your heart and in your mind. I just don't want you getting hurt because you trusted somebody in the church. Christians are just regular people who're trying to be Christ like and we have issues with our flesh everyday just like everyone else," she said as hugged her.

"You know what Justine? I felt too good after testifying about what my Savior has done for me to let what people say stop me from giving my testimony. I know that I can pray for myself because I pray by myself a lot, but I've learned that group prayer is more effective. I lived a rough life but I'm still here by God's grace so I have to give him all the praise and glory he deserves and if other Christians use my testimony as a petty gossip piece, then so be it. They talked about Jesus Christ so who am I?" asked Jackie. She had a lot of skeletons in her closet and it felt good to let some of them out without talking to Toni. She always got good advice from the other Christians and she thought they wouldn't judge her because the Bible spoke against it. She liked Justine, but she didn't like the advice she was trying to give her.

Two weeks later the car that Deacon Jenkins gave her broke down in front of her house. When he gave her the car; he told her that it had been sitting for a long time because he rarely used it. He said he was a mechanic and he would fix it if she needed any work done on it; so she called him when it wouldn't start up. "Hello, can I speak to Deacon Jenkins?" she said into the telephone after dialing his number.

"Well you calling his cell phone," he said with a laugh. "I'm just playing honey, this is Deacon Jenkins, and whom do I have the pleasure of speaking to?" he asked in a phony, sugary voice. He knew that was Jackie's voice on the other end of his phone; and he knew she was calling him because the car he gave her wouldn't start. He's the reason it didn't start because he disconnected a wire up under her hood the night before while she was in the bowling alley with the rest of their Christian social group. He was a forty-five year old, lonely, celibate, widower of five years and he was ready to remarry. He and his wife used to attend the church that Jackie joined and he intended on finding his new wife there. Jackie testified to the whole church about her celibacy and her wishes of getting married several times, and he wanted to be the one she married. She was too beautiful and too sweet to have lived the rough life that she said she lived and he wanted to rescue her. The sooner they got married, the better because he was tired of being celibate and Jackie turned him on every time he was around her. She gave out a lot of church hugs and he felt special whenever she gave him one. He never asked her out on a date, but he was in their Christian social group and felt like the functions they attended together were dates.

"This is Jackie Deacon Jenkins, and I don't mean to bother you but something is wrong with the car. I have to be at work in a couple of hours or I'm gon get an attendance point," she said. Jackie only had two attendance points left and she was willing to take the bus to preserve them if she had to.

"Calm down sweetie, Deacon Jenkins is on his way. If I can't get it going quick enough, I'll just have to drop you off at work. I'll pick you up if I got to drop you off. A woman as pretty as you shouldn't have to work anyway, if you was my wife you wouldn't have to do nothing but take care of me," he said as he silently rebuked the lustful image of him and Jackie out of his mind. There was a long awkward silence until he ended the call. "Well sister I should be there within the next ten or twenty minutes."

"Thank-you Deacon, I'll be looking out for you," said Jackie as she thought, *this gon be the last time I ask him to do anything for me.* Deacon Jenkins looked all right but he was kind of weird and he wasn't Jackie's type. He was 6'3"; real light skinned with freckles and good, curly, sandy brown hair. His eyes were hazel, and his eyebrows were thin and the same color as his hair. He had medium sized teeth and medium sized, pink, lips. He was kind of muscular but he had a pot belly. All of the women in the congregation hated to see him coming because he was always finding ways to accidentally rub up against them and his church hugs were always a little too long.

Five minutes later he was knocking on her door. "Well hello Ms. Jackie. If you'll give me those keys I'll get started fixing old Bessie," he said in a cheery voice when she answered it.

"Here they are. It's eleven o'clock right now and I got to be at work at three, do you think it'll be fixed by then?" Jackie asked as she handed him her keys. She wasn't trying to rush Deacon Jenkins; but she didn't want to get a ride from him in his pick up truck because she would have to sit too close to him and he gave her the creeps.

"I don't know honey, but I'm gon try to get it running as fast as I can for you," he said as he grabbed the keys with a big, goofy grin on his face.

He didn't have plans on being under the hood of the car for long. All he had to do was hook the wire back up and then he had a big surprise for her.

"Oh, you scared me Deacon. You finished already?" asked Jackie in a shaky voice. Deacon Jenkins used her house key to let himself in after he finished fixing her car. She was in the kitchen fixing her lunch for work when she turned around and saw him blocking the doorway between the kitchen and the living room. She had her television on so she didn't hear him come in. She thought he would knock on the door when he was done with the car since she locked it when he went outside. She was very surprised and scared that he was in her house. She never expected him to use her house key to get in; so she didn't feel the need to take it off the key ring when she gave them to him.

"The last thing I want to do was scare you! I'm here to protect you and I'm willing to do it for life. Sister Jackie, will you marry me? I love you and I think you'll be the perfect wife for me," he said as he reached into his pants pocket, took out the two carat diamond engagement ring that he used to propose to his deceased wife; got on one knee, and waited on Jackie's answer. His wife died from cancer at the ripe, young, age of forty-two. He was still paying on her engagement ring and her wedding ring so he kept them to use on his next lucky bride instead of letting them get buried with her.

Jackie felt very awkward because she knew she wouldn't and couldn't marry Deacon Jenkins. They didn't know each other that well and she didn't like what she did know about him. "I'm sorry Deacon Jenkins, but I can't do that. I'm not ready to get married right now," she said trying to let him down easy.

Deacon Jenkins felt crushed and angry. "You can't accept my wedding proposal but you can accept my car and my help. You always asking God to send you somebody, but when he sends me you don't want his gift. Every time I look up, you talking about how you know God gon send you somebody, but when I propose you claim that you ain't ready. Well, I hope you ready to give me some of that pussy, because my wife gave me plenty of hers and that's her car you been riding around in for the last five months," he said as he got up, put the ring back in his pocket, and walked towards Jackie.

She knew she shouldn't have taken that car, but the whole congregation told her to take it. When she tried to give him the couple hundred dollars that she had saved, they told her not to worry about it and to consider it a blessing. Now she was in her own kitchen trying to talk the man who gave her the car out of raping her for it. "Come on now Deacon Jenkins, I know you don't want to waste all of those years of celibacy on raping nobody. You can get that car back if you want it, or I can give you the $300 that I got saved up, but please don't try to rape me in my own house," she pleaded as she started to walk backwards.

"I rather have the pussy. This ain't gon hurt you; you used to sell yo body for money all the time. We ain't got to tell nobody and you never know, you just might like it," he said as he unzipped his pants, pulled his penis out of the hole in his boxers, and walked towards her. "Take them clothes off, it's only gon take a minute," he said as he stroked his long, hard, pink penis.

Jackie blacked out and Toni took over. She turned around, grabbed a big, sharp butcher knife from out of the dish rack, turned back around, and sliced Deacon Jenkins from his shoulder to his elbow with the knife.

"You-you-you-you-cut me," he stuttered. He was in a state of shock and fear took over when he saw Jackie's eyes change from gray to green, saw the menacing look in them, and saw the huge butcher knife she had pointed at him. The pain from the cut and the next words that came out of her mouth heightened the fear he was feeling.

"Motherfucker I know I cut you, you lucky I ain't kill you. Cause that's what's gon happen if you ever try to rape me again. Now grab one of them long dishtowels hanging up and wrap it around yo arm. But first, give me all of my keys including my car keys! I tried to pay you for the car, but you being unreasonable about it and it's already in my name. Sit them on the table and get the fuck out of my house. If I ever see you around here again, I'll kill you! And don't you ever think about calling me again," she said to him as he tried to stop his arm from bleeding. She was only trying to scare him, not kill him. The cut was a warning; he wouldn't be so lucky the next time.

"You can keep that car, I don't want it. I'll stay away from you but I want you to stay away from me too. That's my church, my family owns it, and I been going there my whole life. If I ever see you around there, I'm gon press charges for this. I'll say that you tried to rob me and you know they'll believe me. You a ex-prostituting, convicted felon, and I'm a devout Christian who ain't never been to jail before. You find yo self another church because I'm staying at my home church," he said as he tightened the bloody towel around the long, deep cut, zipped up his pants, and stormed out of her house. He was afraid of her but he was more afraid of anyone in the congregation finding out what happened. This was the closest he came to actually raping one of the female members of the church, but it wasn't the first time he was improper with one of them. It was the fourth time. He was the Pastor's cousin so he received verbal warnings for his past misdeeds. The Pastor told him he was going to ban him from the church the next time he heard of him being inappropriate. He hadn't done anything in two years and most of the members didn't know about the other complaints. The other three females stopped going to the church when the Pastor didn't make Deacon Jenkins leave or give up his post after they told him about his behavior. Jackie was fairly new to the church and she didn't gossip with the church gossipers, so she hadn't heard anything about his past behavior and no one thought to warn her about him. They knew he went a little crazy after he lost his wife; but they thought prayer could cure him better than a psychiatrist could.

Toni was drained and scared after the scuffle and she didn't want to be alone; so she called off of work and called Marcus. He worked first shift and he was still at work; but she heard him tell his boss he had an emergency at home. Then he told her that he was leaving and would be there shortly. While she was waiting for Marcus to come, Jackie tried to come back in the picture until she saw the blood. *"Aw man Toni, what did you do? You didn't kill that man did you? Where is he?"* she asked as she rubbed their hands together.

"Hold on now Jackie, I ain't killed nobody. That disgusting pervert was trying to rape us and I couldn't let him do that. We were powerless when Leon and the police raped us, but we're not anymore. I refuse to let anybody come into our home and takeover the way yo mama and daddy did. When you give somebody control of yo house and yo body, they take complete control of them. I told him not to come back around us and he said he'll call the police on us if we go back to his church. What you cryin' for? We won the fight," Toni replied.

"I felt comfortable at that church and I liked it," said Jackie as she sank to the floor, pulled their knees up to their chest, and rocked back and forth.

"That's the problem, you got too comfortable there. You shouldn't want to go back there after what just happened. Dude said he gon say we tried to rob him and thanks to you telling them all of our business, they'll believe him," Toni said angrily.

"You right, I'm sorry Toni. I can't deal with this right now. Can you please clean up the Deacon's blood?" Jackie asked as she retreated into herself before Toni could answer.

Marcus got there twenty minutes later and when he got there; he helped her clean up the blood Deacon Jenkins had dripped all over her kitchen as he listened to the story. She left out the parts of the story when he referred to them as a prostitute because she was ashamed of that part of their past, even if Jackie wasn't. She just told him that everyone in the church knew that she had been arrested and Deacon Jenkins used that information against her.

After hearing the story, Marcus offered to beat the man up for Jackie, but Toni didn't want to make the situation any worse than it already was so she told him not to. She felt helpless and violated, but she didn't blame God for what happened. She blamed Jackie, because she was the one who told all of those strangers their business. She was happy Marcus didn't go to the church because she had to tell someone what happened; and he was the perfect person to tell because he comforted her. He had some Remy out in the car and he went to get it after they cleaned the kitchen good with Clorox bleach.

Toni didn't know what he was going to get and she was happy when she saw the fifth of Remy Martin in his hand. It was like seeing an old friend. She was grateful that she didn't have the urge to use drugs, but she could use a drink or two. She ended up getting drunk and having sex with Marcus that night. They reconciled and started dating again. Everything was fine for three months, then Erica popped up over Jackie's house to see why she hadn't been to church and busted Marcus out. She told Jackie in his face that he was not worth her sacrificing her salvation over because he was still dating London. Marcus couldn't say anything because it was true. Jackie let Erica believe that Marcus was the reason she wasn't attending church because she was still afraid to tell on Deacon Jenkins. She broke up with Marcus, but remained friends with him because he had been there for her through all the hardships she faced after their first breakup.

(18)

Jackie & Jim

When Jackie got out of jail she put in applications at several car factories, including Premium Motors. PM was the largest car factory in Dayton, Ohio and both of Jackie's previous employers along with most of the other car factories there made parts for it. It was considered one of the best jobs to get without a college degree in Dayton, so Jackie was ecstatic when they called her September 15, 1998 to start the interview process. She was relieved when she passed all the pre-employment tests because all of them were challenging to her. She got her GED in prison, but she had to work extra hard for it. It took her three times to pass the math and reading parts on it so she was frightened when she found out that she had to take similar tests before PM would consider hiring her. She was also terrified of the drug tests they administered, because they tested their future employee's hair for them. Those tests could detect drug use as far back as a year and it had been over a year since she used drugs, but Marcus had smoked weed around her less than a month ago. She'd never been more proud of herself than she was when she got the phone call from the head supervisor, Jim Cartwright, saying she got the job two weeks later. They started her off making twelve dollars an hour which was more than she made working at both of her old jobs. She didn't regret quitting her job at Respect Tool and Die at all. The pay and the benefits at PM were better, the work was easier, and she was didn't have to worry about bumping into Martin anymore. God showed her that he lived once again by answering all of her prayers. She wasn't the perfect Christian she started out trying to be, but she walked away from that terrible experience with Deacon Jenkins still believing in Jesus Christ and the power of prayer.

Jackie didn't plan on making any friends at PM and she knew she could do it since she didn't need anyone. The car Deacon Jenkins gave her still ran good and she put down on a 1998 Lexus when she got her income tax check, so she wasn't going to need a ride from anyone. She went into PM with a no nonsense type of attitude. She read her Bible during all of her breaks or whenever the plant shut down due to technical issues. She didn't engage in any of the conversations the people in her work area had. She didn't laugh at their jokes, and she didn't answer any questions they asked her about her past. She didn't even tell them where she used to work because she made that mistake at Respect and a woman she met knew several people who worked at CTJ with her. The woman heard the whole story about the confrontation she had with Marcus. As soon as Jackie said her name and that she used to work at CTJ the woman told her that she was the infamous woman who caused so much ruckus at the other factory. Jackie wanted to lie and cuss the woman out but she didn't because she was trying to be a Christian. She preferred being antisocial to her new co-workers than making the same mistakes. Whenever someone flirted with her, she ignored their advances. The pain and humiliation she went through with Marcus taught her to never have a relationship in the workplace. She made it clear to anyone who tried to go fishing in her business that she was there to make money, nothing more and nothing less. She wasn't trying to find a man or a friend because she had enough people in her inner circle. She still talked to her sisters and she had sex with Marcus whenever she got horny. She started back drinking and fornicating, but she still had a close relationship with Jesus Christ so all of her needs were met.

Jackie had been working at PM for over a year when she got paged to the office at the end of her shift. It was December 22, 1999, the day before they went on their annual two week shut down. She knew that whatever they were calling her for was bad, but she thought she was alright. She still had seven out of her nine attendance points if they were checking them. She hadn't done any drugs since she got out of the county jail in Dayton, if they were doing random drug tests. She was also a good employee who made her quota everyday. After assessing the situation, she walked to the office proudly with her head held high. When she walked in, the first thing she noticed was that the union representative wasn't present. The only person who was in the office was Jim Cartwright. Jackie was the only person in their work area who didn't suck up to Jim whenever he came in their work area. She didn't like him because he seemed to like the ignorant sexual jokes and the factory gossip the other employees discussed. He was supposed to carry himself like he was in a position of leadership and Jackie felt like he didn't. She didn't know what he wanted with her, but she didn't like being around him by herself. Her confidence began to fade as the strange feeling she used to feel when something was wrong crept into her stomach.

"You can close the door and have a seat Ms. Wright. I hate to do this right before the holidays, but I don't have a choice. We're going to have to let you go, it seems there were some discrepancies on your application. You lied and said you hadn't committed any felonies in the past seven years, but you have a criminal record thick as a book with numerous solicitation charges on it," said Jim as he placed a copy of Jackie's police record from Chicago on the desk in front of her.

"Mr. Cartwright, I know y'all ain't gon fire me right before Christmas! I got bills and rent to pay! Please have some kind of mercy on me; I can't break my lease because I just moved into my apartment! I thought they were asking if I had any cases in Ohio, all of that stuff happened in Chicago, Ill.," said Jackie playing dumb with tears in her eyes. She lied on every application she filled out after CTJ hired her because she thought the jobs in Ohio only checked to make sure there applicants had never committed any felonies in Ohio.

"Jacqueline, maybe we can work something out. I'd hate to see anyone out in the cold, applying for food stamps at the Job Center," said Jim smiling, as he rubbed his penis, and stared at her breasts with lust in his eyes. He was obsessed with her and he tried to approach her several times, but she intimidated him. Her eyebrows and eyes made her look real mean, and every time he went into her work area she was quietly reading the Bible or doing her job. In the winter she wore steel-toe boots, and men's beige Carhartt snowsuits to work. In the summer she wore khaki shorts and plain white t-shirts. Most of the women Jim hired liked attention and tried to look cute coming to work in their cute clothes. Jackie tried to go unnoticed, but she couldn't because her beauty and her presence were too strong.

Jim didn't want to fire Jackie he wanted to have sex with her. That's why he didn't have a union representative in the office. He was willing to pay her for her time but he didn't know how to proposition her. He came up with the plan to threaten her job when she put in a change of address form a week before he called her to his office. He used to date a stripper who lived in Dunbar Manor so he knew she was moving out of the projects into a regular apartment; which meant her rent was going to go up so she was going to need her job. He didn't think she was stupid; he just thought she would be vulnerable with rent and the holidays hanging over her head. But he didn't know Jackie, she wasn't going.

The smile that usually lit up the room; looked menacing; the eye brows that looked so pretty arched; now connected as they crawled up her forehead with their high arch, and her eyes looked more Chinese than the people's eyes in Chinatown looked, as they changed from gray to green, then back gray. Jackie had five dimples in all, two on each cheek and one in her forehead. When she smiled a genuine, happy smile two deep, cute ones popped out of her cheeks. When she was angry and squinting all of them came out, and all of them were out as she mean mugged Jim. He looked at her with fear in his eyes as her face transformed right before his eyes. She looked him in his eyes, with hatred in hers. "Motherfucker I know you ain't just asked me to fuck you to keep this back breaking, death trap y'all call a motherfucking job! You must think I'm stupid or something! As a matter of fact; where the fuck is my union rep? The only thing I'm gon do is forget all that bullshit you just said and decide if I'm gon sue you motherfuckers for sexual harassment," she yelled. She hadn't cussed or let Toni back since the incident between her and Deacon Jenkins and she was very angry that Jim bought the foul language and her alter ego out.

Jackie saw the fear in his eyes as she jumped up out of her chair and started walking towards him. "You must not have read my criminal record all the way! You don't know who you fucking with! Fuck what I got convicted of, look at the charges they couldn't make stick! Most of them assault and batteries were committed on tricks just like yo bitch made ass," she said with a look of disgust in her eyes. Jim was not her type at all because he was too old, fat, and short. He stood 5'3" and Jackie was 5'7". She couldn't begin to guess the color his hair used to be because his whole head was silver. She knew he was over sixty because she heard the people in her area say that he could have retired two years ago. He wasn't obese like Leon, but he was about twenty pounds overweight. He had beautiful, clear, blue eyes, but his big, black framed, dorky glasses covered them. He was very pale, his lips were thin, and his nose was long and pointed. Whenever he got angry, he got red and he perspired profusely so the thought of him on top of her was very disturbing.

Jim flinched when she made it to him because he thought she was going to hit him. He wasn't prepared for her anger at all. She was supposed to be happy that he was offering her a chance to keep her job. She was making thirteen dollars an hour with good benefits. When she first started working at PM she was living in the projects so he thought she would be very appreciative towards him. Her reaction was the total opposite of what he was hoping for. Why couldn't she see that he was trying to be her night in shining armor? Instead of her on her knees, sucking his dick like he envisioned her doing for the past year, she was threatening his job! She was even threatening his life! He saw all of the things she had been arrested for, but he thought Jacqueline Wright was far too beautiful to commit the violent crimes she had been accused of committing. He quickly realized how wrong he was. Jackie was a very dangerous and intelligent woman and all of a sudden, his plan didn't seem like such a good idea. This wasn't the first time he tried to trick a black female employee into his bed; it was just the first time it didn't work. Jim loved black women, but he hated the fact that he loved them. He was born in the south and was raised to be a male chauvinist and a bigot.

"Ms. Wright, I apologize if I offended you, I was just trying to help you out," he said raising his hands to shield his face.

Jackie had to stop herself from laughing out loud at Jim. *Look at his bitch ass, he lucky these motherfuckers got all of my information. This ain't the streets, they got my real name, social security number, and they know my address,* she thought as she calmed herself down.

"Look, I can accept you trying to fuck me. Hell I ain't met a man who didn't try to hit this in years, but I ain't with nobody playing with my intelligence. This job is feeding me but I'm gon eat with or without it. There's a procedure that y'all have to follow before y'all can fire me and it starts with a union representative being present. I'll cry rape if you try to call one in here now and they won't have a choice but to investigate what I'm saying because you didn't follow the proper procedure in the beginning. So, we both know you're not about to fire me. It'll be best if we both forget this shit ever happened. PM don't want no scandal on them, and I don't want to lose my job trying to prove what you just said in court. If you don't tell anyone about my record, I won't tell anyone about this conversation. Now if you don't mind, I'm about to go home and let

203

Calgon take me away," she said as she extended her hand out for Jim to shake.

That was the moment Jim fell in love with Jackie. She had just cussed him out, and threatened his job, but she was right. He felt ashamed of the stunt he tried to pull. He was glad that she had respect for herself because it made him respect her. She earned his respect and he had never respected any woman before the conversation he had with Jackie. She didn't even try to blackmail him. She was very different from any woman he'd ever met. He needed to be put in his place and he liked the way Jackie did it. No one had ever talked to him like that before and he liked it for some strange reason.

Jim breathed a sigh of relief as he stood up and shook her extended hand. "Jacqueline, I am truly sorry for not treating you like the queen that you are. I don't know what came over me. You're the most beautiful woman I've ever met in my life and I haven't been in my right state of mind since I first laid eyes on you. I hope we can still be friends. As a matter of fact, I'd like to give you a little something for Christmas," he said as he pulled fifteen one hundred dollar bills out of his wallet and gave them to her. He was very relieved when she took the money because he felt like he was paying her to keep their meeting a secret. If Jackie told anyone what Jim tried to do, the human resource department would have a field day investigating his misdeeds. He wasn't supposed to have hired a lot of the women he hired over the past ten years, and he was ripping off a lot of the employees who worked for PM by stealing out of their 401 K benefits. Jackie's acquisition would open up a Pandora's Box for him, and the Union would fight hard to defend her. The whole company would be investigated because of him and he would lose his job, his money, and he'd be facing jail time. The $1,500 he gave Jackie was well worth her silence. He would have given her more but he had to meet his wife at the mall to go Christmas shopping right after work and didn't have time to go home to get any more money. The only money he kept in the bank was the money he made honestly and he only paid rent and bills with it. He let the rest of it accumulate interest and spent the money he stole on vacations, gifts, jewelry, and anything else he wanted. He kept that money hidden in his house because he planned on lying about the amount he stole over the years if he ever got caught.

Jackie put the money Jim gave her in her pocket. When she saw that it barely put a dent in his wallet, the wheels in her mind started to turn.

Damn he carry all of that money around on him? she thought. "Thank you Mr. Cartwright, I mean Jim. From now on I'm going to call you Jim and I'd like for you to call me Jackie. You just don't know how much I needed this. I couldn't even buy me none of the items they said I might need for Y2K. Why you looking at me like that? I'd rather be safe than sorry! You know what? I want to take you out to dinner tonight. We can go anywhere you want to go," said Jackie with her hands on her hips and the prettiest smile that Jim had ever seen on her face.

"Damn Jackie, I can't make it tonight but if you're free around eight o'clock tomorrow night then it's a date," said Jim eagerly thinking that being friends with Jackie couldn't be anything but beneficial. He didn't know if she was a friend or foe but he believed in that old saying, "keep your friends close and your enemies closer."

"Tomorrow will be perfect Jim, just give me a call when you're ready or if you can't make it," said Jackie as she handed him the small piece of paper that she had written her telephone number on.

"Oh, I can definitely make it tomorrow night," said Jim smiling brightly, as he looked at his watch. *Today is the best day of my life,* he thought as he watched Jackie switch out of his office. He realized that the gig was up and it was time for him to stop all of his scheming before he lost everything he'd worked so hard to accumulate. He'd never been arrested for anything, and he realized just how close he came to losing his freedom. He felt like the incident with Jackie was a warning from God telling him to fly straight, and to quit ruining people's lives by taking their jobs and their money when they needed them the most. It didn't feel good when the shoe was on the other foot.

The next day Jim took Jackie out to dinner. While they were eating he told her that she really failed her math and reading tests, but he was the only one who knew. He thought she would be appreciative towards him, but that information made her despise him. She was very book smart before Leon took her, so she never doubted her success at passing the tests and knowing that she really failed them hurt her very much. She didn't show Jim her pain, but she felt it very deep and she instantly wanted revenge. She decided to trick him out of as much money as she could since he thought she was just a dumb prostitute. She let the greedy, vindictive prostitute inside of her come out and started lightly flirting with him. As she sat there rubbing his hand and laughing at his corny jokes, the thought of robbing him came to her mind. She banished that thought because she didn't want his blood on her hands if anything went wrong. She still had dreams about Leon and China every now and then, and she didn't want to add another body to her recurring nightmares.

By the end of the night she talked him out of $5,000 for new furniture and by the end of their two week vacation she had talked him into paying off the car note on her Lexus. When they got back to work, she treated him the same way she treated him before they went on vacation and he was furious. The day before they came back she told him that she wanted to keep their friendship a secret, but he wasn't prepared for the cold treatment she displayed towards him. They were the only two people in the cafeteria at one point during the day and she wouldn't even talk to him then. He tried to speak to her and she looked right through him like he didn't exist. That move snapped him out of the love trance she had him in for the past two weeks and left him feeling used and stupid for letting a two dollar whore play him out of more than $22,000. All he got out of her were a few sexy dances in exotic costumes. He was very angry at himself because he'd never allowed anyone to do him like that, and the fact that Jackie was a black woman infuriated him. He walked around barking at all the employees and everyone except Jackie walked around on eggshells until the end of the shift. She got a kick out of watching everyone else scramble around trying to reach the ridiculous quota he gave them for the day, as they tried to figure out why his mood changed so dramatically from that morning to that afternoon.

Jackie was a master manipulator, so it was easy for her to hook Jim again. He planned on accepting his losses and leaving her alone, but he flew over her house with his tail between his legs when she called and told him to come over. She didn't want to talk to him at work and she convinced him that this was for his protection since he was the one who was married. He would've accepted any explanation she gave him to heal his wounded ego. He didn't realize that his anger came from thinking she was through with him and not from her ignoring him until he felt so happy after she called. There was something about her that he couldn't leave alone, and she wasn't about to let him go either. He was the biggest fish she ever caught so she wanted him forever. He was the kind of trick she used to dream of catching while she was on the streets hooking. She had to train him right away if she was going to be able to keep him, and the first thing he needed to learn was that she was the boss when it came to their relationship. She told him not to try to communicate with her at work and that's what she meant. She knew that being as rude as she was towards him would hurt his feelings, but she didn't care because his feelings meant nothing to her.

Jim let Jackie string him along for seven more months without allowing him to touch her. He gave her thousands of dollars to let him jag off while watching her dance seductively. When she finally gave in he thought she did it because he put his foot down, but the real reason was because she decided to have a baby by him. She came up with the plan when he showed her his beautiful baby pictures. He was so pretty that he looked like a girl. He had pictures of himself throughout the different stages in his life and he was very handsome on the ones that were taken before he started to age. Jackie thought they would make a beautiful baby that she could love. Her first two girls came out looking like her rapist so she couldn't love them because their faces were a constant reminder of his. She made Jim meet her at the board of health so they could get tested for HIV and every other STD that existed. He was irritated by her request because he used condoms with everyone including his wife and he told her so. Jackie didn't tell him the real reason she wanted him tested because she felt like it was none of his business. The baby would be hers and hers alone, she wasn't even going to let him help her raise it. If his sperm came back clean, she was going to have sex with him with a condom on. After he left, she was going to use a turkey baster to suck his sperm out of the condom, and then she was going to squeeze it inside of her. She saw a story on the internet where a woman impregnated herself with the sperm of a famous athlete like that. She thought about poking a hole in the condom but it seemed like the sperm would make it to her egg quicker with the turkey baster. The thought of asking him to get her pregnant never crossed her mind because that would have given him the choice of saying no, and that was not an option as far as she was concerned. .

It was going to take two weeks for their HIV test results to come back and Jackie was a nervous wreck while she waited on hers. She prayed that she didn't have the deadly virus everyday that she had to wait; but this was her first HIV test and the fear of getting a positive diagnosis engulfed her. She tried to prepare herself for the worst and ended up convincing herself that she had it. Jim was positive that he didn't have it and that infuriated Jackie. She hated to see him acting like he had nothing to worry about while she thought she had one foot in the grave. She was considered high risk because she used to shoot up, she was an ex-prostitute, and she had been in prison before. She thought it was unfair that Jim wasn't worried because he was twice her age and he had sex with prostitutes for over thirty years. She decided that she was going to poke a hole in her condom and have sex with him if her test came back positive and his came back negative. She hated tricks and he represented them all because he was the one who reminded her of her days as a prostitute and the consequences that came from being one.

Both of their tests came back negative and Jackie was pregnant a month later. She hated having sex with Jim because his penis was small, he sweated a lot, and he smelled like a wet dog when he perspired. But she made him feel like he was the best lover she ever had. She wanted that baby more than anything she had ever wanted in her life. It was going to bring her unconditional love and lots of money. It was going to be her insurance that she would be taken care of for the rest of her life. Jim was a very wealthy man on paper and he was foolish enough to tell Jackie about all of his money. He was a salaried employee who made $60,000 a year and he invested wisely in the stock market. He also owned lots of real estate all over the United States that he made a lot of money from. Jackie wanted to make sure she got her part rather he was dead or alive and the birth of their child was going to insure that she did without having to marry him. She thought about making him leave his wife for her, but she didn't know if he would make her sign a prenuptial agreement and she didn't like his company. She hated being around him because he tried to act like they were in a real relationship.

Jackie didn't tell Jim that she was pregnant until she was four months and too far along for a safe abortion. She thought he was going to be mad but he was extremely happy. He had four kids by his wife and all of them were over thirty with kids of there own. They all lived in different states so he rarely got a chance to see them. He lived in a very exclusive part of Kettering, Ohio and he bought Jackie a condo in his neighborhood the same day he found out she was pregnant. He hadn't been intimate with his wife in years so he offered to leave her for Jackie, but Jackie didn't let him. She only dealt with him on her terms and he didn't know it; but he would always be considered business to her. He didn't know anything about her past or what she did when she wasn't with him, and she kept it that way. He was the only person she was seeing, but she didn't let him know that. He wanted to ask her for a paternity test, but decided to wait until she had the baby.

Jackie got her number changed and quit seeing Marcus as soon as she started sleeping with Jim. He tried popping up at her apartment a few times, but she kept acting like she wasn't there whenever he showed up so he stopped. She didn't care about hurting him because he hurt her in the past. He didn't give her a warning when he decided to sleep with the woman they both worked with, so she didn't feel the need to tell him about the plans she had in store for Jim. He left London years ago and was ready to be with Jackie and Jackie alone, but she no longer wanted him like that. She didn't trust him with her heart anymore so she didn't let him back in it. She learned how to separate her emotions from her vagina when she was a prostitute, and she did that every time she had sex with him after he caused her so much pain. She used him for the pleasure she got from sex like so many men had used her. She didn't tell him anything about her personal life when she wasn't with him so he didn't even know that Jim existed.

Jackie loved how she looked and felt during her pregnancy. Her stomach, breasts, and butt got big; but she didn't mind her body making room for the life that was growing inside of her. Her body stayed filled with love and appreciation for the blessing God blessed her with. She loved her unborn child so much that she read and sang to it daily. She took very good care of herself during her pregnancy. She stopped drinking, started eating right, exercised, took her prenatal vitamins and went to all of her doctor's appointments and Lamaze classes. She was the only woman in her Lamaze class who came by herself, but she didn't care because that was the way she wanted it. She scheduled everything pertaining to their baby during the shift they worked so Jim couldn't come with her.

He invented a job for her to do in the office making seventeen dollars an hour and she turned it into what appeared to be a part time job. She came in at eight and left at noon, but she made him clock her in at five in the morning and out at five in the evening. Those were the hours she was getting before he changed her position without her consent so she made him give them to her. He thought she would be happy that he invented the position for her but she hated it. She still ignored him at work but he didn't care because the cubicle he gave her was right across from his, and he used to invent jobs for her to do so she would have to talk to him. She said as little to him as possible but he didn't care because he got to stare at her for long periods of time. That worked for a couple of days until she told him the new rules for the new job. He got very angry and told her no, but she threatened to expose him to the police, his colleagues, and his wife. He had no choice but to give in to her demands. He'd rather get caught stealing a few hours for her than create a disaster that would crash his entire world. He hated when she pulled power plays but she didn't care. She didn't want him thinking he had control over any aspect of her life; so she punished him every time he made a decision that affected her without consulting her first. She let him come to her condo once a week so she could update him on their child's progress and she enjoyed the pain she saw on his face whenever she described a doctor's visit to him. They didn't have the technology to hear the baby's heartbeat when Jim's wife was having kids, and not being able to enjoy that experience hurt him very deeply. Jackie showed him the ultrasound picture, but she didn't give him one. She claimed that she didn't want his wife to find it, but she just didn't want him to have one.

He hated her and loved her at the same time. While she was pregnant she was the most beautiful woman on earth in his eyes. She let her perm grow out and her long, fine, curly, red hair grew down her back past her butt. She wore maternity clothes that complimented her pregnant figure and her complexion got very light. She was happier than he had ever seen her, but she always managed to be very mean to him. The only time they had sex was when she wanted to, and those times were far and few. He tried hard to please her but she always found fault in everything he did. She was horrible towards him and he took it out on everyone but her. She was mean to him before she got pregnant, but she was downright cruel during her pregnancy. He couldn't wait until she had the baby because he was going to fire her and leave her if it wasn't his. If it was his, he was going to be in his child's life rather she liked it or not. He was prepared to fight her in court if he had to, but he was praying for her to let him be involved without putting up a fight. He hoped she would be nicer after the delivery was over and her hormones were back to normal because deep down in his heart he wanted to be with her.

Jim was used to dealing with strong, aggressive, black women when they were angry, but Jackie's anger was psychotic and weird. He was happy that none of their co-workers thought he was the father of her child because they all gossiped about how crazy she was behind her back. She openly talked to their unborn child like he was right there, but never talked to anyone else unless the conversation pertained to the job. He saw her look through people while rudely ignoring their questions several times. Everyone knew not to touch her stomach because she got into it with a woman who worked there over that. Everyone who saw the argument said she was arguing with the woman and an invisible woman named "Toni", while her eyes rapidly changed colors. He knew they were telling the truth because he saw her eyes change colors like that before and he met Toni. He was ashamed of the feelings he had for Jackie, but they were real and they were strong. He wanted to get her some help, but he was afraid to tell Jackie that she needed help because Toni threatened to kill him if he told Jackie that he knew about her. He took the threat serious because she pulled a razorblade out of her mouth and put it to his penis when she said it.

Jackie gave birth to Bill Cartwright Saturday July 21, 2001, and it was the happiest day of her life. She drove herself to the hospital at two o'clock in the morning and had him at nine. She didn't want to share that moment with anyone, so she didn't call Jim until the day after she had their son. She was happy she didn't because she formed a very special bond with him that day. It started while the doctor was cutting the umbilical cord and Bill looked up into his eyes. She felt a very deep love that was different from any kind of love she had ever felt before. She loved her parents dearly, but it was nothing compared to the love she felt for her son. He melted her frozen heart with his big, blue, Chinese shaped eyes. After cleaning him up, the nurse swaddled him in a blanket and placed him in her arms. Jackie felt her body fill with a ton of good emotions and she couldn't stop smiling as she cried and looked into his face. She was extremely happy because he looked just like her. The only features he had of Jim's were the color of his eyes, and his straight blond hair. He was very light but his ears were only a shade lighter than her complexion, so she knew he was going to get darker and that pleased her. She didn't want her son trying to pass like her grandfather did. She wanted him to be a strong, black man who was proud of his self.

She held him as long as she could before the epidermal she was given; and the exhaustion from giving birth kicked in. She was in labor for thirty-seven hours but she didn't go to the hospital until she couldn't take the pain anymore. Giving birth to her son was much easier than giving birth to her daughters. The midwife who delivered her girls acted like she enjoyed seeing Jackie in pain, the nurses and doctors who delivered her son did everything in their power to make her son's delivery pain free. She got three stitches, but she didn't feel anything. They pampered her while she was in there and that treatment felt much better than the cruel treatment Bertha gave her.

Jim was beyond angry when he found Jackie called him after their child was born. She promised to let him in the delivery room to witness their child being born throughout her pregnancy. He was tired of all the lies she told and the games she played. He was getting ready to go to church with his wife when she called his cellphone and told him that she had the baby. He told his wife that there was an emergency at the plant and rushed to Miami Valley Hospital to see his child. He had every intention on cussing Jackie out and breaking up with her for good, but when he walked into her hospital room and saw her holding their beautiful child he got so happy that he forgot all about his ill intentions. When she handed him their child she filled his heart with pride by telling him that she named him Bill Cartwright after his great-grandfather, like he asked her to do. He wanted to cry several times throughout the two hour visit, but he restrained his self because he didn't want Jackie to think he was weak. Their child's nursery was filled with everything he could possibly need or want, but Jim still went shopping after the visit. He called a florist and surprised Jackie by having flowers, stuffed animals, and balloons delivered all day long. Jim was the only person besides Pam who visited her over the next three days, but she got several phone calls from her family members in Chicago and that was more than enough for her.

(19)

A New Outlook on Life

Jim wanted to get Jackie a nanny, but she didn't want one. She wanted to raise her child on her own, without anyone's help. She couldn't believe the woman she had become. When her girls were newborns Bertha took good care of them throughout the day while she was woke. When they cried in the middle of the night, it was Jackie's job to get up to get them and she hated it, but she did it well. Bertha beat her until she cried both times she let Rhonda wake her up out of her sleep, and Jackie made sure it didn't happen again. She hated getting up with her girls, but she loved getting up with Bill. She made up songs with his name in it and she sang them to him while attending to his needs. She was so stressed out after giving birth the first two times, that her breasts wouldn't produce any milk to feed either one of her girls. They stayed full after she had Bill and she loved breastfeeding him. She felt them get closer and closer every time she felt his tiny lips on her breast. When she was a little girl she wanted kids so she could raise them the way she wished she would've been raised. She had to grow up before her time way before Leon came along, and she always promised not to do her kids the way she had been done as a child. She knew how to care for infants because she had to help her mother take care of her younger siblings from the time she could walk. Technology made the job much easier. Her mother used cloth diapers and glass bottles with her little brothers and sisters and cleaning them was no easy task, but her mother made her do it. She used to wish that her older siblings would have helped her help their mother with their youngest siblings, but they didn't. She was glad when Leon started helping out with their kids, but she didn't allow Jim or anyone else to help her do anything when it came to Bill.

Jackie didn't go back to work until Bill turned four, and she enjoyed those four years more than all the other good moments she had in her life combined. She loved raising her baby and she nurtured him with every ounce of love she had in her body. He softened her heart so much that she helped her youngest daughter, Melissa, move to Ohio. Melissa got her telephone number from information and called her a year after Bill was born. The phone call lasted for eight hours and Jackie was in tears asking Melissa to move to Ohio by the end of it. When Melissa said she was Jackie's daughter, Jackie instantly put up a guard but her curiosity kept her on the phone. She started off by saying that she harbored no ill feelings towards Jackie; she just wanted to get to know her, and her side of the family. She'd recently started going to Dawson Technical College with one of Jackie's nieces and found out that she'd went to high school for four years with a lot of family members, and didn't know it. She went to Phillips on the Southside of Chicago because she didn't want to go to school with Rhonda or any other members on her father's side. They hated her because she started looking like a dark skinned version of Jackie as she got older. Bertha and Rhonda mentally and physically abused her throughout her life, but she was still determined to make something out of herself. She was going to school to get a certified nurses degree. She worked at the same Subway since she was sixteen and made it out of her teenage years without having any kids, doing any drugs, or joining any gangs. She moved into her own apartment when she graduated out of high school, so she was also independent.

Jackie never thought she could be proud of either one of her girls, but she was very proud of Melissa. She defeated the odds that were stacked against every poor, black child growing up in the projects and ghettoes in the inner cities of America. She felt a tremendous amount of guilt after talking to her because she hadn't thought about her since she left her with Bertha. She didn't even ask Rhonda how she was doing when she came to Ohio. She wanted to make it up to her by helping her reach all of her goals. She tried to convince her to drop everything and move to Ohio, but Melissa waited until her semester was over. Jackie was happy that she did wait in the end because it gave her time to get everything together. She found her a nice two bedroom apartment around the corner from Pam's house that she paid a year's worth of rent on. Melissa told her that she didn't have much furniture in her apartment in Chicago, so Jackie surprised her by furnishing her whole apartment by the time she moved in. Pam helper her decorate and it was so beautiful that Melissa cried when she saw it. She also threw her a surprise house warming party that following weekend so she could meet all of her relatives. She felt so good that she even sent Rhonda an invitation. Jackie's mother Janice and all of her kids and grandkids came and they had a real nice time. During the party, Jackie surprised Melissa with a 1997 Ford Explorer. It wasn't brand new, but it was new to her and she was beyond happy. Rhonda got so jealous when Jackie presented Melissa with the truck that she put Leona in it and demanded that Melissa take her home. Melissa didn't want any trouble so she did what Rhonda told her to do and she never came back. Jackie rented out a hall for the event so everyone else stayed until it was over. Jackie was the only one who noticed that Melissa never returned.

Jackie wasn't just being nice when she got Melissa her own apartment; she was also doing it to protect her privacy. She didn't want her crossing paths with Jim outside of work. She got him to get her a job a week before she moved there so she could have her first paycheck by the time she moved in. Jim didn't mind doing it because she was going to actually be working there, unlike Jackie. He knew how to make ghost employees, but he didn't like doing it because it was an easy way of getting caught. He wasn't used to women staying home longer than six weeks after giving birth, and Jackie had already stretched hers out to for a year when she made him put her "cousin" on the payroll. He was furious, but he did it. She was being nicer to him than she had ever been to him since giving birth to their son and he didn't want to make her crazy and angry again.

She let him come over to spend time with Bill every Saturday, and watching how good she took care of him made him want to give her the world. His wife was a career woman who went back to work as soon as she could and let the nannies raise their children. She was jealous of the attention Jim showed them and was kind of cold hearted towards them. Jackie was the complete opposite. She enjoyed raising their child and she liked to see the love Jim had for him. He didn't like changing diapers, feeding babies, or trying to figure out why they were crying, but Jackie did all of those things with a smile on her face and love in her heart. He even loved the little songs she made up for him and the way she called him Billy the Kid. He'd never seen a woman as patient with a screaming baby as Jackie was and he was always amazed at how she knew what each cry meant because they all sounded the same to him. While he was there she cooked delicious meals for him and she kept her house immaculate, so he fantasized of them being a real couple every Saturday. Jackie hadn't had sex with him since she got pregnant and she stopped dancing for him after Billy was born, but he was just happy to be included in their lives. She also proved to be a very smart business woman and she helped make the income he generated outside of PM double within a year. He gave her a weekly allowance that was way more than any child support she could have gotten from the courts, kept her on PM's payroll until she was ready to come back to work, and gave her anything she asked him for, so Jackie was happy too.

After hiring Melissa, Jim made Jackie promise to come back to work after Billy was old enough to go to school. He thought she would cave in and go sooner, but she didn't start back working until the day their son started pre-school. She didn't tell Melissa who Jim was, and she told him not to talk to her while they were at work. He did what Jackie told him to do and didn't say one word to her while she worked there. Jackie told Jim to put her back out on the floor so the people who worked there before she went on maternity leave wouldn't get jealous. He put her in the station Melissa worked in and she had to stop herself from getting angry when she walked in it and saw Melissa kissing a black man. She told her not to get into any relationships at work and not to socialize with anyone in there, but Melissa did both. It seemed like everyone who worked there knew her and she enjoyed the spotlight. Jackie didn't tell her she was going to start back working there, so Melissa didn't feel the need to tell her what she did at work. Jackie bought it to her at lunch and she told her that she needed people in her life besides Jackie and Rhonda and Jackie agreed. Over the past three years, she saw how terrible Rhonda treated her, and she didn't know how to entertain her so she did need a social life. She was young and she had her whole life ahead of her, so Jackie let her be.

She thought they were getting along good and she started loving Melissa almost as much as she loved Bill. She grew up to be a beautiful witty young lady with a good sense of humor and Jackie loved getting to know her. She went to Wright State University while working at PM and Jackie loved the huge amount of energy she had. She didn't converse with her while they were at work, but after work she constantly praised her. She also compared her successes to Rhonda's failures and Melissa secretly hated her for that. Rhonda mistreated her all her life but she felt like

Jackie didn't have the right to speak on it because she could have stopped her if she would have been there. She had a bond with Rhonda that no one could break and she resented Jackie for trying to. She wanted her to stop Rhonda from coming over her house, but Melissa refused to. She preferred Rhonda and her niece Leona's company over Jackie and Billy's any day. She despised Jackie for the way she raised him. They grew up in poverty barely making it from one day to the next, and Jackie was raising her bastard son like he was a king. She hated being around them hearing the stupid songs she invented for him and seeing the love she had for him. She consoled her self by thinking his father wanted nothing to do with them. She hadn't seen him since she'd been there and the one time she was alone with Bill, she asked him who his father was and he just looked at her like she was talking to the air. He was very smart, handsome, and polite, but he was weird like Jackie and Melissa felt strange around them. She started going to school when Jackie started back working there because she hated working with her. She was making fourteen dollars an hour and she got good benefits at PM, so she wasn't going to let Jackie's weird behavior force her to quit before she was able to get a better job. The only way she was going to be able to do that was if she became a registered nurse like she was going to school to become. She was happy that she came to Ohio because she met and loved Pam, she lived closer to Leona and Rhonda, and her goals became larger and more obtainable. She also had a good social life and a man who satisfied her.

(20)

Trouble in Chicago

Jackie was truly enjoying her new life until her sister, Sharon, called August 25, 2006 to tell her that their niece Samantha's six year old daughter, Ralonda, had been shot and killed. The pain she felt after hearing the terrible news was deep and she couldn't move for a minute. Confusion and anger started to seep in and she started questioning God, but she came to her senses and stopped. "Lean not to your own understanding" was one of her favorite quotes in the Bible and she used it to calm down. She knew that she couldn't help the situation if she wasn't in her right state of mind so she cleared her mind and started packing Bill and her some clothes. After she stopped herself from crying she called her sister, Angel, to try to ease some of the pain she was feeling from losing her grandbaby. Angel was inconsolable because she was at the gang picnic with her daughter and her grandkids when the men did the drive-by. She saw the bullet pierce her grandbaby's chest, heard the last words she spoke, and saw her soul leave her body. Jackie didn't know any words that could console her sister so she just cried with her. The pain that Angel felt transferred into Jackie's body as she described the horrible scene in full detail. She was going to wait until the morning to go to Chicago, but Angel said she needed her now so Jackie decided to leave that night.

It was after ten o'clock at night, and Jackie didn't think twice about waking Jim up out of his marital bed to tell him she was taking their son to Chicago. He snuck in his home office to take the call and tried to forbid her from taking Bill with her. As she cussed him out for being racist and insensitive, he stormed out the house in his housecoat and pajamas to try to catch them. They were gone by the time he made it to Jackie's condo and he regretted Jackie being the mother of his child for the first time since Bill was born. He knew she was from the streets, but he never thought about that affecting the safety of their child until it happened. He didn't mean it as a racial slur when he told Jackie that he didn't want his child in that environment around those kinds of people, he was just trying to protect his son. He loved Bill more than life itself and the thought of him being robbed of the chance to see him grow up put a fear in him that was more intense than the fear he felt when he fought in the Korean War. He sunk to his knees in front of Jackie's door and sat there for hours crying. He felt that fear the entire week she was gone, because she didn't call him or accept any of his calls while she was in Chicago.

After hanging up with Jim, Jackie called Pam and Melissa to tell them the bad news and to see if they wanted to ride to Chicago with her and Bill. Melissa sent her condolences but said she couldn't leave out that night. The news hit Pam very hard so she wanted to go. She started going to the family reunions in Chicago with Jackie after meeting all of her great-grandchildren and seeing her daughter Janice, sober at Melissa's house warming party. After Jackie described which grandchild she lost, Pam felt extremely sad. Lil Ralonda always found her at the family events to check on her and to tell her she loved her. She was so pretty with her big, brown eyes, and her long black hair. Pam was happy that the Lord sent Jackie to Dayton, Ohio because she wouldn't have gotten the chance to meet Ralonda if she wouldn't have. She was eighty-seven years old and she thanked God for longevity, but she would have died to let her beautiful grandbaby live. She was glad that she kept a suitcase packed because she didn't have the energy to pack one. She felt her age for the first time in years, but she mustered up enough strength to lock up her house and walk to Jackie's car when she made it there.

Jackie got the phone call at ten o'clock that dreadful Saturday night and made it to Angel's house three o'clock the next morning. The street Angel lived on, Monroe and Pulaski, ran one way and Jackie passed her house by accident, so she had to drive down the block and go back around to get to it. She felt a tremendous amount of pain as she drove down the long block because there were three makeshift memorials on it, and she could tell which one was made in the spot where her great-niece died. It was the only one with a huge, brown teddy bear, and it had the most balloons, flowers, candles, and stuffed animals on it. They both felt something so powerful when they rode past it that it woke Pam up out of her sleep and it bought tears to both of their eyes. She didn't know that the drive-by happened on the same block her sister lived on until she rode down it and saw all the yellow tape and the memorials on it.

When Jackie walked through Angel's door her pain eased up a little bit because her mother, all of her siblings, and her nieces and nephews were there. Jackie had stopped crying before she rung the doorbell, but the water works started up again when Samantha ran into her arms crying, shaking, and hyperventilating. "She gone Auntie, they took my baby from me," she managed to get out as Jackie held her. Jackie loved all of her nieces and nephews, but twenty-three year old Samantha had always been her favorite. She had the same hustle mentality that Jackie had, and she looked just like her except her eyes were brown. Angel was strung out on drugs and Samantha had been helping her mother take care of her household since she was eleven years old. Jackie was in prison then she moved to Ohio, so she didn't know anything that was going on in her sister's lives that they didn't want her to know. She didn't find out that her niece started selling drugs at the age of eleven until she told her at one of their family reunions. She was seventeen with two kids by then so there was nothing Jackie could do about it. She was still with the father of her children, Raymond, and he lived in the house with her, Angel, and her two little brothers Dwayne and Dwight. Jackie even respected the way Samantha handled that situation. Raymond was major in the streets and he took good care of Samantha, their two kids, her two little brothers, her mother, and her mother's drug habit while he was out. He was in jail fighting a murder and Samantha still held down their household while he was gone. Jackie tried to get her to move to Ohio when he got locked up, but she didn't want to leave her mother or her brothers and that raised the level of admiration Jackie had for her.

"I know it's hard to accept, but she's in a much better place baby," Jackie replied. "Come on, lets go run you some bathwater," she said as she released her and walked her through all of her family members and to the bathroom. Samantha still had her daughter's blood on her and getting it off was the first thing Jackie felt needed to be done.

Samantha sat on the toilet, with her head bent, softly crying while Jackie ran her a warm bath with lots of bubbles in it. "How am I supposed to live without my baby Auntie?" she asked as she touched Raymond's chain. Fear overtook her as she realized for the first time that night that he didn't know. "Oh my God Auntie, I missed Raymond's phone call tonight! How am I gon tell him that Ralonda's dead?"

"Baby, I'll tell him if you want me to."

"Thanks Auntie, but I think I need to be the one to tell him. I owe my baby that much. He just got sentenced to seventy years for that murder he was trying to beat last month, so he already got a lot on him. He'll never forgive me if he has to hear about this from anybody besides me."

"Don't worry about nobody's feelings but your own for the time being. I know it sounds selfish, but you can't put all of that added stress on yourself. While you soak in that tub, the only thoughts I want you to let enter your mind are the ones of the good times the Lord allowed you to share with Ralonda," said Jackie as she pulled Samantha up and hugged her.

"Thanks Auntie, I do need a quiet moment to myself," Samantha replied as Jackie released her. Then she left out so Samantha could take her bath in privacy.

Samantha soaked in the tub for a couple of hours and Jackie had the house clear by the time she came out. Everyone promised to come back later on after they got some rest. Pam went home with Janice, and Jackie and Bill stayed at Angel's house. She was happy she bought Bill with her when she saw how good he got along with Samantha's five year old daughter, Ramona. They were inseparable while they were in Chicago and that gave Samantha a lot of free time. Bill was only five, but he was very strong and intelligent. He knew where help was needed and how to provide it. Throughout the entire trip he kept Jackie sane and Ramona happy. Jackie loved her family; and being with them helped her deal with the pain she felt from her beautiful niece getting killed in such a violent way, at such a tender age.

Everyone came back around five that evening. Jack Jr. bought in lots of bags of food from Kentucky Fried Chicken and they all sat around eating, planning Ralonda's funeral, and reminiscing for hours. Since they were sending one of God's angels back to heaven, they all agreed that everyone who attended the funeral should wear white. Samantha's daughters were ten months apart and she dressed them alike every since Ramona was born, and she said that she wanted them dressed alike at the funeral too. Janice's husband was a Pastor and he agreed to preach the sermon and to have the funeral at his church. Jackie was going to write the obituary, Jennifer was going to write a tribute to Ralonda, Samantha was going to write a poem, and Pam, Janice, and Jamika were going to sing individual songs because they all had beautiful voices. Jack Jr. and three of Samantha's cousins were going to be the pallbearers. They planned the funeral during that first meeting, but they got together everyday until the funeral because they felt that Samantha and Angel needed their support and shouldn't be alone during their time of need.

Jackie did every task that needed to be done to make sure the funeral went exactly the way Samantha wanted it to go. She cooked, cleaned, and took care of the kids daily, while making the funeral arrangements. The day before the ceremony Samantha was flat-ironing Ramona's hair and as she was doing it; she told Jackie a story about the way Ralonda used to cry because she wouldn't flat-iron her hair. She said she felt they were too little for that heat in their hair, but she was doing Ramona's because she wanted to see how Ralonda would have looked if she would have done hers. Jackie knew how her girls always had the same hair do; so she went to the funeral home and took down all the little French braids Ralonda had in her hair, flat-ironed it, and put the same kind of white headband her sister was going to wear on it. While they were planning the funeral she offered to pay for it, but Samantha said the chief of her gang, Bullet, was paying for everything. Jackie wanted to do something financially, so she bought Samantha, Ramona, Angel, Dwayne, and Dwight's attire for the funeral. She also purchased so many long-stemmed white roses and tulips for the funeral that the fragrance could be smelled outside the church. The thing Samantha appreciated Jackie for the most was how she helped keep her mother sober. Angel was trying to stay sober because she felt like she owed it to Ralonda. She wouldn't have been able to do it without Jackie's help because the rest of her sisters were still getting high, and they bought their drugs with them every time they came to the family meetings.

People who didn't even know Ralonda attended the funeral. The church was so packed that there was only standing room available by the time the last person arrived, and everyone wore white. The Pastor preached a strong sermon on gang violence in Chicago and the effects it had on its youth. He also spoke on the love that God has for the young and innocent and urged everyone else to repent. There wasn't a dry eye in the church and Samantha constantly broke down. She tried to pick Ralonda up out of the casket when she passed it because she didn't look dead to her; she just looked like she was sleep. She wasn't supposed to be dead before her life began; she was supposed to grow up with her sister. It wasn't natural for a parent to bury their child, especially when it's due to violence and Samantha didn't know how she was going to move on with her life. When they went to the burial, Jackie and Janice had to stop her from jumping in the grave with Ralonda as her casket was being lowered into the ground and the preacher was saying "ashes to ashes and dust to dust". Seeing her baby lowered into the ground was the hardest thing Samantha ever had to do, because she knew she would never see her again. She was very grief-stricken and angry.

Jackie saw all of the anger in Samantha and she tried to get her to let go of some of it before she left, but she knew she hadn't gotten through to her. She couldn't even convince herself not to hate the cold hearted person who killed her great-niece, so how was she going to convince Samantha not to? She didn't even want to think about the way she would feel if Bill ever got killed, but she knew she would be very angry and she would probably want revenge. Samantha was just like her so she understood her need for revenge, and looked the other when she started disappearing from the family meetings at the same time on the three nights before the funeral. She could tell she was going to do some dirt because she changed in all black and crept out. Jackie was very worried about her niece but she knew she wouldn't have been able to stop her so she prayed for her, and watched her daughter while she was gone. She thanked God every night she made it back home safely, and praised him when she noticed that she didn't sneak out on the night of the funeral or the night after.

She wanted to stay in Chicago longer than the week she stayed, but Bill had to go to school. If he wouldn't have had to go she wouldn't have thought twice about staying. She wasn't worried about getting fired because Jim ran things at PM and she ran him. She was so angry at him that she didn't allow him enter her mind while she was gone, but as soon as she got on the highway headed to Dayton he immediately entered it. At the time he disrespected her and her family, getting to Chicago was more important than arguing with him so she hung up and left. She refused to let his reaction interfere with what she felt she had to do. He thought she was calling to ask if she could take Bill, but she was really calling to tell him she was taking him. She felt like Bill was hers and hers alone. She allowed Jim to be in their lives as a courtesy but she felt like she didn't have to, and legally she didn't. Jim didn't know that he was supposed to sign the birth certificate the day Jackie gave birth and she didn't tell him. She wanted complete control over every aspect of her son's life, so the only way she was going to get paternity established was if she had to for financial support. She was no longer angry at him by the time she made it home because she felt like she punished him very well. She knew he was afraid of Bill getting killed while they were in Chicago and that's what she wanted. She thought she had everything figured out, but Jim wasn't a stupid man.

Jackie took Bill in and put him in the tub before she bought her luggage in the house. When she went out to get it, Jim was getting out of his car. "Where's my son you crazy bitch?" he asked as she walked towards him laughing. "I paid a guy who works downtown in the DNA office to do a paternity test with the saliva out of my mouth, and the saliva out of Billy's toothbrush. He's my son and I have proof that he is," he said as he took a folded up piece of paper out of his pocket with a smile on his face. He was starting to hate Jackie so he enjoyed seeing her smile turn into a frown.

"Let's go in, I don't like airing my dirty laundry out in public," Jackie replied as she turned around to go in without waiting for his response. She turned to face Jim after locking the door. She wanted him inside so she could attack him without going to jail if she needed to. She held her composure while they were outside, but she was fuming. "I don't give a fuck what this paper says! You listen and you—"

"No, you listen!" screamed Jim as he grabbed Jackie by the throat with both of his hands. "If you ever take my son out of this fucking state without my permission again I'll do everything in my power to ruin your fucking life. Do you understand?" he asked as he released her. "I hired a private investigator and the file he's given me on you is very interesting thus far," he said to a stunned Jackie.

She hadn't been choked since Leon chocked her and the feeling temporarily immobilized her. When Jim released her and she caught her breath; she sat on the floor, pulled her knees to her chest, and cried. Her reaction caught Jim completely off guard. When the man he hired to watch her condo called and told him they were home, he was prepared to kill her if he had to. Her police record was violent, but it was nothing compared to her street reputation in Chicago so he made sure he bought his derringer pistol. He thought long and hard while Jackie was gone and he came to the realization that he would do anything for his son, including murder. He had a plan if Jackie made him kill her, but he was totally unprepared when she made him comfort her. She broke completely down into a childlike state and Jim didn't know what to do, so he hugged her until Bill called her name and pulled them both back into reality. "Look Jackie, why don't we start over? We both have the power to destroy each other's lives, but if we do Billy will be the one who suffers the most."

"I just want to be happy," Jackie whispered. She was physically and emotionally drained by the thought of the things Jim could have found out about her past. She underestimated how deep his love for their son was and the things he would do to be a part of his life. She wished she would have kept him posted on Bill's well being while they were gone, because she knew he wouldn't have gone as far as he did if she would have. She felt so vulnerable and weak that she no longer felt like bathing Bill or getting her luggage, so Jim did the tasks for her. Jackie thought Jim was going to demand more time with Bill, but he didn't. They fell right back into their old routine and Jackie was grateful towards Jim for that. They came to a mutual unspoken agreement that they both needed to be there for their son because they both had his best interests at heart.

(21)

Sometimes You Gotta Go

Jackie's life took another drastic turn when Angel called her four months after Ralonda got killed to tell her that Bullet, the chief of the gang Samantha was in, was the person who murdered her grandbaby. He wasn't trying to kill her, but he did when he shot back at the men who did the drive-by at their picnic. The detective who was leading the investigation came to their house, and Angel and Samantha identified Bullet in a photo lineup as one of the people who was out there when the shooting occurred. He told them that Bullet got caught with the gun that was used to kill Ralonda. They lived on the block that the Impression Black Souls, Samantha's gang, hung out on so Angel wanted to move. Samantha didn't want to leave their house because she felt like Bullet was in the wrong. She thought her fellow gang members would take her side because they all claimed to love her and her kids, but Jackie knew better. Bullet was a Soul much longer than Samantha and he was the chief of their gang, so there was no way they were going to go against him for her. Telling the police anything was breaking the code of silence which was an unforgivable crime in the streets, and Jackie reminded Samantha that the least the Souls would do to her was beat her in a violation when they found out. Jackie knew Bullet's family personally and they were very dangerous people who would want revenge if he went to jail because of Angel and Samantha's testimony, so the Souls weren't the only people they had to worry about. It took her an hour, but by the end of the conversation she was able to convince Samantha to go down to the Ickes with her mother, brothers, and daughter.

The Wrights had a lot of friends and family down in the Ickes who would protect her sister and her intermediate family, so Jackie tried to convince herself that everything was going to be alright. Whenever her stomach tightened up something always went wrong, and she couldn't relax at all after they hung up, so she called Angel on and off for the rest of the day. The knot in Jackie's stomach wouldn't let her go to sleep, so she was awake when Angel called at one o'clock in the morning to tell her that Samantha had been shot. The police thought Bullet did it because he bonded out before the detective made it back to the station with the picture lineup, and a woman who was affiliated with the Souls was found shot to death with Samantha. Jackie's niece, Malika, told them that Samantha was going to meet the woman on the Westside to sell her some stolen clothes. Samantha was shot in the chest three times and the only reason she didn't bleed to death was because Malika knew where she was going. She was with Samantha when she got the phone call from the woman so she made her give her the address to the house she was going to. After an hour passed and Samantha didn't answer her phone, Malika told Angel everything and Angel had the lead detective meet them at the address which ended up being an abandoned building. Angel's description of the crime scene was so graphic that Jackie felt like she was right there seeing Samantha lying on the filthy floor, still holding the shopping bags, as blood oozed out of her gunshot wounds and onto the clothes that had spilled out. The woman lying beside her was shot in the face several times and the way Angel described how pieces were blown off of it, sent shivers down Jackie's spine. She'd seen and done a lot, but she didn't think she could have walked away in her right state of mind after seeing the things her sister had recently seen done to her daughter and granddaughter.

When Angel finished telling Jackie what happened, they prayed for Samantha's speedy recovery and for Angel to have the strength to stay sober. She hadn't smoked any crack or tooted any heroin since Ralonda died, and she was trying not to but it was hard. Her grandbaby was dead, and she didn't know if her daughter was going to live. She was used to using drugs to briefly escape the trials and tribulations she faced in her life, so it was very difficult not to. She was traumatized behind the events that were occurring and her twin sisters were constantly trying to get her to start back getting high, but she didn't give in. She made it through the physical pains from detoxing cold turkey months ago, but she had a mental struggle everyday. She was proud of herself for staying strong, but she didn't know how long she was going to last if things kept happening. She needed Jackie to be there, and she knew she could always count on her.

After praying, Jackie told Angel that she was going to tell Samantha's father, Rodney, what was going on. She wanted to tell him when Ralonda got killed, but Angel begged her not to and she honored her wishes. Rodney was a Gangster Black Soul and he used to be a professional hit-man so Jackie felt like they needed him. Her street credit died when her brothers died, Jack Jr. couldn't get Bullet, and she wouldn't feel right involving any of her nephews. The only way Samantha was going to be safe was if Bullet died and Rodney was the only person Jackie could get to kill him. She didn't say anything about the hit over the phone, but Angel knew what she was talking about when she said she was going to ask him to come out of retirement. Angel knew that they needed him, but she hated that they did and she told Jackie she did. Jackie never knew why Angel hated the father of her three kids until that conversation. She understood her ill feelings towards Rodney because he got her strung out on drugs, got clean in jail, and left her for his lawyer when he got out, but she still had to contact him to stop Bullet from trying to kill Samantha again. She didn't realize how bitter Angel was until she told her that she moved on the same side of town that Rodney lived on, but she didn't tell him or any of his people her address. She stopped letting him see their kids when he left her ten years ago, so they had no way of knowing how to get in contact with their father and he only lived fifteen minutes away from them.

Jackie asked Melissa to watch Bill while she went to Chicago because she didn't want to put him in harms way. When they went for the funeral, Jackie kept Bill in safe environments. She was on a mission to find Rodney this time and she was going to have to go where his gang hung out in order to find him. Angel gave her his address, but she refused to go to his house because she didn't know or trust his woman. She hadn't been in the streets in years so she didn't know if there were any gang wars going on where she had to go, but she had to do what she had to do so she left her son and bought her twenty-two instead.

Angel told her that a policeman was stationed outside of Samantha's hospital room and that the lead detective put her, Dwayne, Dwight, and Ramona in protective custody so it wasn't necessary to leave right away. She decided to wait until the morning to leave. When she called to tell Jim that she was going to Chicago, but was leaving Bill he begged her not to go. It touched her that he was concerned for her safety but she wasn't scared. She knew how to take care of herself if she needed to, and she didn't think she would. All she had to do was get to Rodney and he'd handle the rest. Jim was so afraid of Jackie being murdered that his fear crept into his nightmares. To try to understand the way she grew up he watched *Colors, Boys in the Hood, Menace to Society,* and every other movie he could find but he still walked away clueless. Jackie was great with Bill and everything was fine when she didn't involve herself in her family's affairs, but when she did he always prepared his self for her death. He understood that she loved them, but he wished she would understand how important she was in his and their son's lives too. He never thought the mother of his child would be black, violent, and schizophrenic but he couldn't think of a better woman for the job. He loved Jackie and he stayed trying to convince himself that she loved him too. He was so happy that she called him throughout her trip in Chicago that he didn't think about the fact that he still didn't get to see or talk to Bill while she was gone.

Jackie made it to Mt. Sinai, the hospital Samantha was in at four o'clock that evening. The hospital was packed with friends and family so Jackie wanted to stay longer than the hour she stayed, but she needed to find Rodney. She wanted Bullet dead before he tried to kill Samantha again. If he was anything like his uncles, he wasn't going to stop until he succeeded. She went in the room and prayed for Samantha before she left and it broke her heart to see her favorite niece in a coma hooked up to several machines. She was so hurt and angry that Toni tried to take over for her, but she didn't let her. She never wanted Bill to meet Toni and she told her that when she was in labor with him. She let Toni take over most of the time while she was pregnant and she didn't like the way she behaved. She was too mean and she didn't have any patience so Jackie was terrified of what she would do to Bill he had one of his infamous temper tantrums. Toni was very understanding and she popped out as fast as she popped in.

Jackie thought Rodney was going to be hard to find, but he was on the corner of Walnut and Homan in front of the store he'd always hung out in front of. She saw the surprise look on his face when she walked up, but she acted like didn't. "What's up partner? How's life been treatin' you?" she asked.

"I can't complain! I ain't got to ask how life's been treatin' you, not with you pushing that fly ass Lexus I don't," Rodney responded.

"I'm alright, but I wish I could say the same for your kids."

"I knew something was wrong when I saw you get out the car. Y'all ain't tried to tell me shit about my kids in ten years, so I know it's bad. What's going on with my babies Jackie?" he asked with deep concern in his voice.

"Let's sit in my car and talk," said Jackie as she turned around and walked to her car without waiting on his answer. "Do you know this Soul who goes by the name Bullet?" she asked as soon as they sat in the car and closed the doors.

"Yeah I know him, he a rowdy motherfucker that calls it for the Souls down on Pulaski. What he got to do with my kids?" he asked as his curiosity and his anger peaked.

"He killed Samantha's daughter Ralonda about three weeks ago, and he shot Samantha this morning. I wanted to tell you about your grandbaby getting killed, but Angel begged me not to. She didn't want me to tell you about Samantha but I couldn't keep that from you, because it's obvious the nigga's got a hit out on them," Jackie said as she started to cry. Rodney started crying when he heard about Ralonda and seeing such a strong, muscle bound, heartless man cry made her cry.

"How could y'all do me like this? I saw that shit about Ralonda all over the news! I never thought she was any kin to me, but it still fucked with me because she was so pretty and young. I started to go to that meeting out west when I heard about it, but you know how much work I put in for the mob so it wasn't mandatory for me to go. I knew Angel was bitter but I didn't know she would go that far. I didn't want to leave Angel, but I was tired of getting high and she wasn't so I had to do what was best for me. She punishing me just because I found me a good woman who's never gotten high and I got my life together. I heard Bullet was on the run for murder, but you sure he killed my grandbaby and tried to kill my daughter?" asked Rodney as he used the bottom of his shirt to wipe his face.

"We positive it was him. The lead detective who was investigating Ralonda's murder came over their house and told them that Bullet got caught with the gun that was used to kill her. I told them to leave their house and go down to the Ickes, but I guess he had some girl lure Sam back on the Westside. He was locked up but he bonded out before the detective gave the new evidence to the prosecutor. I'm sorry for keeping Ralonda's death from you, but Angel would have never forgiven me if I would have told you after she told me not to. I see how wrong we've been towards you over the years but yo daughter needs you now. That nigga ain't gon stop tryin' to kill her until she's dead or he's dead. The police guarding her for the time being, but you know they ain't gon protect her for the rest of her life. They probably shouldn't have told the police anything, but they didn't know what else to do. The only muscle Samantha had came from Bullet's foot soldiers, so she tried to get revenge on him by using the police. The nigga is bogish Rodney! I know he didn't mean to kill Ralonda, but he did. He didn't have to try to kill her mother knowing she got another daughter she has to raise," she said as she took a manila envelope from out of her purse and handed it to Rodney. "I put one of Ralonda's obituaries and some pictures of Dwayne, Bobby, Samantha, and her two daughters in there. I would kill the nigga myself but I don't know how to catch him".

"Naw, you leave that up to me. I know where he hiding out and everything. He fucks with my woman's sister and he told her part of the story. He didn't tell her he killed no little girl and he didn't tell her that the people he beefing with are females. Tell Angel to check on they house because he told his woman that he killed one of the witnesses and he paid some hypes to burn down the house they lived in. His bitch tells my woman everything and my woman turns around and tells me. He told her that he paid for Ralonda's funeral, did he?"

"Yeah, the nigga paid for everything but that don't excuse him from killing her. That actually makes it worse in my eyes. He could've told them that he might have shot her while he was giving them all that dough. I mean shit happens. Some niggas did a drive-by at the picnic he threw on his block, and he returned the gunfire. I'm sure it was an accident, but he still killed her. Damn, I hope he ain't burned down they house because if he did, Angel gon lose her Section Eight."

"I'm just telling you what my woman Tyeshia told me."

"Hold on this Angel," said Jackie when her cell phone rang. "Hello."

"Jackie that motherfucker set our house on fire and he must have taken Sam's car keys because the police said they wasn't on her. I'm about to lose my Section Eight and the police talkin' bout they can't help me keep it! They said they don't know anything about Section Eight, but they're going to do an investigation to make sure the fire was a result of arson. I had them take me to the house when they escorted me from Mount Sinai this morning, and our house was still burning. Our neighbors didn't even have the decency to call the motherfucking fire department. Everything we owned was in that house and these motherfuckers got the nerve to have me way out in the boon docks in some cheap, raggedy ass motel. They said that the Red Cross would give us some clothes but you can imagine the type of clothes they gon give us. When you gon make it to Chicago Jackie? I need you," Angel said into the phone through her tears.

"I'm already here sister. I been up to the hospital to see Sam and everything. I'm sorry about y'all house but at least y'all still alive. Is Ramona, Dwayne and Bobby with you?'

"Yeah, they here. I know we alive but where we gon live, Jackie?"

"Don't worry about that right now. Y'all can come to Ohio with me after Samantha gets out of the hospital and we get all of this shit took care of."

"For real Jackie? Thank-you sister. I don't know what I would do without you."

"You know I got you just like you got me. But look sister, I'm busy right now. I'm gon call you as soon as I finish handling this business," she said trying to end the conversation so she could finish talking to Rodney. She didn't mention him to Angel because she was with the police.

"Alright sister, call me back as soon as you get a chance to. Thanks for everything, I love you, bye," Angel replied.

"I love you too. Bye," said Jackie and hung up her cell phone. "Yup, he burned down their house," she said to Rodney.

"I heard, so you gon let them move to Ohio with you for real?" he asked. He was relieved when he heard her tell Angel they could move out there and he wanted to be sure she meant it.

"Yeah, I'm gon help them get on they feet. But I want that nigga dead. Do you think you can get him? I know you squared up and I hate for you to come out of retirement, but that nigga needs to be in hell with the devil," said Jackie.

"Shit, I'm gon have to kill him because that nigga want my baby dead. This is between us Jackie, you can't tell anyone. Bullet got rank in the mob and I'm supposed to get permission before I kill any Soul, let alone a chief. I can't even tell my woman and we've never had any secrets between us; but I owe it to my baby. I'm serious Jackie, you can't even tell Angel because she spiteful towards me and I can get killed for what I'm about to do."

"I won't Rodney, I owe you that much. But when you kill him, can you leave him somewhere where the police can find him so Angel and the kids can get up out that fake ass witness protection program the police got them in?" she asked. Rodney was known for making his victims disappear when he used to murder people for money.

"Yeah, I can do that. It's fucked up that I don't know nothing about my kids. Were they Souls or something? What were they doing at the picnic?"

"Yeah, Angel moved them on Monroe and Pulaski back in 97'. I told her she should have let you in their lives when she first started having problems out of them with that gangbanging shit."

"She should have listened to you because I would have made sure they didn't get mixed up with any gang. Tell her that I'm gon be in my kids lives rather she likes it or not. As a matter of fact, don't tell the bitch shit. Here's my phone number. Give it to my kids, they old enough to make their own decisions now," he said as took his business card out of his wallet and gave it to her. "I ain't going up to the hospital until I leave this nigga stankin' somewhere, but I'll be up there to see my baby before she gets out. Thanks for the pictures and the head's up. My grandbabies look just like me don't they?" Rodney asked.

"You know what? They do favor you. We always said they looked like they father Raymond from off of Sixteenth Street, but they look like you too."

"I know Raymond; that was my little nigga. That's a damn shame I didn't know he had kids by my daughter because we kicked it and did a lot of business together. I'm glad I didn't know they was dating because he too damn old for her. God knows what he be doing because the nigga got a seventy year bit to do; and I'm so mad at the way my baby been treated that I probably would have murked his ass too. But I love you Jackie and you gon always be my sister regardless of what. Kiss my kids for me and take care of yourself."

"I will. Thanks Rodney, I love you too and I feel the same way. Make sure you make that motherfucker pay for everything he did."

"They ain't gon be able to recognize that bitch when I get through with his ass," Rodney replied while getting out Jackie's car. Bullet was found murdered the next day. Rodney cut out his eyes, cut off his tongue, and set on the bottom half of his body on fire before he shot him in the head.

Samantha was still in a coma, and Angel was in protective custody when the murder occurred so the police didn't suspect them. Jackie didn't have to be in the streets to know that everyone on them, who knew Bullet, knew that whoever killed him did it because of what he did to Samantha. She stayed in Chicago until Samantha came out of her coma three days later and she was able to reprimand her for letting the Souls lure her out of the Ickes. She didn't tell her that they were going to have to move to Ohio when she got out the hospital because Angel asked her not to. She didn't want her to know that they had to start completely over because she didn't want her to worry about anything while she was trying to heal up. The only thing they told her was that Bullet was dead.

Jackie left the day she was able to talk to Samantha because she needed and wanted to go home very bad. Angel begged her to stay, but she couldn't do it. She missed Bill too much and she didn't want to admit it, but she was scared that she would relapse if she stayed. Angel was released from protective custody when Bullet was found murdered and she asked Jackie to stay down in the Ickes with her at their sister Sharon's house. The first night they went in Sharon's house, crack smoke hit them in the face as soon as she opened the door for them. Jackie didn't realize how much she missed the feeling she felt when she smoked crack until she smelled it for the first time in years. It took everything in her power not to ask to hit the crack pipe that was in rotation. All of her sisters accept Angel was at the table getting high, and that reminded her of her days as a crack head. She knew they couldn't stay there when Jamika tried to be funny by offering the pipe to her and Angel, so she tried to convince Angel to let her get them a hotel room. But Angel had convinced herself that the Souls were following them and was too scared to leave the Ickes. They went to Sharon's daughter's house and were hit by marijuana smoke when she opened her door. Jackie wanted to hit the blunt, but she was scared to because they did random drug tests at PM and a pull off a blunt wasn't worth her losing her job. Jim couldn't save her job if she failed a drug test because he didn't work in that department. She was happy that Angel knew how she felt about Bill because she was able to use missing him as an excuse to get out of Chicago with her sobriety intact.

Samantha got released a week after Jackie left and Jackie couldn't wait for them to get to Ohio. She went to the Greyhound Station and paid for their one way tickets to Dayton fifteen minutes after Angel called her with the good news. While she was in Chicago she bought them all clothes, shoes, and coats. She also took Angel to the necessary offices and helped her get her and her intermediate family's important documents, so they were ready. She was so happy that her favorite niece and one of her favorite sisters were moving to Ohio that she didn't know what to do. When she came back from buying the tickets on her unauthorized break, she walked around the factory smiling for the remainder of the day. It was a very beautiful smile but the people at work found it strange and unusual because her face was usually expressionless. Jackie heard the woman she got into it with snicker, so she knew they were talking about her attitude change but she didn't care. Her sister was coming and that's all she was focused on. God had answered another one of her prayers so she let the woman slide and continued smiling.

Pam got Alzheimer's after Ralonda's funeral, but she remembered her more than she remembered Jackie. The disease took her mind quickly and she tried to microwave a pot, so Jackie had to put her in a nursing home. She felt bad for putting her in there because Pam asked her to take her home with her during one of her lucid moments, and she didn't. She would have felt better if the lie she told her about not being able to quit her job were true, but it wasn't. She could've worked at home managing Jim's books if she wanted to, but she didn't. She didn't want anyone at her house because she started back sleeping with Marcus when she got back from Chicago and she liked her privacy. Jim came to her house every Saturday and if she started working for him he would be there a lot more than that. No one knew who the father of her child was and she wanted to keep it that way. She knew she was being selfish so she planned on making it up to Pam by bringing Samantha's other daughter Ramona to see her on a weekly basis when they moved there.

Jackie was so frantic that they were coming, that she picked Bill up from daycare and went to the Greyhound Station to get them two hours before their bus was due to arrive. She was happy until Samantha stepped off the bus with a deep scowl on her face. "What's wrong with you Ms. Thang?"

"Every fucking thing, what's right? First of all, I didn't appreciate you talking all that shit when I was in the hospital and y'all the reason this shit happened. Sierra didn't even know dude killed my baby, so that means none of the Souls knew. If we would have stayed—,"

"If y'all would have stayed it would've been y'all in that house burning instead of y'all shit. What you think they was gon give yo ass a trial? You was already convicted when you told the police whatever the fuck you told them!" yelled Jackie. She couldn't believe how ungrateful Samantha was acting. She tried to control her anger because she knew she was just naïve, but it was hard not to slap her across her face.

"On the Soul, on King Wee I knew I shouldn't have come out here!" said Samantha throwing up her gang sign. She was embarrassed that she told on Bullet, and she didn't appreciate Jackie yelling it. She wished she could have handled it the way Jackie did Leon. She'd always looked up to her and sought her approval and not having it lowered her self-esteem another notch. Jackie told her that she did the right thing the day she told on Bullet and now she had her in Ohio yelling at her like it was a bad decision.

"You look real stupid throwing that shit up and don't nobody out here know what the fuck it means," said Jackie as she laughed and imitated her niece.

"I need to be in the Chi tryna get some paper instead of out here in no man's land depending on the next motherfucker. Fuck this—,"

Jackie's eyes changed colors as she started to get weak. "Fuck what Sam? Look, it ain't shit to get on the next bus home. I'll even pay for the ticket, but you need to think real fucking good about yo next move. I'm just gon keep this shit all the way one hundred with you cause you's a ignorant lil bitch and this my first time seeing that. Them bullets that hit yo first baby weren't meant for her, so that wasn't your fault. If you go back and your other baby gets shot her blood will be on your hands. I know they got a hit out on you, rather you believe it or not. Ain't no love in them streets, them niggas gon send some bullets yo way so you better think about the quality of you and your child's lives before they take it," said Toni without an ounce of compassion in her voice. Samantha had never disrespected Jackie before and she couldn't handle it, so she let Toni back for the first time since Bill was born. She was depressed when Samantha was in the hospital but she handled it on her own. The thought of them moving to Ohio is what kept her strong through it all, and Samantha was threatening to take away her dream. She didn't realize how much she wanted them all there until Samantha threatened to leave. She missed living around family because she didn't like dealing with outsiders. She never reconciled with Rhonda, Mellissa stopped her weekly visits after the advance rent she paid ran out, and half the time Pam wouldn't know who she was if she walked up to her and slapped her. She was starting to feel lonely in Ohio so she wanted all of them there. She wanted Ramona there the most so she could protect and help raise her. The beautiful little girl was like a ray of sunshine to her, Bill, and Pam and the thought of not having that sunshine in their lives was unbearable to Jackie. She would have never said the hurtful things that Toni said to her niece but she didn't stop her when she heard them being said.

Toni's words sucked all of Samantha's energy from her body and she had to lean against the bus to prevent falling as the harsh reality of the words seeped in. The only way she could go back was if Jackie paid for her ticket. She was broke physically, emotionally, and financially. The only job she'd ever had was hustling and no one was going to let her work for them after they found out she'd told on Bullet. She had several felonies so it was going to be hard to get a square job. She used to be able to get money out of men, but her self esteem sunk real low after she got out the hospital and saw herself. She lost a lot of weight and she had a long scar on her chest that she wanted no one to see. They lost their Section Eight and there was no way her mother's SSI checks could cover the high rent in Chicago without the government's assistance; so they would be homeless. Her cousins said they could move with them down in the Ickes but she didn't want to move down there with her daughter or her little brothers. The city of Chicago knocked down a lot of the projects and put the residents from them in the ones they left standing, like the Ickes. They made enemies neighbors which caused a lot of gang wars and Samantha didn't want them getting caught in the crossfire.

She knew there was a hit out on her since somebody had Bullet killed and if Jackie wouldn't have cut her off at the beginning of the conversation she would have told her so. She was glad that she didn't say it because that would have really made her look like a bad mother if she did. She felt real bad for even considering taking her daughter back to Chicago knowing there were people after her. "Wow," was all she could get out as she tried to muster enough strength to stand up on her own.

"You better say more than some motherfucking wow," said Toni. She didn't plan on backing off Samantha until she apologized to Jackie because Bill needed her to be there for him. He was too spoiled and Toni didn't trust her self around him just as much as Jackie didn't.

"Jackie can't you see she crying? Can't we please leave? Y'all embarrassing the shit out of me and it's freezing out here," said Angel speaking up for the first time.

"Hell naw, cause this bitch aint even gettin' in my ride if she on that gang-banging, disrespectful, petty hustling bullshit! I rather pay that lil fifty dollars to send her ass right back to Chicago so them niggas can continue pimpin' her ass," Toni said. Samantha always looked like she had a lot of money so Jackie thought she knew what she was doing, but Angel told her that she was a pack worker and Jackie and Toni didn't approve of that at all. She did it when she was a hype Samantha was too young and smart to be out there. All Jackie wanted to do was help her. Toni didn't care if she went back or not, her mission was to keep Ramona there and she planned on doing that with or without Samantha.

"You women need to get your luggage and let the other passengers get theirs," said the luggage handler. He was enjoying the show like everyone else, but it was cold out there and he was ready to go in.

"Auntie Jackie I aint never sold no pussy," said Samantha as they walked to her 2006 Ford Expedition.

"Baby how long was you on that corner? See, it's not about what you was selling. Anytime you only get 10% of whatever it is you selling, you getting pimped. That shit would have never went down if I was at home. Yo motherfucking father put in a lot of fucking work for the mob, and if yo mama would have been in her right state of mind you would have gotten the respect that you deserved. And shit, I sell pussy it's the easiest thing to sell and it's the only thing that's gon sell at all times," said Jackie laughing as she came back and lightened up the mood. Her happiness returned after they all greeted each other properly and climbed in her truck. Jackie told Mellissa that they were coming after work and she called her phone to talk to Samantha while they were on their way to the Cheesecake Factory for dinner. She didn't think she could get any happier but she did when Samantha hung up the phone and told her that Mellissa, Rhonda, and Leona were going to meet them there. Jackie hadn't seen Leona since Mellissa's house warming party and she didn't realize how much she missed her until she found out she was going to see her.

She didn't want any bad feelings between her and Samantha so she talked to her during the rest of the ride. "Look Sam, I know life dealt you a hell of a hand to play, but baby you got to play that motherfucker. One thing for sure is that bad shit is gon happen rather you like it or not because life is a test. Why do you think when people stand up in church to tell others about their struggles in life, they call those struggles testimonies? Because you are going through a test and rather you pass it or not depends on you. Some people's tests are harder than others but it's the way you handle it that counts. I'm offering you a new life! It ain't gon be glamorous but you ain't gon have to look over your shoulder for the rest of your life. While I was in Chicago I had the Red Cross there contact the one here so they already had y'all file when I called them this morning. They gon give y'all apartments in their emergency housing shelter tomorrow."

"All right Auntie. I'm gon do my best to succeed down here."

"That's what I like to hear baby," said Jackie as she pulled up to the restaurant. She had the same huge smile on her face that she had all day at work throughout dinner.

They had a very nice time at the Cheesecake Factory and Jackie was the life of the celebration, but she was all business the next day. She took off work and took them everywhere they needed to go. Samantha thought she was going to share one of the shelter apartments with her mother, but Jackie made her apply for her own. She was twenty-three and she had a child, so it was time for her to be the woman she always claimed she was. Jackie didn't believe in helping people who didn't help themselves so she took Samantha to apply for welfare right after they filled out the paper they had to fill out for their emergency housing apartments. After leaving the welfare office, she took Angel to the SSI office to get her son's SSI transferred to Dayton. They were tired but she didn't feel sorry for them because she made Rhonda go through everything they were about to go through. She wasn't about to let them move with her in her condo because she enjoyed the privacy she maintained in her home. She was an ex-dope fiend who'd been through hell and back and she was enjoying her new life without other people watching her every move.

When Rhonda lived in emergency housing Jackie never went inside her apartment, but she went inside of Samantha's and Angel's. The furniture they housed the apartments with was hideous, but the apartments were kind of nice. They were townhomes with polished wooden floors and Angel and Samantha were very grateful. When they heard that the apartments were in the projects they thought they were going to look like the ones they lived in in Chicago, but they were a lot nicer. They didn't come with any entertainment so Jackie bought both of them nice television sets and radios. She also bought them all the food, toiletries, cleaning supplies, linen, towels, and kitchen utensils they needed. All of them helped clean Angel's apartment, then Samantha's. Before they left Samantha bought tears to Jackie's eyes because she thanked her and told her that she was happy she came. Jackie was very proud of Samantha but she didn't tell her because she had a long way to go before she deserved a pat on the back.

Samantha treated her emergency housing apartment like it was a real one. She decorated it, kept it spotless, and she had rules that she enforced for anyone who entered it. She'd never lived on her own and she enjoyed the independent feeling she felt living in the shelter. It was just her and Ramona and it felt good being able to raise her daughter without her mother's input. She didn't even mind the ten o'clock curfew that was imposed on them because she didn't want to be out after dark anyway. She job hunted, took care of business, and ran all of her errands while the sun was still out. They were in the hood and she wanted no parts of the street life in Dayton. All she wanted to do was take care of her daughter and find herself a job. She didn't want any boyfriends or female friends there, so she ignored anyone who tried to talk to her. Jackie popped in every now and then during the month she lived in Parkside, but Mellissa, Rhonda, and Leona came over there all the time and that was enough company for her. They were given an emergency status because their house was burned down; so it only took Samantha a month and her mother two to get their apartments. Both of them chose to move to Hilltop because Rhonda lived there.

Jackie planned on getting Samantha a job at PM immediately, but she made her wait until she moved into her apartment because of the way she disrespected her at the Greyhound Station. She didn't communicate with Mellissa at work by choice, but she didn't have to worry about her disrespecting her while they were there. Jackie wanted to make sure Samantha was truly sorry and back to her normal respectable self before she made Jim hire her. Mellissa favored Jackie, but Samantha looked just like her so everyone would know they were related. She needed to make sure she was loyal to her before she was willing to work with her, so she watched her to see how she would act without her help. She wanted to start back respecting Samantha and she did after seeing the way she handled her business. She had her welfare rolling, her daughter and her little brothers enrolled in school, and several job applications in within her first week of being in Ohio; and she did it all on the bus. Her little brothers tried to get a little wild in Parkside but Samantha got a hold of them quickly. They listened to her more than they listened to their mother, and that reminded Jackie of the way she used to take care of her younger siblings.

Samantha tried her best to get a job, but the economy was terrible and the failing automobile industry wiped out seventy-five percent of the jobs in Dayton, Ohio. Jim was trying to fly as straight as he could because the government was starting to wonder why the factories were doing so horribly. He constantly complained to Jackie about the investigations that were going on, so he was pissed when she forced him to hire Samantha. PM couldn't even afford to pay the employees they did have let alone hire any new ones, but Jackie didn't care. She made him give Samantha the position he invented for her when she was pregnant because she had lifting restrictions on her. The doctors could only extract two bullets out of her chest because taking the third one out could have messed up one of her major arteries. Jim was appalled when he heard why she had medical restrictions; but he was angrier than he'd ever been at Jackie when he found out that Samantha was twenty-three years old and had never had a real job in her life, was a ninth grade dropout, and she had numerous felonies on her criminal record. He was so mad that he started to contact Bertha Thompson so they could form a plan to destroy her together. He let the private detective that he hired continue to investigate Jackie and every important person in her life and the file was getting thicker and thicker. He hated her, but he loved her just as much as he hated her so his heart wouldn't let him conspire against her with her enemies in the end. He hired her niece against his better judgment, but Samantha ended up being a delight to work with. She looked like a younger, fresher looking Jackie and was as sweet and smart as she could be. She came to work everyday and learned every task he invented for her very fast.

Mellissa told Samantha to ask Jackie to get her on at PM, but she refused to because she had too much pride. She was happy that she didn't because she hooked her up with a job in the office, and their relationship grew stronger when Jackie saw that she could stand on her own. She didn't even trip when she found out that she had weed in her system, she just told her she had to stop and went to take the drug test for her. Samantha had never been more proud of herself than she was when she when she got hired. Sometimes she had to help out on the floor and that work was hard, but most of the time she worked in the office doing nothing. She loved feeling like a productive member of society and she tried her best to follow the rules. She couldn't believe how drastically her life changed in a year. She would never fully recover from losing Ralonda, but she liked the new life she was living. She knew if she went to work for forty hours, at the end of the week she was going to get paid for working those forty hours. When she sold drugs she worked more than forty hours and sometimes she didn't even see a profit. She'd been robbed by drug addicts and policemen several times, and some of those times she had to work packs for free to pay Bullet back. Then there were the times the police actually did their jobs and arrested her. Sometimes she got bonded out, and sometimes she had to bond herself out and hire her own lawyers. The only way she made any real money was when she sold her own drugs on their spot without them knowing and that was very dangerous. She saw men and women get limbs broken, faces disfigured, and several other cruel punishments for double juggling on Bullet's spots so she was very scared every time she did it. She made a lot of money working on drug spots, but the peace of mind that came with working a square job was priceless. Jim started her off making twelve dollars an hour and that was more than enough to support her and her child very well.

When Samantha started working at PM she was antisocial like Jackie for the first week, but she saw how much fun Mellissa was having and changed her attitude. Jackie tried to stop talking to her at work like she did Mellissa when she started socializing with the other workers, but Samantha didn't let her. She had to go on the floor to collect data from the different work stations, and she stayed in Jackie's area for long periods of time whenever she could. Jackie tried to ignore her the first time she stayed longer than she was supposed to but she couldn't resist when she asked about Bill. She started making Jackie and Mellissa's work stations the last two on her list so she could visit with both of them separately. They had no desire to communicate with each other when Samantha first started working there, but she was able to unite them after two months. Jackie did it but she made them promise not to tell anyone that Mellissa was her daughter. Everyone knew that Samantha was her niece so she told them to say that Mellissa was her niece too. She thought Mellissa was going to object, but she was very happy to oblige. She wanted people to know that she was related to Samantha, and she didn't want to claim Wacky Jackie, (the name Jackie was called behind her back), as her mother. She told everyone that her mother and father died in that hotel room, and that's how she truly felt.

(22)

Why Me?

Jackie didn't realize how much she missed Mellissa until Samantha came into their lives and bought them back together. She loved her, but she didn't like when she called herself trying to teach someone younger than her something, and they didn't listen. Mellissa went out of her way to defy Jackie so she stopped trying to tell her how to do anything and just enjoyed being in the presence of her company. Samantha bought out the best in her and watching them together was a joy for Jackie to see. Mellissa started showing Jackie more respect when she saw how much Samantha respected her and that pleased Jackie. She was able to give Mellissa advice through Samantha, because Samantha did everything Jackie advised her to do and she prospered because of it. Jackie taught them how to invest their money wisely and she enjoyed watching them watch it grow. They didn't know how she did it, but Jackie made Jim let Samantha and Mellissa work during the weeks PM and every factory that worked for them were shutdown. The only other employees working besides them were the technicians who worked on the machines and Jim Cartwright. Samantha started dating Byron, the cutest and highest paid tech at PM, and Jackie taught her how to play him. He left his wife for her after three months of dating and everyone knew they were together because he adored her. He did romantic things like send her roses and gifts while they were working. Every woman who worked at PM besides Mellissa and Jackie envied Samantha when Byron started courting her. Mellissa was even jealous when he left his wife for her because she'd been dating a tech named Jamal for two years, and he still hadn't left his girlfriend for her.

Jackie didn't want to work during shutdown; she wanted to have fun while they were off work. She used the extra time to take Angel, Ramona, Leona, Bill, Dwight and Dwayne on all types of field trips. Angel's sons acted like they didn't want to go to any of the places Jackie planned for them to go, but she saw them enjoying themselves like everyone else at the amusement parks, bowling alleys, skating rings, aquariums, carnivals, museums, and every where else they were "forced" to go to. Angel really enjoyed herself and she showed Jackie a lot of gratitude for taking her sons and her granddaughter to places they would have never went to if Jackie wouldn't have taken them. She was also grateful to her for showing her how to have fun living a clean and sober life. When Jackie got back from Chicago she started back attending NA meetings and Angel started going with her when she moved to Ohio.

Angel missed Ralonda with all her heart, but she felt like God took her back to Heaven with him to wake the rest of them up. Dwight was a nineteen year old, gang-banging, drug dealing, high school drop out when they moved to Ohio. Jackie wanted to teach him how to be a man, so she made him find his own job and he found one in two months. He worked at a gas station around the corner from their house and went to a GED school. Dwayne gang-banged and sold drugs, but he was only fifteen so Angel tried to make him stay in school. She was slowly losing control of him before Ralonda died, but he turned back into the sweet boy that he once was when they moved to Dayton. He got straight A's and even joined the band at the high school he went to. Angel was proud of Samantha the most because she had been through so much and still managed to move forward in her life. She got sad every now and then, but she didn't allow it to turn into depression. She went to the same school Dwight went to for her GED and she went to work everyday rather she felt like it or not. She had a beautiful apartment, a nice car, and a good man who loved her and her daughter dearly. Jackie was proud of everyone including Rhonda and she was really enjoying her life and the people in it.

Marcus asked Jackie to marry him and she wanted to accept his proposal, but she knew that she couldn't. She hadn't been intimate with Jim since she found out she was pregnant and he accepted that, but he forbade her from marrying anyone. Jackie didn't know it, but he knew all about Marcus and he didn't care because she never had him around Bill. Bill spent the night at one of her relatives whenever Marcus stayed overnight. He wasn't mad at Jackie for not being with him because he understood what kind of relationship they had rather he wanted to accept it or not. He loved her so much that he was willing to share her with another man. He was twenty-seven years older than her, had paid his way into her bed, and he spied on her so he didn't blame her for wanting to be with the young, nice looking black man. He was just happy that he got Bill out the deal and that he was able to remain a major factor in her life. The man he hired to scope out her house provided him with pictures of Jackie with Marcus and he could see the love and the longing in her eyes when she was with him, and that gave Jim a sick sense of satisfaction. He was happy that he was able to deny her the love of her life because she was denying him his. He was able to make her live a double life like she was making him do and he loved it.

Jackie loved Marcus but she loved Bill and her lifestyle more. Jim threatened to take Bill and to turn Jackie in to the police if she ever married another man and she thought he was capable of doing them both. They never discussed what the private investigator Jim hired found out or found, but Jim had his way of threatening her with the file without disclosing any of its contents to her which made the threats scarier. He was really bluffing because he didn't have any hardcore evidence that she committed any of the heinous acts people said she did, but she didn't know that. Jackie thought his private investigator found her father's knife or the razor blade she left at the motel when she killed Leon or some other concrete evidence against her so she did what he said and stayed single. When Marcus asked her she said "yes," and accepted the tiny one carat diamond ring he put on her finger, but she knew deep down in her heart that she would never marry him. He didn't even know that Bill existed or that Mellissa was in Ohio and she didn't feel like explaining anything to him. She kept most of the people in her life separate and she preferred it like that so they couldn't tell each other anything she didn't want told. She knew how to be very evasive with Marcus, but he thought he knew everything about her. He told her everything that happened in his past, present and what he wanted to be his future because he thought she was his soul mate. He was tired of trying to replace her with women who couldn't make him feel the way she made him feel; so he was ecstatic when she accepted his proposal. Jackie enjoyed being his fiancée whenever he was around but she only wore the embarrassing ring when he was with her.

Jackie was in her work station thinking about the rendezvous she had with Marcus the night before; when Mellissa ran to her station with tears in her eyes. "Jackie, Sam's hand just got crushed on one of them machines," she yelled when she made it there. She felt terrible because she knew Samantha was about to loose her job and she felt like it was her fault. When Samantha started working there she tried to follow Jackie's rules, but Mellissa convinced her to break as many of them as she could. Jackie told Samantha and Mellissa not to do any drugs because of the random drug tests they did at PM, and Samantha tried not to but Mellissa convinced her to start back smoking after her one year anniversary at PM. Before Samantha started working there, Mellissa got cool with an older lady who agreed to let her pay for clean urine whenever PM did random drug tests, so she thought she had them protected. There was nothing for Samantha, Mellissa, or their boyfriends to do most of time they worked during the shutdown weeks, so they kicked it at work. All of them smoked weed and that's one of the things they did on their long, unauthorized breaks. They smoked on the lunch break they took before Samantha's accident, so Mellissa knew her system was dirty but there was nothing she could do about it. She never thought about them getting hurt on the job so she didn't have a plan that would cover them if they did. PM drug tested everyone who got hurt on the job, so Mellissa knew Samantha was going to get tested. She always thought she was so much smarter than Jackie, but she wished she'd listened to her at that moment.

"I'm bout to go check on her—;" Jackie said before one of her co-workers rudely interrupted her.

"And who the fuck about to do yo work? I'm getting tired of this shit, if you leave I'm leaving!" the disgruntled worker yelled.

Jackie didn't let the woman push her buttons because getting to Samantha was more important. "Honey, I don't care what you do, but my niece is more important than this job to me. Is she that important to you?" she asked her. She knew that the woman wasn't going to leave because she was always complaining about the hours PM was taking from them. She just hated the special privileges Jackie and her nieces got. "Mellissa can you pick Bill up from the daycare for me?" she asked not giving the woman a chance to answer her question. She ignored her as she started slamming parts in the rack because she refused to let her transfer her anger to her. Her tunnel vision was focused on Samantha so it was easy to tune the woman out.

"Yeah, do you need me to pick up Ramona too?" asked Mellissa as she followed Jackie out the work station.

"Naw, Angel gon go get her. Here's my house key in case Bill wants to go home. I'm bout to go to the office to tell them I'm gone," Jackie nervously replied. She was very scared that Samantha was going to loose her hand, but she didn't voice her fears out loud. She worked in factories for years and she'd seen some gruesome injuries. She'd never be able to forgive herself if Samantha lost her hand on the job she got for her. She was trying to help her improve her life, not make it worse.

"Can you please tell her that I love her and I'll be up there as soon as you come and get Bill?" Mellissa asked as crocodile tears started to roll down her face.

"Yeah, I'll tell her. She gon be alright Lissa, just pray for her," said Jackie as she embraced her. She hadn't hugged her daughter in years and it felt good. She made a silent promise to try to get closer to her in the future.

"I will Jackie."

Jackie made it to the hospital in less than ten minutes and the man at the information booth gave her a visitor's pass and told her which room Samantha was in. She talked to the nurse before she went in the room and she calmed her down when she told her that they could definitely save Samantha's hand. A pin was connected to the press that slammed down on her hand so it was smashed and pierced, but the nurse assured her that the hole would close up. None of her bones were broken but her hand was still in pretty bad shape. When Jackie went to tell Jim that she was leaving, he told her that he had Samantha working on the floor because someone took off and he didn't have anything for her to do in the office. Jackie told him to get ready because she was about to sue the shit out of him and PM with his lawyer. She was able to think more clearly when she found out Samantha's hand was going to be saved. She didn't have to try to sue Jim because Samantha had been at PM for over two years, so the job was going to take care of her very well. "Hey, baby. How you feeling?" she asked when she walked in Samantha's room.

"I feel terrible Auntie," Samantha said through her tears.

"Well the nurse said yo hand gone heal up, so you should be happy. You can get workers compensation until you get ready to take the buyout that PM is offering. The plant is about to close down anyway so you can get yo money and bounce," said Jackie with a smile on her face. PM was about to shutdown completely because the price of gas had skyrocketed which caused the sale of trucks to decrease dramatically. The economy was horrible and people weren't buying the big, expensive, gas guzzling trucks that they made in the Moraine Truck and Bus PM Factory Jackie, Samantha, and Mellissa worked at. A lot of the employees were taking the $70,000 buyout the plant was offering and Samantha had been talking about taking hers so she could move out of Hilltop and buy her and Ramona a house. She was even considering moving out of Ohio because most of its jobs were going to be gone when PM shutdown because most of the factories worked for PM. The only jobs left were jobs in the medical field, the mall, and the restaurants. She didn't have a degree to work in the medical field and she refused to work in retail or in a restaurant because they didn't pay the money she was used to making. The crime rate was also rising because a lot of people lost their jobs already and they hustled so they could eat. It seemed like there was a home invasion, a bank robbery, or a person getting robbed on the streets of Dayton everyday.

"I fucked up Auntie."

"Girl it was an accident, everybody makes them. We supposed to be shutdown next week anyway and I think you'll get more from workers compensation than you'll get from unemployment anyway. I'm gon contact my lawyer tomorrow so he'll defend you, and he gon make sure you get paid," said Jackie trying to make Samantha feel better. She didn't have a lawyer but Jim did and she knew she could get him to represent Samantha.

"I aint gon qualify for workers compensation because I got weed in my system. They tested me as soon as I got here and I already know the results," said Samantha as she broke all the way down. She hadn't thought about all the money she messed up until Jackie came in there telling her what she would have been qualified for. She saw all of her dreams disappear in a matter of seconds for a high she could have done without. She was going to be stuck in depressing ass Dayton, Ohio for the rest of her life.

"What the fuck do you mean you got weed in yo system? I told yo stupid ass not to smoke that bullshit anymore! You was with Mellissa wasn't you? I knew you two dumb ass bitches was coming in there actin' silly everyday after lunch! You know what? I'm through with both of y'all! You was right about one thing! You did fuck up! I'm about to tell that bitch to come up here with yo dumb ass because I can't tolerate stupidity! You den threw away everything you had going for yourself for a blunt and you used to try to play yo mama because she used to get high! What's the difference? Drugs are drugs! Her blow cost ten dollars just like yo weed costs ten dollars," Jackie yelled before she stormed out of Samantha's emergency room. Samantha unknowingly confirmed Mellissa's involvement in her decision to start back smoking weed when she ignored the question and turned her head so she didn't have to look her in her face. A move she'd unknowingly done since she was a little girl when Jackie was teaching her not to lie. She was furious at Samantha for being a follower, but she blamed Mellissa the most because she didn't even start smoking weed until Jamal turned her out. She was able to pass her drug test with flying colors when she first got hired. Jackie saw the change in her behavior when she started sleeping with him, but it wasn't a big change and Mellissa refused to take her advice when it came to him so she stayed out of her business. Samantha not only listened to her advice, she also asked for it and Jackie wished it would've been Mellissa who got hurt instead of her. She loved Samantha since birth; she had to learn how to love Mellissa.

She stormed out the hospital into the parking lot and dialed Mellissa's cell phone number. "Yeah, you can come up here with yo little weed buddy! I got you bitches that job and y'all gon play me like I'm a fool! I wish you would've got hurt too so they could fire yo dumb ass right along with this bitch," she yelled into the phone as soon as Mellissa answered it. She hung up in her face after she finished because she didn't want to hear her reply.

(23)

An Unexpected Path

Jackie was so mad that she forgot that she told Angel to meet her at the hospital. She was about to pull off until she saw her pull in. Angel was the type of mother who loved to blame other people for the mistakes her kids made so she was quick to agree with Jackie when she blamed Mellissa for Samantha's mistakes, and that made Jackie even madder. She did a quick breathing exercise while Angel bashed Mellissa. After she was relaxed, she calmly told Angel that she didn't want to be contacted by anyone while PM was on shutdown. It was Friday, so she was ready to start her vacation away from everyone accept Bill. She didn't even want to be bothered with Jim. She was going to be humiliated when he found out Samantha failed her drug test, and she didn't feel like hearing him gloat. He was very remorseful when Jackie left him, but she knew that remorse was going to turn into anger. Jackie regretted using him to help others get ahead for the first time. The government was no longer hiding the internal investigations they were conducting on the entire automobile industry because they were bailing them out. She felt stupid for risking the father of her child's freedom, money, and lifestyle for people who didn't appreciate it. Jim could loose everything he worked for because of her. She promised herself that she was only going to look out for Bill, Jim, and herself in the future. She wasn't inviting anyone else to Ohio, and she wasn't' giving anyone another dime. She was through with making other peoples' problems her own.

She was happy that she did let Angel vent because she forgot that she asked Mellissa to pick up Bill. Seeing them approach her initially bought a smile to her face, but it disappeared when they made it to her and she smelled weed. "I hope smoking that bullshit in front of my baby was worth it because I'm gon make sure you get fired when you go back to work."

"Fuck you, and that job. I'm bout to go see my cousin. You just remember all that shit you talking."

"Naw, you remember it cause I ain't fucking with yo dumb ass no more!"

"You late, I been on that," Mellissa said with a forced laugh. Every word Jackie said to her cut deep. The love she thought she had for her turned to hate and every decision she made from then on was made with a clear conscious. She stood there until Jackie walked to her car with Bill and then she walked into the hospital with Angel.

When Jackie walked into her condo she instantly felt that something was wrong, but she was so depressed that she didn't have the energy to add anything to the battles she was already fighting. Bill felt her mood and got sad to. She cut off her cellphone, unplugged the house phone, put them on their pajamas, cut off all the lights in her house, and carried Bill into her room where they instantly fell asleep. They went to bed at five and didn't wake back up until 8:37 the next night. When they woke up they used the bathroom and Jackie made Bill eat a half of an apple and drink a cup of water. She drank a lot of water then they fell back asleep, and slept all the way through Sunday. They were awakened out of their sleep seven o'clock Monday morning by extra loud banging. Jackie didn't know who it was but she was about to cuss them out. "Who the fuck is banging on my damn door like they the motherfucking police?" she shouted as she yanked open the door without looking through the peephole. Her knees literally buckled when she opened it and saw that it was the police at her door.

"Jacqueline Wright we have a warrant for your arrest for the murder of Leon Thompson. Turn around and put your hands behind your back," the arresting officer said.

"Can I slip some clothes on and call my sister so she can get my son first?" Jackie asked in a shaky voice. She had on pajamas with no underwear on and she didn't want to be arrested in that.

"Sure. Dial your sister's telephone number on my cellphone, I'll tell her what's going on. Mary go with her to her bedroom so that she can change," the detective that Jackie assumed was in charge said.

She thought she was in a bad dream but reality smacked her in the face when she looked in her underwear drawer to get some panties and a wireless bra, and didn't feel her father's diary. At first she thought that Jim turned her in, but when she discovered her father's diary missing she knew Mellissa was behind the knife that stabbed her in the back. She was with Marcus the night before Samantha's accident and forgot to set her alarm clock. She woke up so late that she ended up rushing out before locking her bedroom door like she usually did. She felt hurt, betrayed, and stupid. If they had her father's diary like she suspected, they had all of the evidence they needed to prosecute her. The letter Timothy sent to her and a picture of her father holding the knife she used to castrate Leon were inside of the diary. She planned on getting rid of the evidence years ago but the picture was the only picture of her father that she had; and the diary and the letter were the only words that her deceased father and brother wrote that she had. She felt weak as she started shaking and crying. She was scared for the first time in a long time and she didn't like the feeling. She was worried about Samantha losing her job, but she was about to lose her job, her freedom, her son, and everything else she had worked so hard to get.

"Miss you have to hurry up. Slip on your panties and bra and grab you something to wear right now, we don't have all day," said Mary, the female officer who was sent to Jackie's bedroom with her.

Jackie had taken off her pajamas and she was just standing there, staring into space, naked with her underwear in her hands. "OK," she said as the officer's words snapped her back into her present situation. She slipped on her wireless bra, panties, a pink and black Baby Phat t-shirt, and a black velour Baby Phat jogging suit. Then she grabbed her pink and black Air Max gym shoes from out of her closet and put them on too.

"Mommy why are the police are in the house?" asked Bill as he sat up in Jackie's bed.

"Mommy's got to go with the nice policemen but Auntie Angel's gon come to get you," Jackie replied as she bent down and picked him up in her arms. She held on to him as long as they allowed her to because she knew that it was going to be a long time before she would be able to touch him again.

The detective in charge came into Jackie's room. "The aunt's here. Come on little fellow, I need you to follow me so that you can go with your aunt and your cousin," he said in a friendly voice. He hated arresting people in front of their kids but he didn't have a choice. "Let the older lady come in so she can put the little boy on some clothes, its cold out there," he said into his walkie-talkie.

"What's going on Jackie," Angel yelled when she entered the house.

"They think I killed Leon," Jackie yelled back from her bedroom as she grabbed a coat from out of her closet and put it on. "Stay in my house so that bitch Mellissa can't get back in here, she still got one of my keys. I'll call y'all as soon as I get the chance to."

"Alright, enough of this," said the detective in charge. He didn't let Angel in to discuss Jackie's case, he let her in to get her nephew. "Put your hands behind your head. Jacqueline Wright, you have the right to remain silent. Anything you say can and will be used against you in a court of law. You have the right to speak to an attorney, and to have an attorney present during questioning. If you cannot afford a lawyer, one will be provided for you at the government's expense," he said as he put the handcuffs on her and walked her out to his police car.

When they got outside there were reporters everywhere and as Jackie walked past them she heard one of them saying "a twenty-five year old homicide that occurred in Illinois has been solved and the suspect, Jacqueline Wright, is being arrested for brutally killing her husband." She didn't know that the news was outside so she didn't ask the officers to cover her face, and embarrassment was added to her list of emotions. She could imagine all of the people she worked with and the people she used to work with watching her get arrested for murder. Most of them hated her so she knew they would love seeing her being taken away in handcuffs. Everyone was going to be discussing her. She saw one of her neighbors giving an interview when they rode off.

They took her to the Kettering Police Station and Jackie was allowed to make a phone call as soon as they finished fingerprinting her. She decided to call Jim so he could get her a lawyer. "Jim I'm in jail and I need you to get me the best lawyer money can buy," she said as soon as he answered his cell phone.

"What did they arrest you for? Where is Bill? How much is your bond? What happened?" he asked badgering her with questions without letting her answer any of them.

"They got me for murder Jim. Bill is safe, he's with Angel."

"Murder! Did I just hear you say that you're in jail for murder? Oh my God! What are we going to do?" Jim asked as he thought about the file he had on her and wondered which murder she'd been arrested for.

"Are you going to help me or not Jim? I don't have time for all of these questions your throwing at me! You know I didn't kill anyone! Now contact that big shot lawyer you got on retainer and get me the fuck up out of here!" she yelled into the phone. Then she hung before he had a chance to respond.

Jackie thought she was going to be transferred to the Montgomery County Jail to wait for Illinois to come and get her. She also thought that she would be there for at least a week because her old roommate Jane'een had to wait three weeks for New York to come get her. But Illinois wanted her bad and a couple of officers came to get her two hours after she was arrested. None of them asked her anything, they didn't even talk to her. They just transported her from jail to jail like they already knew she was guilty.

The two officers who came and got her from Ohio took her to the Harrison and Kedzie Police Station where she was finally interrogated by Detective Joseph Monroe Jr., the son of the chief Bertha attacked. Jackie was terrified because of the seriousness of her crime and because Detective Monroe looked exactly like his father. She thought that it was him and the fear she felt twenty-five years ago when his eyes and his questions accused her of murdering Leon was back. She started shaking like a leaf and she thought that her mind was playing tricks on her because he looked a little younger than he looked when he questioned her the last time. But when he read her the Miranda rights, she was sure it was him because their voices sounded just alike.

"Mrs. Thompson do you understand your rights," he asked her for the third time. He knew that she had her last name changed back to Wright years ago and he called her Mrs. Thompson to shake her up. When he read her the Miranda rights he called her Jacqueline Wright though. He didn't want her to get off on such a small technicality.

"Yes."

"So are you going to remain silent or are you going to confess to Leon's murder? It really doesn't matter to me because we got a stack of physical evidence against you! Do you recognize these items," Detective Monroe asked as he sat a box on the table in front of Jackie and took the items out one by one as he described what they were. "Your father's diary, the letter from Timothy, a picture of your father holding the knife you used to kill Leon, the actual knife, and dun-dun, the razor blade that you put in your vagina before you had sex with him. We know that this is the razorblade that you used to immobilize your husband because it has your blood and your cum on it. You actually had an orgasm as you shredded his penis! Did you know that? Did you know that his pain made you cum—,"

"OK that's enough! You're going too far," yelled Detective Carla Snow with a look of disgust on her face. She had been Detective Monroe's partner for two years and she respected him because he was a good cop but sometimes his methods repulsed her. "Look Jackie, I understand why you killed Leon. He took you when you were only fourteen, he killed your father, turned your mother out on drugs, had sex with your twin sisters, and the list goes on and on. I want to help you because I feel like you're a victim too, but I can only help you if you help me. We know that you were at the Palace Motel with Leon, and we know what happened in that room. What my partner didn't tell you was that we also have the pubic hairs that you left on Leon's body and these blood spots and these bloody stiletto footprints on the floor belong to you. The footprints are a size eight and you're a size eight," she said as she pulled out the picture of the crime scene that showed the blood spots and the bloody footprints that led from the bed to the bathroom. "You wiped away your fingerprints, but technology has changed since 1983 and the DNA that you left at the scene proves that you were there. If you write out a confession then the prosecutor might be more lenient on you. Your honesty is the only thing that can save your life at this point. Do you want to write out a confession? It might lift a heavy weight off of your shoulders," she said as she played good cop while handing Jackie a pad of paper and a black ink pen.

Jackie nodded her head as she cried, hyperventilated, and shook profusely. She was tired of lying about killing Leon; she killed him because he needed to die. She was also tired of seeing him in her dreams and in her daydreams. She hoped he disappeared for good after she confessed to his murder. Before she could start writing the confession, the lawyer that Jim hired came in the interrogation room followed by the D.A. "Don't write one word on that pad. My name is Steven Jackson and I'll be representing you Ms. Wright. This interview is over until I talk to my client alone," he said as he stayed standing until they were in the interrogation room by themselves.

"I had your case faxed to me when Jim hired me to represent you, and the only way I can see you making it out of here before you die, is if you strike some kind of deal with the district attorney. Are you willing to?" he asked choosing to be completely honest with Jackie. The State of Illinois had a substantial amount of physical evidence against her for Leon's murder, but the D.A., Edward Johnson, wanted all of the murders mentioned in Timothy's letter solved.

"What kind of deal would I have to make?" she asked in a shaky voice. She'd always looked down on people who snitched and now she found herself ready to make a deal. She loved the life she had become accustomed to living and she was willing to do whatever it took to try to get it back. She had to get out so she could be there for Bill.

"You're going go have to testify against King David and your brothers for the other Thompson murders."

"King David died in a car accident and my brothers who killed the Thompson's are all dead. They killed each other several years ago and the only one living had nothing to do with the hits," Jackie lied. Jack Jr. helped kill the Thompson's but she wasn't going to tell on him. They got back close after Ralonda died and she didn't want to be the reason they fell out again.

"You're going to have to give them something more than a bunch of dead suspects."

"Leon killed two people in front of me and his mother, Bertha Thompson, made me help them cut up the bodies. She's still alive and the police in this precinct hate her," she said with a smile on her face. If they made her spend the rest of her life in jail after she helped them solve seven murders then she decided that that's where God wanted her to be.

"That should do it," he said before he called Edward Johnson back into the room. "My client is willing to tell you what happened, but most of the people involved are deceased."

"What good is that going to do us if everyone's dead?" asked Edward Johnson.

"You'll be solving seven murder investigations instead of one," Steven Jackson replied.

"OK, I'm interested. I know about the Thompson murders and the woman who was with Jason, who're the other two people?"

"First I need to make sure she gets immunity for her involvement in that crime."

"Immunity! So she's involved in the double murder that she's going to tell us about as well? Come on Steven you're killing us here. I don't know how it's done in Ohio, but we convict our murderers in Illinois. She really deserves to be executed for the gruesome murder that she did commit but I'm willing to give her fifteen years in exchange for her testimonies."

"That's ludicrous! You want her to spend fifteen years in prison after she helps you solve six other homicides! We'll take our chances in court! Your so called victim was a child molesting, drug dealing, pimp who took my client out of her parent's home for a drug debt that her father owed when she was only fourteen years old. No jury in America will make her do any time in prison after they hear all the things your victim did to her," said Steven Jackson. He knew things about Leon the police didn't even know because of the file Jim gave him and he planned on telling the jurors all about him if he had to.

"Your client had sex with the deceased with a razor blade in her vagina and when she was finished shredding up his penis, she cut it and his head off. She did these things for money that a street gang paid her, not because he took her childhood from her. She thought about how she was going to kill him before she actually killed him which is called premeditated first degree murder in every courtroom in America," Edward Johnson yelled. He hated when lawyers tried to use a victim's past to get their killer out of trouble. He honestly felt like Leon Thompson didn't deserve to be brutally murdered the way he was, regardless of what he had done in his past or to the defendant.

"I think five years will be fair in exchange for the information my client is willing to tell you guys," Steven replied with a stubborn look on his face.

"How about seven years with the eligibility of parole," Edward Johnson replied. He wanted Jackie to spend the rest of her life in prison, but the possibility of solving seven murders was an opportunity he didn't want to pass up.

"We'll take the seven," said Jackie's lawyer with a look of triumph on his face.

Jackie was able to tell the date that each of the Thompson's were killed, where they were killed, which fingers were missing off of their hands, where they were shot, and what kind of gun was used to shoot them. Juan and Beauty's bodies were found around the time Leon proposed to her and she was also able to tell all of the details surrounding their deaths as well.

When the police went to Beauty's condo and put the luminal down, the rooms they were killed in, the hallway leading to the bathroom, and the bathroom floor and tub shined very blue when they turned the black light on. It was evident that the two John and Jane Doe bodies were indeed killed in Beauty's condo and Jackie was telling the truth about the events that took place on that dreadful night. Bertha was arrested for accessory to their murders and the entire Harrison and Kedzie police department celebrated when she was arrested.

Jackie wasn't given a bond so she was held at the Cook County Jail while she waited to go to court to testify against Bertha. She testified against King David and her brothers via video camera, but she had to go in the courtroom and sit on the stand to testify against Bertha. She loved every minute of it because Rhonda and Mellissa came and she looked at them throughout her entire testimony. She made the D.A. ask her questions about the events that followed Beauty and Juan's deaths and she loved the horrified look on Mellissa's face as she told the courtroom full of people how she was forced to bring them into the world. Bertha's lawyer yelled "objection," and the judge yelled, "Sustained," when she started describing the disgusting rapes in full detail, but Jackie wouldn't stop. They escorted her to the prison psychiatrist after a five year old male personality took over. The little boy stood up while Jackie was in the middle of testifying on the witness stand, pointed to her daughters, and yelled that they were the monkey's Leon put inside of Jackie. Toni's voice was similar to Jackie's so no one was able to tell when she took over, but the little boy's voice sounded like a child's voice and everyone knew she'd cracked. She laughed a ridicules, high-pitch, hysterical laugh as they drug her out. That court date was the first time she'd seen Bertha in over twenty years and seeing her, Rhonda, Mellissa and a lot of other people she wanted to leave in her past was more than she could handle so she lost her sanity completely. She started cracking when Bill was snatched out of her arms but she was able to conceal it. She missed him so much that she spent most of her time in her jail cell talking to him. He was with Samantha and she made sure that Jackie talked to him on the phone daily, but that wasn't enough.

It took six months of therapy and lithium before Jackie was declared competent enough to stand trial and Bertha was dead by then to her dismay. She wanted her to suffer in a jail cell like she was going to have to do for seven years. Finding out about Bertha's death was a devastating blow to Jackie so she thought that things couldn't get any worse for her, but they did. While she was out of her mind, Detective Monroe was thoroughly investigating the other three Thompson cases. His father committed suicide behind those murders so those cases were too personal to him to just take Jackie's word that things went down the way she said they went down. Timothy's letter said that they didn't trust any of their sisters or their mother, and since Jack Jr. was the only living brother Jackie had left; he decided to track him down. His superiors were satisfied that the cold cases were closed, but Detective Monroe thought Jack Jr. played a bigger role than the one Jackie said he played and he was determined to find out. Jack Jr. cracked fifteen minutes into the interrogation, and told him everything he knew. He was arrested for the murder of Jason Thompson, the only one he helped kill. He received ten years for the murder in exchange for his testimony against Jackie. She was shocked, hurt, and angry when she went to her sentencing trial and Jack Jr. was the first witness the state called against her. He felt so bad that he looked down at his hands during his entire testimony; but he still felt the hurt filled stare Jackie looked at him with every second that he was in the courtroom. Jackie got twenty-five years to life plus five years for perjury, thanks to Jack Jr.'s testimony. He told the police that she knew he killed Jason and she was lying to protect him. She lied and said that Timothy killed Jason even though she knew it was Jack Jr. who pulled the trigger. Timothy didn't kill anyone, he just planned the murders.

Jackie started her sentence on March 16, 2009 and had an epiphany on the ride to Dwight. She remembered the day she got released and how she'd begged the warden to let her stay. Now she was about to live there for the rest of her life. That revelation made her feel like she was headed to the place God wanted her to be so she could serve him better. She instantly let go of all the intense anger she had towards everyone she was angry at. She wasn't about to let the devil trick her into living her life with all of that hatred in her heart and that revenge on her mind. She'd already let Toni arrange to get Jack Jr. raped when he made it to Logan Correctional Facility and she felt terrible about that after accepting her fate in life. She decided to stop plotting against Mellissa and Rhonda and was happy that she hadn't put her plans against them into action. She silently prayed for Jack Jr. and felt such a strong feeling of happiness when she was done that she prayed for Rhonda and Mellissa too. She never understood why Christians said to pray for your enemies until she did it. It chipped away the ice she had around her heart and put a huge smile on her face. Her mind was so full of revenge that she'd blocked out everything else that was going on around her. When she emptied it and started listening to the conversations the other inmates were having, she found out that Barack Obama won the presidential election. That piece of information filled her with pride and inspiration. She decided right then and there that she was going to try to help her race succeed as much as she could. If Obama could become president Bill could too, and maybe she was too mentally unstable to get him there. She didn't know how crazy she was until she started getting professional help for it. She'd seen a lot of women just like her go in and out the same prison doors she was about to enter; and she wanted to help them get the spiritual, educational, and mental help they needed while she was incarcerated.

The thought of being needed strengthened her and she had a plan developed by the time they made it to Dwight Penitentiary. She had a lot of money out in the real world and she was going to use it to fund a Christian based group that she was going to call Bill's Rights. She came up with that name because she felt that her son and the children of other women incarcerated had the right to grow up to be successful just like any other child. She wanted Bill's Rights to provide the resources the women would need to walk out of Dwight rehabilitated for real. They were going to try to get the inmates to join by giving out free commissary at the end of each meeting. She felt bad for starting a Christian based organization by luring people to join with commissary, but she knew that was the only way she'd get a big turnout. If the warden let her, she planned on hiring a staff of professionals to provide the women with good psychological help, tutoring services for the ones who went to school, and parenting and marriage counseling for the inmates who had children and husbands at home. She also wanted to get with the Christian Chaplin at Dwight to see if he would teach them about Jesus at all of the Bill's Rights meetings because she wanted everyone who decided to join to give their lives to Christ. She didn't make it mandatory because she knew that Christ wanted people to come to him freely not by force. Jim helped her make a presentation for her plan and she presented it to the warden of the prison a month after being there. Jackie had been in and out of Dwight several times so the warden knew her very well and she was happy to let her start Bill's Rights. She saw the big change in her and she was very proud of the new, calmer, nicer Jackie. She thought she was going to be trouble when she found out about her courtroom antics, but Jackie was the exact opposite of what she expected and that pleased her. Bill's Rights bought Jackie closer to God and gave her a sense of purpose. She learned how to love unselfishly during its formation, so it didn't hurt when she gave Samantha custody of Bill.

Jim agreed to the custody because he was old and didn't have the energy to raise an eight year old boy. He knew Samantha very well, and he couldn't think of a better woman to raise Bill. He bought her a house in Kentucky so she could be in between him and Jackie. She drove to Illinois every month to take Bill to see Jackie and Ramona to see Raymond. Jim drove to her house every Saturday to get Bill. When she first found out who Bill's father was she was very surprised and disgusted, but the more she got to know Jim the more she liked him. He was a good father who took very good care of Bill and Jackie. He gave her $2,000 a month for Bill and that helped her household out a lot. Her hand looked normal, but the machine damaged a lot of nerves in it so she couldn't work if she wanted to, but she was financially stable thanks to Jackie and Jim. She got SSI and she was in school trying to get a paralegal associate's degree because she didn't want to depend on them for the rest of her life, but she was very grateful to them. Her daughter went to the same private school Bill went to, and they went on trips all over the United States and she knew they wouldn't have experienced any of those things if it weren't for their generosity. The best gift they gave her by far was Bill. He became the best friend Ramona needed after losing Ralonda and she didn't heal from the loss of her sister until he moved in with them. Ramona helped him too. He stopped talking to people when Jackie went to jail and she was the one who convinced him to start back. Samantha was happy when she moved out of Ohio and started over. She dropped everyone she met at PM besides Jim after she got fired because she was embarrassed by everything that happened there.

Mellissa snuck in and out of Ohio until she was able to get her buyout money. When she got it she paid for her and Rhonda to relocate to Georgia. They were going to move back to Chicago but their grandmother died, so they didn't have a reason to move back. Before Bertha died, she made them promise to develop a better relationship with each other and they were trying. She tried to call Samantha and Angel but both of them cussed her out, so she moved on with her life with her sister, her niece and her man. Jamal was an asshole but he loved Mellissa so he took his buyout money and moved to Georgia with her after she got settled. Rhonda and

Leona stayed with them for a year until Rhonda's Section Eight came through and she got her own place. She loved Mellissa and she started treating her a lot better after Bertha died.

Two years flew past and Jackie felt great! She was getting the help she needed and she was helping others get the help they needed. Bill's Rights took on a life of it's own as it spread out to several other prisons. Lots of people were getting released from prison properly rehabilitated because of the organization Jackie started and she couldn't have been more proud of herself. The love of God was at work and the crime rate in the Illinois prisons had never been so low. Jackie's case got national attention so Bill's Rights got a lot of free publicity because she was the founder. She became a hero to a lot of people and they held protests to try to get her out, but Jackie refused to put in an appeal. She was happy where she was and she thought she was doing what was best for everyone in her life.

She'd been getting lots of mail since she first got arrested, but the only letters she read were the ones Bill wrote her. She decided to start reading the rest of the mail out the blue one day because she felt like she owed it to her fans. A lot of people donated huge sums of money to Bill's Rights and she needed to start showing her gratitude. The media constantly badgered her for being cold and she didn't care what they said, but she didn't' want to feel like she was a cold-hearted person. She started with the mail she got while she was still in the Cook County Jail because that's when a lot of her fans started writing her. She decided to separate the mail by its writers and while she was doing that, she saw Bertha Thompson's name on one of the envelopes. Her hands started trembling and her heart started beating fast when she read it. Her eyes changed from gray to green when she pulled the letter out the envelope and a recent picture of Bill fell out.